HEARTS OF FIRE

★

HEARTS OF FIRE

★

Ellen Brazer

Writer's Showcase
presented by *Writer's Digest*
San Jose New York Lincoln Shanghai

Hearts of Fire

Writer's Showcase
presented by *Writer's Digest*
an imprint of iUniverse.com, Inc.

For information address:
iUniverse.com, Inc.
5220 S 16th, Ste. 200
Lincoln, NE 68512
www.iuniverse.com

ISBN: 0-595-09963-7

Printed in the United States of America

Dedication

———— ★ ————

*TO MEL BRAZER, MY HUSBAND AND BEST FRIEND
—I COULDN'T HAVE TAKEN THE JOURNEY WITHOUT YOU.*

Acknowledgements

———————— ★ ————————

As with any endeavor, it's the people in our lives that encourage us to set the dream into motion. My thanks to Guela Gat, a founder of the Kabbutz Ayelit Hashakar in the upper Galilee in Israel, her life was the inspiration for my novel; my beloved friend, Menachem Perlmutter, architect of the Negev, humanitarian and survivor of the Holocaust who touched my heart and my soul with his undying love and belief in the goodness of humanity. Special thanks go to my friends, Bobby Tyler and Sally Cameron who encouraged me from the moment I put the first words on paper, and to Mitch Kaplan and Michele Krinsman, at Books & Books in Miami, along with Naline Milne, Yael Ginsberg, Marjorie and Alan Goldberg and Irwin Hyman, Judi Wolowitz for their help and for believing that this book should be published. Thank you to my parents, Esther and Irving Glicken, for everything they are to me and for giving me their unconditional love, and to my family, Todd and Randi Brazer, Joe, Bonnie, Rachel, Ali and Ryan Grote, Mitch, Becky, Matt and Megan Brazer, Barry, Ellen, Heidi and Samantha Brazer. To Carrie, thanks for always believing in me. And a special thanks to my son, Judd for his time, energy and patience, and to his family: Ayda, Tiffany and Julia for giving him that time. Thanks to Barbara Glicken for designing the cover and for reading the book each time it was rewritten. I would be remiss if I didn't add a just a few more special names-My second Mom, Ethel Zweig, and to my beloved Rose Brazer and Rebecca, (Becky) Meltzer-Thank you all.

BOOK I

———————— ★ ————————

Chapter 1

———————— ★ ————————

On this day in 1919 an icy wind swept Berlin's winter streets. Heavy clouds cast a gray metallic hue over the bleak stone buildings lining the broad boulevards. The weather suited the mood of a city, where 250,000 citizens, many embittered ex-World War I soldiers, were unemployed. And while decadent cabarets catered to the boisterous, ostentatious war profiteers, the sick and the starving shrieked their discontent while shivering in ragged clothes.

Paper-thin walls brought the surrounding chaos into the tenement flat where Ingrid Milch lived with her family. Trying to block out the angry sounds, Ingrid placed her hands over her ears, just as a flashing pain splintered through her back. She flinched and cried out, startling her nine-year-old twins.

"I'm OK. Don't worry," she said. Ingrid studied her beautiful children. Their white-blond hair, delicate features, and dancing azure eyes seemed to contradict her current misery. .

At that moment, the apartment door flew open and Ingrid looked up in horror. Sigmund's eyes were streaked with red and he could barely stand. Her husband was not due home for at least three hours, so his appearance could mean only one thing—he had lost his job again. Ingrid knew what would be coming next.

"What are you staring at, bitch?" he snarled, slapping Ingrid brutally across the face.

"What's happened?"

"What the fuck do you think happened?" he slurred, lifting his hand to hit her again.

"Mama!" the twins screamed, running to their mother.

Ingrid rose heavily. She grabbed the children tightly by their arms, dragging them to their cot in the corner of the one-room flat.

"Stay here and don't make a sound. And no matter what happens, don't come out," she whispered, pulling the curtain closed around their bed.

In the shadows, Sigmund had quieted down, Ingrid thought. But hope vanished when she saw that he was holding his swollen erection, stroking it rapidly.

"The baby's coming, Sigmund," she groaned, barely making it to the bed and covering herself with sheets before another pain slammed into her.

Sigmund laughed as he continued to slowly undress.

Ingrid had met Sigmund when she was sixteen and he was twenty. He had been nice looking, with a decent job and a promising future. At the beginning of their marriage, he had been kind to her. Even after the birth of the twins, he had remained affectionate.

When the war came, Sigmund enlisted, genuinely believing he was going to defend the Fatherland against the Allies. He returned four years later a changed man from the one Ingrid had married. Drunken and violent, he had openly turned to the neighborhood whores.

That morning, Sigmund had been laid off at the printing plant, and he had spent the entire day in the neighborhood whorehouse drinking and bantering with his friends.

"My wife's gonna have another kid," Milch had said to his comrades, "and now I have no job. What the hell am I gonna do?"

Sigmund's friends shrugged their shoulders, all too familiar with his predicament.

"Shit!" Sigmund had hissed. "It's all because of those stinking Jews; they get all the jobs. Walking around thinking they're so fucking great, their pockets bulging with gold."

He needed someone to blame for his misery, and as he downed his drink and slammed the glass on the table, the other men grumbled their assent, wisely keeping their distance.

He then grappled his way to the top of the stairs, where he paid his last marks to a whore with big bosoms and a flat belly. The whore took his money greedily, dropping to her knees and rubbing her breasts against his erect penis. Sigmund ejaculated the moment she took him into her mouth.

When the whore began to laugh loudly at how easily she had earned her money, Sigmund punched her in the face, breaking her nose and knocking out a front tooth. Her screams brought the madam, who chased him down the street, screaming obscenities and swearing that she would kill him.

* * *

Now, as he stood naked, glaring down at his writhing wife, the memory of his total humiliation further enraged him.

"We'll see who's the man around here!"

"Please don't touch me, for the sake of the baby," she begged.

Sigmund ripped off the covers, exposing Ingrid's swollen belly and malnourished hips and legs. Purple and yellow bruises, remnants from her last encounter with his brutality, covered her body. Sigmund's erection withered, and his renewed feelings of shame and rage fired his unmerciful beating.

Otto put his hands over his sister's ears, trying to muffle Ingrid's screams, but to no avail. Unable to contain himself any longer, he ran to his mother's side.

"Stop! You're hurting her," he screamed, throwing himself across Ingrid.

Disregarding his son, Sigmund grabbed for his hysterical daughter, who was punching and yelling at him with all the fury her nine-year-old body could muster. Taking a handful of Ilya's golden hair, he brought her tear-streaked face within inches of his own.

"Stop, or I'll fuck you instead!" he hissed, his erection returning.

Otto glanced at his unconscious mother for an instant before tearing his sister from his father. Bounding from the room before Sigmund could react, the twins ran screaming down the stairs and into the street.

* * *

The neighbors brought a doctor, who managed to save the torn, bruised, and emotionally shattered Ingrid. Her infant son was born dead.

The police came later that night looking for Sigmund, but he was gone. When they left, Otto took his sister's hand and pulled her to their bed.

"It's going to be all right. I'll take care of you, Ilya," he vowed, his childish voice trembling from anger and frustration.

"Why couldn't he have died in the war?" Ilya asked.

"Don't worry. I promise you; someday you're going to have beautiful dresses and a lovely home. Someday I'm going to get you out of here," he said.

Ilya smiled. She knew he would.

Chapter 2

──────── ★ ────────

Hundreds of miles away, Jonte Villre climbed up into the droshky's open carriage and quickly covered herself with the wool blanket that had been thrown across the seat.

"The Jewish hospital. Hurry please, my mistress is ill."

The driver slapped the reins across the back of his wretched horse and headed out over the cobblestone streets. Jonte scrunched forward trying to evade the freezing Polish wind. But even before the carriage had clattered off of the Boulevard of Gara Zomkova onto Zyclouska Street, she realized her trembling was less from the cold than from excitement. Jonte sat back and was soon enthralled by the strange and exciting world of Vilna's Jewish Quarter, allowing the sights and sounds of the bustling city to envelop her. She smiled as they passed the Shulhoyf, the Great Synagogue of Vilna. Jewish students talked animatedly in the courtyards, seemingly oblivious to the bitter cold. The droshky moved quickly past the Gaon's Kloyz, the Strashum Library, and the dozens of small Prayer Houses where the Jews of Vilna studied Torah, and rolled uptown past the Science Gymnasium.

It was still all new to the seventeen-year-old who had come to Poland from Paris after her cousin had told her that the Rabinowiszch family was seeking a well-educated, French-speaking nanny for their expected child. Dr. and Mrs. Rabinowiszch had hired her after the first interview, deciding that Jonte's simple face, intelligent and earnest demeanor would serve them well. And Jonte was happy with her new family, even though at times she was dreadfully lonely for her parents and old friends. But now with the baby finally arriving, she was sure she'd be too busy to feel lonely anymore.

On Ulica Zawalma the carriage drew to a halt in front of the Jewish hospital. Jonte felt a pounding in her chest as she lifted her skirt and jumped to the street, calling to the driver to wait for her return.

Bounding up the granite steps and through the front entrance of the hospital, she ran directly into a stately old man wearing the white coat of a doctor.

"Please, sir," she said, "can you find Dr. Rabinowiszch for me? His wife is…" She stammered…in need of assistance." Jonte felt the tingle of embarrassment.

"Wait here, young miss. I'll locate Dr. Rabinowiszch for you. And please do try and calm yourself. Babies are born every day." He winked knowingly as he scurried away.

Jonte pushed her back against the wall to wait, wishing to make herself invisible. Within moments Dr. Rabinowiszch came striding toward her.

Mrs. Sara is so lucky, Jonte thought, as she moved out of the shadows to meet the startlingly handsome man. His close-cropped mustache and beard matched his midnight black hair, which was slicked back and parted fashionably down the middle. She was surprised she hadn't noticed before that Samuel Rabinowiszch had eyes the color of sapphires, which now fixed her sternly, the perspiration on his forehead giving away the concealed tension.

"How is Mrs. Sara?"

"She's very frightened, sir," Jonte answered.

Samuel's face grew pale. "Let's go," he whispered.

* * *

Samuel helped Jonte up into the droshky, a courtesy not lost on the young, impressionable nanny. As he took the seat across from her, Jonte kept her head modestly bowed, her eyes riveted on the floorboards. The sound of the horses' hooves clacking along the cobblestones echoed in Jonte's ears. When she ventured a quick look at Samuel, he seemed oblivious to her presence.

In fact, he was confined in his own mind, reflecting on his own life now that he was about to become a father. From as far back as he could remember, he had always wanted to be a doctor, and his family had encouraged that dream. After his formative years at the Yeshiva, learning the Jewish law and values from the Rabbis, he had graduated from the Science Gymnasium and continued his education at Berlin and St. Petersburg Universities where ultimately he obtained his medical degree.

At thirty-two Samuel had married Sara, fifteen years his junior. In the beginning he had been puzzled by Sara's seemingly unprovoked spells of sadness, but the Rabbis had assured Samuel that most arranged marriages began that way, that once his young wife had a baby, everything would be fine.

* * *

Briefly he smiled as he pictured Sara's sweet and open face, with trusting turquoise eyes, hair the color of toasted wheat, and a heart-shaped mouth that smiled easily. Sara had taught him about another side of life, about the beauty of the universe. He loved Sara and he believed she had come to love him. Now he felt warm tears well up in his eyes and spill onto his cheeks. He shifted in his seat, turning away from Jonte.

"Driver, please go faster!"

Hours later, Samuel delivered Morgan Rebecca Rabinowiszch, named after Sara's beloved maternal grandmother, Rebecca Morganstern, into his wife's arms.

His voice quivered. "Look, Sara. God has blessed us with a perfect baby girl."

Once he had made Sara comfortable, he donned his heavy winter coat and walked out into the garden. Alone at the farthest corner of the property, Samuel stretched his six-foot frame and swung his arms into the air, dancing and abandoning himself to utter joy.

I will always love and protect you, Morgan Rebecca Rabinowiszch. As long as I live, no harm will ever come to you.

Chapter 3

────────────── ★ ──────────────

Samuel held eleven-year-old Morgan's hand protectively, as father and daughter threaded their way through the streets of Vilna. It was 1930, and an unremitting summer sun had turned the alleyways of the Jewish marketplace into a furnace. Oblivious to the heat, the merchants hawked their wares passionately, coloring the noisy market with their piety and gossip.

Skirting the meat stalls where the butchers were carefully displaying their freshly slaughtered chickens, Samuel rushed Morgan past the glazier's hut and the intense heat of the furnace. At the fruit and vegetable section, a vendor swatted flies away from his quickly spoiling food as he called out to Samuel.

Soon after the two men shook hands and began to talk, a small group gathered, asking Samuel's advice on their various afflictions. Samuel listened attentively, prescribing remedies as if his inquisitors had paid to see him in his hospital office. Morgan watched demurely in the background, proud of her father but anxious to be on her way. Samuel was equally proud of his hauntingly beautiful child, with her wavy midnight hair, alabaster skin, and almond-shaped violet eyes.

"You'll have to excuse me now," Samuel said finally, looking at his pocket watch, "I'm taking my daughter to the Yiddish theater."

As they watched Samuel and Morgan walk away, the men murmured their admiration for both.

"Oh, Papa, I'm so excited," Morgan said, hardly able to maintain her ladylike composure as they hurried away.

* * *

Ten minutes later, shadowed by the city's exaggerated Baroque architecture, Morgan tugged on Samuel's arm. "Look! Up there, the Trzy Krzyze," she said, pointing to the Hill of the Three Crosses off in the distance.

Samuel smiled, enchanted by Morgan's joyful curiosity. "It's an architectural wonder. Don't you agree?"

"Oh, yes. I quite agree, but…" Morgan stammered.

"Speak your mind, child. One's opinions only matter when one is willing to speak."

"The crosses frighten me," she said. "Why don't the Christians like us, Papa?"

"That's a very complicated and sad story, one I'll tell you some other time," Samuel said as he urged Morgan away.

Their steps quickened when the Yiddish theater came into view. Samuel had always loved the arts, and he was thrilled to be taking Morgan to her first performance—Shloime Ansky's *The Dybbuk*.

"Yiddish," Samuel said softly as they waited for the performance to begin, "is the language of Jews all over the world. It was born in the beautiful Rhine Valley during the twelfth century as a kind of union between the German language and the Hebrew alphabet. The language is unique because it has never remained stagnant; as our people relocated to various areas of the world—Russia, Lithuania, Poland—the language continued to diversify. Sit back and watch. You'll see what I mean," Samuel said.

From the moment the curtain rose, Morgan was drawn into the fantasy and tragedy of Ansky's tender love story about a young woman possessed by a dybbuk, a demon. And as Morgan watched the young woman manifest her possession, she was gripped by a euphoria that drew her deeper and deeper into the character. In that highly altered state Morgan watched the young woman's exorcism and her eventual return to the mystic and pious world of Hasidism, a world of divine justice and love.

The audience rose to their feet, applauding loudly as the curtain fell. Morgan stood transfixed, her hands stinging from her own enthusiastic clapping.

"Papa, that was so wonderful! When can we come again? I have to come again soon so that I can learn. I'm going to be an actress!" she said, her eyes shimmering with determination.

Samuel stopped and took Morgan gently by the shoulders, looking deeply into her eyes. "Listen to me," he said, his voice barely above a whisper, "I'll be exposing you to many things in your life in the hopes that you'll become a well-rounded young woman. I don't want to be worried that every time you see something new..." He hesitated in frustration, realizing he wasn't getting through. "Look, Morgan, your fate has already been decided. People like you do not ever become actresses. When the time is right, you'll become a wife and mother. That's where you should be focusing your attention."

Outside, Samuel flagged down a taxi, and once inside he tried to talk to Morgan, but she remained distant and uncommunicative. As he helped her from the taxi, he feared that taking Morgan to that play might have been the single biggest mistake of his life.

* * *

Morgan rushed to her rooms to find Jonte in the closet, knee-deep in some old clothing.

"What am I to do?" Morgan asked frantically, throwing herself on the floor beside her nanny.

"Excusez-moi" Jonte asked, not particularly concerned by Morgan's impassioned outburst, having grown used to them over the years. "What seems to be the problem?" she continued in French.

"I want to become an actress when I grow up, and I just know that Papa's never going to let me"

"You're right about that," Jonte said, stealing for what she knew was coming. "I can assure you that girls from proper Jewish families do not become actresses."

"Oh, Jonte, I know that. That's why I'm going to need your help," Morgan said, throwing herself into Jonte's arms.

Jonte loved Morgan as if she were her own child, worrying about her constantly and fearing that Morgan's sensitive and often unpredictable disposition would lead her into trouble.

"I can't go against your parents. Now, I won't have any more of this kind of talk. Here, help me fold this," she said, handing Morgan a stack of clothing.

"Do you love me, Jonte, or are you nice to me because my father pays you to be?" Morgan asked.

"How can you ask me that?" Jonte snapped. "I'm here because I love you, and that's the only reason I'm here."

Morgan looked deeply into Jonte's eyes.

"I'm going to become an actress. I know that just as I know that one day you'll be forced to leave my family because we're Jewish. You'll see," Morgan said.

"Where in the world do you get such outrageous ideas?" Jonte asked, trying to shake off Morgan's ominous proclamation.

"I just know; that's all," Morgan said.

"I'm still not going to talk to your father. Now, can we please change the subject?"

Chapter 4

————— ★ —————

Samuel sat in his study engrossed in a paper he would be presenting to the medical society, when Morgan entered. He looked up and smiled.

"I'm sorry to disturb you, Papa."

"Don't be silly. Have a seat," he said, setting his reading glasses on the desk and wondering what his precocious fifteen-year-old was up to this time.

"Papa, I have so much school work, and I could do it much more effectively at the Strashum Library. I'd like to begin going there on Sundays if you wouldn't mind? "

"The library is quite a distance from here, Morgan. Don't you think you're better off studying at home?" Samuel offered, secretly thrilled that Morgan enjoyed the old library.

"It's not the same, Papa. With the reference books so readily available, I'll be able to do much better work," she said, knowing how much her father wanted her to exercise her intellect.

Samuel eventually agreed, and the following Sunday the chauffeur delivered Morgan to the front door of the library.

She stood inside the library door until she was sure the driver had gone. She then ran from the building and rushed the half-mile to the movie house, her heart pounding wildly all the way.

* * *

The movie house was a wondrous place. The smell of stale tobacco and pungent perfume seeped into the darkest corners, where mysterious looking people sat. Morgan began spending every Sunday there, enchanted by the enormous images that magically filled the screen. Only after the last credits had rolled across the screen and the house lights had been turned up would Morgan leave, hurrying back to the library to await her ride.

During many weeks of the same ritual, Morgan had noticed an older boy who always sat in the back of the theater and also never left until the very end. When they left the theater together, he always smiled at her, nodding his head in recognition. Before long Morgan became intrigued with him, weaving glorious mental stories about the mysterious stranger who never spoke to her.

Eventually the screen images began to affect Morgan's daily life. After seeing Bette Davis in *Jezebel*, she imitated the Davis look, walk, and talk, stupefying unsuspecting teenaged boys by fluttering her eyelashes most provocatively.

Morgan became one of the most popular girls in school, with friends constantly vying for her attention. She understood and cultivated her uniqueness, determined not to spend her life managing a house, raising children, and living with some dull husband.

＊ ＊ ＊

Samuel had been just as determined to keep his rebellious daughter under control by making the concepts of Judaism so much a part of her life that she would willingly give up her unorthodox behavior and conform. Every Friday afternoon and Saturday morning, Samuel would escort his daughter on a forty-minute walk to the "Great Synagogue" of Vilna.

The building was outwardly unimpressive because of a Church decree stating that no synagogue in Poland would be as tall as even the shortest church. Longing for a synagogue with the beauty of catapulting cathedral ceilings and the space for prayer and study, in 1633 the Jews of Vilna had dug two stories into the earth, so that from the street, the "Great Synagogue" looked only three stories tall. But when people entered the sanctuary after descending a long flight of stairs, they were caught breathless—the ceilings soared for five stories.

Women were segregated from the men at the synagogue, but before Morgan menstruated she had been allowed to sit with Samuel in the men's section of the main sanctuary. Here she had first learned Hebrew, snuggling against her father's swaying body, listening to the haunting sounds and rhythms of the ancient language while savoring the aromas of the sweet Sabbath wine on his breath, his hair pomade, and the fragrant soap he used.

* * *

One day after services, when Morgan was outside the synagogue talking with her friends, she spotted the mysterious stranger from the movie house sitting alone on a bench by the sidewall, openly staring at her. Terrified that he might tell someone that he had seen her at the theater, she took a deep breath, gathered all her resolve, and walked up to the young man.

"I've never seen you here before," she said.

"That's true. My family usually attends the Taharath Ha-Kodesh Synagogue. Been to any movies lately?" His eyes sparkled mischievously.

Morgan looked around frantically.

"Listen, I know you don't want to ruin my life, so please don't ever say that again. I'm not supposed to go to the movies," she said. "They think I go to the library."

"Relax, your secret's safe with me. My name's Jacob Gold," he said, offering Morgan his hand.

"Hi. I'm Morgan Rabinowiszch," she answered, shaking his hand enthusiastically, noticing for the first time his French accent. "You're not from around here, are you?"

"No. I'm from Marseille. My father has been assigned here temporarily. He's with the government. I'm only here for a short visit before I have to be back at school."

"Oh, I see," Morgan said. "So I guess your parents don't mind if you spend Sundays in the movie house?"

"No, they don't. As a matter of fact, they have a lot of friends who are entertainers."

"You're kidding."

"Sometimes they even stay with us when they come into town."

Morgan smiled, happy to have finally found someone with interests similar to hers.

* * *

Jacob and Morgan soon became inseparable, sitting together in the movie and meeting after services every Saturday. She learned that he was twenty years old, studying medicine at Cambridge University. More importantly, he too was a dreamer filled with deep intellectual curiosity. He spent a lot of time visiting prayer houses and synagogues throughout Vilna listening to discourses on the Kabbalah, Jewish mysticism. When he discussed what he had been hearing with Morgan, she found the courage to confide her own unorthodox beliefs.

"He's not just the God of the Jews, is He?" she asked Jacob, fearful that her heretical comments would enrage him.

Instead Jacob laughed. "I don't think He belongs specifically to us."

"My father would disagree with you."

"Of course he would, and so would my father. It's what they've been taught, Morgan. And let me assure you, it's not only our people who feel this way. Every religion believes that God belongs to them."

Looking at Morgan thoughtfully, he hoped she might notice the passion in his eyes, but she was too engrossed in her own thoughts. He said, "Your father would be mortified if he ever knew that you entertained such outrageous ideologies, and he wouldn't ever let you see me again if he thought I'd planted them in your head."

"Don't worry, Jacob, I'm not stupid. I'd never tell him," she said as they walked back into the synagogue.

Samuel was standing by the front door, his arms crossed over his chest.

"*Ich habe es eilig,*" he said in German, upset at how long Morgan had been outside.

"*Es tut mir leid,*" Morgan responded stiffly.

She hated speaking German, but her father saw it as the language of the Arts and Sciences and therefore the language of the intelligentsia.

"You must become more respectful of time, my child. Your mother will be waiting for us.

"Yes, Papa."

* * *

Months later at school, Morgan read about an open call that was being held at the Reduta Theater. Knowing full well that Vilna had some of Poland's finest municipal theaters and that many of the country's best actors regularly auditioned there, Morgan decided to try out regardless of her slim chances of getting a part.

Lying to her mother about having to stay after school, she left the campus and waved down a taxi. Fifteen minutes later, her knees shaking, Morgan was standing backstage waiting for her turn to go on.

"Miss Rabinowiszch, please," someone called loudly.

"I'm here," Morgan shouted back, feeling foolish and terrified.

"Five minutes," a hassled woman with nervous eyes said. "When you're called, read the part marked in red."

"My God, she's an incredible looking young woman," the director whispered as Morgan walked onto the stage. "Whenever you're ready, my dear," he said.

Morgan, despite her nervousness, read her lines superbly, enunciating loudly, her voice alive and impassioned. When she finished reading, she took a deep breath and looked up for the first time, trying to see who was sitting in the middle seats of the theater.

"What's your name," the director barked from the darkness.

"Morgan Rabinowiszch, sir."

"And you want to be an actress, do you, Miss Morgan Rabinowiszch?"

Morgan was sure she had made a total fool of herself; with tears spilling from her eyes, she turned to leave.

"Where are you going?" the director bellowed. "The part is yours."

"I don't understand," Morgan said.

From the darkness she heard the gentle sound of laughter. "Tell my assistant, Miss Gottleb, how we can reach you. We'll be in touch."

Morgan was ecstatic when she left the theater. But by the time she arrived home, she had become sick with worry, realizing that now she would have to tell her father.

"What's the matter with you?" Jonte asked, feeling Morgan's fevered head. "I want you in bed this minute," she ordered.

Morgan pushed Jonte's hands away. "Stop it! I'm not sick."

"Are you crazy? Just look at you. Your face is red as a beet."

"Jonte, stop it! Please, just leave me alone."

Jonte, shocked at Morgan's rudeness, walked out of the room, slamming the door behind her. *What's wrong with that girl? Every day she's more and more unpredictable.*

* * *

When Samuel arrived home and walked towards his study, Morgan approached.

"I need to speak with you, Papa," she said.

"Young lady, I think you know me well enough to know that I don't like to engage in conversation until I've had a chance to unwind a bit. Now, if you'll excuse me, please."

"No!" Morgan snapped.

"Are you ill?" he asked, reaching for her forehead.

"I'm not sick. I need to tell you something."

"What is it?" he asked, feeling his pulse quicken.

"I tried out for a role at the Reduta Theater today and I got the part, Papa," she said. "I'm going to be in a play."

Samuel felt relief, and then fury. He stared at Morgan for a moment and then said, "No you're not going to be in a play, and I refuse to discuss this matter any further!" He had shouted, and turning his back on Morgan, he began to enter his study, feeling his heart pounding furiously.

"Papa, please!" Morgan screamed. "Please wait. Don't walk away from me."

Samuel stopped. He turned around, fighting to control his fury. Tears were streaming down her face.

"I've never asked you for anything in my entire life. Please, Papa. Please don't deny me my chance." Her glistening eyes flashed with determination as she continued. "Haven't you always taught me to do my very best? Well, I did, and they chose me, Papa. Me. I was the best one. You should have seen me." She choked back a sob.

"I'm proud of all of your talents, Morgan, and I'm proud you were chosen." He hesitated, feeling heartsick. "Listen to me, child. I've spent my entire life trying to maintain a precarious balance, keeping one foot firmly planted in Judaism and the other planted in a secular world. My soul longed for the confines of Orthodoxy but my intellect wouldn't allow me to deny the existence of the arts and sciences. And when you were born I made a conscious decision to continue on this same path with you. And as I thought you would, you flourished. But now, now you are pushing too hard–asking for too much." His next words sounded empty, even to him. "Besides, a young lady of your standing has absolutely nothing to gain from such activities. It's a complete waste of time."

"But, Papa, I work so hard. I never waste time. Give me a chance. I promise you my school work won't suffer." *I can't give in. I know he means well but I won't let him take this away from me.*

Samuel knew the battle was lost. He had nurtured Morgan, encouraging her determination and single-mindedness. He simply wasn't capable of standing his ground with her even though his intuition told him that this indulgence was a terrible mistake.

* * *

Less than three months later, sixteen-year-old Morgan Rebecca Rabinowiszch appeared in her first play. The local critics wrote rave reviews, predicting she would one day bring fame to Vilna. Samuel and Sara attended that first performance.

During intermission, they sat huddled together, frightened by their daughter's obvious talent.

"What are we going to do, Sara? I didn't raise her for this," Samuel said.

"I don't know. I'm afraid she's really very good," Sara said, proud of Morgan and terrified at where that ability might lead her.

"She's too good. We have to put an end to this foolishness now. It's time she married and settled down," Samuel said.

Sara nodded. "You're right, of course. I'll contact the matchmaker first thing in the morning." Grasping Samuel's hand, she squeezed it reassuringly. "Don't worry, darling, Morgan's a good girl and she'll do the right thing."

Chapter 5

———————— ★ ————————

By 1922 Germany was in chaos. Her economy had collapsed and the inflation that followed brought grievous suffering to the poor and the helpless. Thousands more had died from the rampaging influenza epidemic that killed 20 million people worldwide.

In Berlin, those fortunate enough to have jobs got paid every day, usually at noon. With money in hand they ran to the nearest store to buy anything at any price. The frenzied people paid millions of marks for cuckoo clocks, shoes that didn't fit—anything that could be traded for something else.

The resilient German people were surviving by bartering and ruthless maneuvering. Barbarism prevailed, people were restless, and the streets were dangerous. Snipers shot indiscriminately from the rooftops at anything they saw.

Bitter and angry, the German people turned their hate outward, to anyone or anything foreign, and a frantic nationalism took hold. A generation began to spoil.

In 1922 the Milch twins turned twelve years old. In spite of being tall and gawky, they possessed classic Germanic features, and it was evident that Ilya would be a beauty and Otto would be distinctly handsome.

The twins spent their early years in the streets and became favorites in the neighborhood. Their friendliness prompted the local baker to employ them, and Otto and Ilya spent their teenage years working ten hours every Saturday and every day after school, rarely arriving home before nine at night. The hours were long, the pay was poor, but the work gave the twins refuge from their abusive father. Equally important, they never went hungry in the bakery.

Committed to rising above their poverty, and knowing instinctively that Otto would have to obtain a first rate education, the twins squirreled away every mark they could. Eventually they accumulated the needed tuition for Otto to enter the Friedenau Gymnasium, a school that taught Greek and Latin and espoused the nationalistic beliefs of the Fatherland, and the Reich. At sixteen, Otto's keen intellect was fully stimulated. But because he was the only student in the entire school who came from a working-class family, the teachers and students made his life miserable. But Otto's misery only served to make him more determined to succeed.

In his final year at the Gymnasium, Otto was introduced to the works of Max Wilhelm Wundt, a German psychologist who was generally considered the founder of scientific psychology. Wundt had carried out extensive experimental research on perception, feeling, and apperception, writing more than 500 published works. Otto read them all.

Tantalized by Wundt's occasional references to mind control and hypnosis, he read everything he could find on the subjects. Consumed with the idea of being able to control another human being's mind, he brought books home from the library and spent the hours when he should have been sleeping in study. Endlessly practicing, Otto found that he could hypnotize even his most skeptical friends. Cultivating this skill energized Otto, driving him deeper into his newfound obsession.

Upon his graduation, Otto was promoted to assistant manager of the bakery; and Ilya was promoted to apprentice baker. After extensive discussions, the twins reached two unavoidable conclusions: if they were to protect their mother from their father, they couldn't leave her alone; and if Otto was to attend the Institute of Physiology in Berlin, they had to continue saving as much as they could.

* * *

On a hot night in the middle of July, the owner of the bakery allowed the twins to leave an hour early. Few lights were on as the twins entered their tenement, and the chaos that bid them farewell every morning was absent. In its stead was an ominous silence.

"Have you seen the way he's been looking at me lately? I'm afraid, Otto," Ilya said, stopping at the first landing.

"You don't have to worry, Ilya. I'll protect you if he tries anything," Otto said, his eyes dark with determination.

They were both strikingly good looking, but Otto's father had constantly taunted him, calling him a fairy and a sissy, thinking that the features he found so desirable for his daughter—high cheekbones, full sensuous mouth, and enormous blue eyes—were much too feminine for his son. To offset his father's insults, Otto had asked to work in the receiving room at the bakery, where he had laboriously unloaded the 100-pound sacks of flour from the open carts, many times falling to the ground in a heap from the weight of them. And even though he was always sore and bruised, his childish physique had eventually turned into a solid mass of taut muscles.

"I know you'll protect me as best you can," Ilya said, "but you're no match for him."

"I said I'll take care of you," Otto insisted, taking Ilya by the arm and leading her into the dank two-bedroom apartment.

They made their way quietly to their room, and as they began undressing, they heard their mother's moan. Ilya, dressed only in her panties and bra, ran from the room.

"Oh my God, what's he done to you?" she cried, seeing her mother's face covered in blood.

"It's nothing," Ingrid slurred, trying to cover her face with the blood-soaked sheet.

"I'll kill that bastard," Otto swore, approaching his mother, his body rigid with anger.

Just then the door crashed open behind them. Sigmund, returning from the hallway bathroom, naked except for his filthy nightshirt smeared with his wife's dried blood, sneered as he studied his partially unclad daughter.

"Not bad," he said, licking his lips as he approached. Before either twin could react, he grabbed Ilya and began grinding himself against her. She screamed, but Sigmund took little notice, forcing her to the ground.

"I'm going to teach you to be a woman—a real woman!"

He slobbered drunkenly, pinning her down with his knees, his nakedness rubbing against her belly.

As Otto swung wildly at his father, Sigmund continued his attack on Ilya, tearing off her panties, spreading her legs apart, and brutally trying to penetrate her, oblivious to his son's blows.

"Stop it, you pig! Help me, Otto!" Ilya screamed.

Ingrid charged her husband, digging her nails into his face and shrieking, "No! No! No!"

Otto was still no match for his father's enormous strength. But in that moment, with Sigmund's laughter ringing in his ears, something dark and ugly burst inside of him. With a sudden serge of power, Otto pulled Sigmund off of Ilya and slammed him heavily to the ground. The laughter died in Sigmund's throat.

"I could kill you, you son of a bitch. I could cut your fucking cock off and stuff it down your throat," Otto snarled as his eyes burned like twin lasers into his father's, pinning him to the floor.

Sigmund was terrified and unable to move his eyes from his son's mesmerizing glare. As Otto stood, his blond hair soaked with sweat, he knew he had somehow taken control of his father.

"Get out, you bastard! If you ever come back here again, I swear I'll kill you," Otto said, looking down menacingly at his helpless father.

Sigmund scrambled to his feet, grabbed a handful of clothing, and ran for the door.

"Are you all right, Ilya? Please tell me you're OK," Otto pleaded, taking his twin into his arms.

"Oh, Otto," she said, her body convulsing with sobs, "I thought he was going to—"

"Shh, it's over now," Otto said, caressing his sister's face.

"I can't believe you actually stopped him. How did you do it?" his mother asked.

Otto continued to hold his sister tightly.

"He knew I would kill him, and I would have," he said, seeing for the first time the killer that lurked within. The bile rose in his throat as he realized that not only had he wanted to kill his father, but he would have relished doing it.

"The bastard was terrified, as if he were hypnotized or something," Ingrid said, rushing to the window to get a last view of her fleeing husband.

* * *

Everything changed for the Milch twins after that night. Twenty-two-year-old Otto took full responsibility for his mother and sister, and their daily existence was no longer filled with fear.

But the years of brutality and ridicule had irreparably damaged Otto's self-image, and the trauma of watching Ilya come so close to being raped by his father had simply compounded the problem, disastrously affecting his already fragile libido. He lost all interest in women. And when he felt the need for sexual release, he visualized a grotesque half-man, half-woman, and sustained an erection and reached orgasm only when he saw himself as the brutal aggressor.

Ilya, on the other hand, grew pensive, secretive, and tense, unable to dispel her memories of being defiled and violated, vowing to herself that no man would ever touch her again.

Chapter 6

─────────── ★ ───────────

World War I had not devastated Germany and her factories had remained mostly intact. Therefore, from 1924 through 1929 she was able to begin rebuilding her economic machine. Inflation had made the mark almost worthless, but by selling it abroad and borrowing money from foreign bankers, Germany began expanding and modernizing her plants.

For a time, mass production techniques and cheap labor made the country competitive in the world markets. Unfortunately, high tariff walls raised by competing countries and deflated agricultural prices resulting from world over-production brought a decline in the Republic's purchasing power, and before long the sources for loans began to dry up. Soon German industrial activity began to decline and unemployment began to rise. Frustration, despair, and anger became the foundation of the German consciousness. So when Adolf Hitler's National Socialist Party came upon the scene, the people greeted his hate-filled ideologies with exuberance.

The dynamic and charismatic Hitler promised social and economic reforms, vowing improved living conditions for the 4,000,000 unemployed German citizens and affirming that under his leadership Jews would not be citizens. Many in the professional classes, who felt they were suffering from the keen competition of the Jews in medicine, law, banking, and trades, cheered the promise of the National Socialist anti-Semitic program to rid the economy of its Jews. White-collar workers, students, the unemployed, and the poorly paid joined *en masse.*

On March 5, 1933, Hitler's Nazi party won fifty-two percent of the popular vote. Now, with 288 Nazi representatives and 53 Nationalists, Chancellor Hitler controlled a majority of the 648 seats in the new Reichstag. It had begun.

* * *

While walking together past an abandoned building one afternoon in the fall of 1935, the twenty-five-year-old Milch twins heard impassioned words coming over a public address system from somewhere deep inside the structure.

"Look at our flag! As our beloved Hitler said in his book, *Mein Kampf,* 'in red we see the social idea of the movement, in white, the nationalist idea, and in the swastika, the mission of the struggle for the victory of the Aryan man.'"

"Come on, Ilya," Otto said, pulling her by the hand. "I want to see what's going on."

"You know what's going on. It's a Nazi rally, and we don't have time for such nonsense."

"We don't have to be at work for another two hours," he said, leading his sister into the building.

Inside, hundreds of young people listened intently to a handsome man dressed in the full Nazi regalia of a lieutenant. The lieutenant was mesmerizing the group with Hitler's Aryan philosophy, promising national unity and national resurrection.

"It will begin with you," he said, pointing his finger boldly at his audience. "It begins with the young men and women of Germany!"

"Look at him," Otto said. "Just look at him! I can feel his power from here."

Extolling the need for physical violence, civil and political degradation and economic repression against the Jews, the lieutenant was whipping the crowd into an anti-Semitic frenzy.

His message ricocheted off the power symbols of the Nazi party. Giant insignias personally designed by Hitler were placed strategically throughout the hall, each bearing a black metal swastika perched on top of a silver wreath that was then surmounted by an eagle. On the bottom of the insignia, the initials N.S.D.A.P. were burned into a metal rectangle from which cords with fringe and tassels were hung. Sitting proudly atop of the insignia was a square swastika flag emblazoned with the words, *"Deutschland Erwache!"* (Germany Awake!)

Otto's darting eyes scanned the room, not knowing what to look at first. He watched in fascination as the brown shirt SA soldiers moved among the participants. The SA was used to protect the Nazi rallies, and they could be counted on to disrupt any rally that opposed the Nazi agenda. Otto forced his attention back to the speaker.

"Our Fuhrer chose the *hakenkreuz*, the swastika, as the symbol of our fight. It is a symbol as old as the planet, and if you are chosen to wear it, you must wear it proudly!"

At the end of his speech the young lieutenant moved into the waiting crowd, shaking hands and accepting expected accolades. He was an influential Nazi with a passion for good looking young men, and as the head of the Munich SA, he never ran out of new love interests, always finding what he wanted at the rallies. He spotted Otto.

"Let me introduce myself. I'm Lieutenant Edmund Heines." He raised his hand in the Nazi salute.

Otto smiled. "I'm Otto Milch and this is my sister Ilya."

"Did you enjoy the rally?"

The Lieutenant's attention apparently flattered Otto, whose face flushed a deep red.

"It was inspirational. I feel as if my life has been changed."

Edmund knew instinctively that Otto was an innocent. He put his arm around him and whispered, "Your life has been changed. Would you like me to introduce you to the Fuhrer one day?"

"I would like that very much," Otto said, smiling eagerly.

"We will be great friends, you and I," Heines said as he looked intently at Otto, knowing that it would be much more that that.

Chapter 7

──────── ★ ────────

The crickets chirping filtered through the partially opened window in the anteroom of Sara and Samuel's bedroom. Sara shifted comfortably in her chair as she quietly worked her needlepoint. Samuel, having completed the article he had been reading, set it down and smiled at Sara, enjoying the intimacy of the moment. Sensing that he was watching her, Sara looked up. When their eyes met, they both looked away, realizing they could no longer put off their discussion about Morgan's future.

"Samuel, I know this is going to be difficult for us both," Sara said, feeling her throat tighten, "but we really must meet with the matchmaker."

"I know," Samuel said, "but perhaps we could wait just a little longer," his mind flashing back to Morgan's first steps and first words. *She is my baby, my only child.*

"I don't think that's a good idea. She's already too smitten with being on the stage," Sara said, surprised by Samuel's indecisiveness. "Besides, it could take months to make a proper match."

"Fine. You meet with Mrs. Pekarsky, but you'll have to do it without me. I don't have the time," he said, ashamed by the transparency of his excuse. "In the meantime I don't think Morgan should be told about any of this. It would only upset her." He got up from the chair, his signal that it was time for them to retire for the night.

Once in bed, Samuel turned his back to Sara, feigning sleep. But instead, he relived the precious memories of his daughter's life. He visualized her violet eyes sparkling with joy, then he visualized them filling with tears. *I won't be there to wipe away those tears anymore.* He felt empty at the prospect of losing Morgan, but he was also overcome with guilt for not being there for Sara, who he knew must be as heartsick as he was. He turned over and reached for his wife, but she didn't respond.

Desperately, Samuel began silently praying for guidance and understanding, and soon a new picture began to form in his mind. He saw himself bouncing grandchildren on his knee and he saw a house filled with excitement and noise. *Yes, my Morgan will be a wonderful mother. And she'll learn to be a good wife.* With the sound of children's laughter in his head, Samuel fell into a deep, peaceful sleep.

Sara lay awake for hours, contemplating if she and Samuel had the right to steal their daughter's dreams. On one level, Sara knew that she was simply doing what was expected of her as a mother—keeping faith with the traditions. But on a deeper level, she wasn't sure those traditions were still valid.

Exhausted, her pillow wet from tears, Sara finally acquiesced. *I can do this! I'll find a good husband for Morgan, someone young and full of spirit, someone who will make her happy.*

The next morning, Sara had a note arranging for a meeting delivered to Mrs. Pekarsky.

* * *

Sara awakened early on the day of their appointment. Determined to make a good impression, she dressed carefully and put on her most expensive jewelry.

"Mrs. Pekarsky, how very nice to see you. Won't you please come in and make yourself comfortable," Sara said when the butler brought Mrs. Pekarsky's into the drawing room.

Mrs. Pekarsky paused in the doorway, practically filling it with her ample girth, and openly studied her surroundings.

"Lovely, very lovely," she said after appraising the marquetry desk with its inlay of tortoiseshell and ivory, obviously designed by Roentgen. The desk sat against a wall under a painting by Nicolas Poussin. Four perfectly adorned Louis XVI chairs surrounded a gilt and bronze table mounted on a pink marble base. She moved past it to the tapestry sofa displaying a tawdry scene from the *Fables of La Fontaine*, and sat down heavily. Sara moved one of the Louis XVI chairs directly opposite Mrs. Pekarsky.

"I was so happy to receive your invitation, my dear," the matchmaker said in a high-pitched voice. "After all, by sixteen most proper young women have already been introduced to their intended husbands."

Sara felt embarrassment and guilt. The woman was obviously aghast that she and Samuel had waited so long.

"You know, a miracle worker I'm not. Nice Jewish men don't grow on trees, and I'm afraid it won't be easy finding your daughter a husband. I don't want to hurt your feelings, dear, but I wouldn't be doing my job if I didn't tell you the whole truth right from the beginning. Your daughter's antics—flaunting herself on the stage and all—have not exactly been good for her reputation, let me tell you."

Sara panicked, imagining Mrs. Pekarsky searching through her "nobody wants this one" file.

"Of course," the matchmaker continued, "you know what they say— 'There's a cover for every pot.'" Her laugh was more like a cackle.

She sounds like a hyena.

"Don't you worry, dearie. I'm the best matchmaker in all of Poland. I'll find a match. I'll find one somewhere. Of course, you understand that it may have to be someone who lives far away from Vilna. I'll of course have to find a gentleman who doesn't know about your daughter's activities."

Mrs. Pekarsky made a great show of removing the hanky from her pocketbook and mopping at the beads of perspiration dripping down her face. With great difficulty she rose from the sofa.

"I'll see myself to the door. Hopefully you'll hear from me soon."

Mrs. Pekarsky was gone before Sara could mutter a word. She felt faint and angry.

How dare that woman speak to me in such a manner? I'll never let her step foot in my house again!

But she knew she had no alternatives. Without Mrs. Pekarsky, Morgan would be lost.

Chapter 8

———— ★ ————

In the summer of 1935 Robert Osborne followed the porter through the exuberant throng of people, hardly aware of the commotion he was causing at the Vilna train station. His sweet face, deceptively promising sex and danger, was known throughout Europe, his intense cobalt eyes and enchanting smile effortlessly inviting intimacy.

Jacob Gold easily spotted Robert and hurried to his side.

"Welcome to Vilna," Jacob said, shaking his hand heartily.

"Jacob, what a pleasant surprise. I thought you were in England healing the sick," Robert said, hugging him warmly.

"I'm here on holiday."

"How are your parents?"

"They're great," Jacob said, leading Robert to the waiting automobile.

* * *

Fifteen minutes later the phone rang in Morgan's home.

"Did you hear? Robert Osborne's in Vilna. I swear it, Morgan," her friend Shirley said. "My aunt Ethel saw him at the train station."

"Are you sure?" Morgan asked.

"I'm sure."

"Oh my God. The most famous actor in all of Europe is somewhere in Vilna at this very moment! I could just die," Morgan said, sitting down to catch her breath.

* * *

Jacob wanted it to be the surprise of her life, so he had not called to tell Morgan that Robert Osborne was staying at his home overnight. The actor had befriended Jacob's mother and father years earlier while attending a dinner at the French Prime Minister's residence.

Robert had supper with the Gold's that night, catching up on the events that had transpired since their last meeting almost four years earlier. Over coffee, Jacob asked Robert if he had plans for the evening.

"No, not really. Why? Got something in mind?" Robert asked.

"The Reduta Theater is presenting Wyspianski's *Wesele*, and I thought you might like to go."

"Jacob!" his mother said reproachfully. "You'll have to forgive my son. He has a friend in the production, so I'm afraid he has ulterior motives."

"People say she's going to be a famous actress one day," Jacob said.

"I'm at your disposal," Robert said, laughing mischievously. He loved amateur productions and had planned to search for new talent in Warsaw anyway.

* * *

From the first moment she stepped on stage, Robert was entranced. Morgan's rich blue-black hair cascaded in gentle waves to her shoulders, framing a face so alluring that Robert actually gasped. Her lips were full; her complexion was dove white, and her violet eyes slanted exotically. Her tiny waist, slim hips, firm breasts, and long legs moved with the grace of a ballerina. He couldn't wait to meet her.

At the end of the performance, Robert strode confidently toward the stage. Morgan stood in a corner, surrounded by a buzzing cast, waiting for her turn in the bathroom to wash off her make-up. The buzz became a whisper as Robert and Jacob approached.

Sensing the sudden silence, Morgan glanced up and immediately recognized Jacob approaching.

"I didn't know you where back in…"

Her words caught in her throat as she noticed Robert. Her face turned crimson.

"Morgan," Jacob said, "I'd like you to meet Robert Osborne."

"Miss Rabinowiszch, that was one of the finest performances I've ever had the pleasure of watching. You're a great talent," he said, gently shaking her hand.

Morgan could see his lips moving and she could see the intensity in his eyes, but she couldn't hear him. A thunderous rushing sound filled her head, and the room began to spin. Morgan had never fainted before, but she knew she was going to faint now.

Robert saw the color draining from her face and he reached out to catch Morgan just as she crumpled. He sat on the ground, holding Morgan in his arms while Jacob ran for a cold compress. He was about to place it on Morgan's forehead when she awakened.

She gasped and jerked herself up in embarrassment.

"I'm so sorry," she said while straightening her skirt, her head still spinning. "I guess I should have eaten something before I went on."

"Are you feeling better?" Robert asked, concern in his voice, while he remained cross-legged on the floor.

As Robert studied her intently, she began to lose her embarrassment and found herself fascinated by the sound of his voice and his vibrant blue eyes.

"I think we should get your friend something to eat," Robert said as he stood and brushed himself off.

"You don't have to bother," she said, hoping he would.

"I assure you it's no bother, for either of us," Robert said, looking at Jacob. "Please say that you'll join us."

* * *

Even before they could hail a taxi, Morgan had completely gotten over the initial shock of being in Robert's presence. Her confidence and easy manner returned. She chatted with Robert in flawless French, wanting to know everything about what it was like to be a star. And by the time the three of them reached the restaurant, Morgan had Robert roaring with laughter at the outrageousness of her queries.

They found a booth at the back of the restaurant, and after they had ordered, Robert looked intently at Morgan. "With all the questions you already asked, I'm somewhat amazed you haven't asked me why I'm here in Vilna."

Morgan smiled. "To tell you the truth, I was dying to know, but I would never ask you anything that personal," she replied.

Robert and Jacob chuckled, finding her sudden reticence amusingly contradictory to the uninhibited grilling she had just put him through.

Morgan pouted, determined now to have the answer. "Well, since you brought it up, are you going to tell me or not?" she asked.

Robert smiled. "Actually, I was on my way to Warsaw in search of new talent. At this point in my career I can choose the people I want in my cast, and to tell you the truth, I've become insufferably bored with the usual collection of actors."

Morgan held her breath, almost afraid to hear his next words.

"When I saw you on stage tonight, I was overwhelmed," he said. "It's not just your beauty and talent, there's something else about you, something inexplicably powerful." He hesitated. "I'd like you to be in my next production."

"You don't really mean that, do you? Is this some kind of joke? Are you in on this, Jacob?" she accused.

Jacob shook his head, aghast at what Robert had just said. He had been planning to speak with his parents about arranging a marriage contract with Morgan and he couldn't believe that he may have had some part in this impending fiasco.

"You have no idea what it's like to dream of performing on stage—a real stage in a real production," Morgan continued, "to dream of it all your life, but to know that it's impossible. Then you come along, and to amuse yourself for an evening, you throw a crumb to a little bird. Well, I won't allow you to amuse yourselves at my expense." Morgan felt the hot tears stinging her eyes.

She moved to get up from the booth but Robert put his hand on hers. "Dear God, girl, listen to me. I do know about those dreams. Don't you think I've also had them? I would never, as you say, amuse myself at your expense. You must believe me. Your dream can be realized, Morgan, if you'll just listen to me."

Morgan slid back into the seat, sighing deeply and allowing herself to relax. "No, you have to listen to me. Even if you are serious, this is impossible—my family would never allow it. So there's no point in continuing this discussion."

Robert sensed that no one could stop this girl from doing anything she really wanted to do, so he pushed on. "Morgan, I can help make you a star. I can put the theaters of Europe at your feet, but it won't be easy. Quite the contrary, you'll work harder than you ever imagined." He spoke almost reverently as he continued. "But I have absolutely no doubt that you have all of the qualities and talent of a major performer. If you're willing to put in the work required, you'll make it. Let me help you." Robert was afraid to stop talking, afraid she might bolt out of his life. "I recently decided I'd try my hand at the theater again, and I want to take you with me. There are fabulous new playhouses being built all over Europe. In Germany, they're building a theater that will hold thousands of people. I see you on those stages, Morgan. I see the people rising to their feet in adulation. This is your chance. Please don't let it slip through your fingers."

Jacob crumpled his napkin and threw it on the table. He cursed himself for ever having introduced Robert to Morgan. After what felt like a very long time, Morgan finally spoke. To Jacob it was the voice of a stranger, a voice he had never heard before.

"I need some time to think about this. I'm not promising you anything. As a matter of fact, the answer will probably be no."

Robert was elated. *At least she is willing to think about it. What more can I ask?* "I'll be in Warsaw for a month. At the end of that month I'll come back for your answer."

* * *

Voices echoed inside the cavernous train station, and the musty odor of perspiration from the dozens of passengers who were anxiously milling around assaulted Robert and Jacob's senses as they made their way to the busy lunch counter.

"Two coffees please," Robert said to the star-struck waitress as he noticed her hands shaking so badly she could barely pour. He handed Jacob a cup and the two men moved to a warn wooden bench facing the tracks.

"You're upset with me about last night, aren't you?" Robert asked.

"No, I'm not," Jacob said, his anger barely disguised.

"Are you in love with Morgan?"

"She's my friend and that's all she is," he said without much conviction. "You don't realize what you've done, do you?" Jacob asked.

"What have I done?" Robert asked, honestly dismayed.

"How can I explain this to you? Morgan's different. She has unrealistic dreams and a dangerous wanderlust that will only get her in trouble. You must understand that Morgan could never go with you, not even if she wanted to. She has a responsibility to her family, and whether she likes it or not, she has to live up to their expectations. You have to leave her alone. We're Jews, Robert."

"I can't leave her alone, Jacob," Robert said, intuitively knowing that his feelings for Morgan were much more than infatuation. "I'm twenty-six years old, and I've learned to fight for what I want. And even though I know it displeases you, I intend to fight for Morgan. She may not want me, but damn it, she deserves to be on the stage!"

The whistle screamed the train's imminent departure, giving both men a reprieve from the conversation.

"Have a good trip," Jacob said stiffly as Robert turned to leave.

Chapter 9

— ★ —

In July of 1914, when Robert was only seven, his father, Michael, had walked out, leaving his young wife and son to fend for themselves. In August of that same year the fragile peace that had prevailed in Europe exploded.

Twenty-five-year-old Annabelle Osborne had been barely making ends meet, and as the guns began firing she had grown desperate, certain that she would no longer be able to support and protect her young son. After a frantic search, she got a job as a maid, but that meant leaving Robert with the only person who offered to help–her alcoholic neighbor Kitty. Annabelle, having herself been raised by a mother who drank too much, found the arrangement intolerable. So, when her employer offered to see her home in his carriage one snowy day in November, she accepted. When he made advances towards her, promising to care for her and her young child, she hadn't refused.

Even though Annabelle lacked the skills of an accomplished hostess or the wily mannerisms of a courtesan, she had something more valuable–she was beautiful, fresh, naive, and filled with an unassuming charm. She became the mistress of Henri Conde, a direct descendent of Prince Louis II de Conde, and instantly everything changed for Robert and Annabelle.

Henri moved them into rooms in a respectable neighborhood deep within the countryside of France, away from the terror of an escalating war. When the war ended, he brought Annabelle and Robert back to Paris, setting them up in beautifully appointed rooms not far from the Opera House.

Because Henri possessed enormous wealth and power, and he was married to a fat, ugly, and disagreeable wife, the wealthy matrons of Paris politely received Annabelle. She learned to entertain lavishly in her apartments; and soon it became an honor to receive an invitation to the salon of Annabelle Osborne.

For Henri the arrangement was quite satisfactory. On the one hand he saw Annabelle as a valuable possession. Something selected and paid for; on the other, he loved and was deeply devoted to her. But to Henri, Robert was a constant reminder that Annabelle had in fact been with and loved another man, and his ego couldn't tolerate that.

On the eve of Robert's twelfth birthday, when he was suppose to be sleeping, he slipped out of his bed and stood behind a partially closed door listening to a conversation between Henri and his mother.

"What kind of a life could the boy possibly have here, living in a home filled with only women? There are things a boy needs to be taught, things that neither you nor his nanny can teach him. He needs to build character and resolve. That can only be accomplished through a strict regimen of discipline and education," Henri said.

Robert, as young as he was, knew that Henri wanted to remove him from his life and that his mother was being manipulated. He hated Henri for it, but there was nothing he could do.

"Some of the finest families in Europe send their sons to boarding schools in France. And I'm willing to send your son to one of the finest," Henri said, knowing that Annabelle's greatest wish was to have her son one day accepted into proper European society. Robert could hear the sobs coming from his mother. "There, there, my dear. Don't cry. This isn't the time to be selfish. We must keep the boy's best interests at heart."

Robert wanted to rush into the room and beg his mother not to listen to a word the deceitful man was saying. But he knew it would have only deepened Henri's resolve that "the boy" needed discipline.

* * *

Out of love and devotion to his mother, Robert went off to school without ever voicing his objections.

"It's the best thing for you, my darling. Some day you'll understand," Annabelle had said that cool September day in 1919 as she put her son on the train.

As Robert matured, he eventually concluded that perhaps in some ways his mother actually had been right.

He spent six years at Cordeliers, an exclusive boys school in the South of France, never once coming home during the term for a holiday, because Henri had convinced Annabelle that Robert was better off staying at school. In spite of her love for her son, Annabelle was too occupied with her own fears of abandonment, knowing that without Henri she would have nothing. It was only during the summer months, when Henri was forced to take his wife and five children to his country estate, that Robert had been allowed to come home.

"What can I do? I have no choice," Annabelle had always lamented when her son returned, begging him to forgive her. Robert didn't know what she could do, but he'd grown to resent her, feeling she loved Henri more than she loved him.

For six summers Robert and Annabelle shared a life filled with tainted affection, surviving by pretending that they had a normal and healthy relationship. As Robert matured, he edged further away from the watchful eyes of his mother. Viewing Robert's rebellion as desertion and to allay what she had seen as the ultimate insult, Annabelle began drinking excessively.

Robert, unaware of his mother's drinking problem, busily pursued his own interests, spending most nights prowling the whorehouses and music halls of the city. Until one night, while dining with friends at the L'orangerie, an excessively expensive restaurant located on the river Seine, where he met the Duchess.

In her prime the Duchess had been the most famous and sought after actress in all of France. Her thick blond hair fell in ringlets well past the middle of her back, and she wore it tied in crimson ribbons that complimented her cherry red lips and Nile green eyes. She was broad shouldered, big breasted, and small of waist and hips.

Emboldened by whiskey, one of Robert's friends dared to ask the thirty-eight-year-old Duchess to join them for a drink. The lusty woman slipped into the booth and quickly set her sights on Robert. With the accomplished style of a well-bred courtesan, she began flirting openly with him, and after two more drinks, she placed her hand on Robert's thigh, all the while staring deeply into his eyes.

Robert was dumbfounded by the aggression of the most desirable woman he had ever met and was completely infatuated with her irresistible charm.

"Let's go, my pet," the Duchess whispered, sliding her hand to his pulsating erection. "The Duchess has a wonderful surprise for you."

* * *

Robert, hungry for affection, had soon become addicted to the Duchess. She in turn had become obsessed with the seventeen-year-old Robert, finding his easy curiosity, dangerous good looks, and enticing sexuality an amusing distraction. Robert's whole world began revolving around the Duchess and her pleasures, and eventually he even began to believe that she loved him. But the Duchess needed more than Robert could ever give her, and he was not prepared to compete with her wounded and aging ego. The Duchess was losing her beauty to time, and in her desperate search to prevent the inevitable, she grasped on to young men, boys really, and played hurtful games with their egos and hearts. When Robert felt he could no longer tolerate her affairs with other young men, he dared to question her about it. Her answer had left no room for further discussion.

"Variety, my pet, variety. It only makes me appreciate you more. Never forget how much the Duchess loves you. Now, don't make me angry with your boring jealousy. Make the Duchess happy."

* * *

When Robert returned for his final year of school, he wrote to the Duchess every day. Her replies to Robert were filled with glorious stories of her years on the stage, and they ignited a spark in Robert's soul that inspired him to want to become an actor. The Duchess was pleased with Robert's decision, promising to use her varied influences to help him.

As the frigid winter closed in, Robert grew concerned over how melancholy and depressed her letters had become. She spoke often of death and illness, ending every letter that winter with the same words, "The Theater is my only true love, and only an adoring audience can fulfill my deepest needs. It is their voices I long to hear and their approval I would die for. Nothing else really matters."

Robert felt sick, as he began to understand that she was incapable of ever really loving anyone. He decided that somehow he would have to stop his senseless love affair with her.

The following summer he vowed to repel her amorous advances, but the Duchess found his resolve refreshing and challenging. She flaunted herself in front of Robert, kissing and fondling other men. Finally, unable to control his jealousy, Robert relented and begged her to take him back.

As a reward for his recommitted devotion, the Duchess arranged for Robert to meet the famous actor, poet, and visionary Antonin Artuad, who had recently formed his own theater company with Alfred Jarry, Roger Vitrac, and Robert Aron. After agreeing to allow Robert to attend their daily rehearsals, Artaud began taking an interest in Robert, tutoring him whenever he had a spare moment. Robert proved to be an exceptionally talented student, and by the end of that summer Antonin had arranged for Robert to join a traveling theatrical troupe.

Annabelle sent her son off with her blessings, hoping that Robert's leaving would put an end to his ridiculous affair with the Duchess. But Robert had remained devoted.

At the end of the three-month tour he returned to Paris. He went directly to the duchess's apartment without calling. The maid answered the door but didn't invite him in.

"Where's the Duchess?" he asked, confused by the maid's rudeness.

"You don't know?"

Robert began to tremble. He leaned against the door, shaken by the thought that she might be dead.

"The Duchess is on her honeymoon," the maid replied. "She was married over a month ago. I'm sorry. I thought she surely would have told you."

Stunned, Robert turned and ran blindly from the house, heartsick with the feeling that he had again been abandoned.

* * *

Robert returned to the acting troupe without seeing his mother, not knowing how desperate Annabelle's life had become. She had taken to constant drinking, and Henri had been threatening to leave her if she didn't stop immediately. She didn't–she couldn't–and on a balmy spring day in 1928, Annabelle Osborne threw a rope over the chandelier in her bedroom, stood on a chair, and took her own life.

The news of his mother's suicide produced a pain, fury, and desperation in Robert Osborne that would forever alter his life. He vowed to never again allow others to decide the course of his life. With that decision, everything seemed to come more easily for him. Subconsciously, the tragedy of his mother's death had positively impacted his acting ability, giving him a depth rarely found in someone so young. His passionate portrayals soon caught the attention of the director of le Theatre Francais, who quickly made him a permanent member of the company and starred him in his first performance when he was only twenty. Robert astounded his audiences, and from that performance on his success had been meteoric.

Through determined discipline, Robert had also managed to maintain a personal life uncluttered by the complications of any serious involvements.

Chapter 10

──────── ★ ────────

Jacob tried to talk to Morgan about Robert's proposal, but she refused to discuss it.

"Too many other things are going on in my life. I can't even consider it."

That lie only increased her self-loathing and drove her even deeper into herself. Sleep evaded her, food made her sick and conversation became insufferably boring. She thought her image of Robert would fade, but it only grew sharper. She spent hours daydreaming about him and life in Paris. She wanted to see him, to be near him again, and she wanted everything he represented–adventure, fame, and love.

The reality thrust upon her by Robert's proposition also gave her a sense of new power. She began to realize that her destiny was in her own hands. She saw two distinct paths: one had been walked by generations of her predecessors, women who donned the veil of obedience and fulfilled their duties as wife and mother; the other, littered with uncertainty and scorn, would surely desecrate the principles so dear to the people she loved so much.

If she chose the second path, she wondered if she was brave enough to walk away from the safety and security of her family, if she had the courage to allow her dreams to carry her past her cowardice and her guilt.

While Morgan pondered, the powers of fate moved unavoidably forward. Exactly two weeks after Sara's visit with Mrs. Pekarsky, a letter arrived by messenger. Sara sat with it on her lap, turning it over in her hand, lightly gingering the script before tearing it open, her own desperate resolve weakening.

* * *

Dear Mrs. Rabinowiszch,

I have located a suitable husband for you daughter. I will be available to meet with you tomorrow afternoon at precisely two o'clock. I await your reply.

Respectfully yours,
Mrs. Ethel Pekarsky

* * *

At two the next day, Mrs. Pekarsky was shown into the drawing room, but this time both women shared the sofa. Sara went through the amenities of serving tea and cookies, but by the time Mrs. Pekarsky had eaten her sixth cookie, Sara was unable to contain herself any longer.

"Would you please tell me about the young man," Sara demanded, aware that she was blatantly disregarding protocol by not waiting for the matchmaker to first bring up the subject.

Mrs. Pekarsky slowly finished her cookie, wiped her face, and then smiled at Sara.

Oh, for God's sake, get on with it!

"Well, my dear, I can tell you it wasn't easy finding a suitable young man. As expected, I had absolutely no luck with any of the prominent families in Vilna. Don't misunderstand; they all have the utmost respect for you and your fine husband. It's just they want a daughter-in-law with a lot less...notoriety. And to be perfectly honest, they want someone a little more docile.

"Anyway" she continued, "I've found the perfect match. He's a doctor. As a matter of fact, he comes from a very long line of doctors. His name is Howard Dworsky and he's twenty-six years old. He works in a hospital in Warsaw, which is, as you know, not all that far from here. He owns a lovely set of rooms–that I saw with my own eyes–in a very prestigious building in the city. As you can well imagine, he's been sought after by every matchmaker in the area. But he was, believe it or not, holding out for someone with real intelligence and some spirit. When I heard that, I almost plotzed. So I took the first train I could grab, and I went to meet this young man in person. What an exhausting trip it was, so many hours on the train. So ask me if it was worth it? He was just perfect!"

Sara opened her mouth to respond, but Mrs. Pekarsky waved her hand at the wrist and said, "Do you know how lucky you are to have called me, how lucky you are I have so many connections?"

You pompous...

Before Sara could find the appropriate noun in her head, the arrogant matchmaker continued.

"So OK, my dear, it's now up to you to introduce the happy couple. We'll work out my fee and a contract after they've met. I invited him to join you for Shabbas dinner one week from tomorrow night. He'll arrive at six o'clock if that's convenient for you?"

Sara held her head high and looked directly at Mrs. Pekarsky. "That sounds just fine. I have one question," she said, her voice dropping an octave. "What does he look like?" Sara knew that at twenty-six he was going to seem like and old man to Morgan.

"What matters my dear woman is whether or not the prospective young man is of equal station in life." Ethel Pekarsky was incredulous, having never been asked that question before. "What is this world coming too?"

"I was simply curious," Sara said, knowing with some satisfaction that she had clearly crossed the boundaries of propriety. She gave Mrs. Pekarsky her most charming smile. "You've done a wonderful job. Now, would you like more cookies?"

* * *

When Samuel arrived home at seven that evening, Sara was at the front door waiting for him.

"What is it, Sara? Has something happened?" he asked, handing Sara his hat after kissing her cheek.

"Oh, Samuel, I have the most wonderful news. Mrs. Pekarsky was here today, and she's found a husband for Morgan. A wonderful young man, a doctor." Sara watched closely for Samuel's reaction, having already decided that Morgan's fate was sealed.

She knew that Samuel had been trying to prepare himself for this moment, but when the words were actually spoken, he looked as if he'd been kicked in the stomach.

"Samuel, are you OK?" Sara asked, seeing the color drain from his face.

"Of course. A job well done, my dear. With God's blessing we'll fill this house with grandchildren. Come and sit. I want to hear all the details," he said, taking Sara's hand as they moved into the drawing room. "What's my new son-in-law like? he asked, trying to convince Sara–and himself–that he was really pleased.

Sara snuggled against Samuel on the sofa and reiterated the details of her conversation with Mrs. Pekarsky. When she described her impressions of the matchmaker, they both couldn't contain their laughter.

"You wouldn't have believed it, Samuel. God forgive me for saying this, but the woman is an absolute sow!"

Their laughter renewed them, making the task ahead seem much less ominous.

"When do you think we should tell Morgan?" Sara asked a short time later.

"I'll tell her tomorrow night after Shabbas dinner. This way she'll have an entire week to get adjusted to the idea," Samuel said. "It will also give me an entire evening to figure out just how to break the news to her. We are doing the right thing, aren't we, Sara?"

His vulnerability touched Sara deeply. She put her arms around him and whispered, "This acting business has gone way too far and we must stop it now. Besides, we only want for her what we have. How can that be wrong? What else could she do with her life? She's to be a wife and mother, that's her duty."

* * *

In the Rabinowiszch's observant home, Friday evening was a time of great festivity. The Sabbath table was adorned with the family's finest china and silver, and the fragrance from the freshly baked challah, chicken soup, and brisket filled the house. It was a time for gentle conversation and witty repartee. Still, Morgan could feel a tension in the air as she slowly picked at her meal.

At first she was concerned that her mother might be ill, considering how strangely she'd been acting over the past few weeks. The thought terrified her, bringing on a rare headache.

"*Ketsul,* come and take a walk with me in the garden," Samuel said when dinner was finally over.

Morgan hadn't heard Samuel use that particular term of endearment for years, and his use now intensified her concerns.

Stars glistened overhead and only the hoot of a barn owl off in the distance broke the stillness of the lush garden. Samuel faced Morgan and smiled, noting how beautiful and vulnerable she looked with the moonlight reflecting off her childlike face.

"You've grown into a lovely young woman, and I want you to know that your mother and I are very proud of you."

Morgan looked closely at Samuel, trying to fathom what he was trying to say.

"There comes a time," he said, clearing his throat self-consciously, "when a young woman needs to think about getting married. And your mother and I have decided that you're now at that age."

Morgan gasped.

"We've found a wonderful young doctor who'll be a very good husband for you. And while your mother and I regret that you'll have to live in Warsaw for now, I'm quite sure I'll be able to arrange a position for him right here in Vilna." Samuel stopped. He was looking into Morgan's eyes, and for a moment Morgan feared he detected her terror.

Morgan opened her mouth to speak, but nothing would come out. She gasped for air and tried again. From somewhere deep inside of herself she heard a scream, a bursting, a fire exploding, but no sound escaped her mouth.

"I understand this is a shock, but you'll grow used to the idea. I'm sure when you meet the young man next Friday, you'll be well pleased," Samuel said, feeling utterly exhausted.

He took Morgan's icy hand in his and put his arm around her, leading her back into the house.

Sara had been waiting expectantly, and when she saw her vacant-eyed, trembling child; she rushed to her, encircling Morgan in her arms.

"It's going to be all right, Morgan. I know you'll be happy," Sara said brightly, despite Morgan's damnatory expression.

"This is all a little too overwhelming. If you'll please excuse me, I'd like to go to my room now," Morgan said, her voice cooler than the evening air.

"Do you think she's all right? She looked so strange," Sara said to Samuel after Morgan had gone.

"She'll be fine. She just needs time. She's a good girl. She'll soon realize that she has a duty to herself and to us," Samuel said with more conviction than he actually felt.

Chapter 11

─────── ★ ───────

Morgan spent the next three days in bed with a raging fever. When she slept, her dreams were filled with vivid pictures. Sometimes she would see herself as the perfect wife and mother, leading a proper life, one that would make all the people she loved happy. And at other times, when her fever was at its worst, she would see Robert and hear his voice pleading, "Come with me, Morgan. Don't let your chance slip by."

Sara checked on her daughter every few hours.

"Speak to me, darling. Let me help you. I understand so much more than you think I do."

Morgan looked at her mother vacantly, then shook her head and closed her eyes, deciding her dreams were much better than reality.

In the evenings, Samuel would come. He would just sit and stare at her, so Morgan forced herself to speak, unable to bear the pain on his face.

"I'm OK, Papa. It'll pass."

"It's my fault. I never should have let you go out into the chill night air. If I'd paid better attention, you wouldn't have gotten sick."

"Papa, it's only a cold. I'll be fine."

By Friday afternoon Morgan had made up her mind to bravely face her future, and as six o'clock approached, she began dressing. Her arms felt like lead weights as she slipped the heavy velvet dress over her head. She looked into the mirror and thought; I just might look ugly enough to scare off Dr. Dworsky. Her alabaster complexion was sallow, so she pinched her cheeks. Her midnight tresses cascaded down her back in wild splendor and her violet eyes sparkled, but Morgan couldn't see her exquisite beauty; she could only see the anguish.

Samuel watched Morgan slowly descend the main staircase. His breath caught in his throat as he thought how really beautiful and fragile she looked. And for a moment he feared he might begin to cry. Fighting off the urge, he straightened his back.

"You look lovely," he said, gently embracing her. "You know, darling, if you still feel ill, we could make your excuses."

"I feel much better. I'll just go and sit in the library until Dr. Dworsky arrives," she said.

"You know, Morgan, the first time I met your mother, I was so nervous I almost got sick on her front doorstep. I never told her that. Actually I never told anyone that before," Samuel said.

Morgan reached up and kissed her father on the cheek.

"Papa, it'll be OK. I understand how difficult this must be for you as well."

Morgan heard the knock on the front door, and she heard the butler invite the young man in. Her parents greeted him and they went into the living room. She spent the next ten minutes pacing before the three of them entered the library. Seeing the joy on her parents' faces, she knew that the young man must have made a favorable impression.

"Morgan, I'd like to introduce you to Dr. Howard Dworsky," Samuel said.

Howard nodded his head almost imperceptibly and then extended his hand to Morgan.

"It's such a pleasure to meet you, Miss Rabinowiszch."

In a glance Morgan decided he wasn't bad looking, although his voice was a little too high-pitched for her taste. He had dark brown curly hair, small intense eyes that were hidden behind very thick glasses, and a mouth that seemed to be perpetually smiling. His nose was prominent but not overly so, and Morgan found herself smiling warmly at him, enjoying how disheveled he looked in what was obviously a brand new suit.

"It's nice to meet you as well," she said. "I understand you're a doctor. What's your specialty, if you don't mind my asking?" Morgan said as they sat on the dual couches that dominated the room.

"Actually, I'm in research, and I spend most of my time in a laboratory," he said, obviously expecting a look of disappointment to cross Morgan's face.

"I think that's absolutely marvelous. I'm sure the medical profession needs men like you who are willing to spend their lives searching for cures. You should be very proud of yourself."

Dinner was filled with animated conversation, and Morgan found Howard delightful. After dinner, Samuel suggested that she and Howard take a stroll in the garden.

The evening was warm, and Morgan slipped her arm easily through Howard's as they followed the path to the gazebo. The moon, full and bright, hung in the sky like a beacon as they sat down to talk.

"You have such a nice family. You're a very lucky young woman," he said.

"Thank you. I love them very much."

"I'm sure the thought of leaving them must be a source of great turmoil for you, so please let me put your concerns to rest. You may visit them whenever you like, and of course they'll always be welcome in our home." He smiled at Morgan.

What makes him think he can tell me what I can and cannot do, no matter how nicely he says it?

"If you don't mind, I'd like to tell you a little about myself," he said, apparently not noticing the anger in Morgan's eyes. "I've spent the last several years deeply involved in my work. Some people say I'm antisocial, but I don't think you'll find that to be necessarily true. I'm just easily preoccupied. It's true that I can be rather disorganized but I'll certainly do my best not to clutter up our home." He paused and looked down at his tightly clenched hands. "Look, Miss Rabinowiszch, I know to someone like you I must not seem like much of a catch, but I'll be a good husband. I promise you that."

Morgan felt her anger evaporating.

"Has anyone told you about me, I mean really told you about me?"

"I don't know what you mean," Howard said.

"The truth is, all I've ever wanted is to be a professional actress. And besides that, I'm strong minded—even pig-headed at times—and that's certainly not a quality you want in your wife."

"You'll be a fine wife. I like you just the way you are, so stop worrying. It'll all work out perfectly," he said.

They continued to talk a while longer, and when he left at ten, he promised to return the following Shabbas.

"He's a fine young man," Samuel offered the moment the door was closed.

"Yes, he is, Papa, and I liked him very much," Morgan said, noting the look of relief on her parents' faces. "Now, if you'll please excuse me, I'm a little tired."

"Of course you are, darling. We'll talk all about this in the morning," her mother said, kissing Morgan gently on the cheek. "I'm so proud of you. He's a very lucky young man."

"Indeed he is," Samuel said, hugging Morgan.

* * *

The next few weeks moved in slow motion for Morgan, as she grew pensive and depressed trying to come to terms with her fate.

Her mother, accepting Morgan's withdrawn behavior as unavoidable, kept busy by meeting with florists, stationers, and chefs. And Jonte, whom Sara had promoted to her private secretary years earlier, was present at every meeting, feeling equally responsible for making sure that Morgan's wedding was perfect.

"I'm worried about her," Sara said to Jonte one afternoon as they were adding more names to the guest list. "It's not like Morgan to be so docile. Do you think she's really accepting all of this, or is it an act?"

"I'm not sure. It's as if she isn't really aware of what's going on. She's always had an illusive quality about her, but I've never seen her like this," Jonte said.

"What can we do?"

"There's nothing we can do, Sara. She really has no other choice, and the sooner Morgan accepts that, the better off she'll be."

"Of course you're right, Jonte. There's nothing that can be done," Sara said.

* * *

Morgan left rehearsal on the following Wednesday afternoon in tears, after having been reprimanded by the director for not paying attention. She set out to walk home, and hadn't gone fifty feet when a limousine passed by and squealed to a halt. It backed up dangerously on the busy street, the door opened, and out stepped Robert Osborne.

Rushing to Morgan's side, he took her hand and brought it to his lips. "It's wonderful to see you again," he said, caressing her with his eyes.

"I didn't expect you for a few more days," Morgan stammered, hoping she didn't sound displeased to see him.

"I'm afraid I've been called back to Paris sooner than I expected, but I couldn't go back without seeing you first," he said.

"Well, I'm happy to see you, Robert. A little shocked, but still very happy."

"Can you have dinner with me now?"

Morgan hesitated, wondering if she dare go out in public with him now that everyone in town knew she was betrothed.

"I'd like that," she said, deciding there was nothing wrong with having dinner with a friend. "And I know the perfect place. It has lovely gardens, bubbling fountains, and it's so close we can walk."

"That sounds wonderful."

"I need to call my mother before we go," Morgan said. "I'll be back in a minute."

Inside the rehearsal hall, Morgan called Sara. She told her mother that she was going to a friend's house. Her adrenalin pumping wildly, she hurried back to Robert.

The sun was setting in a sky filled with clouds of organdy, white, and red. They walked in silence, content with simply being together. At some point, as if it was the most natural thing in the world, Robert took Morgan's hand and held it protectively. She sighed, wanting the moment to last forever.

It was 5:30 when they arrived at the restaurant, and they requested a table in the back. Over glasses of sherry, Morgan found herself opening up to Robert as if he was her oldest friend. In turn Robert found himself divulging things to Morgan that he had never told another human being.

Time flew by, and when Morgan realized that it was almost seven o'clock, she excused herself and called her mother, saying she was still at a friend's house studying.

When dinner was eventually served, they ate ravenously, deciding they had never tasted better food. Over coffee Robert reached across and took Morgan's hand. "Tonight I'm happier then I've ever been in my life," he said. "But I'm afraid about tomorrow." He hesitated, seeing the tears fill Morgan's eyes. "I never expected to feel this way about you or anyone else for that matter. But now that I do, we have to figure out what comes next."

"A lot has happened since I last saw you, Robert." Morgan stopped as tears spilled down her face. She fought to regain her composure, accepting his handkerchief. "I've been promised in marriage. The wedding plans have already begun."

"Do you love this man?"

"Of course I don't love him. How could I?" she said so softly, Robert had to lean closer to hear her. "My parents made the arrangements through a matchmaker."

"I can't believe it. That's absolutely ridiculous and archaic. What in God's name is wrong with your family? This is the twentieth century, and people don't have other people arranging their lives like neat little antiseptic packages."

"I can't expect you to understand any of this," Morgan said, "but it's the way of my people, and it's been that way for thousands of years. What can I do? Even if I hadn't been promised, I'm a Jew. You're a Gentile. Those are the facts. It's impossible for us."

"I don't believe in impossible. Please don't make this mistake. It isn't fair. Not for you and not for me. Just keep your mind open and listen to me for one more minute. Then I'll leave you alone to make your decision," he said, deciding to play his final card. "I'm leaving for Paris at nine o'clock tomorrow morning. I'll purchase two tickets and two sleeping berths. If you really want to be an actress, you'll be on that train in the morning. If you choose to stay here and give up your dreams, I can't stop you. The only promise I can make to you is that if you come with me, you'll have your opportunity to fulfill your dream of becoming a great actress. Do it for yourself, Morgan."

He stood and took her hand. Passionately he kissed her palm, never taking his eyes off of her.

Chapter 12

————— ✱ —————

Morgan sat for a while inside the taxi parked in front of her house, realizing that everything she had ever been taught to believe was hanging by a thin thread. She paid the driver and entered the house, immediately going into the dining room in search of her parents.

"Morgan, my dear, won't you come in and join us for some coffee and dessert?" her mother asked.

"You remember the Rosen's, don't you, sweetheart?" her papa asked.

"Yes, of course I do. It's lovely to see you again. I know your son, Herschel. We went to school together. I understand he's at the University in Germany. You must be very proud of him. Is he doing well?" Morgan was trying to be polite, despite her disappointment that her parents had company tonight of all nights.

"He's doing very well. Thank you for asking," Mrs. Rosen said.

"Well, it was nice seeing you all. I just came in to say good night." Morgan hesitated. "Papa, I'm sorry to interrupt you, but could I please speak with you?"

Samuel pushed back his chair and turned to his guests. "Please excuse me for a moment."

Morgan turned and moved quickly to her mother, and before Sara could react, Morgan gently touched her face and bent down to kiss her cheek. In a voice only Sara could hear, Morgan said, "I love you, Mother. I love you more than you'll ever know."

Sara began to tremble as Morgan turned and walked away.

"Is something wrong, Morgan?" Samuel asked once they were in the hallway.

"Not really, Papa. I was just thinking about my life and feeling a little blue. I'm sorry I interrupted your dinner."

"Don't be silly, Morgan. Nothing in my life is more important than you."

Morgan watched Samuel as he spoke. She wanted to always remember him as he was tonight. Her eyes filled with tears. "I want to tell you I love you, Papa. You've been a wonderful father. You taught me to be independent and determined. You gave me those values, and I just wanted to thank you." Morgan's voice broke, she put her arms around him, and they held each other tightly.

After the long hug, Samuel pushed away and held her at arm's length. "I'm very touched by those beautiful words. I understand leaving your family is a very difficult thing to do. But I'm sure Howard will be a wonderful husband. You've made your mother and me very proud." Samuel smiled and gently kissed Morgan on the cheek. "I really should go back to my company. I'll see you in the morning. Sleep well, darling."

Morgan walked slowly up to her room, each step resounding in her ears. She wanted to remember which steps creaked and which light switches were temperamental. She ran her hand along the banister, and the feel of the wood recalled the childhood sounds of laughter. Morgan had always loved to slide down the banister, and Jonte had always allowed her to. They both had giggled at the absolute impropriety of it all, knowing that if Sara had ever seen them, they would have both been in serious trouble.

* * *

Morgan left the house at six the next morning carrying a small valise. As she walked forlornly away, she tried to formulate exactly how she would ever make her parents understand why she had to leave.

The streets were damp from an early morning rain. She stepped into the first available drosky. Morgan sat back and surveyed her beloved city while the bright sun heralded a new day.

As they pulled into the station, Morgan spotted Robert leaning against a wall by the entrance doors. When he saw Morgan, he waved, running towards her. Lifting his arms, he helped her down from the drosky. The touch of his hand sent shivers of excitement through her.

"I was so afraid you weren't coming," he said. "I died a thousand deaths last night. I swear, I'll never let you out of my sight again."

* * *

Sunday in the Rabinowiszch home always started later than other days. Breakfast was served at ten because Samuel liked to read the paper in bed while drinking his coffee—one of his few self-indulgences.

Morgan was usually downstairs waiting for them, complaining she would starve to death if they didn't eat soon. So when she hadn't appeared by 10:15, Samuel and Sara became concerned.

"She must have been exhausted from all of the excitement this week. I'll go see what's keeping her," Samuel said.

He walked gingerly up the stairs. The sun was reflecting off the walls and the wind was gently blowing through the open windows as he knocked softly on Morgan's door. When there was no answer, he knocked a little harder before slowly opening the door.

Samuel sensed that something was wrong. Everything was the same as it always had been, and yet as he walked through her sitting area with its chintz-covered couches and chairs and its vases filled with freshly cut wildflowers, he couldn't feel her presence and knew instinctively that Morgan was gone. Samuel went directly into the bedroom.

In the bedroom all Samuel saw was an empty bed with a note propped up against one of the pillows. He sat on the bed and picked up the note, his hands trembling so badly he could hardly read the words. His mind howled in excruciating pain.

When Samuel failed to return, Sara and the staff ran into the hallway and up the stairs. Sara was beyond terror, unable to imagine what might be happening in Morgan's room. But somehow she knew without a doubt that whatever was happening in that room would bring a darkness into her world.

*   *   *

Samuel lay on the floor next to Morgan's bed, his face a white mask frozen in shock. Sara ran to him and fell to her knees.

"Samuel, talk to me. Talk to me!" She laid her head on his chest. "I can hear his heart beating. Thank God, he's alive. Call Dr. Brzezinski!" she cried, tears blurring her vision.

Jonte took Sara in her arms as the butler and chauffeur lifted Samuel onto the bed.

"He's going to be all right, Sara," Jonte said, squeezing Sara's hand. "The doctor will be here soon. Try to be strong for a while longer."

"But what if he...Oh, Jonte, what am I going to do? I couldn't live without him."

"Shh. Everything's going to be fine."

*   *   *

Dr. Brzezinski arrived fifteen minutes later; and after making a cursory examination of Samuel, he ordered everyone out of the room.

"What in God's name is wrong with him?" Sara asked.

"I don't know yet, my dear." Looking over at Jonte, the doctor said, "Why don't you take Mrs. Rabinowiszch into the study. I'll join you there when I've completed my examination." Sara hesitated. "Go on, Sara," he urged, smiling confidently.

After carefully examining Samuel, Dr. Brzezinski called the hospital and made arrangements for Samuel to be immediately moved. He then rolled down his sleeves and went to find Sara.

"Will he be all right? What's wrong with him?" Sara asked.

The doctor moved a chair next to Sara and took her hand.

"It seems that Samuel's had a slight stroke, but his heart is very strong and his chances for a full recovery are excellent," he said.

"What caused it? Why?"

"I found this in Samuel's hand." The doctor held up the note, saying before he gave it to her, "You must be strong, Sara. Samuel's going to need you."

"Oh, my God, no!" she said before handing Jonte the note. "Tell me this isn't happening!"

Jonte read with trembling hands.

Dearest Mother and Father,

By the time you read this, I'll be gone. I wish there was an easier way for me to break this to you, but I can think of none. I have the opportunity to become an actress in Paris, and since that is the only thing I've ever really wanted, I've decided to follow my dreams. I feel it is my destiny. I know I'm disappointing you both and that I'm being terribly selfish, but I can only hope that one day you'll understand why I had to do this and that you'll find it in your hearts to forgive me.

Please give my regrets to Dr. Dworsky and assure him that it was nothing personal. I would have been a terrible wife. You can rest assured that I will always conduct my personal life in a manner that will make you proud. I know who I am and where I come from. You have my word that I'll never forget that. I'll call you as soon as I'm settled.

Your loving daughter,
Morgan

* * *

Jonte let go of the note and watched it flutter to the floor. She gathered Sara in her arms and both women wept. Eventually Sara pulled herself away from Jonte.

"We can't do this now, Jonte. We have to get Samuel well. There will be time for this later."

Chapter 13

———————— ★ ————————

At 6:30 AM only a few people were around to gawk at Robert and Morgan in the Vilna train station.

"I'm so glad you came," he said, putting his arm protectively around Morgan as they walked along the platform.

She shivered.

"It's chilly," Robert said, slipping his jacket off and wrapping it around her trembling shoulders as he helped her up the train's steps.

"Bonjour, Mr. Osborne. Please follow me," the steward said, taking charge of Morgan's valise and leading them through two cars to their compartment.

Morgan hesitated at the threshold for an instant before entering, aware that her next steps would take her forever away from the safety of her family and the life she had known so well. Continuing to tremble, she sat, her back rigid, her expression frozen.

"I'll have your suitcases taken to the sleeping berths. Please don't hesitate to call on me if you need anything at all," the steward said before leaving.

Robert sat next to Morgan. He reached for her hand. Morgan's breathing became ragged as she fought to hold back her tears.

"Are you all right?"

"I'm just so scared. I've never been so scared. I still can't believe what I've done."

"It's going to be OK, Morgan. I promise you."

"How? How can it ever be OK? I wanted to come with you, I wanted it so badly," she said as the train whistle sounded. The sound terrified her and she pulled her hand away.

"Did you really have an alternative? Staying would have meant marrying a man you didn't love and giving up everything you ever wanted. It's your life and you have a right to live it the way you see fit. You must try to stay focused on those thoughts and not the others."

"But I know I've broken my parents' hearts," she said.

"They'll get over it and forgive you. They just need some time."

"Do you really think so?"

"Do you think you're the first kid who ever struck out on her own? Sometimes we have to break with tradition, and that usually involves making sacrifices."

His words mollified Morgan and she began to relax.

"Think about it, Morgan. You're on your way to Paris."

"Am I really going to be an actress?" she asked, her eyes flashing with renewed excitement.

Robert smiled.

"What's it going to be like?"

"Well, you're going to have to work terribly hard, because that's what it takes to become a success. But when you aren't working, I'll show you every fabulous secret Paris has to offer. We'll walk down every street, eat in every bistro, and dance in every club."

Morgan leaned over and kissed him quickly on the cheek.

"I have a surprise for you," he said, reaching into his bag and taking out a brightly wrapped package.

"Oh, Robert, how kind of you." She tore open the package and couldn't hold back a gleeful squeal. "How could you have known?" she said, cradling the books, a collection of Shakespeare's works.

"I'm so glad it pleases you."

"Pleases me? I adore Shakespeare. You couldn't have given me anything I'd have enjoyed more."

"I was hoping that would be the case. We now have one more thing in common, Miss Rabinowiszch, because I too love the classics. Tell me, which is your favorite?"

"Tolstoy's *Anna Karenina.*"

"Why is that your favorite?"

"Anna and Levin, they had such love for each other and such courage." She looked away shyly. "What's your favorite?"

He smiled. "Why don't we continue our conversation over lunch? Are you hungry?"

"I'm starved."

* * *

When they entered the dinning car all conversations seemed to stop. The maitre'd approached, seemingly unconcerned at having such a famous celebrity to seat. "This way please, Mr. Osborne," he said, showing them to a table.

On the way past the other diners, Morgan heard pieces of their conversations.

"It's him. They said he'd be on board, and he really is."

At another table she heard, "That young woman is magnificent. I wonder who she is? Do you think she's an actress or just another one of his lady friends?"

"Does that happen everywhere you go?" Morgan asked, intoxicated by all the attention.

"What price fame?" Robert said, smiling wickedly. "It won't be long before it's you they're craning their necks to see. Just wait. You'll grow to adore all the attention; it's shamefully addictive."

When lunch was served Morgan became immediately absorbed in her meal.

"I've never seen anyone enjoy eating as much as you apparently do. What happens when you have a bad meal?" he asked.

Morgan laughed. "I've never had one. I'll eat anything."

Once coffee was served, people began approaching their table. Most wanted autographs; others just wanted to introduce themselves. The compliments he received made Morgan blush, but he seemed to take it all in stride. And when they finally managed to escape back to their compartment, Morgan was still excited.

* * *

"Robert, that was absolutely fantastic. I loved it! Imagine, all those people, all that attention, and all you had to do to get it was act." Morgan saw the crestfallen look on Robert's face. "Oh, come on. You know what I mean. Of course you're a great actor, but you have to admit it's not exactly the most difficult job in the world."

"You really have no idea, no idea at all, but you will. You'll learn what it's like to work hard, six, sometimes seven days a week. And you'll find out how difficult it is to give your all and find out that sometimes it's still not enough. One day I'll take great pleasure in reminding you of this conversation."

"How can you call acting work? I love it too much, and it's too much fun to be called work."

Robert smiled. "You'll see."

Morgan looked out the window and quickly became mesmerized by the passing vistas. "Am I really on my way to Paris?"

* * *

The warm sun filtered through the cloudy panes of glass and Robert quietly watched Morgan drift off to sleep.

For a very long time he was unable to take his eyes off of her, overcome by the feeling that she was the treasure he had been searching for all his life. Sustained by his feelings of love, Robert leaned over and kissed Morgan softly on the forehead. She sighed deeply, stirred for a moment, and then fell back to sleep.

* * *

For two days, Samuel remained unconscious. And even though Dr. Brzezinski put nurses on around the clock, Sara refused to leave Samuel's side. She took catnaps in the chair next to his bed but she was afraid to sleep, afraid that he might stir and she wouldn't see it. Sara prayed constantly that God would be merciful and return her husband to her.

Late in the afternoon of the third day, Samuel began his journey back to consciousness. He felt himself being lifted from the abyss. When he opened his eyes, Sara was standing over him, and he knew that Sara had been what was pulling him back.

His voice barely audible, he asked, "What happened to me?"

Sara reached for his hand as tears cascaded down her face. "You've been asleep, my darling. How do you feel?"

Samuel realized instantly that the sight in his left eye was blurred. *I can't see! I'm finished as a doctor.* Then he saw the fear in his wife's face.

"Don't worry, Sara," he said, "I'm going to be fine."

Sara looked at the nurse standing on the other side of the bed feeling Samuel's pulse.

"You're doing very nicely, Dr. Rabinowiszch. I'll go call Dr. Brzezinski now."

Samuel looked at the nurse for the first time. *Does she know that I'm not really fine? Can she tell?* "Yes, do that please. I would like to see him immediately."

Sara and Samuel sat in silence waiting for the doctor. Sara was busy thanking God while Samuel made a cursory inventory of the moving parts on his body. Sara was afraid to speak, afraid of bringing back the memory of Morgan's note. And Samuel didn't speak because he knew that something devastating had happened in his life, and he was afraid he might remember what it was.

When Dr. Brzezinski came striding into the room, he said, "Well, it's about time, Samuel. It's good to have you back, my friend. He placed his hand on Samuel's shoulder and looked at Sara. "Why don't you and the nurse wait outside while I give this man a good going over?"

Both women left the room smiling, and for the first time in days Sara allowed herself to believe that she again had a future worth living.

Samuel looked at his friend Simon. They had taken their medical school training together and they were like brothers.

"I've had a stroke, haven't I? The vision in my left eye is blurred, and my right hand won't respond. I can't even make a fist."

"OK, Samuel, let's not jump to conclusions until I examine you thoroughly. We both know that a stroke patient's recovery rate is excellent when the trauma is localized. You've regained almost total control of your motor skills and your verbal skills are normal. Those are all good signs, and you know it. Now just relax and let me do what I do best."

At the conclusion of the hour-long examination, they both knew the stroke had been very mild and that with therapy Samuel would most likely recover the use of his hand. They also knew that his eyesight would probably never return to normal.

"I'll never operate again, never deliver another baby. Will I, Simon?"

"Damn it, Samuel, be grateful you're alive. You're still a doctor and you can still care for your patients."

* * *

Sara was happy that physical therapy would begin immediately, knowing that at least Samuel's mind would be kept occupied. And she was thankful that for the time being he was still totally confused about the events that had prompted his stroke.

"Where's Morgan? Why haven't I seen her?" he asked on the way down to physical therapy.

"She came down with another cold, darling," Sara said. "It's nothing to worry about, but Simon doesn't want her near you. He's afraid you might catch it. I speak with her every hour, and she sends you her love."

Chapter 14

———————— ★ ————————

From outward appearances the Fire Tavern was just another men's club in Berlin. Inside, it was decorated in subtly masculine tones, a band played romantic music as the clientele sat quietly talking and drinking. That clientele was exclusively wealthy and well-connected homosexual Germans. It was the first place Lieutenant Edmund Heines took Otto when their romance had begun months earlier.

"Come, my pet, and dance with me," Lieutenant Heines said to Otto.

Otto allowed himself to be led onto the darkened dance floor. Edmund took the young man into his arms, holding him tightly, rubbing himself against the firm body. Otto sighed, nuzzling Edmund's neck. Pressing himself closer, he let the music carry him as he rhythmically followed Edmund's lead. "Let's go," Edmund said a short time later, his breath coming in short gasps.

"After the party, my love," Otto said, relishing his control over Edmund.

"I haven't seen you in days. The party can wait."

Otto pushed himself away from Edmund, glaring. "Himmler will be at that party and I want to go. If you don't want to," he threatened, "I'll go without you."

Edmund looked hungrily at the young and virile Otto. He longed to be in bed with him, but he feared his unpredictable moods and anger enough to acquiesce.

"Whatever makes you happy," Edmund said.

Otto smiled. He didn't doubt that the coveted place he held in the Lieutenant's life was tenuous. But it was useful. He intended to become an integral part of the Nazi elite, and if Lieutenant Edmund Heines would open the doors for him, he would take advantage of the fool's infatuation. And he knew that tonight's party would be the payoff for all the months he had endured the tedious affair with Heines. Tonight Otto would meet Heinrich Himmler, the newly appointed head of the SS Schutzstaffels.

The limousine ride took Otto and Edmund into the very heart of Berlin, past the Reichstag building, and onto the Unter Den Linden. Passing by the Brandenburg Gate, the car took a sharp left.

Looming off in the distance stood the private estate of Werner Gott, an enormously wealthy Berliner and a personal friend of Adolf Hitler. Long, sleek limousines lined both sides of the driveway, and the front gardens were aglow with hundreds of twinkling lights as Edmund and Otto pulled in. A white-gloved attendant opened the door for them, greeting Heines by name.

Inside the house, they accepted champagne from a passing waiter and were soon deep in conversation with Heines's friends when Himmler approached.

"Ah, so this is the young man you've been telling me so much about, Lieutenant Heines," Himmler said, looking at Otto. "I was hoping I'd meet you this evening."

Otto smiled; delighted that Edmund had been keeping Himmler abreast of his activities.

Otto had taken an active role in the brutal persecution of the Berlin Jews, looting stores, and burning synagogues. And then, with Edmund as his mentor, he had become a Storm Trooper, helping to arrest thousands of innocent Jews. Taking part in mass executions, Otto had proved himself to be a remorseless, cold-blooded killer.

Himmler introduced his SA Chief Roehm to Otto. Roehm nodded, then shook Edmund's hand, staring at him coldly. He had always hated

Edmund and had heard about his relationship with Otto. Now he watched in joyous anticipation as Himmler continued.

"Lieutenant Heines here thinks very highly of you, so I'm considering assigning you to the Dachau Concentration Camp, where we have an opening in our exclusive Death's Head Unit of the SS."

Handing his glass to a dumbstruck Edmund Heines, Otto clicked his heals smartly and raised his arm in the Nazi salute.

"Thank you. I'd like nothing better than the opportunity to serve the Reich."

"We'll talk again soon," Himmler said, walking away with the smiling SA chief at his side.

Edmund shuddered. This was not what he had planned. He had been lobbying to have Otto stay with him in Berlin. He pulled Otto aside.

"When he offers you the appointment, you must refuse," he demanded. "I can't live without you."

Otto snickered. "Refuse? Why would I do that? This is more important than either of us. But you don't see that, do you, Edmund?"

"See what?" he stuttered. "What are you talking about? I've done nothing but talk about what a fine asset you'd be to the Reich. It's because of me that they've made you this offer. And I'm sure if you requested it, they would allow you to stay in Berlin." Edmund insisted, his face flushing in anger.

"You're a selfish man, Edmund, and I don't think we should see each other anymore," Otto whispered, turning his back on Edmund.

"No, wait! Give me another chance," Edmund wailed, reaching for Otto.

"Stay the fuck away from me," Otto said, moving to the group where SA Chief Roehm and Himmler were holding court.

Chapter 15

——————— ★ ———————

In 1936, twenty-five-year-old Otto Milch was assigned to the Death's Head Unit of the very first Nazi concentration camp—Dachau. Built in 1933 for the incarceration of German political prisoners and enemies of the Reich, the camp was now a symbol of terror, meant to deter anyone from even contemplating resistance to Nazi rule.

Located about eighteen kilometers northwest of Munich on the Amper River, Dachau was constructed in the shape of a large rectangle. In its center was a barren three-block square surrounded by two-and three-story, wooden prisoner barracks, and other buildings for the administration of the camp. Electrified fences and high walls, as well as starving, vicious dogs and a huge force of guards, kept the prisoners confined. Outside, beautiful stone building housed the Nazi SS officers and officials.

* * *

Dachau's Commandant, Theodore Eicke, having been warned that his newest recruit was being personally groomed by Himmler for SS leadership, did everything he could to accommodate Otto. Impressed with Otto's interrogation techniques, Eicke sent glowing reports to headquarters, always mentioning his outstanding new initiate.

In the meantime, Himmler teamed up with Goering to establish another arm of the SS—the Gestapo Secret State Police. And as Himmler's power within the Reich grew, he continued to take interest in Otto's progress within the Reich.

* * *

Otto's first ten months at Dachau were the happiest days of his life. He only regretted having to leave his twin and his mother behind. Sprawled out on his bunk, he reread his sister's letter for the hundredth time, still finding it hard to believe that his mother had died of a heart attack.

He had begun writing to Ilya, vowing that he would send for her as soon as possible, when Commandant Eicke entered his room. Jumping to his feet, he hurriedly adjusted his uniform. "Heil Hitler," Otto said formally, raising his arm. He remained standing at attention, waiting for Eicke to speak.

"At ease, Milch," Eicke ordered. "This came for you today," he said, handing an invitation to Otto. "It seems you've been invited to a dinner party being held in Himmler's honor in Munich. I've taken the liberty of arranging for my personal car and driver to take you."

Otto read the invitation twice, as Eicke watched, knowing he would have to cultivate Otto's friendship even more now that he was being invited into Himmler's inner circle.

"Please be sure to send my regards to Herr Himmler," Eicke said.

* * *

Otto was nervous as the limousine pulled up in front of a private home on the outskirts of the city. But he felt thrilled and important when a handsome blond-haired, blue-eyed young man helped him out of the car and accompanied him into the party.

The mansion's main dining hall had been turned into a gallery celebrating the works of *Die Blaue Vier* (The Blue Four) and its artists— Alexey Jawlensky, Kandinsky, Paul Klee, and Lyonel Feininger—who were holding court at the far end of the room.

Otto stood holding a drink in his hand, taking in the glorious lines and colors of the modernistic paintings, when he felt a light tap on his shoulder. He turned to find himself face to face with Edmund.

Otto nodded politely. "How nice to see you, Lieutenant," he said.

"I've missed you so much. Why haven't you returned my calls or answered my notes? How could you do this to me? You used me!" Edmund said.

"Please don't make a scene, for God's sake!" Taking Edmund's arm, Otto led him through the crowd. "Let's go outside. We'll get some fresh air and talk," he said.

Himmler watched Otto lead Edmund from the house. He was concerned, because he had heard that Edmund had been drinking heavily and behaving erratically lately, so he excused himself from his friends and followed them. He stood in the shadows, watching.

"You're a lying, cheating bitch!" Edmund said, grabbing Otto's arm.

Otto pushed him away. "Why did you come here anyway, Edmund?"

"Why? I belong here, that's why. It's you that doesn't belong here, and I intend to make sure they all know it."

"What are you raving about?" Otto asked.

"You owe me, damn it! I love you. I need you."

Otto's hands shook. "Did you ever think I really gave a shit about you? My God, you're a nobody. Have you looked in the mirror lately? Just seeing you makes me want to vomit."

Edmund slapped Otto across the face and screamed, "Shut the fuck up!"

Realizing what he had done, Edmund began to cry.

Otto took Edmund by the shoulders roughly and pulled him close. "Look at me, Edmund," he ordered, lowering his voice and staring directly into his eyes. Edmund's rage vanished and he became deathly still.

Reaching into his breast pocket, Otto painstakingly removed a silver cigarette case. With deliberateness he flipped open the case. A tin-like sound emerged–the unmistakable cadence of a music box. The tune was only a few bars long. It was the kind of melody that seemed immediately familiar. The kind of melody that remained in your ears long after the music stopped. "Take a deep breath, my love," Otto said, his voice a purr. "Trust me, go deep inside your mind," he intoned quietly, his inflection monotonous, beckoning. Otto spoke ever softer, the words drifting around Edmond.

"I just want to die…to end the misery," Edmund said finally, his voice devoid of all emotion.

Otto moved abruptly away from Edmund, a vicious smile contorting his handsome face. "If that's what you want, then do it. Just wait until I'm inside before you pull the trigger," Otto said without a hint of emotion.

Himmler watched in fascination. He could only pick up bits and pieces of the conversation, but it was enough to get the gist of what was happening, and he grew tense with anticipation. He waited to see the scene play to its completion.

Tears were streaming down Edmund's bloated face as he watched Otto leave. He stood riveted for a good five minutes before unsnapping his gun and removing it from its holster. He slowly raised the pistol, placed the barrel into his mouth, and pulled the trigger. The blast reverberated as Lieutenant Edmund Heines's blood and brains spewed everywhere.

"Get him out of here," Himmler ordered as his shocked comrades rushed to the porch. He then moved inside, looking for Otto.

He found him sitting on a sofa talking intently to a lovely young girl who was obviously unaware of what had just taken place outside. Himmler walked up slowly.

"Excuse me, Herr Milch," Himmler said.

Otto jumped to his feet.

"I'd like you to join me for a drink in the study?"

Otto followed Himmler up the winding staircase and into the book-lined room. Himmler closed the door quietly, turning towards Otto while lighting a cigarette. He intentionally blew the smoke into Otto's face.

"I saw what happened in the garden, Milch. I think you're a very dangerous and devious young man. You've taken out one of the Reich's best men on a whim, and that is unacceptable."

Otto began to tremble as the blood drained from his face.

"Heines was a pathetic little man, but he was your superior and you killed him," Himmler said, pointing his finger in Otto's face. "I could have you shot, you know."

Otto remained silently wide-eyed with fear.

Himmler sat. "I still can't believe it. If I hadn't seen it with my own eyes, I wouldn't have believed it was possible to make a man kill himself," he said more to himself then to Otto. "How did you do it?"

"I simply made a suggestion."

"That's impossible."

"I know it seems impossible, but you saw for yourself. I must admit, I really didn't expect him to do it. He must have really wanted to die."

Himmler rubbed his hands together. "Sit down," he ordered. "I want to know how and where you learned to do that."

"I've been studying hypnosis for years, Herr Himmler. In the beginning, I must admit, it was simply a young boy's folly, a hobby really, but when I began to understand the implications–it became my obsession. While learning, I followed all of the acceptable techniques; having the subject go through a tedious relaxation exercise and then having the subject visualize my suggestions. But it never took them deep enough. I never got enough control." Otto's eyes flashed cold. "So, I began to improvise. I added music, intimidation and continuous repetition and—you saw tonight for yourself what's possible."

Himmler's mind was reeling with the staggering possibilities. "I'm going to spare your life, Milch, but only because the Reich needs you. I intend to set up a special position for you, and I'll be watching you carefully. Do we understand each other?"

Otto nodded.

"You're to tell no one what you did here tonight. I'll see to it that you have everything you need—the proper facilities and as many subjects as you request. We'll take them from the camps. You're work is to be kept secret and you are to report directly to me."

* * *

After being dismissed, Otto walked arrogantly from his meeting with Himmler, a new sense of power coursing through his veins. He looked lovingly at the armband that he wore so proudly, reaffirming his commitment to the cause of German supremacy.

* * *

Two months after the death of their mother, Ilya Milch arrived in Dachau. Working as a secretary in the Commandant's office, for the first time in her life she wore nice clothing and had a decent place to live. To show her appreciation and to make her brother proud, Ilya worked long and hard, making herself indispensable within weeks of her arrival.

For lunch, Ilya would sit alone in the employee cafeteria, eating quickly, refusing to befriend her fellow workers. As she unwrapped her sandwich one noontime, a stranger approached.

"Please forgive me for intruding on your privacy. I just had to come over and introduce myself. It's not often that one sees such beauty in a place like this. I'm Dr. Hans Wells." He reached over to shake hands with Ilya.

Normally she would recoil from a man's touch, but for some reason she didn't fear him. When she gave Hans her hand, he brought it to his lips and kissed it. She pulled it away as if she'd been burned.

"Fraulein, please, I certainly didn't mean to offend you. Forgive me."

Ilya had never met anyone with such obvious breeding and self-confidence. She studied him carefully, noting how strikingly handsome he was. He had a straight nose, intense green eyes, and thick curly blond hair that he wore slicked back. His beard was neatly trimmed, and he was dressed impeccably.

"My name is Ilya Milch," she said shyly. Having never made small talk with a man before, she had no idea what to do or say next.

"May I sit down and join you for lunch?" Hans asked.

Ilya nodded and continued eating.

"Fraulein, I've been brought here to work with a man named Otto Milch. Is he a relation of yours?"

Ilya looked at the doctor more closely now. She had heard about a brilliant psychiatrist who was being brought to the camp to work with Otto. "He's my twin brother," she said.

"In that case, I've been doubly blessed. Now I'll have many excuses to see you again. You'll see that I'm easy to talk with, and I'm sure we'll become great friends."

Ilya continued eating, never looking up again. When she was finished, she stood up, glanced over at him, and walked away.

Hans watched Ilya leave, contemplating how he could manipulate her to his advantage. He was good at what he did, and he knew instinctively that this lovely young woman was neurotic and could be easily controlled to further his career.

Chapter 16

————— ★ —————

Whenever the train stopped to take on more coal and passengers, Morgan would rush Robert through the streets of the tiny villages, determined not to miss a thing. In the evening after dinner, they played cards and talked, their conversations growing more intimate; and before long, they both began to feel as if they'd known each other for years. Inevitably Morgan found herself in Robert's arms.

She had spent nights dreaming of this moment, and as he kissed her passionately, she closed her eyes, allowing the sweetness of his touch to envelope her.

Robert deepened his kiss and pressed her tightly against him. Moving his lips from hers, he began tracing his mouth down the alabaster column of her throat. Morgan moaned and leaned her head to the side, offering her sensitive neck to Robert's kisses.

"I want you, Morgan. I want you so much."

His voice jarred Morgan back to awareness.

When she stiffened, he pulled away.

"I'm sorry, Robert. I know that everything that I've done must have lead you to believe that I was willing to…but I'm not ready. This isn't what I intended when I agreed to go with you," she said, tears welling in her eyes.

"I'm sorry, Morgan. I got carried away. I'd never do anything to hurt you. It won't happen again," he vowed. "You're not going to be mad at me, are you?" he asked, pinching her cheek playfully.

She smiled. "Believe me, I had as much to do with it as you did. I hope it will happen again, but I need some time."

In the back of her mind lurked the agonizing thought of her parents. She was becoming more and more anxious to arrive in Paris so that she could call, knowing how worried they must be.

* * *

Robert's chauffeur met them at the station, and Morgan was wide-eyed as they drove through the streets of Paris.

"I want you to be my Empress, my Marie-Louise," Robert teased as they passed by the Arc de Triomphe.

"Only if you'll be my Napoleon," Morgan answered.

"I see you know your French history," Robert said.

"I should. Jonte, my French nanny, fed me French history along with my bottle," Morgan said. She had fallen instantly in love with the broad boulevards, stylish cafes, and unassuming elegance and romance of Paris. "Oh Robert, I can't believe it. Am I really here?"

"This is only the beginning…only the beginning."

Morgan looked at him and smiled.

* * *

Robert had booked them into the Paris Ritz, a converted eighteenth century townhouse considered to be one of the finest hotels in the world.

"It's such a pleasure to have you back with us, sir. We always look forward to your arrival. Shall I show you to the Edward VII suite?" the hotel manager asked, fussing over Robert the moment they entered the lobby.

"That would be fine, Pierre," Robert said.

"Please allow me to take charge of your belongings." He snapped his fingers and five valets appeared to gather their valises.

Morgan gasped as she entered the Edward VII suite. The furniture was covered in a richly patterned brocade of off-white, silver, and gold; and the walls were adorned with huge Aubusson tapestries.

In the bedroom, featuring a four-poster bed tented by a hand-brocaded silk canopy, the porters pulled back draperies, fluffed up sofa cushions, and rearranged the spring flowers in cut crystal vases next to the bed and on the coffee tables.

"This is the connecting door into the other suite," Monsieur Osborne.

"*Merci*. That will be all," Robert said, showing the porters out.

Morgan immediately picked up the phone, gave instructions to the hotel operator, and sat down on the sofa to wait for the call to come through.

Robert, looking suspiciously mischievous, began ceremoniously opening his valises. And Morgan watched in stunned silence as he removed magnificent gowns fashioned of the finest organza, silks, and velvets from his suitcases.

"These are for you," he said. "I spent a lot of time in Warsaw picking them out."

"I can't accept such extravagant gifts, Robert. I just can't," Morgan said. "I really appreciate your thoughtfulness, but it's out of the question."

"Hold on." Robert said. "If you're uncomfortable accepting my gifts, don't think of them as gifts. You can pay me back when you have the money."

"That's fair enough," Morgan said, looking hungrily at the gowns. "Don't move. I want to try them on right now." She gathered them in her arms and hurried into the dressing room.

"Wait until Paris society meets you!" Robert beamed as Morgan modeled every gown.

She was giggling when the phone rang. Her mood changed abruptly as she rushed to answer it.

"Yes, I placed the call to Dr. or Mrs. Rabinowiszch," Morgan said. "I see. Well thank you anyway." She put the receiver down. "That's really strange. Neither one of them is at home. How can that be?" Worry and disappointment were apparent in her voice.

Robert came to Morgan and held her in his arms. "We'll try again later, darling. It's almost dinnertime. They must be out to dinner."

* * *

When the phone rang at their home, Sara was beside Samuel's bed in the Vilna hospital. As if the ringing phone had caused some kind of cosmic reaction, Samuel's confused mind cleared.

"Oh my God! My daughter's been taken away from me!" he said in anguish.

"It's all right, Samuel. She'll be fine," Sara said, looking deeply into Samuel's eyes. "I know it's difficult to adjust to, but we'll learn. Please don't upset yourself so. It's not as if she were dead."

"You're wrong, very wrong. My daughter is dead." Samuel choked, sounding as if he was smothering. He reached up and tore at his pajama top.

"Stop that!" Sara screeched, grabbing for his hand to stop him from tearing his clothing, a symbol of mourning for a Jew. "You can't do this. I won't let you! She's our daughter, our only child. Samuel, please," Sara begged, collapsing in hysterics.

Samuel looked at his wife as if she were a stranger, feeling neither concern nor sadness. His emotions had been deadened.

"I want you to leave immediately," he ordered. "Cover every mirror and prepare our home for sitting Shiva. We will mourn the death of our daughter. I'll call the rabbi and make the other needed arrangements. And one more thing, Sara—you're never to speak her name to me again. Do you understand?" he said without love or compassion. "Go now!" he yelled.

Samuel rang for his nurse.

"I want you to arrange for my immediate release. I need transportation to my home, and I may require some assistance.

"But, doctor, I can't do that," the nurse said incredulously.

"You've been given your instructions. Now see to them!"

The nurse left the room and rushed to find Dr. Brzezinski.

"What's all of this about? Why are you ordering my staff about?" Simon asked, arriving at Samuel's room minutes later. Seeing the agony in Samuel's eyes, he instantly realized his friend's memory must have returned. "Samuel, I must insist that you stay in the hospital. You're not ready to leave, and I won't be responsible for any consequences that may result from your asinine behavior."

"My only child is dead. I'm going home to mourn. Can you deny me that right?"

Simon sat down next to the bed and placed his hand over Samuel's.

"Are you sure you know what you're doing? I read the note. I found it in your hand after you collapsed," he admitted. "It doesn't have to be this way, my friend. You can learn to live with what she's done."

Samuel looked fiercely at Simon. His voice was filled with stony resolve as he responded, "My daughter is dead."

Chapter 17

———— ★ ————

Soft music from the radio drifted into the bathroom as Morgan slid further into the bubble-filled tub. She sighed deeply. She spent over an hour soaking, until the water cooled. Soon she was cuddled beneath a down comforter. She closed her eyes and tried to sleep, but she was too excited about being in Paris and too worried about her parents to sleep. She placed another call home.

"I have Mrs. Rabinowiszch on the line for you. Go ahead please," the operator said crisply ten minutes later.

"Mother! Is it really you?" Morgan asked, breaking down in tears the second she heard Sara's voice. "Can you ever forgive me?"

"Are you all right? We were so—"

"I'm fantastic," Morgan said, regaining her composure. "You can't imagine how fabulous Paris is! You'll never believe it. I'm going to be doing a reading for a fabulous new play, *La Mort du Docteur Faust*. A Belgian dramatist named Michel De Ghelderode wrote it. Robert's sure I'll get it. I won't have a very large part, but it's a start. Oh, Mother, it's such a wonderful story! It might be a bit too satirical for your taste, but I think father will adore it." Morgan prattled on, fearful of silence. "The play is scheduled to open in just a few months. And Robert Osborne is the star of the show. You and Papa will just have to come to the opening. Promise me you will, Mother," Morgan said.

Sara held her breath for a moment as she decided exactly how to respond. "Morgan, dear, I'm afraid your father isn't feeling well. He won't be able to travel for a while," she said.

Morgan gasped. "What's the matter with him?"

"He's had a slight stroke, but he's going to be just fine," Sara said.

"That can't be true!"

"I'm afraid it is true," Sara replied.

"I'll be on the next train home," Morgan said. "You tell Papa I'm on my way. You tell him that for me, Mother, OK?"

Sara cleared her throat and said, "Morgan, listen to me. Your papa is just fine now. He's out of danger."

"I'm coming home anyway. He needs me," Morgan said.

"You must not do that!" Sara said. "It's just...well...you see, he's very upset with you. He's going to need some time to get over what you've done. You'll have to have patience, Morgan."

"Mother, do you feel the same way? Are you angry with me too?" Morgan asked.

Sara was heartbroken and desperate. "This has been a terrible shock, but I'm not angry. In a way I even understand why you've done what you've done."

"Thank you, Mother. Thank you for that."

A short while later Morgan hung up the phone. The pain of her mother's words burned her soul. She sobbed as the full implications of Sara's words began to register in her mind. *My God, I expected them to be upset. But why is Papa so angry? I never thought I could do anything to make him sick. It's all my fault.*

* * *

Robert had to fight through the crowd at the hotel bar to find his friend.

"Well, well, well, I can't believe that after two weeks of being back, you've actually found some time in your busy schedule to meet with your old buddy," William said as Robert approached him.

Robert's agent wore his sandy blond hair unfashionably short, further accentuating his large nose and the thick horn-rimmed glasses that magnified his cloudy gray eyes. Perpetually smiling, William had the kind of face that people immediately trusted.

"God, it's good to see you. It's been too long, Robert."

William adjusted his bow tie and cleared his throat. "You know I like Morgan a lot and I can certainly see why you're so smitten, but what about me? How about some equal time?"

Robert laughed and slapped William on the back, realizing how much he had missed him. "OK, I get the message," Robert said. "If you're trying to tell me you missed me…well, I missed you too."

Over drinks they discussed their plans, but inevitably their conversation turned to the subject that was on the minds of everyone in Europe.

"You know if Mussolini continues his aggression in Abyssinia," Robert said, "and the League of Nations continues to remain so impotent, you and I could be fighting men before long."

William shook his head. "I may live in France but I'm a Brit at heart, old man," he said, switching to English. "And if there's a war, I'll be fighting for England. But I don't think we have anything to worry about. We're about to ratify a pact with the Soviet Union. Neither the Germans nor the Italians would dare move on France. The French army would have them for lunch."

"I hope you're right, William. This Hitler fellow's making threats against everybody," Robert said. "I heard one of his speeches when I was in Germany last year, and I want to tell you, that man's dangerous, really dangerous.

After the second round of drinks was served, Robert said, "I need your help, William. I have a problem."

"Say no more. Your wish is my command, sire." William laughed, but Robert didn't.

"This is serious, William. It's not just a war that I'm worried about. This Hitler seems bent on destroying the Jews. I hear thousands of Jews are leaving Germany every day." Robert put his face in his hands for a moment, then he looked intently at his friend. "I'm frightened for Morgan. I want you to take her papers, and no matter what it costs, I want her name changed to just Morgan. Any records containing her last name or the fact she's Jewish must be altered or destroyed. Can you do it?"

"You don't fool around when you ask a favor, do you, my friend?" William said, nervously fingering a pack of cigarettes. "I have a few connections that could make the arrangements. But have you really thought this through? You're wiping out Morgan's identity. Have you spoken with her about it?"

"She doesn't know," he said, "and I don't want her to ever know. She sees her Jewishness as an integral part of who she is. It took me days to convince her to drop her last name and go by the stage name Morgan. She wouldn't have ever agreed to do that if she thought I was trying to conceal that she's a Jew."

"I'm not sure this is the right thing to do, but if it's what you want, I'll start working on it right away. Do you have her papers with you?"

"Yes," Robert said as he handed them over. The moment William took the papers, Robert felt relieved.

* * *

La Comedie Francaise, the French national theater, was located on the Boulevard du Temple on Paris' Right Bank, and it was in that fine old theater that Morgan and Robert first shared a stage. They spent hours in rehearsal; and when they weren't rehearsing, they were memorizing lines together.

Morgan completely immersed herself in the character she was playing in an effort to escape the guilt that had become like a cancer, attaching itself to her very being.

The cast of *The Death of Dr. Faust* realized that Morgan was an exciting new talent. She was seen as a charming and slightly eccentric young ingénue who had managed to captivate the notoriously jaded Robert Osborne, despite her careless approach to her beauty. She soon became the talk of Paris.

"Please, Morgan," the director pleaded one morning, "you have to do something with your hair. It's always hanging in your face. How can I direct you when I can't even see your face?" Throwing his script to the floor, he yelled, "Someone put her hair up!"

The hairdressers took almost twenty minutes to get Morgan's heavy black curls to stay in place. But by the end of the day, her hair was again hanging in her eyes and sticking out in every direction.

To alleviate any further problems, Morgan bought a man's black bowler hat that she took to wearing all the time. Before long, the hat became her trademark, and soon bowlers began showing up on women's heads all over Paris.

* * *

Morgan sat at her dressing table, her hand resting on the telephone, as she willed her emotions to stay under control. She was determined that her weekly calls to her mother and her desperate desire to speak with her papa were not going to get her down. She couldn't help being lonely for her family and friends, but it had been her decision to break away from all of them, and she was resolved to make the best of it.

An unexpected knock on her dressing room door came as a welcomed distraction. "Who is it?" she asked, trying to sound cheerful.

"Excuse me, mademoiselle, my name is Claire Sornet and I've been instructed to do a fitting for you," said the beautiful young girl.

"Come in. Where's Rene? Is she ill?"

"No, mademoiselle, I'm her assistant. I hope you don't mind?"

"Of course not. If Rene sent you, you must be very talented," Morgan said. She thrust out her hand. "My name's Morgan. Mademoiselle is too formal."

"Of course, Morgan," Claire said.

Morgan caught herself staring at the girl. Claire had straight, lustrous, strawberry blond hair worn in a swing cut just below her chin. Her heart-shaped face had tiny freckles that surrounded an up-tilted nose. Thick golden lashes shaded her green eyes, and even though she was at least two inches taller than Morgan, she was so thin she seemed petite.

Morgan took the dress that Claire had brought for the fitting.

"It's really lovely. Do you enjoy being a seamstress? Me, I can't even sew a stitch. My mother tried to teach me but I was all thumbs."

"It's OK. I'm going to the University, and it helps pay my tuition."

"You're kidding! I didn't know women were allowed. You must really be proud of yourself."

Claire looked intently at Morgan, smiling sweetly. "I am proud of myself. But look at you! I hear you're about to become the most famous actress in Europe. And you're so young."

Morgan handed the costume to Claire and moved over to the stool. She unbuttoned her dress and pulled it over her head. Claire helped her put on the crinolines and then the costume.

"What are you studying?" Morgan asked as Claire began measuring and pining.

"Psychology."

"Wow, that's really interesting. I never even knew that women could do that sort of thing. Actually, where I come from, a woman can't. But that has more to do with religion than anything else. Jewish women are expected to stay at home."

"I can't believe you're Jewish."

Morgan felt herself flinch and draw back.

Claire smiled and continued, "Oh, it's not like that. I'm not prejudiced or anything. My boyfriend Saul is Jewish. That causes us a lot of problems. Not that I care, because I don't. But he sure does. How about you? Is it a problem for you and Robert?"

This girl's frankness was totally foreign to Morgan, and she found herself captivated by it. "It's a problem, but it's only one of many."

Seeing that her question had troubled Morgan, Claire changed the subject. "Have you been to the Louvre yet?"

"Robert and I spent a few hours there, but I would love to go back."

"Perfect! I'll take you. I bet you didn't see my very favorite painting, Ingres's *La Grande Odalisque*. It's French exoticism at its best. You just tell me when it's convenient for you, and we'll go. I'm on break from school, and I have lots of free time after work."

"I could go Saturday morning."

"Then it's a date. I'm finished with the fitting," Claire said, carefully lifting the dress over Morgan's head.

"Claire, may I ask you a favor?"

"Sure. Just name it."

Morgan lifted her head proudly. "I left my home in Vilna to become an actress and to be with Robert, and I'm not sorry. I've had so many wonderful experiences and he's been so kind, but I've been so lonely for a girlfriend." She hesitated for a moment. Shyly she asked, "Would you be my friend?"

Claire threw her arms around Morgan. "I already am, silly girl. But I have to warn you; I'm like a bad smell. Once I'm your friend, I'm impossible to get rid of."

* * *

The play opened to rave reviews, firmly reestablishing Robert as one of the great stage performers, and life took on a gentle routine.

The girls began to spend a lot of time together. Maintaining anonymity was easy, because without Robert, Morgan was just another pretty face that wasn't quite recognizable. The girls laughed, talked about the show, and gossiped endlessly as they explored the museums of Paris. Because Claire was so honest about her relationship with Saul and because life was so much more liberal in Paris, Morgan felt safe in confiding to Claire.

"I think something's wrong with me, Claire. When Robert brings me back to my room at night, he doesn't even ask to come in. You would think by now he would have tried something."

"I'm sure he wants to, darling. That's the problem. You're just too irresistible, and I'm sure he thinks he couldn't control himself. Stop worrying about it. Just be happy that he loves you that much."

"Do you really think that's it?" Morgan asked.

"I'd bet my life on it."

Chapter 18

———— ★ ————

Christmas 1936 was approaching, and Morgan and Robert were about to open in their second play together. Earlier in the day they had a dress rehearsal and Morgan was still in her make-up. Now she stood in front of the bathroom mirror closely studying herself. The mascara had run a little, making her look tired. She reached for the soap, and five minutes later her face was scrubbed. Untying her hair, she allowed the curls to fall softly around her face. Satisfied with how she looked, she moved into the bedroom.

The gown she had intended to wear to the party that evening had been pressed and was lying on the bed. Morgan picked it up and placed it back into the closet. She then took out a pair of baggy men's trousers and a white, men's dress shirt she had bought in a second-hand store on the Left Bank.

Just as Morgan finished dressing, she heard a knock on the door. She opened it, and when Robert saw her, he stood there open-mouthed, staring.

"You're gorgeous," he said, stepping inside and spinning Morgan around.

"Put me down," Morgan said, pretending to be annoyed.

"What are you up to, young lady?" he asked, grinning.

"Well," Morgan said, "I thought it might be really nice if we just stayed in tonight and maybe…you know." She began to blush. "We could skip the party." She held her breath waiting for his response.

"That just may be the best idea you've ever had." Robert smiled as he removed his suit jacket and threw it on the chair before loosening his tie.

"Come with me. I have a little surprise for you," Morgan said as she reached for his hand and walked him into the sitting room. Soft music was playing in the background, and candles were flickering on the table, casting a golden light over the room.

"For you, kind sir," Morgan said, escorting him to the sofa, I've ordered dinner to be sent up, and I even ordered champagne."

"This is great," Robert said, "but aren't we celebrating a bit early? The show hasn't even opened yet. We don't usually celebrate until we're sure we have a hit."

"This isn't about the play. It's simply my way of saying that no matter what happens, I've had the most wonderful time. I never thought my life could ever be like this."

Robert took Morgan's hand and pressed it to his lips. "I love you, Morgan."

* * *

Well past midnight Robert watched Morgan begin to doze off, the effects of the dinner and champagne obviously taking their toll. "Hey, you big party pooper," he said, poking her in the ribs, "is this how a romantic evening ends? No princess goes to sleep without a waltz." Robert pulled Morgan to her feet. "Come dance with me."

As they danced, Robert kissed Morgan deeply, and she responded passionately. His hands traced the curve of her breasts and Morgan sighed. "Robert, we must stop," she said, realizing how close she was to the edge.

Robert pulled away from her. His hands were trembling. "I've never wanted or needed anyone as much as I want and need you. Keeping my hands off of you has been the most difficult thing I've ever had to do. You're going to owe me a thousand nights, Morgan. And rest assured I'm going to collect one day," Robert said.

Morgan sat down on the sofa, motioning Robert to join her. He put his arm around her and she snuggled into him, closing her eyes and quickly falling asleep.

Robert sat holding her for a very long time before gently lifting her and carrying her to the bed. Pulling the coverlet over her, he kissed her on the mouth and whispered, "Pleasant dreams, my love."

Morgan awakened the next day thinking about her enchanting evening with Robert, but her peace soon gave way to self-recrimination. She had intended to use the previous night to discuss her nagging concerns with Robert, but the night had been too perfect to ruin. Deciding that she could no longer put it off, she picked up the phone and dialed his room.

"Hello," he said, his voice thick with sleep.

"Robert, would you mind meeting me downstairs? We can have some breakfast in the shop across the street. I really have to talk with you," she said.

"I think you're forgetting something, my sweet. If you want to talk and not be bombarded by our devoted public, you'll have to pick a place a little less conspicuous…like my room for instance," he said.

"I'll come to your room in half an hour," Morgan said, hanging up the phone before Robert could respond.

* * *

Thirty minutes later she was standing in Robert's room. He couldn't help noticing that her eyes were solemn and her lips pale, as he held her in his arms.

"What's the matter, Morgan?" he said. When she didn't answer, he took her hand. "I have breakfast being delivered in a little while. Why don't we talk before it arrives"?

Morgan nodded and they moved into the living room. She sat in the club chair and Robert sat opposite her.

"I'm lonely for my family," Morgan said. "My mother tells me so little, and I miss my father terribly. It's not that I don't love you. It's just that I have this giant hole in me…like something's missing. I don't want to pressure you, but I was hoping we could go home and see them. I know we can't go now, but maybe we could go when the play closes. I'm sure by then my father will have forgiven me," she said.

"Of course we can, and we will," Robert said, relieved. "And tell me, Miss Rabinowiszch, how would you like to go home as Mrs. Robert Osborne?" he said, shocking himself as much as Morgan.

Robert watched Morgan's face and was caught completely off balance by the anger he saw in her eyes.

"Robert, I love you but I can never marry you."

"What are you talking about?" he asked.

"Please, just listen," she said. "I've been very lonely, and I realize that some of that loneliness is due to my lack of contact with my own kind." She held up her hand to prevent Robert from interrupting her. "Please, if there's any hope for us, you must listen to me."

Robert felt trapped, fearful that her religion was going to stand in the way of their marrying. He forced himself to appear calm.

"I guess I took the easy way out. I should have told you sooner, but I just couldn't," Morgan said. "For the last couple of weeks, at every party we've gone to, people have discussed what they'll do or where they'll go on Christmas Eve and Christmas day. Not once has Chanukah been mentioned. And please don't misunderstand; I'm not blaming you. You didn't even know that my holiday begins in less than a week. I should have told you. It's just that I've never had Christian friends." She took a deep breath.

"Then last Saturday afternoon Claire took me to meet her Jewish neighbors, the Feinsteins. They greeted me as if I were a part of their family, and seconds after meeting them I felt as if I'd gone back home. They invited me to join them for the Sabbath lunch.

"Ruth is a lovely and gentle woman. She has two young sons, Nathan and Abraham. Their father is a soft-spoken, intellectual professor of history at the Sorbonne. After lunch he told me that stories were filtering in from Germany, stories being carried by Jews fleeing for their lives. Have you any idea what's going on there?" Morgan said. "Have you ever heard of the Nuremberg Laws?"

Before Robert could answer, Morgan continued. "The German Jews have lost their citizenship rights and I didn't even know about it, I've been so wrapped up in my own life," she said, the pain and guilt showing clearly on her face. "Did you know that it is now illegal for a Jew to marry a gentile in Germany? Illegal! Where would that put us, Robert, if we lived in Germany?

"Over half the Jews living there are without work. They have no milk for their babies because the Jewish farmers aren't allowed to farm. They're being punished because they're Jews. That's their crime," Morgan said as tears welled in her eyes. "This is 1936 for God's sake! We are supposed to be an evolving civilization. What is going on?"

Robert moved his chair closer to hers and took her trembling hands in his. "Morgan, please, I'm not the enemy. I would never hurt you."

"I know that. That's not the point," she said. "Dr. Feinstein told me that in 1933 the first laws were passed, rescinding a Jew's right to hold any kind of public office. Those laws eradicated all Jewish political leaders and all civil service jobs. One day the Jews were an important part of the community, and the next day they were non-persons.

"The artists, actors, and the journalists have all been silenced. My father always used to tell me that the Jews are the record keepers, the written conscience of humanity, but I guess this animal Hitler is seeing to it that the Jews are not keeping records in his Germany.

"Your friend, William, was in Germany for the Olympics. He must have seen what was going on. Didn't he tell you anything? Wasn't he concerned?" Morgan started sobbing.

Robert sat numbly, trying to remember the conversations he had had with William. They had spoken about William's impressions of Hitler's Germany, and he had decided not to tell Morgan any of it.

* * *

William had returned understandably impressed by the political and economic situation of the country. Unemployment, a problem that was running rampant in all of the other European countries, was almost nonexistent in Germany. But the racial laws had infuriated him.

"The Germans see themselves as the Master Race, and they see the Jew as the enemy," William had said. "The Germans I met, the ones involved with the theater or the arts, were outraged over the expulsion of the Jews from their trades, but they defended themselves by saying that one man could do nothing. They also argued that if the world cares so much for its Jews, what were all of the tourists doing in Berlin when they could have easily boycotted the Olympics?

"I must tell you, my friend," William had said, "I didn't have any answers. I'm still trying to comprehend the uncanny passivity of the German people. They're like a bunch of unthinking automatons allowing themselves to be herded and controlled. I couldn't wait to get the hell out of Germany. I think changing Morgan's name may have been the smartest thing you ever did."

The two friends, angry and frustrated, had gone out that night and drunk themselves into oblivion, all the while cursing Adolf Hitler and his Nazi followers.

*   *   *

Robert forced himself back to the present. He had been afraid of this all along. He'd worked so diligently at protecting Morgan. When conversations turned political Robert always glossed over the news, assuring her that the dire predictions were an overreaction. He had gone so far as to order the hotel staff not to deliver a newspaper with Morgan's breakfast. But Robert couldn't avoid the fact that Morgan was an intensely curious, intelligent woman who thrived on being kept abreast of world news.

As if she were reading his mind, Morgan said, "I'm so angry with myself. My God, I've been so self-centered, so selfish! I didn't even realize what was happening around me. I was raised to have an opinion, to have a voice that would be heard. I refuse to waste my time and my intelligence on the people we've been associating with. They only care about themselves. They're the shallowest people I've ever known." Morgan was furious. "I don't want to become like them," she said, slow tears brimming from her eyes.

"Morgan, please," Robert said. "This is all my fault." He told her everything—his conversations with William, his decision to protect her, and the great lengths he had gone to keep her uninformed. "From now on, I swear to you, you'll pick your own friends," he said, knowing full well the implications of that promise.

Morgan was quiet for a short time, and then she said, "Will you give me your word that from now on we'll be open and honest with each other?"

"Yes, I promise. But you must realize that you could find yourself in some very uncomfortable situations by exposing yourself to this so-called intellectual society. It's rampant with Socialists and anti-Semites."

"I was raised in Poland. They hate their Jews. I survived." Morgan spoke with a finality that frightened Robert.

The real world, the world Robert had desperately tried to gloss in violets and pinks, now turned suddenly black. Still, he was determined to marry Morgan.

"I've listened to you. Now give me my turn," Robert said. "I've been wrong. I underestimated you. But you must try to put us—us and not the world issues—into focus. No, we're not lucky enough to have been born into the same religion, but that doesn't make us less suited for each other. I'll learn your customs. I can't be Jewish, but I'll join you in your holidays, in your happy ones and your sad ones. Just don't deny us our happiness. Without you, my life has no value."

"Robert, I pray you're right, because I don't want to live without you either."

And as they reached out for each other, Robert finally accepted what he had known all along—Morgan would have to experience her own pain if she was to grow and fully reach her potential.

Chapter 19

———— ★ ————

On January 15, 1936, Robert and Morgan opened in Shakespeare's *Romeo and Juliet.*

Morgan would never forget that opening night. She stood on the stage waiting for the curtain to rise, her stomach so cramped she thought she would be sick, but when the music from the orchestra started, she was elevated past her fear. For the remainder of the evening she was Juliet, giving the finest performance of her life. When the curtain came down, the audience responded with a standing ovation that lasted through five curtain calls.

In a matter of days the entire winter season was sold out. The Paris papers called Morgan one of the most exciting and talented actresses to ever grace a European stage. The critics, always enamored with Robert, dubbed him "The King."

* * *

Morgan had always adored the mornings, but now, out of sheer exhaustion, she slept until noon. Her daily routine began with room service and three newspapers. She took no phone calls and received no visitors until her reading was completed.

Before the opening, Morgan had loved walking the boulevards of Paris in the late afternoons, but now her sudden fame had made her quiet walks impossible. The attention from her adoring fans made her self-conscious and claustrophobic. She had never dreamed that the notoriety Robert so enjoyed and she had so envied on the train would become such a burden.

Determined to find some release, Morgan decided to have a talk with Claire. She found her in the wardrobe room repairing a downed hem.

"I need to discuss something with you," Morgan said, sitting down cross-legged on the floor. "But you have to swear first that you won't laugh when I tell you."

"Oh, it's one of those problems—the kind I wished I had," Claire said.

"Claire!" Morgan said, scowling.

"OK, I swear I won't laugh."

Morgan held on to her friend's arm. "I hate being famous. I wish I was invisible."

"Sorry, I can't help you with that one," Claire said as she bit her lip to keep from giggling.

"Come on, I'm serious," Morgan said, squeezing Claire's arm.

"What's going on? Claire asked, finally realizing that her best friend was really upset.

Morgan stared off into space. "When I was a child, my father use to take me on long walks. Sometimes we would sit in the park for hours just watching. It was my way of getting energy and inspiration," she said, "but now I'm the one always being watched. I can't take it, Claire. I feel like I'm smothering."

Claire put her arm around Morgan. "Relax. You've come to the right place. After the show tonight I'll teach you a few tricks of the trade."

* * *

Well past midnight the two girls slipped into the wardrobe room. Morgan held the flashlight as Claire poked into drawers and cupboards, greedily stuffing her pockets and purse.

"Aha! This is exactly what I was looking for." She held up a short blond wig. "Let's get out of here before we get caught."

They ran through the building and out the front door. Robert was leaning against the limousine, tapping his foot.

"And just where have you two been?" he asked.

Morgan smiled and kissed Robert. "We had something to do, that's all."

"Sure," Robert said as he reached over and kissed Claire on the cheek. "You both look guilty. I don't trust either one of you."

Claire laughed and looked directly into Robert's eyes. "And well you shouldn't," she said.

Once they were safely back at Morgan's hotel rooms, Claire said, "This, my dear, is the secret to your invisibility." She held the wig high in the air.

"It looks like a dead animal," Morgan said.

"Right you are, but I'm a master of disguises. When I'm finished with you, your own mother won't recognize you."

Claire laid out pencils, brushes, and hairpins.

"First we lighten your eyebrows with this blond pencil. We'll use this blush to make your complexion ruddier."

For over an hour they experimented. And when they were finished, Morgan looked like an entirely different person.

"You're a genius!" Morgan said, hugging Claire.

"I know," Claire said, collapsing on the bed. "I hope you don't mind if I sleep on your couch? I'm pooped."

* * *

When Morgan learned to transform herself, a whole new, magical world opened to her. The city's Jewish Quarter, the Marais, became her favorite haunt, where she spent hours walking and observing–there Morgan found her greatest solace and her greatest pain.

The Jews of Paris had become rightfully suspicious of outsiders; and even though she visited the same stores and restaurants each week, no one ever greeted her or acknowledged her presence. Many times she overheard them saying in Yiddish, "What is that shiksa doing here? Be careful what you say. You never know."

Morgan wanted to scream out, "Look at me. I'm a Jew! I want to be acknowledged. Why won't you let me in?" But she said nothing; content knowing she would be going home soon.

*   *   *

Morgan was almost twenty-years old as the winter of 1938 drew to a close. Months earlier the announcement had been made that *Romeo and Juliet* would be closing. Immediately, invitations from the finest theaters in Europe began pouring in. The offers were spectacular— unheard of sums of money and living accommodations in English castles, Italian villas, and Swiss chalets.

Proper scheduling of those performances was critical, and Robert and William spent hours deciding when and where they would take the troupe.

"My friend," William said, "I've been doing some investigating into America's booming motion picture industry, and I've come to the conclusion that if the situation in Europe continues to disintegrate, we should consider going there. What do you think?"

Robert nodded. "I've had the same thoughts."

"Good," William said, "I've already sent inquiries to various producers, and I feel confident the responses will be favorable. When the time comes, if it does, I want to be able to get the hell out of here."

"I know you're right," Robert said, "but we have one small problem—Morgan only knows the limited English I've taught her."

"So, she'll learn," William said, slapping Robert gingerly on the back.

"That's not going to be as easy as it sounds. If Morgan thinks even for a moment that we're considering leaving the continent, I know she'll refuse to learn," Robert said, remembering how strongly Morgan felt about leaving Europe, consumed as she was by the frightful premonition that if she ever left, she would never see her family again.

Waiting for their fifteen-minute curtain call one evening, Robert walked deliberately into Morgan's dressing room.

"William's had a marvelous inquiry from London. They want us to book in for an extended stay once we finish touring. Think about it, Morgan, it's a dream come true. Imagine, the home of Shakespeare, you and I together on the stage."

"That sounds wonderful," she said, hugging him, "but what about the language? Do you think I could learn it well enough?"

"Of course you can learn," Robert said. "I'll make arrangements for a teacher."

* * *

He hired a tutor and Morgan spent months studying in earnest, mastering the basics of language quickly.

As the scheduled closing grew closer, Robert became increasingly agitated, rambling on to William, "How can we be sure where to go? One day the world seems safe and the next day, who knows? We can't bury our heads, can we? We have to be aware of the rumblings of war. Maybe we should leave Europe now."

"If that's what you want, that's what we'll do," William said. "But you may be over-reacting. Consider what you want to do carefully. We can always get out. You are famous after all, and that does afford you certain privileges."

"You're right, of course," Robert said. "I really must try to stay more focused."

William's strategy was to remain only eight weeks in any one location, thereby assuring a sellout in every city. But that type of scheduling had its drawbacks: part of the cast and crew would have to be left behind, and extras and support crews would have to be hired along the way.

They decided that Morgan and Robert would take four weeks off to rest before beginning their tour, leaving William to make the arrangements for the movement of cast, crew, and wardrobe. And as the departure time drew nearer, Morgan became increasingly restless.

Early one morning, two months before the play closed in Paris, Robert knocked on Morgan's door. The break in her rigorous routine unnerved her as she answered the door.

"Robert, it's only eleven. What are you doing here?"

"I've come to take you on a picnic, so hustle your cute little bustle and get dressed. I'll wait out here for you."

"What a nice surprise, but don't you think it's a little chilly for a picnic?"

"Not if you dress warmly. It's March and it's time for us to come out of hibernation," Robert said.

An hour later they were sprawled across a blanket basking in the sunshine. Their picnic basket overflowed with cheese, warm bread, and wine. Robert felt lazy and peaceful, but Morgan was too excited to relax.

"Hey, you," Robert said, "this is a romantic afternoon. We're young and in love. You're supposed to be playing that part to perfection. At this rate your reviews will be horrible."

"I'm sorry. I'm just too excited to be romantic. The thought of what lies ahead is making me crazy. Every dream I've ever had in my life is about to come true—all of Europe at my feet, just as you promised. It's more than I can bear."

Morgan's eyes sparkled as she continued. "And soon we'll go home. Just wait until Papa and Mother meet you. They'll love you so much. I just know they will."

* * *

Morgan called Sara often. She had been trying hard to be an adult, but she missed her family badly.

Sara also missed Morgan, but she felt trapped in a deep, dark hole with no way out. Her only light was Morgan's calls. Nothing could rob Sara of the love and pride she felt for her daughter, and despite Samuel's instructions to have no contact with Morgan, she was determined to hold on to her only child.

"The other day I was passing a news stand, and there you were staring out at me from the cover of a French magazine," Sara said during one of their weekly phone calls. "I almost fainted. Jonte read the article to me. They love you, Morgan, really love you," she said, as tears filled her eyes. "You look so wonderful, darling. You're so grown up, and so very lovely." I can't believe it's been five years since I saw her, she thought.

"Thank you, Mother," Morgan said. "I'm so happy. If only you and Papa could be here with me, everything would be perfect." It wasn't the first time she had said that, and even though Morgan knew that it was a waste of words, she refused to stop trying. "I can't wait until the play closes so I can come home," she said.

"Have patience, darling. Soon you can come home. Soon."

Sara's words were empty, and they both knew it.

After every call, Morgan would hang up and cry. She would then go into the bathroom, wash her face, and become a little stronger and a little tougher, building an inner strength she was not even aware of.

Sara, too, would hang up and cry. Unlike Morgan, she was growing more fragile with each passing day.

* * *

Morgan and Robert had vowed to try to understand their differences. They spent hours learning about each other's religion, and soon the breach began to close as they discerned the similarities of their beliefs.

Discovering that the Old Testament was also Christianity's beginnings and that the New Testament was simply Christianity's continuation gave them a place to begin their studies. But what they found disturbed them both greatly.

"Why can't they leave us alone? Why are they always trying to convert us?" Morgan asked with anger and frustration.

Robert tried to answer her questions as they painfully forged through history, studying the Romans and the Crusades.

"The Church has established control by teaching fear and hatred, and they've used that to maintain control over the masses. Jesus spoke of love and compassion. His message was peace and love. I can't explain why that message hasn't been heard," Robert said one afternoon.

Morgan put her arms around Robert and held him closely. She said, "I don't believe that God ever intended for religion to be used as a divider. Perhaps one day things will change."

"Listen, Morgan, I know we've discussed this before," he said, his eyes burning into hers, "but I want to marry you." She started to say something but Robert put his finger to her lips. "Shh. I have something for you." Reaching into his pocket, Robert handed Morgan a blue velvet box. "Open it," he said.

Morgan slowly removed the five-carat, square-cut diamond solitaire. "Robert," her eyes filled with tears, "what can I say?"

"Just say that you love me as much as I love you. Just say that someday you'll marry me."

"I do love you. God help me, I do. And I will marry you," she said, slipping the ring onto her finger.

Chapter 20

───── ★ ─────

Samuel arose each day before dawn to go to the synagogue, where he took part in morning prayers for the dead. Sara tried everything to convince her husband to stop the travesty of mourning for Morgan, but her pleading and tears were to no avail. When she continued to defy him by refusing to end her telephone conversations with Morgan, Samuel retreated totally, closing her out of his life. He moved to a separate bedroom and avoided her whenever possible.

He spent his days at the hospital and at his office, taking his dinners at the Doctors' Club and never arriving home before ten at night. Samuel's life revolved around his patients, while Sara's revolved around Morgan's phone calls. She never questioned her love for Samuel; despite his actions, he was her husband and she would remain loyal to that commitment.

For Samuel, the question of loving Sara was much more complicated. Sometimes he would steal a look at her and his heart would bleed. *She's only forty years old, still young and yet look at her. She's become as fragile as a porcelain doll. All I have to do is hold her and everything will be right again.* But then he would tell himself that it wasn't about love; it was about a wife's obligation to respect and obey her husband. Sara had defied a hundred generations of tradition by disobeying him. He truly believed that Morgan's headstrong behavior was a direct result of Sara's indulgences, and for that reason alone he was incapable of forgiveness.

Sara had resigned herself to the truth that before long she would have to tell Morgan that she could never come home again, and Sara wasn't sure that she would be able to survive that confrontation. Inevitably, the day came when the phone rang and Morgan said the words Sara had most feared.

"Mother, the play closes in just two weeks and I'm coming home. I'll be off for an entire month. Won't that be fabulous?" When Sara didn't respond Morgan continued, "And, Mother, I won't be coming alone; I'm bringing Robert with me. We're engaged to be married."

Sara gasped as Morgan continued excitedly, "I know you and Papa will love him, just as much as I do. He's handsome and brilliant. I just know you're going to be crazy about him."

Morgan took a long, deep breath; silently praying that God wouldn't let her down. There was complete silence. "Mother, talk to me. Please talk to me!"

Sara could feel the pain as she heard her daughter begin to sob. Sara was crying as well, choking on the words she so loathed to utter. When she regained her composure, she said, "You can't come home. You can never come home. As far as your papa is concerned, you're dead!"

Morgan screamed, "You're lying! Why are you lying to me, Mother? You don't want me to come home. Don't you love me? Why are you making all of this up? You want Papa all to yourself, don't you?"

Sara couldn't believe what she was hearing. All of the suffering she had done, and this was how she was repaid. She had been on the verge of collapse, and Morgan's last words pushed her over the edge.

Quietly, Sara said to her only child, "Your precious papa sat Shiva for you. Do you understand? For him, you're dead. You're dead and I have no life, no daughter, and no husband."

Morgan dropped the phone as the room began to spin and she felt herself slipping into darkness.

Sara held on to the phone for a very long time. She talked lovingly into it, telling the empty line how much she loved her daughter and her husband, and that everything was going to work out just fine.

When Jonte found Sara, she was singing softly into the phone. Gently Jonte pried the phone from Sara's hand. The two women looked into each other's eyes, and then they both began to sob. Sara was mourning now, for in fact she had lost her only child. Jonte held Sara and rocked her, cooing soothing words and singing a gentle lullaby.

* * *

Robert called Morgan at two the next day, and when she didn't answer he assumed she had gone out for one of her walks. When evening came and he still was unable to reach her, he became concerned. They always had dinner together before each performance. He thought nervously, this is totally out of character for Morgan.

He called Claire, and when she said she hadn't seen or heard from Morgan all day, he panicked. Claire was also frightened, but she was determined to hide her fear.

"Relax," she said lightly. "I'm pretty sure she told me she was spending the afternoon with Professor Feinstein. You know how involved Morgan gets. She's probably let the time get away from her. You go on to the theater and I'll go find her."

At seven Claire rushed into the theater.

"The Professor hasn't seen her, Robert," she said.

Robert began pacing the room, clenching and unclenching his fists. "Where could she be? I've called her room a dozen times."

When William entered the room, he saw the anguish on Robert's face. "What's going on here? Where's our star?"

Robert reached for William's hand. "Something's happened to Morgan. I haven't seen her all day and neither has anyone else. Help me, William. I don't know where to begin to look." His voice was shaking.

William glanced at Claire. The look in her eyes clearly signaled that this was a serious matter. "OK, we obviously have a problem, but we'll find her. If we lose our heads we won't get anywhere." William felt the bile begin to rise in his throat. He had a performance beginning in fifteen minutes, and he was missing one star and the other star was incapable of going on.

"Listen, old buddy," William said, "you stay right here, don't move. I have to go tell two understudies they're about to have the biggest break of their lives."

* * *

William returned and took control. "First of all," he said, "we'll go back to the hotel and have the manager open Morgan's room. It may well be that she's left you a note or at least some clues as to where she might have gone."

He put his arm around Claire. "We have a show to do, and they really need you in wardrobe. We'll find her, don't you worry," he said.

Claire held Robert's hand tightly. "I know she's not in danger. I know it as well as I know my own name. You have to believe that, Robert, you just have to."

The ride to the hotel seemed to take hours. Robert couldn't help thinking; this isn't something Morgan would ever do. She would never miss a performance unless she was in desperate trouble.

William, Robert, and the manager rode up to Morgan's rooms in silence. The door was opened. The rooms were dark. Still, Robert sensed Morgan's presence.

When the manager turned on the lights, they saw her sitting in a chair staring out the window. She was unaware of their presence. Robert motioned for the manager and William to leave.

He whispered to William, "I'll call you later when I find out what the hell is going on here."

Robert moved slowly towards Morgan, not wanting to startle her. He knelt and searched her eyes for recognition. They were vacant violet pools. He took her freezing hand in his. "Tell me, my darling, tell me what's happened? I'll help you. I swear to God, whatever it is, I'll help you."

Morgan sensed his presence and she abruptly returned to reality. As she moved into Robert's arms, she knew instinctively that the time had come for the broken child to be replaced by a woman, a woman who could survive.

With renewed determination and purpose Morgan related to Robert her entire conversation with her mother—every word, every painful pause, every inflection.

When Morgan finished her story, Robert held her. At first he felt no response, but then he began to sense her renewed empowerment.

"Robert, do you still want to marry me?" Morgan asked.

"Of course I do, my darling."

"I love you, and nothing is ever going to keep us apart again."

* * *

Sara, in her own search for strength, asked Jonte to leave her alone. She then moved trance-like across the hallway into Samuel's rooms. Walking into his dressing area, she caressed his clothing, bringing his shirts to her lips, smelling the fragrance, breathing in his essence. "I'm alive, and by God, I'm going to have my life back!" Sara said aloud as she moved into his bedroom and lowered herself onto his bed, intending to simply lie there for a minute or two, wanting only to be where he lay and to touch what he touched. More exhausted then she realized, within moments Sara fell asleep.

When she opened her eyes, Samuel was looking down at her. Still half asleep, Sara reached for Samuel, pulling him to her. At first he resisted, but only for an instant. He was hungry for her touch, hungry for her warmth. They held on to each other, at first tentatively. Then the anger and pain began to fall away.

"Forgive me, Samuel. I'll be a good wife to you from this moment on. I promise I'll make you happy. Please don't go away from me again."

Sara was fighting for her life. She was begging and didn't even care. Samuel was all she had left and she was not going to lose him.

"It's all right, Sara. It's all right," Samuel said as he kissed her damp cheeks.

* * *

Morgan and Robert were married in a civil ceremony on April 5, 1938. Morgan wore a white organza Balenciaga suit and a Coco Chanel hat, and she carried a bouquet of white roses, buttercups, and daisies. Robert wore a black morning suit. Claire served as Morgan's maid of honor and William stood up as Robert's best man. Saul, Claire's boyfriend, was the only other person in attendance. The rings were exchanged and the judge was about to complete the ceremony when Robert stopped him.

"One moment, please, your honor."

"Are you chickening out on me?" Morgan chided.

"Quite the contrary, my darling," Robert said lovingly, looking at Saul.

Saul produced a wine glass wrapped in a napkin. He placed the glass on the floor and Robert smashed it with his foot.

"Mazel tov, good luck!" Saul said with a smile.

"I now pronounce you man and wife," the judge said.

Robert kissed Morgan, and Claire moved to embrace her friend. When Saul kissed Morgan, he said, "You've taken a step worthy of Queen Esther, and I applaud your courage. He's a good man, Morgan. A very good man."

"Thank you, Saul, and thank you for reminding me that I'm a Jew and that I'll always be a Jew, no matter what," she said embracing him warmly.

They had wanted a quiet, simple wedding with no fanfare or commotion, so the hoard of reporters waiting for them when they descended the steps of the courthouse made Robert angry.

"I don't even have to ask how they found out, do I, William?" Robert said.

"Come on, Robert," William said, "you're the most talked about couple in Paris. The papers would have crucified us if I hadn't told them where and when. They only want a couple of photographs and a few minutes of your time. Remember, you picked this life and you belong to your fans, whether you like it or not."

Morgan smiled at Robert. "Since we didn't give him his way about a big wedding, I guess we can humor them for a few minutes," Morgan said.

"Thank you. I'm forever in your debt," William said with relief. He turned to the reporters and announced, "Five minutes. That's all the time you get."

After posing and answering a few questions, the couple got into the limo and drove away.

"Robert, I'm so nervous. I can't believe this is really happening," Morgan said.

"I can't believe it either. Do you know how many hearts we're breaking today?" he said, laughing as he pinched her cheek and pulled her to him. "Just remember one thing, young lady," he whispered, "you owe me a thousand nights, and I'm about to call in that debt."

Morgan tried to act shocked. "That's not the way a gentleman speaks to a lady. I'm aghast at your behavior, sir."

"Not as aghast as you're going to be," Robert said.

* * *

Back in Robert's rooms, they drank an entire bottle of champagne. Morgan felt giddy and slightly drunk.

"I'm going to change into something more comfortable," she said. Then she turned and looked at Robert. "Can you believe I said that?"

Robert joined her laughter, reaching to kiss her. "You better put a move on," he said, "or you may not get to show off your new nightie."

Morgan took her time undressing. She checked herself in the mirror from every direction, dabbing cologne on her neck, her shoulders, and between her breasts. As an afterthought, she dabbed some on her inner thighs. Finally, she slipped into her handmade silk nightgown and with all the courage she could muster, opened the bathroom door and entered the bedroom.

"Morgan," Robert said, "you're more beautiful than words could ever say."

He gently took her into his arms. Their long, deep kiss continued as he lifted her and carried her to the bed. Morgan made love with fervor that both surprised and delighted Robert. She was uninhibited, earthy, inquisitive, and lusty. They couldn't get close enough as they pressed into each other and merged, pulled away, and merged again. Night became day and day became night. Room service came and went, and the radio was turned on and then off. The papers were read, thrown aside, and then read again. They stayed secluded, going out only to be refreshed by the sights, sounds, and fragrances of Paris.

Chapter 21

————— ★ —————

The reporters had crowded around William, grilling him for details on the nuptials, as Claire held tightly to Saul's arm.

"Let's get out of here," Saul said, placing his arm around Claire. "We'll see you later, William," he said offhandedly, hailing a cab. He directed the driver to Dodin's, a quaint brasserie with a superb view of the Seine and Notre Dame.

They drank brandy, happily toasting Morgan and Robert. The liqueur quickly warmed and relaxed them.

"Claire, I couldn't help thinking, watching Morgan and Robert, that it could have been us today," Saul said.

"I thought the same thing, Saul. They managed to overcome all of their problems." Claire lifted her head proudly, "If they can do it, I'm sure we can too."

"You know, I realized something today. The difference in our religions doesn't bother me so much anymore. It's taking you away from the safety of your home and family that's killing me," Saul said.

"Look, Saul, we've had this conversation a hundred times. I understand your commitment to Zionism, and I understand why you have to go to Palestine, so why can't you understand that I want to go with you? My life would be nothing without you. I love you, you big dummy."

"I love you too. That's the problem. I love you too much to expose you to the danger of being surrounded by Arabs who will hate us and living conditions that will be horrible at best. How can I take you in good conscience?" he said. "The establishment of a Jewish homeland is the responsibility of Jews, not gentiles. Claire, it's not your fight."

"It will be," she said, hesitating so that the full impact of her next words would penetrate Saul's stubbornness. "It will be once I convert."

"You would do that for me?" he asked.

"I would do it for us," she said. "For us and for our children."

Saul looked deeply into Claire's eyes. He seemed to be on the verge of a decision and Claire waited, holding her breath and praying.

"There's a ship sailing for Palestine in ten days. Let's be on it, Claire," he said. "Will you marry me?"

"Oh, Saul, of course I will. But I would have gone with you even if you hadn't wanted to marry me."

"Let's go see if we can find someone to marry us," Saul said.

Claire was stunned. "Wait a minute! I have to tell my family. I have plans to make."

A dark look crossed Saul's face. "I'm asking you to accompany me, to marry me now. We'll go together to your family after we're married."

Claire's mind was roaring. Tears blinded her eyes as she questioned his lack of sensitivity. "What's the matter with you? I'm giving you my life, and all I'm asking for in return is one day," she said. "I have obligations to the people I love; and if you really love me as much as you say you do, you'll let me do it my way." Claire's eyes drilled into Saul.

He lowered his eyes. "I'm sorry," he said. "I have no idea what you see in me. This is the happiest day of my life and I'm acting like a jackass. I don't want to lose you, Claire."

"You won't lose me, not ever," she said.

* * *

Saul put Claire into a cab, agreeing that they would meet back at his flat by seven that evening. Then he hailed his own cab and instructed the driver to take him into the Jewish Quarter.

As the car moved through the congested streets, Saul was wishing that he too had parents to visit, parents to share the news with, but past scars and pain had taken that option away. He wouldn't call them, not now and maybe not ever.

Saul's extremely wealthy family divided their time between summers with the Vanderbilt's and their winters in Switzerland. But his parents were emotionally cold people whose sole goal in life had been to be accepted into gentile society.

Despite his father's disapproval, at thirteen Saul had gone through the rights of passage into manhood by being Bar Mitzvah. During that time, when he was so openly defying his parents, his Zionism had been born. The rabbi had given him Theodore Herzl's book *The Jewish State* as a Bar Mitzvah gift, and by the time he had turned the last page, Saul had become a zealot, vowing to one-day help his people return to Israel.

At fourteen Saul was sent off to a boarding school, where he was expected to attend weekly church services. When he protested that this was an insult to his ideals, his parents laughed him off. For Saul that was the ultimate insult; he turned away from them and began accepting invitations to go home with his friends, sometimes for entire summers. He thought he was punishing them, but in truth his absence was a relief to his parents.

Saul believed that scientists would become the backbone of Israel once the Balfour Declaration was implemented and Israel became a state, so he majored in physics at the University. Now, with Claire by his side, he would use his inheritance, the money he so detested, to help build a Jewish homeland.

* * *

In the heart of the Jewish Quarter, Saul got out of the cab and walked the crowded streets in search of a synagogue—a place he hadn't been to in years. At three different synagogues the rabbis refused to officiate a marriage between a Jew and a gentile. Saul, frustrated and exhausted, decided to try one more rabbi. If he were refused again, he would find a judge to marry them.

He wandered until he found a tiny synagogue nestled at the end of an alley in the poorest section of the Quarter. Along the way he had passed several much larger more affluent houses of worship, but something had told him not to stop; something had pulled him to this place. He had never been here before, yet it seemed familiar. Saul walked up to the front door and tried the latch. It was locked. *This can't be happening. I know I'm supposed to be here.*

From behind him he heard a rustling. He turned around and was face to face with a very old man dressed in orthodox attire: a long black coat, fur-trimmed black hat, and coarse, black, woolen trousers. His beard was pure white and he wore the long side curls of an ultra-religious Jew. However, it was the old man's eyes that pulled his attention; they were the eyes of a holy man, a seer.

The rabbi looked at Saul and smiled. "Have you lost your way, my son? Can I help you?"

Saul looked pleadingly at the rabbi. "I certainly hope you can."

The rabbi pushed past Saul. "Come with me. We'll have some tea and then we'll talk. I'm an old man, so these days I think better on my bottom than I do on my feet."

Saul followed the rabbi inside, where they moved into a tiny sitting room furnished with a tattered couch and chair. Open books lay everywhere and the dust flew as the rabbi moved some of them so that Saul could sit.

"Wait here, please. I'll fix us some hot tea and then I'll see if I can help you," he said, disappearing into the back of the building and leaving Saul with the feeling that the old rabbi knew why he had come. It was as if the books, the very walls, were speaking to him.

When the rabbi returned, he sat down next to Saul and gently put his hand on Saul's arm.

"What's happening to me?" Saul asked.

"Don't be alarmed. There are times in our lives when the voice of the Lord reaches our ears. The times are all too few, but when it does happen, we must learn to listen and to be grateful. Now, tell me how I can help you?"

Saul shook his head, trying to make himself feel more alert. "I'm going to Palestine, but I have a problem. You see, I've fallen in love with a wonderful girl who isn't Jewish." Saul waited for a reaction from the rabbi. When none came, he continued. "She's willing to convert, only we don't have time now to go through all of that because we're leaving in a few days. No one will marry us, Rabbi." Saul paused and braced himself for another disappointment.

"I see," the rabbi said. "And why are you going to Palestine?"

"I'm going home."

The old man smiled and patted Saul's hand. "There are no right or wrong answers to my question as to why you're going to Palestine, but I can tell you that your answer made the angels sing. So tell me, when can I meet this young woman?" the rabbi asked.

Saul hesitated, not wanting to be rude. "Would tomorrow evening be too soon?"

The rabbi smiled. "Come back at 5:30. We have many things to talk about and much to do."

He stood up and walked Saul to the door. "You're a blessing for our people," the rabbi said as he closed the door.

Saul felt as if he should prostrate himself on the rabbi's doorstep, knowing he had been in the company of a just and holy man and that that experience had forever changed him.

He found a cab and went directly to the shipping office to secure passage. He stood in line for over an hour before an agent with eyes like a weasel told him that no tickets were available. Realizing that the doors were beginning to close on Jews trying to escape Europe, Saul produced a billfold full of money. The agent's eyes lit up and he quickly issued two tickets.

When Saul finally arrived back in his room, he was exhausted and filled with nervous expectation. He was concerned about Claire and the reaction of her family.

*   *   *

She knocked on his door promptly at six, and when he opened the door, she threw herself into his arms.

"God, I missed you! I feel so all alone when you're gone," he said. "Now, tell me about your day. I want to hear every word. What did Philippe and Stephanie say?"

Claire sat down on the bed and kicked off her shoes. She said pensively, "Saul, it was so difficult. My mother kept crying. I felt so sad for her. My dad just sat there with this incredibly stoic look on his face, not saying a word."

Claire laid back on the bed and put a pillow on her stomach, looking up at the ceiling while she continued talking, as much to herself as to Saul.

"My childhood kept coming back to me. They gave so much of themselves to their children. I can remember so many instances where they went without so that all of us could have." Claire fought for composure. "I told them all about the Middle East and Palestine. I must admit I painted a somewhat rosy picture, but I don't want them worrying about me." She looked at Saul hopefully and said, "I promised them I would come home often."

Saul nodded. "You will, my darling. I promise you that."

"My mother asked me what I was going to do about religion? I was afraid to answer her. She was already so upset. Finally I said, 'Mother, I love Saul and I don't want to lose him. I'll do whatever it takes to make him happy.' I can't explain what happened next. I guess she must have been impressed by my resolve and sincerity. She looked at me and said, 'You really do love him, don't you?' After a long silence my father finally spoke. I think I'll hear his words in my head for the rest of my life. He reached for my mother's hand and held it to his heart. He said, 'Giving up a child is very difficult. You came from the union of our love, and down deep we always hoped to keep you nearby. We knew in our hearts you were only on loan to us from God, but we were selfish. We didn't want you to ever leave us. But now, it's your time. Saul is a good man and I believe he truly loves you. You have our blessings.'"

Claire hugged the pillow and began to cry. Saul reached for her, but she pulled away.

"Not now, Saul. I need to be alone. Please, just give me a little time."

He backed away and waited.

When Claire finally sat up, she wiped away her tears and said, "Do you know what the most wonderful part of the whole day was?"

Saul shook his head.

"I never once doubted what I was doing. I'll miss them. They're my family and I love them, but now it's our time, yours and mine."

Chapter 22

─────────── ★ ───────────

The next afternoon, Saul gave the driver directions to the synagogue at the edge of the Jewish Quarter. He knocked on the door and the old rabbi opened it, smiling.

"Come in, come in," he said. "We must hurry. Shabbas ends at sunset, and sunset begins in a very few moments. Young man, help yourself to a tallis, yarmulke, and siddur while I show this lovely woman where she must go."

Saul looked at her, apologizing with his eyes. He'd completely forgotten about the Havdalah service that was performed at the end of every Sabbath. He hoped Claire wouldn't be too upset about not being allowed to sit with him. Claire's smiling face told him his fears were unfounded.

Claire waved at Saul and winked as she followed the rabbi to a rickety old stairway. He looked closely at Claire, making her feel momentarily self-conscious. "Follow the steps; follow your heart and you'll learn."

Claire was puzzled as she walked up the stairs and entered the empty room at the top. Neat little wooden chairs were lined up in a row overlooking the downstairs prayer hall. She had been in enough synagogues with friends over the years to be familiar with the sights and sounds, yet she felt uneasy and unsure of herself.

What did the Rabbi mean? Learn? How can I learn when there's no one here to teach me? And I don't understand one word in these Hebrew books.

Claire sat in the front row, feeling frustrated and a little angry. She eventually picked up a prayer book. It felt hot as she held it against her breast and closed her eyes. She began daydreaming, floating on a cloud, sailing through time…

A whispering sound, like the wind calling to her, brought her back. When she opened her eyes, a woman dressed in white was sitting next to her.

"My people have suffered unspeakably for their beliefs, and yet we've maintained our faith, our humanity, and our love for humankind," the woman said, her soft, spellbinding voice captivating Claire. "You now wish to join our numbers, and we welcome you with open arms. You'll become a woman of greatness, a queen. But your crown will not be one of jewels. It will be fashioned from mud and toil, tears and joy. Your name will be heralded upon all of the Earth, but it won't be man who sings your praises; it will be the trees and flowers, the animals and the birds. They'll sing your name to the winds. Now, give me your hand and I'll teach you all that you need to know."

Claire reached toward the image and closed her eyes. She immediately felt herself being lifted as they traveled together. The wind blew against Claire's face while she soared above the clouds and into the heavens, where they sat on a throne of roses, watching as the generations moved past.

Each soul had words for Claire as they looked lovingly into her eyes. They spoke directly to her soul, giving her the entire history of the Jewish experience. Eternity passed in front of her in an instant. Time was nonexistent in the dimension Claire was visiting. When she finally opened her eyes, she was alone. Convinced that she'd had an incredible dream, she reached up to smooth her wind-blown hair.

* * *

Saul sat at the very end of the pew, feeling out of place with the ultra-religious men in their prayer shawls and long black coats. They were from a time gone by, a time Saul couldn't relate to. The rapid Hebrew and the unfamiliar service confused him. He could feel the perspiration breaking out on his face, and he took a deep breath, forcing himself to relax, as he peered intently at the open prayer book.

Within moments his body began to sway to the songs and melodies. The generations were reaching out for him, calling his name, speaking in whispers of love.

The service ended and the men noisily filed out, but Saul remained, wanting to savor the moment and to let the feelings penetrate his soul.

When the rabbi appeared with Claire by his side, the couple's eyes met and held. Each one was reaching out for the other, trying to communicate in thoughts what had happened, because the words were not there for them and never would be.

The rabbi said softly, "I want you to follow me. We're going for a short walk."

Claire and Saul followed him out the back door of the synagogue and into a dark alley. In a few minutes they came to what appeared to be an ancient cemetery surrounded by a rusty metal fence. They walked through the front gate, and Saul looked questioningly at the rabbi.

The old man spoke directly to Claire. "Your young man seems surprised to be here among the dead, but you, my dear, are not."

She smiled at the rabbi. "Did the woman in white come from here?"

"No," the rabbi answered. "She came from the soul of the Jewish people, from our matriarchs—Sara, Rebecca, and Deborah. She came from the very being of all the brave young women who dared to have the courage to believe in the power of the Lord."

The rabbi touched the top of Claire's head with his open hands. In a loud, clear voice he said, "You need no conversion, you are one of them. Every woman of valor who has ever lived is with you here tonight. Go to the land of our people. Go and learn from the land, and the land will learn from you."

Claire felt the light of God fill her soul.

The rabbi then turned to Saul. "We have come to this place for you, my son," he said. "Look around you. Tell me what you see."

Saul was uncomfortable. He had no idea what was going on, either with him or with Claire. He glanced around the cemetery. "I see an overgrown field and a lot of headstones. That's what I see," he answered.

"What else do you see?"

Saul didn't know what the rabbi wanted him to say.

Before Saul could answer, the rabbi spoke again. "Many times we see with our hearts, not our eyes. See with your heart now, and tell me what you see."

Saul felt himself moving hypnotically from one grave to the next. Each soul gave him a message. He felt their prodding encouragement and their love. When Saul next spoke, he felt God had inspired his words.

"I see beauty here, in the souls that have passed. I see eternal hope and I see the light of God. I see heart's of fire."

The rabbi began to sway as he raised his eyes. "Join hands, my children, and bow your heads." He lifted his hands over the couple's lowered heads. "May the Lord bless you and keep you. May the Lord cause his countenance to shine upon you and be gracious unto you. May the Lord bestow his favor upon you and grant you peace, love, and happiness." The rabbi lowered his hands and his voice. "Here, in front of these witnesses with their blessings and approval, I pronounce you husband and wife."

Claire and Saul stood dazed.

"So, kiss your bride all ready," the rabbi said. "Hurry, we have much more to do."

Saul kissed Claire gently on the lips.

The rabbi walked back out through the gate, waving cheerfully at the smiling couple. "Hurry. Come with me."

Back in his study, the rabbi said, "Sit, sit. I'll be back in an instant."

When he returned, his arms overflowing with objects. Saul moved to help him, but the old man shook his head.

"I'm burdened with the memories of our past, not with these few precious items of our future," he said solemnly.

Claire and Saul watched as he placed a silver wine goblet, a wine bottle, and a candle in a silver candleholder on the table. Once the rabbi was satisfied with the arrangement, he reached into his pocket and removed a glass and a white cloth. He carefully wrapped the cloth around the glass and placed it on the table.

"Come to me, my children," he said.

As they stood across the table from him, he began, "I pour this wine into a single glass, and you will each sip from it, remembering for all time that while you're each separate, unique beings, in God's eyes you are now one, drinking from the same source." He poured the wine and brought the cup to Claire's lips. He then held the cup for Saul to drink.

"Now we'll light the candle that represents the eternal flame burning within us all. It is the light of all people everywhere. When nurtured, it burns pure and bright." The old man struck a match. "Each of you put your hand on mine, and together we'll kindle the flame."

The light from the candle cast a golden glow over the room as the rabbi then bent over and placed the wrapped glass on the floor.

"You'll break this glass with your foot in the tradition of our people." The rabbi's eyes glazed over and when he continued, he seemed to be in pain. "The breaking of the glass is used as a symbol to remind us of the destruction of our ancient temple in Jerusalem in 70 C.E. You must always remember, as well, the broken lives of your brothers and sisters who may not be as fortunate as you. In the end, my children, it's your joy and love that will nurture the universe. Now, break the glass!" he shouted jubilantly.

Saul smashed the glass with his foot.

"Mazel tov! Good luck!" The rabbi said.

Claire's eyes were shining as the old man removed a scroll from the bookshelf and unrolled it on the table.

"This is a Ketubah, your marriage license. I'll fill it out now so that you are officially married. What's your Hebrew name?" he asked Saul.

"It's Smuel. I was named after my grandfather."

The rabbi nodded. "What is your father's name?"

Saul shuddered, and then he smiled, holding his head high. "My father's name is Morris."

The rabbi smiled. "From this moment on your Hebrew name will be Smuel Ben Moshe Chai—Saul, son of Morris, son of Life." He then turned his attention to Claire. "You, we will call Rebecca, the carrier of love and light."

The rabbi looked at them as tears filled his eyes. "You've made an old man very happy, for even though I've broken with the law as it is written, I've never felt more righteous. You'll need God's love and protection. I'll pray for you both."

They left the synagogue knowing they had been given a gift that would forever remain wrapped in a golden light. A vision was shared, individually and collectively. They were now one, joined by the blessings of those gone by.

Chapter 23

─────────── ★ ───────────

Even though Claire was now a married woman, she slept at home in her own bed that night, deciding that it would be easier to tell her parents the news in the morning.

At daybreak, unable to sleep, she dressed and went into the kitchen. When her father came in a while later, Claire burst into tears.

"What's the matter?" he asked, his face growing pale.

"Oh, Father, how are you ever going to forgive me?" Claire said, throwing herself into his arms.

"What in the world's going on down here," her mother said, padding into the room in her bathrobe.

"You both better sit down," Claire said, trying to get her guilt under control. She then tried to explain the circumstances under which she had been wed.

"I'm so sorry you couldn't be there, but I had no choice. I love him and I couldn't let him leave without me," she said.

"It's OK, darling. We understand. We really do. Don't we, Philippe?" her mother said.

Seeing the pain on her father's face, Claire buried her head in her hands sobbing. Her father, desperately unhappy for making her cry, took Claire into his arms.

"Just be happy, my child," he said. "That's all we want for you. Just be happy."

The three of them spent the rest of the morning talking, reliving treasured memories from the past and going over Claire's hopes for the future.

At noon Claire excused herself and went to call Morgan.

"Hi. What are you up to?" Claire asked lightly.

"My God, girl, it's the middle of the night," Morgan said, groaning and muttering something unintelligible.

Claire laughed. "No it's not, unless you call high noon the middle of the night."

"Claire, is everything all right? Morgan asked.

"Everything's fine. It's just that…I need to see you."

"I can't imagine what's happened," Morgan said to Robert after agreeing to meet Claire at 1:00 and then hanging up. "You better get up," she said, shoving him playfully.

"I'll get up, all right," he said. "But first…" He reached for Morgan.

* * *

After sitting with her family for another forty-five minutes, Claire said, "I really must go now. Morgan is expecting me."

"Of course, dear," her mother said. Her parents smiled sadly as she kissed them goodbye.

Claire settled into the cab, contemplating how difficult it was going to be to tell Morgan that she was going to Palestine. They had often discussed how their lives were going in different directions and how at times they might be separated for months, but this was different. Claire knew Morgan would be happy for her, but the thought of separation from her dearest friend was already beginning to sadden her.

Anxiety was churning Claire's stomach as she rode the elevator to Morgan's floor. When she gathered enough courage to knock on the door, Morgan opened it and the girls hugged.

"You look so beautiful," Claire said, "like a flower in bloom."

Morgan reached for Claire's hand, dragging her through the doorway.

"Come in. I've missed you so much," Morgan said.

Coffee and croissants were waiting for them as they settled on the living room couch.

"So where's Mister Wonderful?" Claire asked.

"He went to see William. He figured he might as well take advantage of the few hours I've given him. They're still making last minute arrangements. Can you believe it? We'll be leaving in seven days. I can't wait. Now, enough about me. I'm dying to hear what's going on with you."

Claire reached for Morgan's hand. "I have to warn you, you're about to be shocked right out of your socks," Claire said.

"Honey, after everything I've been through in the last couple of days, I won't be easy to shock."

"Saul and I were married last night."

"You're kidding?" Morgan said, looking open-mouthed at Claire. "My God, you're not kidding. Holy cow, I'm so happy for you!" Morgan said, wrapping her arms around Claire. "Mazel tov, my dear friend. Tell me everything, I mean every minute detail, and then maybe I'll find it in my heart to forgive you," Morgan said a little more seriously than she had intended.

"I'm sorry you weren't there, Morgan," Claire said.

"You don't have to be sorry. You know me—I'm just too sensitive. I'll get over it. Now, talk."

* * *

The two friends sat for hours, Claire telling Morgan everything, even about the woman in white, knowing that Morgan would understand.

"How strange all of this is," Morgan said, wiping her eyes and blowing her nose. "You'll carry on the work of my people. You, my dearest friend, have been given that honor. I feel so guilty that you're doing what I and every one of my people should be doing. I'm so proud to have known you and to have been a part of your life. But we've had so little time together, and I'm going to miss you so much," Morgan said, openly trembling. "I'll pray for you every day. I think you're the finest woman I have ever known."

Claire felt as if her heart were being torn from her body. "If I'm blessed to have a daughter, I'll name her Morgan," Claire said. "I'll tell her she was named after the best friend I ever had, and I'll tell her you taught me to believe that anything is possible, and most of all..." The words caught in Claire's throat as she choked with emotion. Morgan reached for her and rocked her in her arms.

Regaining her composure, Claire continued, "You knew what you wanted, Morgan, and you didn't let anything stand in your way. Your courage gave me the courage to marry Saul. I'll never forget you, not ever."

"Will you listen to us? We sound so maudlin, as if we're never going to see each other again. And that's ridiculous," Morgan said.

"You're right. There's absolutely no reason why we shouldn't see each other, and we can write letters. That way we'll always feel a part of each others lives," Claire said.

They talked, laughed, and cried away the rest of the day. Regardless of what they said, each harbored the same unspoken premonition that they might never see each other again.

* * *

Saul and Claire would be setting sail three days after Robert and Morgan departed, so they agreed to have their final farewells at the train station.

Robert had the trunks delivered to the station early in the day so that when they arrived they would only have to board the train. He understood better than anyone just how difficult it was going to be for Morgan to leave Claire.

"This is a little different than the last train ride we took. This time I won't have to be the perfect gentlemen. As a matter of fact, I intend to act just the opposite. You'll be lucky if I let you out of the berth at all," Robert said as the limousine neared their destination.

Morgan laughed halfheartedly. Robert sensed her inattention, but he was determined to try to put her mind on other things besides her impending separation from Claire.

"You know, our accommodations in Nice are going to be fabulous. No hotel for us this time. We'll be in a villa overlooking the sea, with servants and automobiles at our disposal twenty-four hours a day. You'll become so spoiled; you won't want to dress yourself. So I'm offering to be the one to dress you."

"Well, well, wouldn't that be a change," Morgan said as she pulled at the sleeve of his suit, "dressing instead of undressing me."

When the driver pulled up to the station, Morgan's mood shifted to panic.

"I don't know how I'm going to do this, Robert. All I have in the entire world besides you is Claire?"

"Morgan, you're doing what you want to do. You're fulfilling your dreams and so is Claire. You must try and remember that," he said.

Morgan knew he was right, and she kept repeating his words to herself as they got out of the car. They were immediately recognized by a group of traveling students.

"You're on your own," she said, giving Robert a gentle shove. "I'm going to find Claire. Please, just keep your fans off of my trail."

Robert moved over to the group as Morgan slipped away.

She spotted Claire clutching Saul's arm on the platform. The girls hugged and then Morgan hugged Saul.

"You're one lucky man, you know," she said. "Claire's the best thing that ever happened to either one of us."

"I know that," Saul said, looking tenderly at Claire. "She'll be in good hands, Morgan. I'll take care of her, I promise you that. And now you have to promise me you'll come visit us often."

"Of course I'll come. You can count on it."

The two girls fought back the tears they both knew were inevitable.

"I hate goodbyes," Claire said. "I always cry and make an absolute fool out of myself."

Morgan laughed. "I have a great idea. Let's not say goodbye. We'll pretend that all of this isn't really happening."

"You're the great actress," Claire said. "So let's see if you can pull that one off. I know I can't. By the way, our little group seems to me missing someone. Where's Robert?"

"I left him in the clutches of a group of teenagers. I'm sure he's loving every moment," Morgan said as she took Claire and Saul's hands. "Come on, you two, let's rescue him before he kills me."

"Nice of you to come back," Robert said as he pulled himself away from the group of giggling young girls.

"I thought maybe you wanted a little more time with them," Morgan said.

The train whistle sounded.

Morgan clutched Claire tightly.

"May God be with you, Claire. I love you so much. Thanks for being my friend." Morgan took deep breaths as she fought to stay calm.

Claire looked deeply into Morgan's eyes, feeling as if she were looking directly into her soul. A cold wind blew across her face and she began to shake, feeling a fear for Morgan that confused her. She brought both of Morgan's hands to her trembling lips and kissed them. "If you ever need me, if you ever need me for anything, I'll come. Promise me you'll always remember that," Claire beseeched.

"You have my word. If I ever need you, I'll find a way to reach you," Morgan said.

Saul and Robert hugged; wanting to put an end to the pain the women they loved were going through.

"Good luck, my friend. I hope to see you again one day very soon," Saul said, slapping Robert on the back. The men spoke to each other with their eyes. They too were devoted to one another; they just didn't have the words.

Morgan and Robert boarded the train and Morgan shouted back, "You better take good care of her, Saul!"

Claire stood on the platform until long after the train was out of sight. When she and Saul finally got into the waiting car, she collapsed, her head falling against Saul's chest. "She's in danger, Saul. I feel it and it scares me. Something terrible is going to happen to Morgan. I just know it."

"Darling, she'll be fine. She's in good hands. You're just tired and overwrought," Saul said, not revealing his own fears.

Chapter 24

———————— ★ ————————

Not wanting a repeat of the emotional trauma at the train station, Claire convinced her family to say their goodbyes at home.

On April 24, 1938, at the seaport outside of Nantes, she and Saul boarded their ship.

They made their way to the top deck and found cabin 311. The small porthole permitted entry of some natural daylight, which cast a gray shadow over the two single beds and small desk. The tiny space at least included private bathroom facilities, but having never been on a ship before, Claire became instantly claustrophobic.

Saul tickled her playfully, reading her thoughts. "You'll get use to it, darling. Now, let's go get some fresh air."

* * *

They stood on deck as the ship pulled out to sea, lost in their own individual thoughts, saying their own private farewells.

"Come on, Claire," Saul said as the port grew faint in the distance, "let's get back inside. It's getting cool out here and I don't want you catching a cold."

"You're right, I'm freezing," Claire replied, slipping her arm through Saul's as they walked to their cabin.

Opening the door, Saul looked at Claire and thought again how lucky they were to be getting out of Europe. Thousands of European Jews were fleeing to save themselves and their loved ones from the ever-escalating Nazi threat.

Saul was feeling too restless to relax. "I'd like to get my bearings. Do you mind if I have a look around the ship?" Saul asked.

Claire understood Saul's restlessness. "Don't be silly. Why would I mind? Besides, I want to unpack and rest for a while."

* * *

Saul walked briskly around the third-floor deck, enjoying the feeling of the wind slashing at his face. He went inside to the first-class dining room, where he sat enjoying the rocking motion of the ship. He then walked down to the second deck, where he found the crew quarters and wheelhouse. At mid-ship he discovered the communal showers and bathrooms that served this deck. Peering through the open cabin doors, Saul saw rooms not much larger than closets, but the happy faces in the corridors told him that these passengers were perfectly content with their accommodations.

When he came to a set of stairs with a signed that read "Freight & Food Storage," he became curious as to what cargo the ship was carrying. But just as he was about to descend the stairway, he felt a hand on his shoulder.

"May I help you, sir?" the uniformed ship's officer asked.

Saul turned and said, "No thank you. I'm just having a look around."

"I don't think you want to go down there, sir. We've been forced to use the space for passengers. It's very crowded and it's certainly no place for a gentleman like yourself."

"Is this area of the ship off limits?" Saul asked.

"No sir, it's not. I'm simply suggesting that you return to your cabin and forget about this area of the ship. It really doesn't concern you. Many of those people are ill, and it could be quite dangerous for you to go down there."

"If you don't mind, I'll decide for myself where I will and will not go, sir," Saul replied, moving slowly down the stairs.

When he reached the last step, he had to stop and wait for his eyes to acclimate to the darkness. What he eventually was able to see was so shocking he gasped out loud.

The bowels of the ship were packed. People everywhere, crowded together like cattle, with barely enough room to walk without stepping on someone. Mothers held their children protectively, trying to keep them warm, as babies wailed from hunger. Naked light bulbs encased in wire prisons swung precariously overhead, casting an eerie light over the hoard of humanity.

He could smell the people long before he could see them clearly. There were obviously no toilet facilities, and the odor made him gag. His body began to tremble from the freezing dampness, as he tried to imagine what it would be like down here after nightfall.

These people must have been here for days.

Saul saw the fear and pain in their faces. He had never experienced anything like this before. He felt as if the living dead surrounded him.

He walked furtively among the desperate people, feeling sad and lost, until he stood over a handsome young man dressed in the heavy garb of an orthodox Jew. The young man's stare had stopped him, so he sat down, squeezing his way in beside him.

"May I have a few words with you?" Saul asked in Yiddish.

"What can I tell you, sir?" the young man said more as a statement than a question.

"Where are you from?" Saul asked.

"I'm from Vienna." He looked away, his eyes filling with tears.

"I'm so sorry, so very sorry," Saul said with only remote understanding. "Will you tell me about it?"

"Why?" the young man said. "Why should I tell you? Will it change anything? Can you help me now? Can you give me back my family, my life?"

Saul suddenly feared what the young man might tell him. He wanted to run away, but he knew he couldn't. "What happened when the Germans captured Austria? Are the stories true?"

The boy pulled himself erect. "I'll tell you what I know, what I saw with my own eyes. The rest you'll have to find out from the others." His eyes glazed over as he recalled recent events.

"It was a day much like any other day—cold and clear—March 15. Remember that day...always remember that day. It was the beginning of the end for all of us."

Saul could feel the boy's anguish, wishing now that he hadn't asked him to relive his pain.

"I was a student at the University. My life was good, until one day Hitler marched into Vienna and claimed all of Austria. Overnight he captured all of the Jews, making us prisoners of the Reich—all 180,000 of us."

The young man pounded his chest with his fists. "We'd been warned, but we'd refused to listen. How could we believe that it would ever come to this? When Hitler entered Vienna, we still didn't believe it. That soon changed as the Austrians greeted the Nazis with open arms," he said.

"Jews were beaten and tortured. New proclamations were posted every day. They told us that they had set up work camps because the Reich needed workers to ensure the victory of the new order, and we Jews were to be their workers. Deportation began immediately.

"My father was a doctor, a vital resource for them. He was sent to a camp called Dachau two days after Hitler's arrival. When my mother tried to stop the Nazis from taking him, she was killed for her efforts, but not before they beat and raped her, right in front of my father and little sister."

The young man stopped, using his inner strength to send the visions and memories of his mother to some dark hidden place in his mind.

"Do you see these clothes that I'm wearing? The Nazis made an old Orthodox man strip in the middle of the street purely for the fun of humiliating him, and then they made me put on his clothes. The old man's heart gave out, and as he lay dying, I promised him I would bury his clothes in the earth of Palestine. I swore that I'd go there for him and pray at the Wailing Wall, and I will even though I hate the God who has allowed this to happen to my people. I'll do it for that old man. I'll keep that promise or I'll die in the process."

Saul could say nothing as he waited for the young man to go on.

The boy covered his eyes with his hands. "People who had called themselves friends stood by and watched as Viennese mobs looted and destroyed Jewish businesses. When the shops were empty, the Nazi SA bastards forced the Jews to march in processions through the streets of Vienna." The boy's eyes flashed with rage. "The people spat at them when they passed, and then the Nazis led them into dark alleys, where the Austrians beat them. Do you hear what I am telling you? It was the Austrians beating them, not the Nazis!" His voice grew quiet. "I keep asking myself, why? Can you tell me why?" He implored. "The old men were left to die. The healthy men, the ones that had withstood the beatings, were sent off to the camps.

The people you see here," he said looking around, "we were the lucky ones. We escaped." The boy laughed an angry guttural laugh. "We haven't been told where we're going. As a matter of fact, they haven't told us anything. We were smuggled into France by the underground, but we've become an embarrassment to the French government because they don't know what to do with us."

He bowed his head. "I'm no coward. I didn't want to leave. My family made me. I was supposed to carry the word out—to tell people what was happening." He stared at Saul. "Do you know what a joke that is? They don't want to know. They won't let us speak to anyone in authority. They just keep moving us around."

Saul touched the boy's arm gently. "Tell me your name," he urged.

"David. But no one's left to call me that...no one's left to remember my name." He began to cry again. "Please go away. I don't want to talk anymore."

Saul stood up. "My name is Saul. I'll be back to see you again, David."

Saul left and went back to his cabin, where he rushed to the bathroom and vomited. He cleaned himself up and then told a bewildered Claire everything.

Claire sat weeping, as she listened to Saul, her own anger building. "I'll go with you to see the captain. We must help these people," she said.

* * *

Getting an appointment with the captain was more difficult than Saul had expected. By the time the first officer arranged for the meeting in the captain's private quarters, the sun had set.

"Welcome to my ship," the captain said. He was a comely looking seaman: hair silver white, eyes sea green and a ruddy lined complexion registering a lifetime of exposure to the elements. "I'm so sorry I couldn't see you sooner, but there's so much to do when the ship first leaves port and moves into international waters. Please have a seat and make yourselves comfortable. May I have my steward bring you something to drink?"

Claire and Saul both declined, taking their seats as the captain asked, "How can I be of service to you?"

Saul began, reminding himself that he must try to stay in control. "Sir, I was walking around the ship earlier, and I visited the people being transported in the cargo area. I found the conditions there deplorable.

I'm here to formally complain and to implore you to do something about it."

The captain's face turned red. "I've been a captain for over twenty years, and I've always been conscientious and competent," he said. "This nightmare has been thrust upon me without my consent, and I'm doing the best I can. I've been waiting for instructions as to where I'm suppose to take them, but so far no country has agreed to take them in."

Saul looked incredulously at the captain. "That's ridiculous! We're going to Palestine; they'll just go there with us. The British have certain agreements with my people. Surely they'll take them in."

"Young man, you've got a lot to learn, and I'm sorry that I'm the one who'll be your teacher. On April 1 the British limited the immigration of Jewish refugees to no more then 2,000 immigrants of independent means. In addition, they're only allowing the immigration of one thousand—shall we call them—workers. The quota has already been filled. Supposedly in September they're going to reevaluate it." The captain stopped, waiting for his comments to register. "I can see by your face that you're quite surprised. Well don't be. Your people don't have many options at this moment, and that includes that pitiful lot that are now passengers in the cargo hold of my ship."

Saul began to speak, and then he stopped. He would buy their way in, even if it took every penny he had.

"Sir, I've been blessed to be born into a very wealthy family. I can pay for them all. There must be a way to get by the authorities. For God's sake, you must help us!" Saul begged.

Somberly, the captain said, "I can do nothing, and you can do nothing. We'll have barely enough food to keep them alive until we reach Palestine. I've been told we won't be allowed into the port of Haifa. Skiffs will be sent out to take those who have the proper papers ashore. They'll ferry out rations for the remaining passengers, and then we'll be on our way. God only knows where we'll be headed. Do yourself a favor; forget about what you've seen. Go about your business. You can do nothing." The captain stood, making it clear that he was dismissing Claire and Saul.

They had no choice but to leave. The captain looked intently at them. "These people are in God's hands. All you can do is pray for them. But there will be more, thousands more. Work to help save the rest. For your own good, I'm putting the bottom deck of this ship off limits."

"You can't do that!" Saul screamed. "We can help them."

"You can do nothing!" The captain shouted. "They'll take care of themselves. I can't risk you contracting some communicable disease and infecting the rest of my paying passengers. I must now insist that you excuse me. I have a ship to run."

* * *

The following weeks taught Saul and Claire the lessons of futility as their fragile hearts began to harden. They both had their first lessons in hatred, first welcoming it as an outlet and then pushing it away when they decided that hatred would only serve to destroy them.

David appeared in Saul's dreams nightly—David in the black coat, David with his determined eyes and purposeful stare, accusingly pointing his finger, admonishing Saul. "You promised to help me. You broke your promise. You never returned."

Chapter 25

─────── ★ ───────

Morgan and Robert had a triumphant year on the theater circuit, reaching new heights, as audiences all over Europe opened their arms and hearts to them.

While relishing their success, they remained self-contained and reclusive, selfishly guarding their precious time alone. When the tour was finally over, Robert took Morgan to a villa on the French Riviera, where they spent their days playing in the Mediterranean and their nights making love.

They became the toast of the Riviera, as every influential and powerful person who passed through Nice vied for the opportunity to meet them. The only dim light in Morgan's otherwise perfect life was her growing concern with the impending war in Europe and her ever-growing loneliness and despair for her family. To ease her pain, she wrote long letters telling them everything, praying that they would at least read her letters.

Morgan was sitting on the beach, wrapped in a heavy woolen sweater, one afternoon when she heard Robert excitedly calling her name.

"Morgan!" he yelled, running toward her, waving a telegram in his hand. He dragged her to her feet, swinging her in his arms. "It's here! My dream has come true. We're going to England—a command performance! King George himself has requested that we play *Romeo and Juliet* on the London stage."

"Oh, Robert," Morgan said, "that's absolutely fantastic."

As they dropped to the blanket, Robert said, "Darling, I know how much you love it here, and I wouldn't ask you to leave unless it was really necessary. But I have to go to London for three or four weeks to make arrangements."

Morgan held Robert's hand against her breast. "Darling, would you mind terribly if I stayed here?" she asked. "I'm simply exhausted." She searched his face, watching as the fire left his eyes.

"Morgan, are you ill?" Robert asked with alarm.

"No, silly, I'm fine."

Robert, his jaw set stubbornly, tried to imagine being without Morgan, and the thought made him feel sick.

"How soon would you have to leave?" Morgan asked.

"In a few days."

"Are you pouting, Robert Osborne?" Morgan asked, tickling him under the chin.

"No, damn it! I've become so spoiled with all of this." He stopped, thinking about his words. "Then again, who really cares about any of this? I'll miss you so much." He smiled sadly and bent down to gently kiss her lips.

* * *

On September 1, 1939, the day Robert and William sailed for England, Morgan sat bundled up at the beach reading, feeling unnerved and anxious, her intuition gradually turning her stomach sour.

She went to sleep early that night, refusing a dinner invitation from the American Ambassador. When she awoke the next morning the maid brought her coffee and the local newspaper.

"Germany Invades Poland!" was the bold headline. Morgan jumped from the bed, sending the coffee and tray crashing to the floor. No!" she howled. "No! No! No! It can't be true!"

The maid, hearing Morgan's anguished cries, rushed into the room. "Madame, are you all right?" she asked.

"I'll need my car. Have the driver waiting, I'll be down in a few minutes."

"Shall I help you dress, Madame?"

"No, just go and arrange for my driver," Morgan ordered.

With shaking hands Morgan dialed the Polish Embassy, but the line was continuously busy. She dressed hastily and rushed from the villa.

Twenty minutes later Morgan arrived at the Embassy gate, but she was refused entry. Feeling no need for genteel politeness, she said, "Tell the Ambassador that Morgan is here and that I must see him immediately!"

"That's impossible, Madame," the guard said. "He's in meetings and has left word that he's not to be disturbed under any circumstances."

"Fine. I'll just go inside and wait…unless you plan on stopping me," Morgan said, defiance burning in her eyes.

The guard, knowing that Morgan was a friend of the Ambassador, shrugged his shoulders. "Follow me please," he said, opening the car door for her. "But I must insist that your car and driver wait here. The compound is on full security alert, and I'm risking a reprimand as it is by letting you enter."

* * *

During the three long hours Morgan waited for the Ambassador, her mind swirled in horror as she imagined what might be happening to her parents. As each hour passed she grew more and more determined to get home, realizing that without the Ambassador's help she would never make it. Finally the Ambassador entered the waiting room. He was a stout man in his late 50's with a massive belly that protruded from his expensively tailored suit. His face was round, his eyes hooded, surrounded by bushy eyebrows, and a long angular nose and stern lips.

"Morgan, my dear, I'm so sorry you've been kept waiting. As I'm sure you know, we're in a terrible state of confusion. Now, what can I do for you?"

"I must get to Vilna immediately."

The Ambassador laughed. "My dear, people are running away from Poland, not running to it. I'm sorry, but it's out of the question. It's much too dangerous. Anyway, why in the world would you even consider it?"

The blood rushed to her head and the room began to spin. The Ambassador grabbed her just as she was about to collapse, holding on to her until she regained her composure. "I'm so sorry. I've been thoughtless and rude. Come and sit down in my office. I'll get you some tea and we'll talk," he said with genuine concern.

Morgan allowed him to help her into his office. Once seated, she said, "My family lives in Vilna. I'll need travel documents in order to go there. I must go! Will you help me?"

"Morgan, this is a very serious situation. I'm sure your family will be fine. After all, from what I hear the only ones in immediate danger are the Jews."

Morgan gasped. *He doesn't know that I'm Jewish.* "Sir, I appreciate your kind concern, but if my parents are fine—as you say—you have no reason to fear for my safety either. I'm determined to go. Now, will you help me or not?"

He looked long and hard at Morgan. "I feel I'm going to regret this one day," he said. "I'm sure I can help get you in, but…I can't help you get back out. We no longer have any authority. You must understand that this is like buying a one way ticket to hell." The Ambassador put his arm gently around Morgan, smiling sadly. "Morgan, if they recognize you going in, they'll arrest you for having false papers. They might even kill you. Do you understand that?"

Morgan nodded.

"After you arrive, your fame may be your only hope of ever getting back out alive, but we have no way of knowing that for sure. Please reconsider your request," he pleaded.

Morgan stared at him unflinchingly.

The Ambassador shook his head as he stood up slowly. "It's going to take some time, so make yourself at home. I'll be back as soon as I've made the needed arrangements."

He returned an hour later and handed Morgan the necessary documents. "You must avoid talking with anyone, especially anyone in uniform. When they ask for your papers, tell them you're a journalist covering the war," he said. "Go home now, my dear. You must figure out a way to make yourself look different—really different. Then come back here and we'll have your photograph taken."

The Ambassador led Morgan to the door. "This isn't going to be an easy trip. You'll probably have to change trains many times before you reach your destination." He kissed her softly on both cheeks. "I'll be praying for you, my dear. I wish you good luck."

"I can never thank you enough," Morgan said.

"Yes you can. Come back safely. That will be my thanks."

* * *

When Morgan boarded the train that would take her on the first leg of her journey, she was unrecognizable. She wore her blond wig, large black-framed glasses, and a frumpy dress that made her look overweight and unattractive. She carried a tattered overnight bag filled with clothing she had purchased from the maid.

Knowing that she couldn't reach Robert until his ship docked in England, Morgan left a note for him explaining her reasons for leaving. And as the train pulled out of the station, she prayed he would understand.

Each day of her trip across Europe included more disheartening news. Every stop and every newspaper story served to reinforce her worst fears. The papers declared that the fight had been "horses against tanks." The German army had caught most of the Polish Air Force on the ground, where they had bombed them into oblivion.

It was the world's first experience with a blitzkrieg, as a million and a half Germans entered Poland. Krakow, the second largest city in Poland, fell on September 6. The Polish army was decimated, and by September 17, only scattered remnants of resistance remained.

The few times Morgan managed to fall asleep, her dreams were filled with a recurring nightmare. Robert, Claire, and Saul were sitting in downy soft chairs on a freshly mown lawn, quietly talking. Morgan was overjoyed at finally seeing them all, but when she reached out to touch them, they couldn't feel her touch or see her. After she awoke, the dream continued to haunt her. She sensed that she was being given a glimpse at her destiny.

Chapter 26

———— ★ ————

Robert threw his travel documents on the bed, reaching immediately for the phone. William instructed the bellhop where to place the luggage while Robert placed his call. He desperately needed to hear Morgan's voice, never dreaming that he would be so miserable without her. He sat on the bed mumbling to himself as he waited for the operator.

"Are you talking to me?" William asked.

"I guess so," Robert said. "I'm flying back to France the instant our business is completed."

William smiled. "Have a nice flight. I'll go by sea, thank you. If God wanted me to fly, he would have given me wings."

"Have it your way. But I don't want to be away from Morgan one second longer than I have to be."

"I'm going down to the lobby for some newspapers. I'll see you in a little while," William said, as Robert gave the operator Morgan's number.

Robert was still waiting for the operator to call back when William returned with the newspapers. He looked at Robert, a distraught grimace on his face.

"My friend, I have some very bad news for you. Germany has invaded Poland. The Germans have taken control of the entire country. From what I can decipher, the Russians are now making a deal with Hitler to partition the areas along her borders."

Robert looked at William. He was overcome with anguish just thinking about what Morgan might be feeling or doing.

"William, you don't think…Morgan wouldn't do anything foolish, would she? Tell me I'm being stupid. Tell me my wife is going to be exactly where I left her!" Robert held onto the side of the table, willing the phone to ring. When it did, he lunged for it, knocking over a vase filled with flowers.

"Yes, operator, I'll stay on the line," he said.

"I'm sorry, sir, Mrs. Osborne is not there," the faceless voice said coldly.

"Wait, operator! I'll speak to whoever answered the phone," he said.

"This is the Osborne residence. Who's calling?"

"Anna, where's Mrs. Osborne?" Robert asked.

"She's gone, sir."

"What do you mean, gone? Gone where?"

Anna held her breath, afraid to answer. "She…Sir, I don't know how to tell you this," she said. "Mrs. Osborne has gone off to Poland to find her parents."

"When did she leave? Can she be stopped?" Robert screamed as his throat constricted, making him feel as if he were smothering.

"She left yesterday, sir. I tried to stop her, but I couldn't. She was frantic; she wouldn't stay. I begged her to wait until she talked with you, but she said it would be too late by then." Anna was crying and Robert was having trouble understanding her.

"Anna, get a hold of yourself! You must tell me everything you know, every last detail."

Anna told Robert the little she knew. He listened to every word and asked questions that he knew Anna couldn't possibly answer. When he finally did hang up, he looked at William for help. But William could do no more than try to offer him solace.

Robert's head felt as if it were going to explode. The rushing in his ears was like the ocean and he couldn't focus his eyes or catch his breath. William helped him to the bed.

"I'm going to find a doctor," William said.

"The hell you are!" Robert snapped. "We've got to do something, William. We can't just sit here. Who do we know? Who can we call? Think, man. Don't just sit there. Think!"

"I'll call the French Ambassador. Perhaps he can help," William said, reaching for the phone. William spoke with five different people at the Embassy, but the final word was that the Ambassador was unavailable.

"Don't bother coming here. He's seeing no one," his aide told William.

They spent the rest of the day calling everyone they could think of, but to no avail. No one could help. Communication into Poland was nonexistent and the news coming out was sketchy at best. The consensus was that if Morgan did manage to get into Poland, she probably would not get back out until relations normalized—if, in fact, they ever did.

Finally Robert placed a call to the Royal Palace. After all, the King had personally requested his appearance, so he might be willing to help. The King was kind enough to take Robert's call.

"Keep heart, my good man. Morgan is an international celebrity. She couldn't just disappear. I'll make some discreet inquiries to see if I can find out anything. I'll be in touch," the King said.

Morgan had managed to avoid drawing attention to herself on her move across Europe. The only people who talked to her were the soldiers, who repeatedly told her they thought she was crazy for going to Poland. "But then again, all journalists are crazy."

When the train finally pulled into Vilna on a bleak September day, Morgan was numb with exhaustion. Transportation from the station was not available, so she stored her luggage in a locker and began walking home.

She decided against calling her parents, thinking it might be too dangerous. Despite everything, she was glad to be home. She thought angrily, the country may be temporarily in the hands of those German pigs, but it won't be for long.

Morgan walked slowly down the familiar streets and boulevards of her youth. Everything looked the same, and yet, everything was different. The Jewish Quarter was deserted. *Where are the students? Where has everyone gone?* She walked for hours, as time lost all meaning. It had taken weeks to get here, and now that she was here, she was afraid to go home. *What if they won't see me? What if they're injured? How will I survive if they're not all right?* To Morgan's sudden amazement, she was standing in front of her parents' home.

With shaking knees, she walked to the front door and knocked loudly. A stranger opened the door and Morgan thought, I've been gone so long they've hired a new butler.

"Can I help you?" the man asked in a surly manner.

"Yes, will you please tell Dr. and Mrs. Rabinowiszch that Morgan is here to see them?" "I don't know anyone by that name. You must have the wrong house," he said, moving to close the door. But Morgan put out her foot and blocked it.

"How long have you been the butler here?" she demanded.

He kicked her foot out of the door, sneering at her. "The Jews are gone. This house has been taken over by the German Reich. You'd better leave, and if you were friends with the pigs that lived in this house, you'd better forget about them. They're finished. Gone," he said, slamming the door in Morgan's face.

She stood there in shame and disbelief. Shame that she had let him talk to her in such a manner and disbelief at the words that he had spoken. There must be an explanation for all of this, she thought. They couldn't just disappear. If the Germans took their home, they must have moved them somewhere else. I've got to find them.

Morgan left her childhood home and went next door to her gentile neighbors, believing that they would know something and that they would be willing to help her. Morgan pulled the wig from her head. She knocked on the door. Mrs. Pedafesky opened it and gasped.

"My God, child, what are you doing here? You must be crazy. You'll get us all killed."

She tried to slam the door in Morgan's face, but Morgan was not about to let that happen again. She forced her way inside, slamming the door shut.

"Get out of my home, get out now!" Mrs. Pedafesky yelled.

Morgan grabbed her shoulders and began shaking her. "You've known me all of my life. What's wrong with you? You must help me!"

"If I help you, they'll kill me. Go away!" she said.

Morgan began to cry. "OK, if you won't help me, at least tell me where my parents are?" she begged.

"I have no idea. One minute they were here, and the next they were gone."

Morgan could not accept what the woman was saying. "The servants, where are the servants?" she asked.

"They're also gone," Mrs. Pedafesky said. "I did hear that Jonte moved in with her cousin. Maybe she can help you. Now you must go!" she insisted, pushing open the door and shoving Morgan out. "Go back where you came from. Forget all of this. You can do nothing!" she shouted, slamming the door.

Morgan felt some relief, knowing that she at least had a place to look next. She had visited Jonte's cousin many times over the years, and she knew the route well. She took short cuts through back alleys and dark streets, feeling more afraid than she had ever been in her life. She knew that evil had overtaken the very being of her fellow countrymen and women and she agonized over their plight.

It had begun to rain a cold, bone-chilling rain, but Morgan was hardly aware of it as she moved silently through the streets. Arriving finally at Jonte's cousin's home, she stood at the door shaking uncontrollably, wondering if she would only be turned away again. She knocked softly on the door, silently praying.

"Who is it?" a women's voice asked.

"I'm a friend of Jonte's. Please let me in," Morgan begged.

The woman opened the door, immediately recognizing Morgan. "My God, you're soaked. You'll catch pneumonia," she said warmly. "Come in, come in."

Morgan entered the parlor. Jonte had heard the knock and had cautiously edged into the room. Seeing Morgan, she gasped, reaching to steady herself against the wall.

The two women stared at each other, neither one of them moving. Morgan was overcome with sadness at how pale and sickly Jonte looked, fearing that if she spoke, Jonte might disappear forever.

Jonte's worst fears were now facing her. How could she ever tell this child, her child, what had happened? She had prayed that she would die with her story buried in the dark recesses of her mind.

When the spell was finally broken, the two women fell into each other's arms and wept. At least for now they had the warmth of each other's love.

Morgan tried to speak, but her words were garbled. She wanted to know so many things, but she was terrified to ask.

Jonte looked deeply into the violet eyes that she so dearly loved. "You must get out of those wet clothes this minute. Once you're changed, we'll have some nice warm tea and then we'll talk, just you and I, just like we did when you were a little girl."

Morgan continued to cry as she allowed Jonte to help her change into a robe. Her exhaustion was quickly closing in on her.

Jonte sat with Morgan on the sofa, and Morgan laid her head on Jonte's shoulder. Within seconds she was asleep. Jonte didn't move, wanting only to bask in the closeness of the moment. Morgan being here, next to her, was so bittersweet. She prayed for the strength and for the words to tell her what she knew she would have to say.

* * *

Himmler and Heinrich had been assigned by Hitler to eliminate the Jews of Poland, and within a week of taking over the country their mission had begun. The wealthy Jews were savagely expelled from their homes. Hitler, fearful that men capable of leadership might be sent to the Reich concentration camps where they could cause trouble, decreed that all the Jewish intelligentsia were to be liquidated.

Unfortunately, Samuel had fit into that category, and he and Sara had found their names posted on a list with others ordered to appear in the town square at precisely one o'clock the following day.

"It's not fair! It's just not fair!" Sara wailed, clinging to Samuel. They had finally found that precious time and place where peace and love overshadowed all else, and now it was all being shattered. Samuel held his weeping Sara in his arms.

"I know…I know," he said, holding more tightly. "Life isn't fair. Life is what man makes it. When we let the evil side of our nature take control, all is lost, but we still have a choice, Sara. We can allow our lives to be manipulated by these despicable Germans, or we can refuse. Although I feel in my soul that we're already lost, I won't allow them to force me out of my home. You'll need to make your own decision, Sara, but for me, there is no choice."

"What can we do? We can't fight them. I don't want to die, Samuel. I don't want to die." Sara looked to Samuel for help.

Samuel desperately wanted to make things better for his Sara, but he couldn't. He couldn't make it better, so he was going to do it his way.

"Sara, I won't leave my home," he said. "I won't allow them to herd me away like a helpless animal."

"And I won't leave you, Samuel," Sara said firmly.

The decision had been made. They would sit and wait for the inevitable knock on the door.

Chapter 27

———— ★ ————

On September 3, Britain declared a state of war between herself and Germany. Robert was desperate to return to France, but transportation was limited to priority travel only. France was mobilizing her army, calling for all able-bodied men to enlist.

Robert had always thought of himself as a dove, most of his adult life espousing world understanding and peace. But not now, he wanted Germany to bleed until she was obliterated.

He would awaken in the middle of the night in a cold sweat. His dreams were filled with anger and frustration. The little boy was alone again; Morgan had left him just like his mother and the Duchess had. And each night he would dream he was in battle, bleeding, obsessed with killing, and fighting the fear of being killed.

One day he announced to William, "I'm going mad. I can't just sit here and do nothing. I'm going to join the army and personally see to it that those fucking Nazis are annihilated!"

Once the words were spoken, he became a compulsive, driven man. Phone calls were placed, people were bribed, and passage on a military transport was secured. Robert knew that his life as he had known it was over. On September 25, 1939, he arrived back in Paris and went directly to the recruitment center to enlist.

Before his examination and indoctrination was even completed, the press arrived. When Robert exited the center, flash bulbs began popping and he patiently answered questions, not really caring what he said. When one reporter asked, "What about Morgan. Where is she?" Robert didn't hesitate.

"Morgan went to Vilna, Poland, to help her family, and we haven't heard from her since she left," he answered, hoping that if the world knew Morgan was trapped inside Poland, pressure would be applied and she would be released.

Two days later Robert Osborne, actor turned soldier, reported for active duty.

* * *

Morgan slept with her head on Jonte's shoulder for hours. It was a time of respite for Jonte, a time to gather her thoughts.

"Oh, my God!" Morgan cried, awakening with a shudder. "How long have I been asleep?"

"Not so long, my sweet," Jonte said, her pulse quickening.

"I need you to tell me what happened," Morgan said. "I have to know."

Jonte took a deep breath. She had forced the horror out of her mind, but now the images came flooding back. Talking as if she were an automaton, Jonte began.

"I had been working on some correspondence when your parents summoned the entire housekeeping staff to the sitting room. Samuel and Sara were huddled together on the love seat holding hands when we entered. Sara was my best friend, we didn't need words, we never did. I knew all had been lost the moment I saw her. Your father thanked all of us for the years of loyal service we had given to them, and then he apologized, because all of their assets had been confiscated and he didn't have any money to pay us. My God, Morgan, we didn't care about that, none of us cared, but your father gave us their most valuable possessions—paintings, silver, and jewelry—saying it would be better used by us than by the Nazis. Then he dismissed us, insisting we all leave before nightfall.

"They all left that evening, everyone but me. How could I leave them? My God, they were my family, my life." Jonte began to cry.

"Please go on, Jonte," Morgan urged.

"When two days passed and your parents hadn't shown up at the appointed time and place, the Nazis came to the house in the middle of the night, pounding on the door, insisting to be let in. Samuel and Sara were on their way downstairs when the Gestapo broke down the front door. I heard the commotion, and when I realized what was happening, I hid, watching from behind a partially closed door.

"'Are you Herr Doctor Samuel Rabinowiszch?' the Nazi had asked.

"'Yes I am,' your father said.

"The Nazi took off his glove and slapped your father across the face with it. 'How dare you disobey the orders of the Fuhrer! You're a Jew pig.'"

Jonte began to cry again. "I can't tell you any more, Morgan. I just can't."

"Please, Jonte. I have to know," Morgan pleaded.

"I can still hear it in my head. Your father said to your mother, 'Forgive me for what I am about to do,' as he struck the Nazi in the face, cutting his lip.

"The Nazi pulled his gun out of its holster and grinned. 'You foolish bastard. You'll pay with this!' Then he pointed the gun at Sara. I thought I was dreaming. The Nazi put the gun in your mother's face and pulled the trigger." Jonte covered her face with her hands as she fought the gruesome images that erupted in her mind.

"Samuel screamed and ran for your mother. He held her in his arms, rocking her, crying, intoning the Jewish prayer for the dead. In a tortured voice your father sung out to his God. Even in the end, he called to his God, believing.

"The Nazi laughed and then a second shot rang out and it was all over. Your father was the bravest man I ever knew," Jonte said, choking on her pain.

Morgan sat frozen in her seat, too mortified to even cry. With every word that Jonte spoke, Morgan had retreated further and further back into herself, trying to hide from the pain. Her subconscious tried desperately to veil the visions coming into her mind.

"I need to be alone for a little while, please. Is there somewhere I can go?"

"Of course, Morgan. Come to my room."

Jonte led Morgan down a narrow hallway. The wallpaper was stained and peeling off of the walls. The ceiling had an exposed light bulb that threw off an eerie shimmer, giving the hallway a surrealistic glow.

The bedroom was small and crowded with furniture. Morgan was surprised to see so many pictures. Jonte had obviously taken most of the family snapshots with her before she left the house.

Jonte seemed embarrassed. "I hope you don't mind that I took the photographs? They're yours, of course. I just didn't want to leave them."

Morgan smiled. "Thank you for taking the time to care about them," Morgan said as she touched each one lovingly as if they might break. Each represented a day and a time that made up the moments in a family—her life…her family.

"I'll leave you now, Morgan, but please try to remember that you're not alone and that I love you very much," Jonte said.

Morgan sat down on the floor. She needed to feel the hard surface beneath her. More than anything she wanted to be uncomfortable, to feel pain, to feel something. She stared at the photographs until the light faded and she could see nothing. The darkness brought her some peace.

Morgan fell asleep and dreamt of her parents. They reached out to her, speaking softly, lovingly. She saw her papa dressed in white and glowing with the light of God. She looked into his loving eyes and touched his kind and gentle face.

"I never stopped loving you, my child. I'm sorry I couldn't get past my own pride. I was wrong. I should have held you close to me. I know that now. I'm proud of you, Morgan, really proud."

He began to fade away as Morgan reached for him. "There's nothing to be afraid of, my child. I'm with you and I always will be. You'll hear me in the call of a bird's song, in the melody of the wind, in the face of a cloud. Open yourself and watch for me."

Papa vanished and Mother was there. She smiled at Morgan and spoke in a quiet voice.

"We're here with you, Morgan, watching and waiting. Please try not to give up. You have so much more to do. Fight with everything you have in you. The world has run amuck. Evil has taken control, but you are filled with love and light, and you can help."

Morgan sat up with a start, confused and furious. Standing up, she reached for the lamp on the night table. She straightened her clothing and brushed her tangled hair out of her eyes. *I won't let them win, I won't! If I lose, I'll lose fighting just as my parents did.*

She walked into the hallway and into the light of the living room.

Jonte looked up, sensing that Morgan was somehow reborn, alive and strong.

"Jonte, I'm not going to sit here and wait to be discovered. I'm going to try to figure out a way to get back to France. Mother and Papa wouldn't want me to fall apart, and I'm not going to. They died for nothing, and I don't intend to repeat that mistake."

"Morgan, life's not the same as it was before. If you walk out that door and someone asks to see your papers…" she hesitated and gave Morgan a knowing look. "Just stay put for a few days. Let me make some inquiries. Maybe I can locate someone who'll be willing to help us."

Jonte spent the next several days looking for help, but people were afraid for their lives and refused. She came home at the end of every day sad and discouraged.

* * *

Hitler had all the news reports published throughout the world monitored. The small bit of news about Morgan had caught the eye of one of his readers, and eventually word reached the German high command that Morgan was in Vilna. The Reich, wanting the world to see them as fair and decent people, decided to use Morgan as an example by finding her and sending her back to France.

Himmler was put on alert by an angry German command wanting to know how a famous actress could just lose herself inside the tight net that had been laid throughout Poland.

"This actress has become an embarrassment to the Reich. She's to be found immediately," said the memo Himmler received from the Fuhrer's headquarters.

* * *

Otto was enjoying working with Dr. Hans Wells. Their work was going along nicely, considering the snail's pace at which they were forced to work because of Hitler's other priorities.

He and Hans were trying hypnosis as an anesthetic on a priest with a gangrenous toe when he was called to the camp commandant's office. Eicke wasted no time getting to the point.

"I've had direct correspondence from Poland's Governor General. Himmler has ordered that you go immediately to Vilna. I'm sure you know what will be required of you." He stood ramrod straight and riveted his eyes on Otto. "I want you on the next train. Heil Hitler. That is all. You're dismissed."

Otto was furious, not understanding why Himmler was interrupting his work.

When he arrived in Vilna, he was met at the train station by Himmler's aide, who handed him a communiqué: "You are to locate and detain the actress known as Morgan. She traveled into Poland from France with false papers. We have been notified that she is in Vilna, where her family is believed to have lived. She is to be treated with respect. Notify me the moment she is located." It was signed Heinrich Himmler.

The aide waited until Otto finished reading before he spoke.

"Herr Himmler wants the Fraulein to leave Poland believing that a peaceful transition has taken place here and that nothing out of the ordinary is happening. Herr Himmler said you would understand how to do that."

Otto smiled, finally understanding why he had been brought from Dachau. But still he worried about being away from Ilya; especially with all the attention Hans had been paying to her lately. Knowing how naive Ilya was when it came to men, Otto worried that the charming and devious doctor was taking advantage of her. Otto decided that he would complete his mission and return to Dachau as quickly as possible.

For the next five days and nights Otto researched every bit of information available on Morgan. He easily found out who she really was and where her family lived. He could have taken her in right then, but from the moment he saw her picture, he had become obsessed. He wanted to know everything about her—what she liked, where she went to school, and who her friends were. He visited her neighborhood, her school, the theater, and the synagogue.

When he located Jonte's home, he spent hours sitting in the back seat of his car hoping for a glimpse of Morgan. But the only people who ever ventured out were Jonte and her cousin.

After days of constant watching, Otto was ready to make his move.

Chapter 28

———— ★ ————

At midnight Otto walked to Jonte's door and knocked loudly. Jonte and Morgan jumped quickly from the bed.

"Morgan, we've practiced this for days and you know what to do," Jonte said, trying to sound calm.

They pulled the armoire away from the wall so that Morgan could slip behind it. Jonte and her cousin then pushed it back into place.

"Just stay quiet and don't come out, no matter what happens," Jonte said, moving quickly to the front door after ordering her cousin to hide in the kitchen.

She opened the door slowly and found herself standing face to face with a man dressed in the black uniform of the SS. His face was strikingly handsome, yet there was a sinister look in his eyes that instantly terrified Jonte. She looked over his shoulder, surprised to see that he was alone. She was instantly hopeful.

"May I help you?" she asked in the most polite voice she could muster.

"Yes, Fraulein, you can help me. You can go and get Fraulein Morgan. I'll wait in here," Otto said, pushing past Jonte and moving into the living room. "Don't be long. I'm not a patient man."

"I don't know what you're talking about. There's no one here but me and my cousin."

Otto grabbed Jonte's hair and pulled it back until she was sure he would pull it out of her head. He brought her face up to within inches of his. "I know that Morgan's here, and you can be quite sure that I'll kill you and burn this house to the ground if you don't cooperate this minute," he said, slapping Jonte across the face.

Morgan heard Jonte scream and quickly slipped out from behind the armoire. Otto sensed Morgan's presence in the room and turned to look at her.

Morgan said, "Don't you dare hurt her! Who do you think you are?"

Otto smiled. *She has so much spirit. This is going to be even better than I'd hoped.*

"I'm so sorry if I've upset you, Fraulein," Otto said, taking in everything about Morgan hungrily. Her hair was mussed from sleep and her robe had come partially undone, revealing the gentle curve of her breasts as they pushed against the too tight robe. Her eyes sparkled angrily and Otto felt himself growing hard with desire.

"What do you want?" Morgan barked.

Otto had to catch himself from answering the truth. "The Reich sent me to find you. It seems you have many important friends concerned about your safety. I'm here to offer you the hospitality and protection of the Third Reich. You'll dress now and come with me."

"I'm not going anywhere with you, not anywhere!" Morgan said.

Otto sensed his temper slipping as he reached for Morgan. "You'll do exactly as I say, or I'll have to hurt you, and I don't want to do that," he said. "Now, I know that you don't want that either, so behave yourself and do as I say."

Jonte reached for Morgan, leading her out of the room. "I'll get her ready. It'll take just a few minutes."

"That's very nice of you. And to show you that I'm a fair man, I'll keep your participation in all of this a secret."

Otto sat down to wait for Morgan's return, realizing finally that he had a problem. Morgan's Jewishness instantly made her an enemy of the state, erasing all hope of her being treated favorably. Otto smiled to himself as he contemplated his next move. He would see to it that

Morgan was sent to Dachau as a participant for his research. He knew that once Morgan saw how important he was, she would fall in love with him.

Jonte and Morgan hurried to the bedroom and Jonte began gathering Morgan's clothing. Morgan said, "That man's crazy. Did you see how he acted? He actually tried to be polite to me after what he did to you. I'm not going with him. I'd rather die right here."

Jonte's eyes flashed with anger as she reached for Morgan, gripping her tightly. "You listen to me, young lady. You're not going to die. I saw that happen once, and I'm not going to allow it to happen again. This man is obviously taken with you, Morgan. You can survive if you play up to him. Please do it! If you don't, they'll win again. Is that what you want? Is that how you want to honor the memory of your parents?"

Morgan felt herself shudder, knowing that she could perform her way through this and maybe even survive. The question was, did she want to?

"Try to remember that he's not the one who killed your parents. He might even have some decency in him. If he does, you must find it," Jonte said while brushing Morgan's hair. "Let me look at you," she said, smiling sadly. "You look lovely. Now I want you to go out there and be charming. Be the star you were born to be."

Otto leered at Morgan as they returned, then ushered her immediately out the door, refusing to allow her time to bid Jonte a proper goodbye.

"Now my problem is what to do with you," Otto said as the limousine pulled away from the curb. "If you want me to protect you, you must do exactly as I say. But if you don't want that, you'll be turned over to the Gestapo. And take my word; you won't like that at all. They can be very unpleasant."

Morgan smiled disarmingly at Otto. "I appreciate your kind offer, and I look forward to our friendship," she said swallowing hard.

I knew it. She's crazy about me. "Driver, take me back to headquarters," Otto instructed.

"Unfortunately, as a Jew, you have no future," he said, watching the color seep from Morgan's face and enjoying every minute of her pain. "But you needn't worry, because I intend to use my influence—and my influence is great—to get you transferred to a work camp called Dachau. My sister works there and she likes it, so I'm sure you will as well. She works in the printing shop; it's a very nice office. Maybe you could work there sometimes," he said, pulling Morgan over to him and sliding his arm around her shoulder.

Morgan felt an overwhelming repulsion as bile rose in her throat. The thought of vomiting on him overwhelmed her, and she felt total panic. Near hysteria, she began to giggle.

Otto assumed she was laughing at him. He lost all control, violently striking Morgan's face with his fists. She tried to protect herself, crying out in pain as he continued to hit her.

By the time Otto regained control of himself, Morgan's eye was badly cut and swelling, and her lip was broken and bleeding. When he realized what he had done, he experienced shame for the first time in his life.

"I didn't mean to hurt you. I would never hurt you. Tell me you forgive me. Tell me that you'll forget this ever happened," he begged.

Morgan knew her very existence depended on how she treated this maniac. She held the corner of her dress up to her bleeding mouth. "I forgive you, but why did you hit me?"

Otto began to rub the top of his head with his open palm. "You must never, never laugh at me. I'll kill you if you ever do it again. No one laughs at me, not even those I love. Do you understand?"

At that moment the car arrived at the local headquarters. "You'll come with me now," he said.

Otto was again the black-suited SS man as he helped Morgan from the car. Just as she got her footing on the sidewalk, he pulled her to him and forced his tongue into her broken and bleeding mouth. The taste of her blood aroused him, moving him to the first orgasm he had ever experienced from the touch of a woman.

Morgan swallowed her revulsion as he rubbed himself against her. She could only think of one thing as he fondled and touched her. *I can't go through with this. I'll never be with this man. I'll kill myself first!*

The building was crowded with hundreds of Nazis, all looking important and busy. Otto saluted many of his comrades; obviously enjoying all the attention he was getting because of Morgan, despite her bruised and bleeding face. They walked down long, brightly lit hallways, turning often. Eventually they entered a small, poorly lit room.

"You'll wait here for me," Otto said as he left, closing and locking the door behind him.

Morgan sat down on the only chair in the room and began to cry, not understanding why God was letting this happen to her. She went over her life, grudgingly admitting that she'd made mistakes, but not mistakes great enough to cause this type of punishment.

Purposefully, she opened her purse, took out a mirror, and smashed it against the wall. She watched it break into dozens of ragged pieces as her eyes overflowed with tears. She thought about her beloved Robert, somehow knowing that no matter what she did, he was lost to her forever.

As the realization of what she was going to do became reality, she felt an unexpected sense of freedom. She dropped to her knees, feeling tiny splinters of glass cutting her as she picked up the largest piece of mirror and held it in her trembling hand, deciding that if she hesitated for even a second, she would loose the courage necessary. "I'm sorry, Mother and Papa. I just can't let him touch me. I'd rather die," she said aloud as she slashed at her wrist with the glass, tearing the artery. Warmth spread through Morgan's body as she lost consciousness.

* * *

Otto went directly to the office of Himmler's most trusted aide, where he smugly reported his success in locating Morgan.

"Good work. We knew you wouldn't let us down. I'll notify Himmler immediately. I'm sure I'll have more definite instructions for you in the morning," the aide said.

Otto realized that if he kept quiet about Morgan being a Jew, she would be sent away from him, and that was something he wasn't about to let happen.

"I'm not sure you grasp the entire picture. You see our little actress is a Jew. That surely changes things, doesn't it?" Otto asked.

The aide began to pace. "You may be right. I will hold you responsible for her until I speak with Herr Himmler," he said, showing Otto to the door.

Otto hurried back to the tiny room where he had left Morgan. When he opened the door, he saw her lying on the floor, apparently asleep, so he flipped off the light and moved quietly in.

He took Morgan in his arms, becoming furious when she didn't respond to his caresses. He began to shake her, but still she didn't move. Then he felt the wet slickness on her arms and rushed to flip on the light. He saw the growing puddle of blood surrounding her. Realizing what she had done, he ran to the hall and called for help. The room quickly filled with frantic activity.

"Get an ambulance," someone said.

Otto ripped a piece of Morgan's skirt and then quickly tore it into strips, wrapping them tightly around her wrist.

"I'll take her in my car. Call ahead to the hospital and tell them what's happened," he ordered, lifting Morgan in his arms, devastated and enraged by what Morgan had done.

* * *

By the time Otto and Morgan arrived at the hospital, she was barely alive. The doctor worked frantically, telling Otto that he held very little hope for her survival.

Otto moved behind the doctor, leaning close to his ear. "You can be sure she'll live, because if she dies, you will have to die as well."

Chapter 29

───────── ★ ─────────

The telex sent from Vilna on October 27, 1939, read: "Dateline—Vilna, Poland—It is with great sorrow that the government of Poland announces the death of one of its most beloved citizens and greatest stars. Morgan died of complications from a viral infection she contracted while visiting the city of her birth. Born on January 23, 1919—Died September 25, 1939."

Robert was still in basic training when notification came. For weeks he remained in agony, refusing to believe he would never see Morgan again. He found himself searching for her in crowds, and he would begin trembling whenever he saw someone with hair the same shade or a walk that was similar. His commanding officer tried to encourage Robert to take a furlough, but he stubbornly refused.

Eventually the numbness began to subside and in its place a gruesome guilt planted itself in Robert's gut like a seed taking root in fertile soil. Robert knew that if he hadn't left her alone, she would still be alive. He fell deeper into despair, never believing for a moment that Morgan had died of a virus.

In time his despair turned to fury, and in that dark, angry place he found comfort. Robert befriended hate, becoming the most dangerous kind of soldier there is—one who doesn't fear death. But his desire to fight was put on hold, because the French leadership had seemingly reneged on a pact they had made with Poland. After promising to launch offensive operations in defense of Poland if and when Germany ever attacked, they did nothing.

* * *

"You want to know why we're sitting here with our thumbs stuck up our asses?" Robert asked one of the other enlisted men as they sat playing a game of poker. "It's because of the slaughter our army was forced to endure in the First World War. Our generals have never gotten over it. They're afraid we'll get wiped out again if we attack the Germans. What the hell? We've already waited too long. The Polish Army is demolished and now there's nothing to buffer us against a German attack," Robert said.

"The French leadership is acting like a bunch of frightened children. They even had the unmitigated audacity to insist that the British not bomb Germany. And do you know why? It's because France is afraid Germany will retaliate by bombing us. I'm telling you, we'll be sorry we're not being the aggressor. We'll pay for this broken promise with the lives of everyone we hold dear. Mark my words. If you're lucky enough to live through the coming years, remember that I told you cowardice and treachery makes us no better than those Nazi bastards. We made a promise to a friend, and when that friend needed us, we weren't there. We'll pay for that. Just wait and see. We'll pay."

Most of Robert's fellow soldiers found his observations too controversial, and they were clearly put off by his comments. He was seen as a renegade, but he was also respected and trusted. And when the battle came, as they all knew it would, his fellow soldiers intended to be standing with Robert Osborne.

* * *

Claire and Saul's ship dropped anchor at the northern tip of Haifa Bay near the ancient city of Acre. It was the middle of May 1938.

As the beach and shoreline came into view, every muscle in Saul's body tightened. His eyes felt as if they would pop out from his head and sweat drenched his body. He found the sight incomparable, but he was also overwhelmed with a feeling of incredible sorrow.

Saul thought about David. He knew that this wasn't the time to look back, but the thought of leaving him seared Saul's heart. He had spent the entire voyage anguishing for a way to help David. And now that he was leaving, he only wanted to tell David to his face that he had tried to help him.

On the horizon the skiffs that would carry them to land appeared, and as Saul and Claire moved hurriedly into line, the Captain approached them.

"I have something to say to you before you disembark," he said. "I just wanted to tell you how sorry I am that your people aren't getting off this God forsaken ship. If it were in my power, I'd release them all. I tell you this not so you'll praise me but so you'll forgive me."

He was holding a cumbersome package wrapped in tattered brown paper. "I have a package for you from a young man named David. He somehow got this delivered to my cabin with this note." He handed the note to Saul. "When I read it, I realized it was for you, not me. Read it later if you don't mind. Now, please hurry," the Captain said, giving Saul the package and leading them to the gangway.

Saul reached for the Captain's hand. "We don't blame you. We only pray you'll deliver them to some safe harbor."

* * *

Claire and Saul stepped from the dingy to the welcoming sands of Palestine. The dawning sky sparkled silver and off in the distance Mount Carmel beckoned.

Dozens of enthusiastic Jews greeted them. Claire found herself being hugged by total strangers, each offering words of encouragement. She felt uneasy and a little frightened at first, but the friendship being offered was so genuine that she soon relaxed.

Saul on the other hand was instantly enchanted, hugging his fellow Jews as if he had come home from a distant journey into the arms of his beloved family. His chest ached with gladness as he reached for Claire, kissing her passionately.

"Thank you," he whispered.

"For what?"

"For coming home with me," he answered, tenderly taking her hand. He led her toward the waiting bus.

* * *

Hugging the shoreline of the Mediterranean, they traveled on to Tel-Aviv, which since 1931 had seen its population grow from 45,000 to 145,000, largely because of the large-scale emigration of Jews from Germany.

At a small guesthouse, Saul and Claire quickly registered and went to their room. Before they even unpacked, Saul opened David's letter.

* * *

Dear Saul,

First of all, I want to tell you that I understand why you never returned. It was really so strange. I was the one who had every reason in the world to feel betrayed and lost, and yet I found myself feeling very sorry for you. I knew that a broken promise would be a very heavy burden for you. Because I believe you have that type of character, I'm taking the liberty of asking you to help me keep my promise.

Since you're reading this letter, I'll assume you have been given the package. You remember the story I told you about the old man and his clothing? Well, it looks like my promise to bury his clothes in the soil of Palestine may have to be broken unless you can keep it for me. I know it was simply a symbolic gesture for an old man, a way to put part of him into the land; but for me it means so much more.

Please find a secret spot, a spot that feels right, and say Kaddish for him. You'll notice I haven't asked you to say the Kaddish for me. No, I don't think I'll require those words. I fully intend to tap you on the shoulder one day and say, 'so here I am. Give me a job!' I fully intend to marry and make babies in the land of our people. I'll be in Palestine one day. Maybe not as soon as I would like, but I'll be there!

I want to thank you in advance. Help us by building a place for us to come home to.

Until we meet again,
David

* * *

Saul ran his fingers over the words, allowing himself to feel close to David. He understood better now why the young man had reached so deeply into his heart. David had the kind of determination that made a man proud to be a man.

Claire watched Saul closely as he read the letter. And when he handed it to her, she read it and felt all the pain and love that Saul had for David.

He would now be a part of her life, a friend to pray for, to hold close, to dream about.

Saul smiled. "You know, I really believe I'll see him again. I just know he'll somehow make it back here," Saul said, placing the letter in his breast pocket. "When we go to Jerusalem, we'll find the proper place."

* * *

Arriving in Jerusalem in the early afternoon, Saul and Claire checked into a hotel that overlooked the Old City walls. That afternoon as they sat on their veranda, they were magically drawn into the spell of the ancient city.

Crenellated walls, domes, spires, and minarets dotted the horizon and beckoned to be explored. On their first day in Jerusalem they visited Mount Zion, King David's Tomb, and the Western Wall of the ancient Temple. On their second day they made their way up to St. Stephen's Gate and on to the Church of the Holy Sepulcher. The Christian and Jewish sights brought history to life for both of them and they delighted in every experience.

That evening as dusk fell, they made their way to the Mount of Olives. Hiking to the northernmost summit, they arrived at Mount Scopus. They dug at the earth with their bare hands as giant olive trees rustled in the gentle breeze. And at the home of the Hebrew University, Saul said the prayer over the dead as he buried the old man's clothing.

"Bring David to me and I promise to care for him like a brother. Make me worthy of his presence and I'll cherish him as if he were blood of my blood," Saul vowed as the last of the dirt was placed over the shallow grave.

* * *

Nearly 400,000 Jews, mostly refugees from Eastern and Central Europe, now lived in Palestine. The minority influx of extraordinarily cultured German, Austrian, and Czech immigrants from Central Europe had an enormous impact on the country. These highly skilled Central Europeans brought with them investment capital and economic know-how along with a commitment to education and a better quality of life.

Saul and Claire were kept busy day and night, learning Hebrew and becoming acquainted with the complications of life in Palestine, as they agonized over decisions about where they would live. Because of Saul's strong Zionist leanings, he was drawn to the kibbutz movement of collective farming villages. This socialistic movement, in which everything was shared and nothing was owned, was still somewhat experimental, but it fit the idealized image Saul had brought with him. He believed that the Jews should become farmers, working the soil and turning to the earth for sustenance and survival.

They were determined not to be naive, so they attended many lectures, keeping open minds as they tried to visualize what life in a collective settlement would be like. They were told that to survive they would work until their hands bled, sacrificing daily, living in sparse lodgings, with a limited diet, on a land that was grim and colorless, harsh and demanding.

Saul and Claire realized that they could remain in the newly developing Tel Aviv or even in Jerusalem, but the kibbutzniks counted on each other for their economical and physical survival; and Saul and Claire wanted to be a part of that. Claire had talked about starting a family right away and raising her children in the love and warmth she had known as a child. The kibbutz would give her the security of a ready-made family.

The fact that many of Palestine's emerging political leaders were coming from the kibbutz movement impressed Saul. He believed that for the Jewish dream to become reality, men such as he would have to become involved politically. He had decided to use his extensive education and dogged determination to aggressively seek political recognition.

After hours of debate and introspection, Saul and Claire decided they would settle in the growing kibbutz of Ayelet Haba-ah on the northern border of Palestine a few miles from the Syrian boarder. When the time came for the creation of a Jewish State, the kibbutz would become a front line bastion against Arab infiltration.

The first settlers of Ayelet Haba-ah had suffered greatly in the development of their kibbutz, and while they needed and wanted newcomers, they were reserved and leery. They only wanted dedicated, committed "Olem," new arrivals, to share in the fruits of their labor.

* * *

A young woman greeted Saul and Claire as they unloaded their hired car.

"Shalom. My name is Yegal. I'll be your guide and companion while you get settled in," she said, smiling. The strength of her handshake surprised Saul. She was tall, thin and muscular.

Yegal then hugged Claire warmly. "Don't be afraid. I know all of this seems so primitive, but you'll learn to love it," she whispered encouragingly in Claire's ear.

Claire felt an immediate kinship for this raven-haired beauty who seemed to be able to read her thoughts.

Yegal glanced at their luggage. "Oh, just leave it. We'll come back for it later. First let me show you around."

They followed her down paths dug from the earth and marked with rocks and flowers. Small homes lined both sides of the walkways.

"I've never smelled air so sweet. It's as if the mountains and the trees have a fragrance all their own," Claire said.

Yegal reached over and took Claire's hand. "You're going to fit in here just fine. I can tell already."

When they arrived at the children's house, Yegal said, "It won't matter what else you see today; this is the most important place on the kibbutz. The children all sleep together in this one building so we can protect them. The Arabs learned early on that we Jews are most vulnerable when it comes to our children; and of course, they're right. Children who live on the kibbutz belong to everyone on the kibbutz. We know that when one child dies, an entire generation dies with that child, stealing away the potential of that life; but we're here to make sure that doesn't happen. We vow to be shields for the children, protecting them at all costs. You'll spend many a night keeping guard over them."

Yegal kissed both Claire and Saul on their cheeks. "Welcome, Mother. Welcome, Father. Come in and meet your children," she said. "You'll soon know how it feels to be the parents of fifty children." She led them to the entrance of the children's house, where they were introduced to Jacob.

"Nice to meet you, and welcome. Please keep your voices down when you go in. The little ones are having their afternoon nap."

"Would we wake them, Jacob?" Yegal said, smiling at him warmly, their affection obvious.

Yegal squeezed Claire's hand as they moved away. "Get that silly grin off your face. You don't know me well enough yet. But you're right, I'm crazy about him."

They moved inside. "Look over here," Yegal said with enthusiasm. "Each child has a cubby for storing clothing." As they followed her into the bathroom, she said, "We've built the sinks low so that the children can reach them. We've done the same with all of the necessities in the house. This way they can brush their teeth and tinkle all by themselves."

In the main sleeping quarters, she continued, "All these cots will be filled tonight. You never saw such beautiful children in your life." The room was lined with beds, each with some type of stuffed animal or doll on it.

Claire looked over at Saul and reached for his hand. "It feels so warm and safe in here," she said.

Yegal smiled. "Come on, I'll show you the nursery—where the real little guys live."

The darkened room smelled of powder and the sweet aroma of babies. One of the babies was whimpering in his sleep, and Claire instinctively wanted to pick it up. She looked at Yegal beseechingly.

"Pick him up. It's OK. More than anything else, these children need love and reassurance. They need to feel the beat of your heart; they need to smell the fragrance of love." Yegal's face grew pale as she continued, "Many of these children were sent to Palestine without their parents. They were given to us to care for and protect until their parents could come. Unfortunately, many of the parents will never come. They were killed when the Nazis arrived. Sometimes I have nightmares about what it must have been like for the mothers and the fathers who had to give their children away," Yegal said, wiping the tears away with the back of her hand. "Don't mind me. They call me Mush because I cry so easily. You'll get used to it after you know me for a while."

The baby settled down the moment Claire held him to her breast. Yegal stroked the child's head while Claire held him.

"This is Yisrael. We named him that because he's the hope for our future."

Saul and Claire felt connected with the universe through this tiny little life that had struggled to survive. After a very long time, some of the other babies began to stir and fuss.

"Hey, you guys, it's not my turn. I want out of here before I wind up changing twenty dirty diapers. Take my word, you'll both have plenty of chances to do that, so let's get out of here," Yegal said.

Claire placed Yisrael, cooing and gurgling, back in his crib.

"I'll be back to see you, young fellow. We'll be great friends, you and I," Claire said.

As they walked through the front door, Jacob swatted Yegal on her backside. She pretended to be insulted.

"I'll get you later," Yegal jeered.

"OK, you two, let me show you to your rooms and help you get settled. Dinner is promptly at six. If you're late, you don't eat," she said with a warm smile.

* * *

Saul held Claire in his arms that night, as the gentle, cold, winter wind tried to reach through the walls and chill them. But they were warmed with the sights and the sounds of their new home. Sleep eluded them.

"Let's see if we can make that baby you're always talking about," Saul said, snuggling against Claire's neck.

Claire looked at Saul. "I know that I always said I wanted to have children right away, but now I hope it won't happen for a while."

"What changed your mind?" he asked.

"Everything, Saul—Yegal, the kibbutz, Palestine. I have so much to learn and the opportunities are so much different here. Ever since I was a small child I dreamed of having my own clinic one day. That's why I studied psychology. In Paris it was only a dream, but here it could become reality."

Saul hugged Claire, knowing that her dreams were attainable, because here on the kibbutz, women worked side by side with the men, enjoying complete equality and independence. He knew that was one overriding reason for Claire's wanting to live on a kibbutz. She had seen how restrictive the secular life of a Jewish woman would have been and she wanted no part of it. She was too determined to make a difference in the world.

Chapter 30

———————— ★ ————————

Dr. Hans Wells sat in the back of the chauffeured limousine, contemplating why he had been summoned to Supreme Headquarters. He was confident it had to do with his current research. Allowing himself to sink into the soft leather seats, he thought smugly about how good life had been to him. His mind-control work was going well, even without his partner Otto, and his personal life couldn't have been better.

Otto had been temporarily reassigned in Poland, where he was interrogating the wealthy Jews about where they had hidden their money, valuables, and art. Millions of dollars were at stake, and Otto had proven himself to be a brilliant and expedient hypnotic interrogator, obtaining information that could have otherwise been lost. Otto wrote to Hans, telling him that because of his great success he was now a part of Himmler's personal entourage, moving with him as they conquered new regions.

Hans had been disappointed at first; wanting Otto's talents for his own research, but he soon realized that winning Ilya over would be much easier if Otto were not around.

Hans barely noticed the rain beating furiously against the roof of the car. He was too busy gloating to himself about the progress he'd made with Ilya, turning her into a completely dependent and docile creature that would do anything he asked. He thought about the glorious agony he had put her through, recalling the sequence of events that had led to Ilya's downfall.

* * *

After meeting Ilya that day in the cafeteria, Hans had inundated her with flowers and daily phone calls, not even asking to see her. She was flattered, but cautious and reserved. Then, with no warning, he stopped calling her. Two weeks later he began calling again, never telling her where he'd been or why she hadn't heard from him. He began courting her then in earnest, taking her out every day, demanding nothing, working hard to please her.

When Ilya began to feel confident that Hans really cared for her, he stopped calling again, this time for a whole month. When he reappeared and claimed his undying love for her, vowing never to leave her again, she became his, mind and soul. Hans thought about Ilya and laughed aloud, knowing that in her terror of losing him she was now his slave.

Hans' final step in Ilya's demise had been her initiation into the world of her sexuality. In the beginning he had gently made love to Ilya, never asking her to touch him, in fact not allowing her to. This receiving without having to give was the final hook for Ilya, a hook she couldn't dislodge. Once she became hungry and lustful, Hans became more sexually demanding. But when she tried to refuse his aggression, he verbally abused her, threatening never to see her again. Ilya had become convinced that she was incapable of existing without Hans, so she relented and eventually learned to enjoy the dark side of his desires. Hans' complete control over Ilya gave him access to what he wanted more than anything else in the world—Otto. Hans knew that as long as he held on to Ilya, Otto's continued presence in his research would be assured.

* * *

Hans arrived in Berlin a little past ten in the morning. The air was freezing as he stepped from the car and walked into the heavily guarded building. The sound of his boots striking the marble floors resounded as he walked through the cavernous hallways.

Hans felt secure and confident as he moved into the meeting room and began shaking hands and talking with his illustrious colleagues. He was greeted amicably by fellow scholars who viewed Hans' controversial theories on the relationship between the subconscious and conscious mind with guarded interest.

The tension built in the room as word circulated that the Fuehrer himself was coming. Everyone was ordered to take their places at the enormous rosewood table in the middle of the room. When Hitler entered, they stood, arms outstretched, saluting their master.

Hans thought the Fuehrer looked quite good considering the strain he had been under. His eyes were bloodshot and his hands trembled slightly, but other then that he seemed well.

As Hitler moved to the head of the table, all eyes were on him. He began without preamble, his magnetism and power immediately sucking the air from the room.

"A new era has begun. I look to you as the architects. You must build a Thousand Year Reich for Germany." He balled his fist and struck his chest, like an exclamation mark at the end of a sentence. "I have selected you because you are the greatest minds in all of Germany." Hitler paused, allowing his words to penetrate.

Hans basked in the Fuehrer's praise.

"We will reign supreme! Our pure Aryan blood will produce tomorrow's world leaders. With patience and foresight, Germany will rule the world!"

Hans found himself shaking with excitement.

"You will begin immediately. Children must be carefully selected. These children will be raised with only one goal in mind—world domination for the continuation of our ideals." Hitler scanned the room, taking in every face. "You will be the masterminds of this organization. We will infiltrate the world!

"The children will be educated in the best schools and empowered through wealth to achieve greatness. Money is the only voice that the capitalist mind understands, and money is a resource we have in unlimited supply. We'll buy our way to power!" He closed his eyes, his voice turning soft. "I can see it now—in the United States, in South America, Central America, Asia…" His eyes flew open and his voice thundered, "Every one of those countries will one day have Nazi leadership, but they won't know it until it's too late!" Hitler laughed loudly.

Hans was quite sure the entire scheme was pure madness, and he lost track of what the Fuehrer was saying until he heard his own name mentioned.

"Yes," the Fuehrer was saying, "Herr Doctor Wells, along with many others, is researching new ways of controlling the mind. As I said in *Mein Kampf*, the political opinion of the masses represents nothing but the final result of an incredibly tenacious and thorough manipulation of the mind and soul. The immortality of the Reich is in your hands!"

Hitler leaned forward and placed his hands on the table, his words echoing loudly throughout the room. The Fuehrer's eyes had taken on a glazed look and spittle ran down the corner of his mouth.

Hans knew he was witnessing a grossly compulsive personality, a man out of control and out of touch with reality, but he also understood that every great man in the history of the world had been, at the very least, a little insane.

Hitler continued, "You'll be my guests for the next few weeks, remaining here until every detail has been worked through. All of Germany is depending on you. Heil Hitler!" The Fuehrer raised his arm before he turned and walked from the room.

Himmler took Hitler's place at the front of the table. With maddening deliberateness he studied every face, moving his eyes slowly from one to the other. Fear began to permeate the room. Hans could smell and taste it. He shivered involuntarily.

"Today you each embark on a mission—a top secret mission." He smiled.

No one moved.

"We begin work immediately."

* * *

Hans was sequestered in a room with twenty scientists, who were debriefed intermittently by Himmler and other top Nazi leaders. The plan was complicated and yet beautifully simplistic: when the War ended, these twenty men would be smuggled into various countries throughout the world. Their job, once settled, would be to indoctrinate and educate their charges, their ultimate goal being to infiltrate the government of their adopted country with Nazi leadership.

The men were told that similar debriefings were occurring in other locations throughout Germany. Secrecy was paramount and contact between the participants would remain on a need to know basis.

Three weeks later, having been given the heady appointment to participate with the project in the United States, Hans was seated comfortably in a big limousine heading back to Dachau. As the car wove in and out of heavy traffic, proceeding towards the countryside, a plan to insure Hans' own immortality began to emerge in his mind.

He considered the possibilities of fathering the child that would one day control politics in the United States. Unfortunately, he thought, he certainly couldn't use Ilya as the biological mother because of the obvious imperfections in her psyche. On the other hand, the beautiful young actress, Morgan, the one who had been put in his care, just might be suitable. True, she had very little mind left, but he had read numerous profiles that portrayed her as a brilliant and gifted woman.

Her dementia was a direct result of trauma, not genetics, and that made all of the difference in the world to Hans. The fact that she was a Jew didn't matter at all to him. No one would ever know, so what difference did it make?

* * *

Morgan had been sent to Dachau as soon as she had been well enough to travel. Otto had done his best to get reassigned to the camp, but his services were too badly needed elsewhere, so he struck a deal with his friend Himmler, seeing to it that Morgan was sent to his sister for safekeeping. Otto sent strict instructions to Ilya about Morgan, going even so far as to intimate that he had very personal feelings for her.

None of this made any difference to Morgan, because she wasn't aware of who or where she was. The moment she had held that broken glass to her wrist, deciding to take her own life, her mind had snapped. She was incapable of enduring the grave indignities that would have been thrust upon her, so she chose the only path acceptable to her. But her attempt failed, although she did manage to go away—to retreat back to a fantasy world where only love and warmth prevailed, a place where no one could reach her.

* * *

Morgan lived in a 10' x 10' room next door to the infirmary. Each day she was escorted to meals and then returned to her room. Occasionally Ilya would take her but because Morgan refused to speak, smile or react, Ilya dreaded being with her and managed to slough off the task most days to one of her coworkers.

Morgan spent her time remembering the sights and sounds of her youth: how it felt to hold Papa's hand as they walked to the Great

Synagogue, the gentle sound of her nanny's voice, the caresses of her mother.

Morgan only became confused when Robert would enter her mind and make love to her. This Robert seemed so different, demanding so much more from her than she could remember from the past, but he was her beloved and she was so happy when he came to her.

Chapter 31

────────── ★ ──────────

When Hans married Ilya, he sent Otto a telegram to give him the news. When Otto read it, he flew into a sadistic rage.

After the marriage, Ilya transferred all the trust and loyalty she had in her brother to her new husband. The only problem that developed— one anticipated by Hans—was Ilya's utter jealousy of everyone Hans dealt with. Hans' response to her obsession with him was to introduce her to drugs, keeping her semi-sedated and complacent.

Once the baby was born, Hans intended to get Ilya off the drugs. He knew he would have to make sure that when Otto finally did return, he never learned that his sister had previously been purposefully placed in a drugged stupor.

Copulating with Ilya had become a distasteful chore for Hans, who tolerated it only as a means of procreation. The more he became disgusted with Ilya, the more attractive Morgan became. He couldn't forget the first time he had held her in his arms, determined not to rape the woman who would mother his child.

When he had first touched Morgan, she had looked at him with tears streaking her face. "Robert, where have you been?" she had asked. "It's been so lonely and dark here without you."

Hans understood immediately what was happening in Morgan's mind and he didn't hesitate in his response.

"I'm here now, my darling. You have nothing to fear anymore. I won't leave you again."

The lovemaking that followed was Hans' first experience with passion that developed and emerged from love rather than lust. After that he couldn't keep his hands off of Morgan, and at times he didn't even care if she became pregnant. Hans Wells was hopelessly in love.

Although Hans knew that he was not the real object of Morgan's love, it didn't matter. In fact, it made it better for him—the ultimate agony, the ultimate torture. His pain was exquisite.

To insure Morgan's total dedication to him alone, he continuously wrote to Otto, telling him that Morgan was making wonderful progress and that she had even begun to ask for him. He also insisted that if she were to see Otto too soon, she might slip back into the black hole and never emerge again. He assured Otto that he would let him know when he could come to see Morgan.

* * *

When Ilya found out she was pregnant, she contemplated suicide. She hated children and was sure that the sight of an ungainly belly would repulse Hans. Hans had anticipated her revulsion and depression.

"Ilya, my pet, you've made me the happiest man alive. I wanted a child more than you could ever know," he said, swearing to himself that he would never enter her foul body again.

Ilya mistook his passion for love and she reached hungrily for her husband.

Sneering at her, he pulled away. Reaching into the night table drawer, Hans handed Ilya two sleeping pills. "Take this, my dear, you need your rest."

* * *

Morgan also became pregnant. Unfortunately, as her belly grew, she stopped responding to Hans' love making. He became frantic, missing the aphrodisiac of her passion.

Hans used every form of psychiatric treatment he knew, but he still couldn't reach her. Eventually he began to accept the fact that Morgan was lost to him forever, taking solace in knowing that at least he would have her child.

* * *

Ilya gave birth to a son on December 20, 1940. Hans attended to the birth himself, insisting on total privacy. Ilya's labor was long and painful but eventually the child was born; drug addicted and underweight.

Hans delivered his son with his own hands, and then he placed the infant in a plastic bag. After the child smothered, Hans wrapped the bag in newspaper and dumped the child into the garbage. He saw the entire event as nothing more than an inconvenience.

For weeks after the birth, Ilya was kept deeply sedated, so that she never even asked the sex of the child or where it was.

* * *

On January 8, 1941, Morgan went into labor. The pain pulled her out of the darkness and she screamed in terror as she felt the life in her struggling to be born. Hans was standing over her, his expression guarded. She didn't recognize him but felt intuitively that he was going to help her. She cried out in agony, "What's happening to me? Help me! Help me, please."

Hans glanced nervously over his shoulder, making sure that the Jew he had selected as Morgan's surgeon was ready. Dr. Jacob Gold watched his beloved Morgan wreathing in agony. His brain felt like it was about to explode as he remembered the enchanted afternoons he and Morgan had spent in Vilna watching movies, talking, becoming friends,…until Robert came along and took her away.

Over the past months he had tried so desperately to reach her, bringing her to the infirmary, spending hours reminding her of her life in Vilna and her life with Robert. But his knowledge of psychiatry was extremely limited and his attempts to bring Morgan out of her stupor failed.

Someday I'm going to kill the sick bastard. His hands trembled violently as he took a step forward. He had seen so much since coming to Dachau–his mind and heart wounded beyond repair. *I've got to help Morgan. But I swear to God, someday…*

The Nazi looked at his watch. Hard labor had begun almost six hours earlier. "What's happening?"

A pain seared Morgan's body and she stifled a scream. For months she had been one of the walking dead, unaware until now of the child growing inside her body. She searched Hans' face.

Realizing that Morgan was cognizant of him, Hans' eye began to twitch and he started to sweat profusely.

"There are some difficulties. The child is breach and hasn't yet dropped into position," Jacob replied tersely.

"I can't do this anymore. You have to help me," Morgan whimpered. She reached for Hans' hand and dug her nails into his palm. Her touch was searing, filling him with desire. He backed away. Tripping on his own feet, he almost fell.

"You have to help me! My baby will die if you don't do something," Morgan pleaded.

No matter what, this child will be born, even if we have to rip it from her body. Forcibly blocking out the memory of the moments he had spent feeling love for her, Hans grabbed her soaking wet hair and pulled it until she screamed.

"Do this right, Jew bitch. Push!" he hissed.

I can do this. I can. Morgan tried; she pushed, grunted and pushed again. But nothing would budge her unborn child.

Jacob placed the stethoscope against her writhing stomach, listening to the ever-weakening heartbeat of Morgan's child.

"The baby will have to be taken by caesarean section," Jacob said finally. "It's the only way we can save them. I'll need some ether."

"You need nothing! Don't worry about the Jew whore. Just get me the child."

"Please. It would only take a little," Jacob begged.

"Don't fuck with me. If you can't do this I'll get someone who can."

Jacob trembled as he reached for the scalpel. Leaning close to Morgan's ear he cooed, "Morgan, it's me, Jacob. You'll be all right, I promise you."

Morgan screamed as the knife cut into her belly, mercifully darkness came quickly.

She regained consciousness as Jacob gently lifted the baby from her belly. He cut the cord and the infant began to cry.

Hans took the child from Jacob. For a moment he was disappointed that the child was a girl, but that disappointment vanished as Hans held his daughter.

Morgan used the strength that remained to tug at Hans' coat. Seeing her lips moving, he leaned closer.

"Before I die, show me my baby. Please…"

Hans looked at Jacob, realizing that any show of compassion would be taken as weakness. Laughing, he turned from Morgan and walked away.

Morgan knew she was dying. The black vastness pulled at her. Off in the distance a light beckoned. Spiral clouds of silver danced over her and she hungered for their warmth.

Mother, is that you? Oh, Papa, you really are here. Embracing them, she felt herself merging into them. But even in the midst of such ecstasy Morgan felt that something had been forgotten. It came to her gently, like the dew falling from the petals of a lily.

"Morgan! Morgan, can you hear me? Fight. You must fight. I'm not going to let you die," the familiar voice of Jacob called.

* * *

Hans supervised as his daughter was cleaned. He felt no remorse for Morgan. He had simply done what needed to be done for the greater cause.

Holding his daughter in his arms, Hans experienced a sense of responsibility towards another human being for the first time. Having a son would have made his obligation to the Reich much easier to fulfill, but he would somehow overcome that problem. There would be a way and he would find it.

* * *

A week later, Hans was ready to present Ilya with her baby. He entered her room as dawn was breaking, sitting down stiffly next to her on the bed.

"We have a couple of very important items to discuss before I bring you your daughter," he said harshly. "You have failed your brother."

Ilya's eyes grew wide. "What? How?"

"The Jew whore Morgan is dead. You shouldn't have allowed her to get pregnant. Otherwise, she would still be alive. Otto will, of course, blame you. You know if you hadn't insisted on all of those morphine shots, you might have been able to keep a better eye on her for your brother."

"He'll kill me! You have to help me, Hans. You must tell me what to do."

"Don't get hysterical. Of course I'll help you," he said. "You must listen carefully and do exactly as I say. Otto must never know she was pregnant. We'll tell him she contracted pneumonia and died. We'll assure him we spent twenty-four hours a day trying to save her, and you'll tell him that as soon as we knew she was seriously ill, we sent word to him. The most important thing you must tell him is that she asked for him constantly. He must believe that she asked for him up until the very end. Do you understand all of this?" Ilya nodded as she wiped away the mucus flowing from her nose.

Hans patted her shoulder and said, "Good girl. I knew you would. Now, the next small problem we have..." He hesitated.

Ilya grew impatient and asked, "What other problem?"

Hans grinned. "You're going to have to stop taking your shots."

Ilya reached for Hans' shirt. Her touch infuriated him, but he restrained himself.

"You know I can't stop. I'm not myself without my medication. You said so yourself."

"You're a mother now, and that alone is reason enough to stop. I'll help you. You'll be just fine," he said. "Now, my darling, I want to introduce you to your daughter."

He clapped his hands and a nurse appeared, handing the small bundle to Ilya. Hans watched her closely, resentful that she was touching his daughter but mindful that she was a necessary part of his plan. After a few moments the baby was given back to the nurse. Ilya had lost interest. "I think I want to rest now," she said.

Hans sent word of Morgan's illness to Otto on a letter dated a week earlier. He wanted his brother-in-law to think the courier had somehow been delayed. He also wanted to be present when Otto learned of Morgan's death. Their futures were intertwined. Hans needed Otto, and he couldn't risk him going over the edge.

* * *

When Hans arrived at Auschwitz, a newly established extermination camp, in the Polish city of Oswiecim, he went directly to the commandant's office, introducing himself as Otto's brother-in-law. The commandant showed Hans into an antiseptic waiting area.

Otto entered the room a short time later. "This is a surprise." He begrudgingly shook Hans' hand, still resentful that his twin had married without his presence or approval. "I should think you would be with my sister. She must still be recovering from the birth."

Hans knew he was on precarious ground. He spoke carefully. "Your sister sends you her love. She's doing just fine and so is your namesake, Jotto."

Otto's mouth dropped open in disbelief. "You named the child after me? Jotto? Tell me all about her. What's she like? Does she look like me? I mean does she look like Ilya? Oh hell, it's all the same." He was clearly embarrassed.

Hans smiled. "She looks exactly like the two of you. As a matter of fact, I don't know where I figured into it at all. And she's such a good baby."

Otto grinned at Hans.

"Your sister…well, you just wouldn't believe it. She was born to motherhood. She never puts the baby down. She just sits and rocks little Jotto and coos her name over and over again."

Otto said, "I'll go back with you. I want to see my niece."

Hans put his arm around Otto and said, "Come and sit down, my friend. I have some desperately sad news to tell you. Did you receive my correspondence, the correspondence I sent to you over a week ago?"

Otto shook his head. "What's all this about? What's happened?"

Hans proceeded cautiously. "Morgan became very ill with pneumonia. We tried everything we knew, every medicine, but we couldn't save her. I'm sorry, Otto," he said watching him carefully. "She professed her love for you right until the very end."

Otto began to shriek. He picked up a chair and smashed it against the wall. The noise instantly brought the SS black shirts running. They took one look at Otto and retreated.

Hans waited until Otto had played out his anger. When his brother-in-law collapsed, Hans called for the SS to carry Otto to his quarters. Hans sedated him and then sat down in a chair next to the bed.

* * *

After two days Otto managed to pull himself together. He was anxious to resume his work and to do that he wanted Hans to leave. He needed to find a release for his agony and disappointment—and he knew just how to do that. He walked his brother-in-law to the front gate.

"You tell my sister I'll see her soon."

Hans slapped Otto on the back. "You're a great soldier. One day, you and I and Jotto, and, of course, Ilya will all be together again."

Otto fought to control his rage as he watched Hans' car pull away from the gate. *You can fucking bet on that.*

Chapter 32

───────── ★ ─────────

Captain Gerard had tried desperately to find a home for his bedraggled and ill passengers, but no country would take them in. Sick at heart and out of alternatives, he was forced to dock in Germany. There the Captain was told his passengers would be taken to the Auschwitz concentration camp.

The Captain approached his first mate.

"Do you remember giving me that package weeks ago?" Captain Gerard asked casually.

"Yes sir, I certainly do."

"And do you think you could point out the young man who gave it to you?"

The first mate looked past the Nazi soldiers milling around the passengers as he searched for David.

"I'm sure I could. As a matter of fact, he's right over there, fifth on the left."

The Captain approached David.

"Don't look around, just follow me," he whispered.

They moved unnoticed to the far end of the ship, where the Captain unlocked a storage room door and pulled David inside. He smiled sadly, fear clearly showing in his eyes.

"You must wait here until dark, and then I'll see to it that my men look the other way when you leave the ship."

David stood in shock and confusion. "Why are you doing this for me?"

"I have to do something," Captain Gerard said. "I only wish it could be more. As it is, I don't know if this is a favor or a disservice, but you're young and strong and if anyone's going to survive, you will," he said, reaching to shake David's hand. "Good luck and may God be with you."

Hours later David made his way off the ship, escaping into the night, hopeful but naive to the horrors that lay ahead.

* * *

David eventually made his way to Poland, where he wandered through jungle-like forests for many months. He learned to walk without sound as he roved like the wild boar and packs of wolves that populated the forest. He ate anything he could find, even dead animals not yet devoured by other predators, but mostly he subsisted on wild berries and food stolen from farmers.

When he finally ran into a group of partisans, he stayed with them for a few months, gaining a little weight and enjoying the camaraderie of their group. But he had other plans. His new friends tried to keep him from leaving, insisting that he would be much safer if he remained with them, but David refused. His goal was Byelorussia, the homeland of his grandfather, and he intended to continue on until he reached her border. He wanted to believe that in Byelorussia he would find safe refuge.

By the time David reached Byelorussia, the Russians had regained control of the western portion, which had infuriated the Byelorussian Nationalists, who were sympathetic to the Nazis, believing the propaganda of a Jewish-Bolshevik world conspiracy.

Fleeing ahead of the advancing Red Army, these Nationalists picked up new recruits along the way, and by the time they reached the Third Reich's army, the large group was more then willing to join Hitler's forces in helping to exterminate the Jews. The Nazis accepted the Byelorussians gladly and immediately began placing them in important positions in the towns they conquered, thereby fooling the local populace into believing that their fellow patriots were now administrating the local governments. The people of Byelorussia had no idea that their own countrymen were betraying them as they pointed out and then helped to liquidate Communist officials, partisans, and Jews still in hiding on the eastern front.

* * *

David was forced to hide not only from the advancing Nationalists but from the Russians as well.

As he sat on his haunches in the muck and mire of the flooded spring marshes of Byelorussia, he thought back to when he had left the ship not yet knowing what real fear, hunger, or pain were, but he had learned and had somehow managed to survive, finding out along the way that when necessary he could and would do anything to remain alive.

David had learned to step over a dead body with little or no feeling, thankful that it wasn't him. He had numbed himself to the sounds of exploding bombs, concentrating on the only things that really mattered to him—food and sleep. Everything else, he could and did live without.

Hiding deep within a forest outside the city of Minsk, David sat inside a fallen log that had become his home. It was the summer of 1941, and he had been caught in the crossfire as the Germans assaulted the Russian army.

The people of Minsk, cut off from news of the outside world, had no idea what the Nazis had planned for them. Foolishly, when the bombing was finished, the Jews actually returned to Minsk, believing they would have the same freedoms they had enjoyed with the German occupation during World War I. As David watched the Russians begin their retreat, he knew what would be coming next for the Jews of Minsk.

He was startled by the rat-a-tat of machine guns. Not understanding how or why anyone would be firing off so many rounds of ammunition, and fearing the worst, he made his way to a clearing, where he watched in horror as the Nazis slaughtered hundreds of captured Russian soldiers in total disregard for the Geneva Convention.

"Where are you, God? Why have you deserted us? Where the fuck are you? Aren't there rules even in war?" he screamed, as he made his way back to the log.

Hours later, David returned to the site of the massacre. A plan had formed in his mind, and he hoped that God would forgive him for what he was about to do and for what he had become.

He waited until a few hours before sunrise before going into the open field where the bodies of the fallen soldiers lay. David cut himself badly as he crawled under the barbed wire, but he continued on, disregarding the injury. The stench of the decomposing bodies overwhelmed him, forcing him to stop twice to vomit. He resented losing what little nourishment his body had, and that made him almost as angry as what he saw.

When he reached the first body, he found the papers that held the dead soldier's identification. The darkness prevented David from reading his new name, but just having the papers gave him the first sense of security he'd had in weeks. He managed to remove the dead man's coat before being forced to stop.

Hearing a dog in the distance, he began to shudder. He had seen what the dogs could do, and they terrified him. Remaining belly down, he moved back under the barbed wire, gashing himself again.

Bleeding profusely, he made his way back to his hiding place deep within the forest.

He lay beside the fallen log for days, lapsing in and out of consciousness, unable to eat as the infection from his wounds raged through his body, until he felt someone shake him. He thought he was hallucinating when he opened his eyes and saw a girl no more than fourteen or fifteen staring at him.

"Leave me alone. Just let me die," he said.

Obviously frightened, she momentarily backed away.

David saw a resolute look pass over her face as she squared her shoulders and moved back towards him. She had enormous eyes and coal-black hair that fell halfway down the middle of her back. She wore a long dress, and dozens of bangles decorated her wrists and neck. David had never seen a Gypsy before, but he was sure he was seeing one now.

"What's your name?" he asked weakly.

She looked at him and smiled, shaking her head from side to side as she reached for his hand and brought it slowly to her mouth. For a moment David thought she was going to bite him, until he realized what she was showing him—her tongue had been cut out.

David gasped. "You poor child, how could anyone do that to you?"

She shrugged and smiled sadly as she moved behind David, prodding him to turn on his side. Proceeding carefully, she began removing his shirt, but it was stuck to his wounds and she couldn't get it off. She tore a piece of fabric from her skirt and stuffed it into David's mouth, before ripping the shirt away from his festering wound.

The cool air felt good on David's back, easing the pain, and she soon removed the gag.

"Thank you for trying to help me, but I'm afraid you're wasting your time," he said in Russian, silently thanking his grandfather for teaching him the language but not knowing if she understood what he was saying.

She patted David's shoulder and moved silently away into the woods.

The young girl returned a while later, her arms loaded down with plants. David watched as she smashed the plants in a small vessel, adding all sorts of strange things to her brew. He didn't know whether to laugh or cry when he saw her snatch a spider from the log and add it to the mixture.

"If you don't kill me, I'll certainly have a story to tell my grandchildren," he said, smiling.

She carefully slathered the poultice over his wounds and David quickly felt its soothing results. He watched as she began to peel the bark from his log with a dagger.

"Hey, you're taking my house apart," he said.

The little Gypsy smiled at him as she continued working. Then she placed the bark over David's wound like a bandage.

The Gypsy never left David's side. When he opened his eyes, she was there, and when he fell asleep, she was there, always staring, as if her very presence could keep him alive. She fed him a bittersweet soup that she miraculously produced every time he awakened.

Soon he grew strong enough to sit up and hold his own spoon; and before long he began taking short walks, his little Gypsy girl always close by, watching and waiting.

David was shivering in his sleep the night she came to him. Enfolding her in his arms, he delighted in kisses that tasted of honey as she gave herself willingly, holding back nothing.

He fell deeply in love with the little Gypsy that night, worrying how he would protect her in the coming months. Deciding to deal with it in the morning, he fell into a fitful sleep.

When the sun rose the next day, she was gone. David frantically scoured the forest for days before resigning himself to the fact that she was lost to him forever. But he knew she would always be a part of him, perhaps the very best part.

Chapter 33

Passing himself off as the Russian soldier, Vladimir Vloriscoff, from the Caspian Sea port town of Baku in southern Russia, David began his trek to Moscow, aware that he was no more than a couple of days ahead of the advancing German Army.

He felt that Hitler had badly miscalculated the Russian people, thinking that without a viable air force their defeat was imminent. Hitler hadn't counted on them being such fierce and determined soldiers, unwilling to even consider defeat.

David spent his nights on the move, sleeping during the daytime in old deserted barns or in overgrown wheat fields along the way. By the time he reached Moscow, he was a shell of the man he had once been. Still, he had a fire in his eyes that bespoke of his undiminished determination. After wandering around Moscow for days, he mustered the nerve to go to Soviet Military Headquarters.

"My name is Vladimir Vloriscoff. I was caught in the German strike at Minsk," David said gravely to the officer, envisioning the carnage he had seen. "We were rounded up like dogs, and then those Nazi sons of bitches turned their machine guns on us. I fell to the ground with the first volley of shots, pretending to be dead. That night I escaped through the barbed wire." Lifting his shirt, he showed the officer the deep, ragged cuts on his back. The arduous walk had taken its toll—his wounds had reopened, again spreading infection throughout his body.

"It's taken me weeks to get here. I need rest and food, and then I want to go back to the front lines so I can fight those Nazi bastards," he said.

The officer put his arm around David. "Vladimir, you're a fine soldier. Come tell your story to my commandant, and then we'll get you to the hospital."

David retold his story to the commandant, embellishing some as his confidence grew.

"We shall arrange for a visit from your family as soon as you feel up to it."

"Thank you sir. But I have no family. My parents are dead and I was an only child." It was the closest words to the truth he had muttered since arriving in Moscow.

* * *

David was taken to a military hospital deep within the bowels of Moscow, where he was kept in isolation. His superiors were afraid that his story would erode the fragile morale of the Red Army.

Each night before David fell off to sleep, he would repeat over and over in his head, my name is Vladimir Vloriscoff. My name is Vladimir Vloriscoff. He knew he had to see himself as that man, forgetting who and what he use to be.

He spent a month in the hospital fighting the infection that had spread to his blood. At 5'9", he weighed only 120 pounds and looked more dead than alive. His eyes were circular orbs of darkness and his skin was a sallow gray.

Russian officers visited him often, speaking frequently about his heroism, his place within the Soviet hierarchy, and his upcoming promotion to captain. Vladimir, as he now thought of himself, didn't care about the politics of his newly adopted country; he only wanted to fight, and to die if necessary, to exact his revenge against the Nazis.

I'll never bow to anyone again…not like David had…not ever again!

* * *

Vladimir was only twenty when he was given his first command, but he had the wisdom, fortitude, and compassion of a man twice his age, and he was determined to share that knowledge with his troops.

The Nazis, following Napoleon's route, moved towards Moscow, and by the beginning of December 1941, they were closing in on the city. But they were not prepared to weather a Russian winter. By November, snow covered the ground and temperatures dropped below zero, paralyzing the sophisticated Panzer tanks. Supplies and clothing stopped reaching the Nazi soldiers as transports were under constant attack from the partisans.

The tide was turning against Hitler as the Russians pushed the Nazis back for the first time in the war. This was to be the turning point. Hitler's army began to realize that they were no longer invincible.

* * *

On his days off, to rebuild his strength and relieve his frustration, Vladimir began to compete in one of Russia's great pastimes—wrestling. He found that he had natural ability, and before long he had difficulty finding a partner who could challenge him. He had seen the coaches watching him, so he wasn't surprised when one of them asked to speak with him in private.

"You're not good yet, but you have potential, young man," the coach said. "I could teach you to be great. What do you think?"

Vladimir studied the man, taking note of his bull-like build and excellent physical condition. He estimated the coach to be at least forty years old. "If I wanted to be trained—and I'm not saying I want to be— why would I select you as my teacher?" he asked.

"Ah," the coach said, "you all think you're so good these days, too good to learn from a master. Why I waste my time I don't know," he said angrily.

"Wait!" Vladimir said. "I was rude and I'm sorry. May I buy you a drink after my workout?"

The coach smiled, showing several teeth covered with gold caps, a sign of wealth and prestige in the USSR. "I'll meet you.

I must learn not to pass up opportunities. One never knows where they could lead.

* * *

The two men sat across from each other at a tiny round table in a crowded bar not far from the gym. Vladimir now weighed almost 180 pounds. Working diligently with weights, he had cultivated the look and bulk of a wrestler. His eyes were dark, wide-set, and intense, and his brow was heavy. When he smiled, his eyes crinkled and his face took on an alluring kindness.

The coach lifted his vodka in a toast. "L'Chaim," he said, draining his drink in one gulp.

Vladimir almost choked. The coach had just made an age-old Yiddish toast that meant "To life." Vladimir decided not to say anything in case it was a set-up.

"You're new to Moscow, this is obvious," the coach said.

"And how do you know that?"

"If you were from Moscow, you'd know who I am. My name is Boris Blanchack, the Russian gold medal wrestling champion from the 1920

Olympics in Antwerp. I also happen to be the most sought after trainer in all of the USSR. I train champions, and only champions. I don't see raw talent like yours very often. And you have something else—something unique in a man so young—a killer instinct. There's no fun in what you do; you play not like it's a game. You compete as if your life depended on it, and I like that."

Only a year and half ago Vladimir had arrived in Moscow, weak as a kitten and barely alive, and now he was being offered the opportunity to compete on a professional level in a sport, a game. My God, life certainly takes strange turns, he thought.

He said, "I'm very flattered by your offer, but I'm a soldier in the Soviet Army, and I really don't have the time to devote to you and your teaching. I'm afraid my superiors would object—"

"We don't take our sports lightly in Russia. You should know that. Every man I've ever worked with has been a soldier; it's mandatory. Don't underestimate me, Vladimir. I've already spoken with your commanding officers, and they would like nothing better than for you to turn yourself over to me. They tell me you're a hero, but you could become even more of a hero if you have the guts to try," he said. "But before you give me your answer, you should know what you'd be getting into. If you come with me, you'll work your ass off. I'll expect you to get in shape for wrestling by learning to run faster than you ever dreamed possible, and to swim farther and longer then you can even begin to imagine. You'll be allowed to eat only what I tell you, and you'll sleep when I say sleep. For all practical purposes, Vladimir Vloriscoff, you'll belong to me. If you can't accept that, I don't want you."

Vladimir slammed his fist on the table. "I belong to no one but myself! I'd rather be dead. Do you think I survived so that I could have someone else take over my life? If you want me, it will be on my terms. I'll train harder than anyone you've ever trained, and I'll become a champion, but I must remain my own person or you can forget it."

The two men stared into each other's eyes, each waiting for the other to turn away. Boris desperately wanted to add Vladimir to his team. Vladimir, on the other hand, had surprised himself. He wasn't even sure he wanted to do this thing. Boris poured another drink and raised it to Vladimir. "To our next champion! I hope you have what it takes."

* * *

Vladimir spent the rest of the war in a battle with his body, spending many nights sleeping on the training table, too sore and too exhausted to make it to his rooms. He became everything Boris had hoped for; and because Boris had no children, he began to think of Vladimir as his son, pushing him even harder.

* * *

When the war ended in 1945, the truth began to emerge about the German atrocities against the Jews—a truth the world had refused to believe until newspapers began printing pictures from the liberated concentration camps.

"How could this have happened?" Vladimir asked Boris. "It's all bullshit. They knew; they all knew. They just didn't give a damn. One man can't kill six million people all by himself. He needed help, and damn it, he found all the help he could ever need!"

"You're political views are very dangerous, and they have no place in your work. You must learn more self-control or you're libel to find yourself being shipped out to Siberia—no matter how good you are. Now let's get back to work," Boris said, wishing he could express his own views. But he had learned long ago to keep his opinions to himself, understanding only too well that unlike Vladimir, most Russians hated the Jews.

"Come to dinner on Friday night. We'll talk then," Boris said.

* * *

Sadie, Boris' wife of twenty years, greeted Vladimir warmly at the door. She was a heavyset woman with curly, graying hair and a heavy bosom.

"Come in, Vladimir. It's so good to see you again. We'll sit and talk until Boris gets home; he had to go out for a little while," she said, having sent Boris away so that she could talk with Vladimir alone. She led him to their utilitarian living room where she handed him a cracker covered in chopped liver.

Sadie was an exceptional woman. An intellect, she was considered one of the most knowledgeable professors on ancient Rome in all of Russia. Students waited on long lists to be admitted to her classroom.

"Tell me, Sadie, I've never seen you without that Cameo you wear on your shoulder. Does it have some special significance?"

"My mother wore this cameo every day of her life, and when she passed away, I continued the tradition. This pin," she said softly, "reminds me of her. She was a very good woman."

"Now, tell me, young man. What are you interested in? What would you like to be when you're finished with all of these little boy games you're playing?" she asked.

Vladimir laughed. "Boris would take great exception to that comment. But if you really want to know, I'm especially fascinated by this new science of atomic energy."

Sadie's eyes caught fire. "How wonderful! You couldn't have picked a better field of study. The Russian intellects are anxious to build a stable of scientists to secure our place in the coming scientific revolution. So, it is decided"

"What are you talking about?"

"You'll go to University and that's final!" Sadie had a well-deserved reputation for being stubborn and she had grown use to having her own way.

Vladimir warmed to the idea instantly.

"Sorry, I'm late," Boris said, striding into the room. He kissed Sadie and shook Vladimir's hand. "What's with all the serious looks? Have you been filling the boy's head with nonsense?"

"I'm talking to Vladimir about beginning his studies."

"Are you crazy, Sadie? Vladimir has no time. It will have to wait."

Sadie gave Boris a withering look. "Would you have him wind up like you? Every morning of your life you awaken in so much pain it takes you an hour to dress. Vladimir has a good mind, and it's a sin against God for him not to use it. You will let him use both his body and his mind, or I'll never forgive you."

Boris sighed. "Woman," he muttered under his breath. "He'll still have to practice four hours every day or it's no deal," Boris said sternly. "Now, can we eat now? It's almost sundown."

As often as Vladimir had been to dinner at Sadie and Boris' home, he had never been invited for a Friday night dinner. When he sat down at the lace-covered table and saw the silver candelabrum, the silver chalice, and the tattered Hebrew prayer book, he was astounded. And when Boris sang out the ancient Sabbath prayers, he felt as if his heart would break, as memories of his father, mother, and grandfather flashed through his mind. Guilt washed over him as he chastised himself for breaking faith with his people by living his life as a lie. Believing that he had no right to be with Boris and Sadie on Shabbat, Vladimir pushed himself away from the table and fled without a word

"Is that any way for him to act?" Boris said, staring at the empty chair. "I told you he's been acting crazy lately. I'm telling you, something really terrible is going on in that boy's head."

* * *

Vladimir walked the streets of Moscow for hours, berating himself for hurting Boris and Sadie. Stopping at a local bar, he quickly drank two glasses of vodka, allowing the clear liquid to burn its way down his throat, calming him and giving him courage.

He left the bar and made his way back to the Blanchack's door, knowing that if he didn't confront them now, he never would. He knocked lightly and when they didn't answer, he banged loudly.

"OK, OK. Don't break down the door," Boris hollered. "Who is it?" he asked.

"It's only me," Vladimir said.

Boris threw open the door and pulled Vladimir inside, hugging him tightly. "It's Ok, son. Everything is going to be all right."

Sadie's eyes filled with tears at hearing Boris call Vladimir son. At that moment Sadie accepted what she had avoid admitting to herself for so long—she loved this lonely young man as she would have loved her own son.

Leaving them, she went into the kitchen to boil some water for tea, and when she returned, she found them sitting together on the sofa. Boris was pouring a drink for Vladimir from an already half-empty bottle of vodka.

"Stop drinking, already," she said. "I've made some hot tea and you'll drink that now. Enough with the liquor; it solves nothing."

Vladimir emptied his heart that night, trying as best he could to recapture for them David's life and the events that had led him to this point. "I just can't understand. How could six million Jews have perished? I never should have left my parents. The pain I feel, it never goes away," Vladimir said. "I can't even tell anyone that I'm a Jew," he said miserably. "If only I could get to Palestine, then I could do something to help our people."

"Stop feeling sorry for yourself," Boris said. "You have nothing to be ashamed of. You're a Jew and no one can take that away from you. You did what you had to do to stay alive. It was God's will."

Changing the focus, Boris continued, "I've heard talk that the British are thinking about giving the Jews Palestine. It won't happen tomorrow, but I believe it will happen one day, and you must be ready. You'll go there one day, my son, if you believe. But for now, you must remain Vladimir, the model soldier, athlete, and soon-to-be student. That's a heavy enough burden for anyone to carry."

Chapter 34

In July of 1944, Otto Milch arrived at Auschwitz unannounced. Dr. Hans Wells was stunned by Otto's appearance as he ushered him into his private office. Otto's hair had gone from blond to almost white, and he had lost so much weight that his head appeared too big for his body. Hans stared at Otto, thinking that he had never before seen eyes so dead.

"My God, what's happened to you?" Hans asked.

"You can't even begin to imagine. The Allied forces invaded Normandy with thousands of ships and planes, and Berlin is a city in ruin. It's only a matter of time before Germany falls. When these camps are liberated, the Jews are going to slaughter every Nazi they can find. We've got to get out of here now."

"Fuck!" Hans snarled, rubbing his beard. "Still, if you think about this rationally, our goals haven't really changed. We must stay alive and we will. We'll leave under cover of darkness, but we'll have to be very careful. We'll pass ourselves off as Polish civilians waiting for the Allies to liberate us. It'll be all right, Otto. Just leave everything to me."

* * *

By war's end, most people and nations believed that the Nazi threat had been eradicated. This false sense of security gave men like Hans Wells and Otto Milch fertile ground to plant the seeds of their scheme.

Hitler's secretly appointed "procurers of a new world order" took advantage of their new-found obscurity by systematically selling off the stolen resources they had kept hidden in hundreds of vaults throughout Europe. The Nazis had no difficulty disposing of their treasures to a greedy world hungry for possessions, putting hundreds of millions of dollars into Nazi coffers to ensure that these diabolical men would have enough money to create the next generation of world leaders.

* * *

Otto, Hans, Ilya and Jotto stole away from Dachau in the dead of night. In their possession were forged identity papers that listed them as prisoners of war, part of the Free Polish Forces. The United States military interrogated them, along with tens of thousands of other displaced persons. They were processed and released. Their still powerful connections arranged transportation for them into war-ravaged France, where they immediately went into hiding in the partially destroyed home of a fellow conspirator.

"We'll wait here until the opportunity presents itself for us to gain entrance into the United States," Otto said.

"I hate it here," Ilya complained. "Can't you do something, Otto?"

"Don't worry, my pet, it won't be long."

* * *

Hans took it upon himself to leave the house before dawn and not return until dark each day, as he combed the taverns and streets for information.

"I heard an interesting bit of information today," Hans said to Otto as they sat drinking a cheap red wine. "It seems the Americans are very worried about the Soviet involvement in research and development of atomic power. It also seems that our friends the Americans are convinced that Soviet Communists have deeply infiltrated the United States and are planning to take over control of Eastern Europe. I read in the newspaper today that Winston Churchill told Truman that an iron curtain is being drawn down across Europe by the Russians. The word is that the Americans are looking for collaborators who have access to information on captured Soviet patriots.

"This could be the chance we've been waiting for," Otto said. "I've fucking had it with this place, and I want to get out of here. Why don't you see what else you can find out?"

Hans and Otto saw that the time was right to offer their knowledge to the desperate United States government. But first they would reveal their intentions to their fellow conspirators.

* * *

The meeting took place in a dank basement in the old Jewish Quarter of Paris.

"If the Americans want information, I say we give it to them," Hans insisted. "We already know how gullible the men of the CIA and CIC are. Those pompous asses are so desperate and so afraid of the Russians they'll believe anything we tell them," Hans said. The men nodded in agreement.

Otto stalked the room, his eyes darting from one man's face to the next. "If the United States wants information, then information they'll get."

"Then it's settled. We'll make our move immediately," Hans said firmly. "Heil Hitler!"

* * *

The Nazis wasted no time offering their services to the United States government, assuring their new friends that they had an established Nazi spy network within France capable of supplying the United States with pertinent information about the Russians. The Americans welcomed them with open arms. They accepted as truth the information they were given; and even though they could never officially recognize the network established by the Nazis, they did make clandestine deals with them. As payment for their help, special positions were created for the now cooperative Nazi collaborators. Hans was given a job with the United Nations Relief and Rehabilitation Agency, and Otto was made a Refugee Rations Officer.

Continuous Nazi pressure convinced the CIA and the CIC to allow an elite group of Nazis into the U.S., directly violating laws passed by Congress that strictly prohibited Nazi immigration.

"We can't both go. Jotto must be taken to the United States, you know that!" Hans said vehemently to Otto.

It was impossible for the Americans to smuggle all of the Nazi collaborators into the U.S., and Hans had begun to be concerned that Otto's erratic behavior might give them away.

"I won't go without you," Ilya cried, hanging on to her twin. "Let Hans take the baby, and I'll go with you to South America," she said hysterically.

The brothers-in-law looked at each other sadly, knowing that Ilya felt no motherly attachment to Jotto, whom they both adored. Otto became furious at his sister for her lack of commitment, remembering his own desolate life as a child. He slapped Ilya across the face so hard that his handprint left its mark.

"You'll go with your husband to America. I'm going to Bolivia and that's final."

Ilya pouted for days, refusing all conversation with Otto. It wasn't until he took them to the ship and Hans was busy with the porters that she finally spoke with her brother.

"Don't make me go with him, Otto. He doesn't love me. Please take me with you," she begged.

"Of course he loves you, you're being ridiculous. Besides, haven't I always taken care of you?"

Ilya nodded.

"That's a good girl, now wipe your eyes," Otto said lovingly as he handed her his handkerchief. "You should be so proud, Ilya. Your daughter has been selected above all others! Our bloodline, my beloved, yours and mine, will be responsible for the continuation of the Third Reich. Think about it Ilya, and remember how far we've come. That's what's important, my beautiful sister…that's all that matters," he said, reaching over to kiss his niece goodbye. Gathering Jotto in his arms he hugged her tightly. "The future of Germany will be in your hands one day, my precious angel. Until then, remember that your Uncle Otto loves you very much."

BOOK II

Chapter 35

———————— ★ ————————

Shortly after their arrival in the United States, using the funds he'd smuggled in from Germany, Hans bought a magnificent beach front home overlooking the aqua blue waters on the Gulf of Mexico, in the tiny yet prosperous city of Naples, Florida.

Its west coast location was only a couple of hours drive from the thriving city of Miami and its international airport, giving Hans exactly what he needed: easy access to his brother-in-law in Bolivia, and his fellow Nazis, some of whom had located to the east coast of the United States.

His eight co-conspirators, all of whom had been given refuge in the United States with their children months before Hans, had established an enclave for themselves in the sleepy little town of South River, New Jersey. They had chosen South River as their new home because three of Hans' Nazi comrades, all renowned scientists, had been offered full professorships at Rutgers, thanks to recommendations given to the University directly from the United States government.

The remaining five Nazis, all accomplished business men, had negotiated the purchase of a one hundred year old manufacturing plant for five million dollars, thereby firmly establishing themselves into the capitalistic business community. That acquisition enabled them to make generous donations into the campaigns of influential and greedy politicians. Leaving nothing to chance, the Nazis simultaneously began keeping extensive dossiers on the politicians they couldn't buy, noting who had mistresses and who had tastes that far exceeded their incomes, fully intending to use that information if it ever became necessary.

* * *

Hans's first order of business, thanks to the connections his comrades had established, had been to obtain a Florida birth certificate for Jotto, legitimizing her as an American citizen, and while that bit of illegal business cost him nearly ten thousand dollars, Hans knew that it would be imperative to his daughter's future.

Naples, a city devoid of Jews, served as a winter playground for the giants of American industry who came there to play golf, and to languish in their sprawling mansions that they occupied only when the weather up north became too frigid.

That scenario served as the perfect backdrop for Hans, motivating him to sit for the Florida Medical Boards and the E.C.F.M.G. National Boards. He passed them easily, and once licensed, he established an exclusive psychiatric practice, more for the exposure it would give him within the community than for his desire to ever practice medicine again.

The wealthy and bored matrons quickly filled Hans' appointment book, delighting in his qualifications, European accent and incredible good looks. It didn't take long for Doctor Hans Wells to become a celebrity, and it didn't take long for the gossip to begin.

"Did you hear?" Ann Macmillan asked her friend Janet over lunch at the Beach Club. "Sally McBride invited Doctor Wells to her home for dinner on Tuesday evening, and from what her servant told mine…they were in her bedroom for hours. Can you imagine?" Ann asked with a catty sneer, her Georgia accent drawing out every word. "Why he didn't even leave until almost one o'clock in the morning, and when he did leave I hear she accompanied him to the front door in a dressing gown so sheer you could see everything! To tell you the truth, I don't understand what he sees in her in the first place. Have you seen the way she's been dressing lately? It's just plain disgusting, I tell you, just disgusting."

The women delighted in their unkind chatter, neither one knowing that the other had tried unsuccessfully to seduce Hans. But Hans had chosen Sally because, unlike her friends whose husbands came home for the weekends, Sally's millionaire husband was off in Europe for the entire winter. That made having an affair with Sally wonderfully uncomplicated, even though Hans had found both Ann and Janet more to his liking.

Having husbands who came home on weekends did have its advantages; it afforded the ladies the luxury of inviting the doctor to their homes for dinner parties. Explaining that his wife was chronically ill, Hans swept, unencumbered, into the posh society of Naples.

Life would have been close to idyllic for Hans if not for Ilya and her desperate moods and miserable disposition.

"I hate this God forsaken shit hole!" Ilya screamed in German as Hans was reading the morning newspaper, ignoring her outrage.

"I can't even walk out the door because it's so damn hot, and the fucking mosquitoes are impossible," she whined, violently scratching her newest bites. "I'm sick of being left behind while you're off traveling with your fancy friends," she spat, pulling the paper violently out of Hans' hands.

"I'm talking to you!" Ilya hissed.

Hans glared at her, hoping that his look would be enough to stop her, but it didn't.

"It's not bad enough you leave me here, but you leave me here with that spoiled rotten little girl that you think is so wonderful!" Ilya said, referring to Jo with disgust. "Aren't you afraid I might hurt your precious little darling?" she asked tauntingly.

"That's enough, Ilya!" he whispered, his face purple with rage. "I won't have you speaking that way about our daughter! What do you want from me?" he asked pleadingly. "You know what my life is, and you know I have to travel, it's…"

"Bull shit!" Ilya screamed, interrupting him. "You travel to get away from me because you hate me!" She wailed, crying pitifully.

Hans could smell the liquor on her breath, and it disgusted him.

* * *

Hans had carefully orchestrated their lives so that Ilya had little contact with Jo, seeing to it that she was off to school before Ilya awakened, and making sure that Jo was never left alone with her mother. When Hans went out of town, Ilya's full time nurse gave Ilya injections of a potent tranquilizer every four hours to keep her docile.

The servants felt sorry for Hans, and they never missed an opportunity to discuss the family's problems.

"Why do you think he stays with that bitch?" the maid asked the cook over breakfast.

"The man's sainted, that's why. It's really so sad, him being a doctor and all. It must frustrate him to no end that he can't even help his own wife. Have you ever seen a more dedicated husband and father? Let me tell you, if I had a man that looked and acted like he does, I'd do anything to keep him happy. That woman's just crazy; that's the only thing I can figure; she's just plain crazy," the cook said with conviction.

Hans enjoyed the role he played as the long-suffering husband and father, but he never lost sight of his mission: indoctrinating his daughter into the Nazi ideology.

* * *

By the time Jo was 8 years old she was a seasoned survivor, fending off her mother's neglect and disapproval by becoming as close to invisible as possible. But veiling herself in obscurity was impossible–she was too beautiful. Her hair was the color of freshly harvested wheat, blond and curly, like her father's, and, like her birth-mother Morgan; she had almond shaped, violet eyes that sparkled gloriously when she smiled, drawing stares. She looked like a delicate porcelain doll: magnolia-white skin, high cheekbones and a heart-shaped mouth. But Jo saw none of that when she looked in the mirror. She viewed herself as ungainly: legs too long and skinny, with Olive Oyl size feet that would have made Popeye laugh. She hated her hair and was convinced that being ugly was her fate. She withdrew into a world of fantasy, creating a life through her dolls.

"I love you very much," she cooed, sitting on the floor of her enormous bedroom with her favorite doll, Betsy. "Here comes daddy. Let's put on your new dress so that you'll look beautiful."

Delicate fingers negotiated the buttons as Jo changed her baby lovingly. She then picked up her designated father doll, whose hair she had cut short. Lowering her voice to a masculine level Jo pretended to be the father. "Here's my beautiful little girl. Did your mommy take you for a walk on the beach today? She did…that's wonderful."

Jo picked up her most glamorous doll, and again her voice changed, this time into a deep-throated sophisticate. "My dear husband, how handsome you look and how very much I missed you. Come here and give me a kiss." She had the dolls embrace, adding kissing sounds and words of endearment.

Jo knew that people in the house talked about her. She had heard the servants whispering and knew that they worried about her, fearing she would end up like her mother. Jo didn't care what people said; in her world of dolls and make believe life was gentle and safe.

Lying in bed each night, surrounded by her dolls, Jo prayed, "Please God, just let my dolls come alive. Just let them talk to me and I swear I'll do anything you want for the rest of my life." And each night before she fell off to sleep Jo took roll call, calling out to each doll, waiting for a response but wishing wasn't always enough.

* * *

The morning sun reflected off the windowpane, bathing the room in white and gold. A cardinal perched itself on the windowsill, pecking on the glass. Jo awakened with a start. Seeing the bird, she moved silently from the bed for a better look, praying that her movement would not frighten the creature away.

The door opened without warning.

"Good morning. I hope you slept well?" her father, Hans said, tapping his foot on the floor, fidgeting with the newspaper he held firmly in his hands. Dressed in a navy blue pin stripped suit, his tie securely in place. "You seem to be running a little bit late this morning."

"I'm sorry, father," she stammered, glancing quickly at the clock on her night table, her stomach fluttering in distress. "I didn't realize it was so..."

"Late?"

"Yes, sir."

"Just because it's Saturday doesn't mean you can squander the day away. Get dressed. The newspapers have arrived and we have many issues to discuss.

Jo dressed quickly, pulling on khaki slacks and a white oxford shirt. Using her fingers as a comb, she pulled at the tangles in her hair. Slipping into sandals, she ran down the circular staircase noisily, sliding across the marble floor, jumping over the Persian rug in the hallway. Her breath coming in short little gasps, she tucked in her blouse and squared her shoulders before tiptoeing onto the porch.

His mustache seeded with toast crumbs, Hans used the linen napkin to slowly wipe his face, never taking his eyes from Jo. "Would you care for some breakfast?"

"Thank you, father."

Hans rang the little sterling bell beside him on the table; the maid appeared. "Miss Well's is ready to be served, " he said, meticulously placing the newspapers so that the front page of the New York Times and The Washington Post were clearly legible.

It was October 24, 1951. Jo was 10 years old.

"Look at this!" Hans blurted, noticing a story halfway down the page. "The United States has officially declared an end to the state of war with Germany." He ranted in German; Jo knew he was swearing. "Read," Hans ordered, shoving the paper towards her, his face purple rage.

Jo trembled; it was going to be a bad morning. She read the article aloud, daring not to glance up or even pause for breath.

"The war with Germany has been over for years. This is just a political ploy to embarrass the Germans once again. It's the fucking Jews, putting that fool Truman in the White House," Hans hissed, his normally subdued demeanor vanishing; he became a ragging vile-mouthed racist.

Everything wrong in the world he blames on the Jews, Jo thought, confused by her father's outrage.

"Come with me," Hans said, throwing the paper on the ground and stamping it with his foot. "We need to talk."

* * *

And so it went, day after day: up at dawn, newspapers read and discussed, schoolwork scrutinized, and books read: World history, American history, political science.

Instead of friends, Jo had etiquette lessons, instead of blue jeans, Jo dressed for dinner, instead of going to Church; Jo had her own private Protestant Minister teaching her religion.

* * *

At precisely 9 o'clock every evening Jo went to her room. She undressed and got into bed. Five minutes later Hans arrived. But today was her eleventh birthday and she had decided to assert herself.

"Good evening, father," she said, her body shivering in dread as he entered the room.

"I hope that your birthday was pleasant. Have you completed your days assignments?"

"Yes, sir."

"Then we shall begin?" Hans took out a book written in German. He fingered the pages lovingly, his bible, Mein Kampf. Reaching into his suit pocket, he removed a silver cigarette case, an exact replica of his brother-in-law's cigarette case. He flipped it open. The haunting theme from Beethoven's Fur Elise began to play.

"Please Father, I don't"...*Here goes.* "I don't like being put to bed every night. I'm not a baby, and besides, I don't understand a word you're saying when you read that dumb old book. " Her hand flew to her mouth, she was so scared she thought she would vomit, but having finally spoken her feelings Jo also felt heady delight.

"A baby! A dumb old book?" Hans sputtered, mortified. He had hypnotized Jo nightly from the time she was five years old, and when his brother-in law, Otto visited they worked together, reinforcing and indoctrinating Jo with their ideals. She had never before questioned him. "I'm your father and you'll do exactly as I say." His mouth twitched. "Close your eyes and listen to my voice. Feel yourself relaxing, feel your neck and shoulders relax, feel your arms become relaxed and light as feathers," he said, his cadence all too familiar.

Jo closed her eyes. She fought the sound of his voice, thinking of other things, willing herself not to hear.

Hans opened the book purposely. He read for a very long time, translating every word lovingly, his voice pulling at Jo.

After years of conditioning, Jo's mind pulled her toward the words, but she fought, blocking out his commands. He spoke that night about the radiant splendor of Germany, the purity of the race and Jo's need to understand her duty to the Reich. Jo was confused by the rhetoric, and frightened by his impassioned fervor. She worshiped her father, and wanted desperately to please him, spending her young life pretending to be happy, willing to forgive him for stealing away her naiveté and youth by making her see the world in all its ugly truths. But Jo was Morgan's child as well, and the soul and spirit of her mother was emerging as she grew, resisting Hans' evil smothering attitudes and ideology. It was happening despite all the years of contrary conditioning.

I love my father. I do love him…I do.

She eventually drifted off to sleep, her mind mustering itself to do battle in a fight she was only beginning to comprehend.

* * *

Concerned with Jo's emerging self-will, Hans visited his brother-in-law in Bolivia in early December of 1951 to discuss alternative methods for her indoctrination.

Otto, having spent every summer with Jo since the Wells' move to Naples, gave his advice confidently, and the two men enjoyed a week of quiet conversation as they discussed various approaches to the problems Hans was having with Jo.

Each morning before breakfast, Hans' would visit his favorite room in his brother-in-law's mansion: the library annex that was added as a renovation. It was here that Hans spent much of his time reading and answering correspondence from his allies in Uruguay.

"Sorry to disturb you," Otto said apologetically upon entering the library. "I just came to tell you that I'd be gone for the rest of the day. There's some problems with a land deal I've been negotiating, and I have to go into town."

"Would you like me to go with you?" Hans asked cordially.

"Thank you, but no."

* * *

By late afternoon Hans began feeling bored and claustrophobic, so he decided to take a walk, exploring some areas of the estate that he'd never seen before.

Twenty minutes into his walk Hans came upon a cottage on the very edge of the estate, a mile from the main house. Thinking how strange it was that Otto would have a cottage stuck so far away from everything, he walked up to the window and peered in. To his surprise the window was covered in grime, something completely out of character for his fanatically clean brother-in-law. Hans tried unsuccessfully to wipe off the grime in order to see in, but the film was on the inside of the windows as well.

Moving to the front door Hans turned the handle, and upon finding it unlocked he entered. He was instantly overcome with revulsion. Otto was standing with his back to the door, holding a black leather whip in his hand. A young boy no more than 12 years old was suspended naked from the ceiling by chains. Otto was laughing loudly as the blood from the young boy's slashed and bleeding back dripped onto his head.

"I'll take you down soon, my beloved," Otto said in Spanish to the semi-conscious boy. "And then we'll make love," he cooed, his voice heavy with desire.

Hans grabbed the whip out of Otto's hands.

"Are you crazy? Do you want to ruin everything?" Hans screamed, quickly working to free the boy. "Get me something to clean him up, you son of a bitch," Hans ordered, laying the boy gently down on the giant bed that occupied the entire corner of the room.

Otto watched with anger as the boys' blood spilled onto his white velvet comforter. Throwing pillows to the floor in order to have better access to the now unconscious boy, Hans smashed his hand against iron stirrups that had been welded to the end of the bed.

"What the fuck are these, more toys?" Hans asked furiously as he began tending to the boys torn flesh. Otto watched dispassionately, not offering any assistance.

"Go back to the house and wait for me," Hans ordered disgustedly.

* * *

Carrying his charge to the servant's quarters a half of a mile away, Hans turned the injured boy over to the gardener, instructing him to find a doctor. Reaching purposefully into his pocket, Hans pulled out three twenty-dollar bills, an enormous amount of money in a third world country like Bolivia.

"I found the boy badly beaten, and lying unconscious on the grounds while I was out walking. I have no idea who could have done this to him, but I don't want any problems," Hans said, handing the bills to the gardener.

"With boys like this one, Senor," the gardener said knowingly, "these things happen all the time. Don't worry about anything, I'll take care of the him…there won't be any problems or questions, I can assure you."

* * *

"What am I going to do with you?" Hans asked Otto murderously after arriving back at the main house. Looking accusingly at Otto, Hans knocked an expensive vase to the floor in a fit of temper and frustration. "I think it's time for you to come back to the states with me…permanently." Hans watched carefully for Otto's reaction.

"I like it here!" Otto said stubbornly. "This is Bolivia, for Christ's sake, and he's nothing more than a poor street urchin. What are you so worried about?"

"It's not your perversions that worry me; it's Jotto's future that I'm concerned with, and unfortunately for all of us, your power is greater than mine, and I need you. Don't you see? We must put our personal differences aside, and do what's best for Jotto."

Otto puffed out his chest, forgetting his anger. "She's really got quite a strong personality, doesn't she?" Otto asked, turning his thoughts adoringly towards his niece.

"That she does, and it will serve her well as she matures, but for now it's become a problem." Hans looked intently at Otto. "I know you love Jo as much as I do, and I know that you wouldn't do anything to spoil our plans…so you must do as I say, Otto. You've indulged yourself long enough. It's time you found a wife and settled down."

Otto snickered as he tried to imagine himself married. Rubbing his beard with the back of his hand, Otto contemplated Hans' words.

"For Jo's sake…I'll come to the states. But don't push me Hans…remember you're nothing without me."

Chapter 36

————— ★ —————

The summer sky over Naples had turned from turquoise to gray as the thunder cracked and the clouds burst, spilling cooling rain on to the simmering ground. Otto and Hans, getting instantly drenched, moved from the open veranda into the main house, carrying their drinks. Once dried off and settled, Hans broached a subject that had been on his mind for weeks.

"Jo will be 12 before we know it, and I'm worried that outside influences are impacting negatively on her. We must...," Hans faltered, clearing his throat. "We must send her to a private boarding school where..."

"So soon? Otto interrupted. "You said yourself the child needs further teaching, and now you want to send her away. I don't understand."

"We have no choice. She has to start making the right kind of friends, and we both know that can't happen here. We'll still have the summers with her, and if we use that time wisely it should be enough."

"Is this why you brought me here? I could have stayed in Bolivia where at least I had a life!"

"Let's not digress, Otto. You aren't here just for Jotto, and you know that."

Otto sipped at his drink, begrudgingly admitting to himself that Hans had been right to bring him to the United States. His twin, Ilya, had become an alcoholic just like their father had been, and she needed his help.

When Otto first came to Naples and saw Ilya, he had been mortified, and he had insisted that she be immediately hospitalized, but Hans had refused, pointing out that it would be a waste of time because Ilya was beyond help. Otto, believing that Ilya could get well, took it upon himself to work with her.

It had been months, and Ilya was still drinking but at least with Otto around she got dressed every day and maintained some semblance of normalcy.

* * *

When Jo came home from school Hans and Otto were waiting for her on the front porch.

"Did you have a nice day, sweetheart?" Otto asked adoringly as he kissed his niece on the cheek. His enormous blue eye sparkled with love; he was a brilliantly handsome man.

"It was fine, Uncle Otto," Jo said suspiciously.

Hans put his arm around Jo and led her into the house.

"Is something wrong?" she asked.

"Come and sit down, we need to talk," her father said.

Jo moved to the recliner, and sat down with a sigh. Her heart was pounding in her chest, and her throat felt dry.

"Uncle Otto and I believe it would be in your best interest if you went to boarding school next term," Hans said decisively.

"But why? I'm getting all A's. Why would you want to send me away? It's because of mother, isn't it? She doesn't want me here!"

Otto flinched and began nervously to bite his fingernails–wishing his sister didn't drink.

"Where did you ever get such a ridiculous idea?" Hans asked angrily. "Your mother is very ill, and that makes her short tempered, but that's certainly not the reason we're sending you away to school."

"It's not fair. I don't want to go!" Jo said disrespectfully, fearing change.

"Don't talk back to me, young lady," Hans snapped. "Naples has been a lovely place for you to grow up, but it has always been my intention to send you away when the time came. And as your father, I have decided that the time for you to go is now.

"As for your grades, I expect nothing less than A's. You must always be exceptional...always exceptional," Hans ordered menacingly. "Do you hear what I'm telling you, Jotto Wells?"

"Yes, Father."

"I expect you to become friends with the best people, the kind of people that will run this country one day, because you too will be an important person some day, and that can't be accomplished with you going to a tiny little school in Naples, Florida!"

* * *

Jo spent the next six years in boarding schools. Brilliant, she excelled in all her subjects and she was truly happy for the first time in her young life. Away from her father and uncle, she had a freedom that was heady and a metamorphosis began to take place.

Tall and lovely, her vivacious beauty and unbridled curiosity became a great attraction and friends were drawn to her. She was determined to experience life and was willing to try anything. A natural athlete, she skied the slopes in Switzerland with her friend Celia's family over the Christmas holidays like a child born of the snow. And tempted by the excitement, she wrangled a mountain climbing trip to Nepal with her friend, Claudia. She fell and broke her ankle and had to be flown back to the States. She recuperated at her friend's home, never telling her father about the accident.

*   *   *

Despite all her antics and outward appearances of confidence, Jo remained terrified of her father, never certain that she would be able to live up to his expectations.

During the summer months, Jo returned home to Naples, where she spent long hours under the scrutiny of her father and uncle. When she was feeling strong and her attention was focused she could ward off their advances, pretending to be hypnotized. But when she was tired or distracted, they managed to lull Jo into a stupor. Jo was confused and frightened. She retreated, blocking out those things she could not bare to think about.

To save her sanity, Jo escaped each morning at sunrise, taking refuge in the Gulf waters that lay only 150 feet from her back door.

*   *   *

It was her first day home for spring break of her senior year, and the sea was shimmering glass. Jo carried her raft out past the breakers, hopping on and paddling strongly. She stopped only when the shore became a smooth line on the horizon.

The sea made her feel alive and at peace as she held her breath and dove into the steel blue waters, reveling in the freedom and solitude she found at these magical moments. Drifting for hours, always knowing the sea would protect her and never carry her too far away, Jo allowed herself time to reflect over the past few months.

*   *   *

Her school, Wellsberry, outside of Boston, and the neighboring boys' school, Mildrith, held mandatory group dances that the painfully shy Jo had always attended with dread.

At seventeen Jotto Wells had turned into a strikingly beautiful young woman, and except for the blond hair, she was an exact replica of the mother she never knew; violet eyes, porcelain complexion and all. But Jo still didn't see herself as beautiful. At five foot eight, Jo felt awkwardly tall around men and entirely too smart.

Sitting stiffly in a wooden chair decorated with streamers and balloons, Jo listened halfheartedly to her friends as they gossiped about the boys who were so valiantly trying to get up enough courage to ask one of them to dance.

"Oh my God. There's Robbie Taxton, and I think he's headed this way," Judy Smollen said to Jo excitedly. "He's so fabulous looking, I think I'm gonna faint. Oh please, God. Let him ask me to dance," she squealed, straightening her skirt and throwing back her shoulders, revealing abundant breasts.

Despite herself, even Jo felt a quiver of anticipation watching him approach. He was; after all, quarterback of the Mildrith football team and without a doubt the school's best looking young man.

"How about dancing with me, beautiful?" Robbie said, looking directly at Jo.

"No thank you," Jo said, blushing with embarrassment. "I don't dance." "Look, I've just made a five dollar bet with my friends that you'd dance with me. I've been watching you for months, and I'm not leaving here tonight without dancing with you at least once!" Robbie said, crossing his arms over his chest and pouting.

Jo had never seen a male pout before, and she thought it made him look vulnerable and adorable.

He continued melodramatically, "You can't turn me down; my life would be ruined. I'd never regain my self-confidence, and all my dreams of being famous would bite the dust! Do you really want that on your conscience?"

Jo laughed. She stood up, gratefully realizing that Robbie was a good six inches taller than she was. Leading her out to the dance floor, he put his arms around her, holding her at a respectful distance as the band played a slow waltz.

"My name's Reginald Taxton but my friends call me Robbie."

"Nice to meet you, Robbie. I'm Jotto Wells, and my friends call me Jo."

Jo was instantly taken with Robbie's doe-like eyes that sparkled mischievously when he smiled, revealing perfect white teeth. His olive colored skin, and light brown hair fell into his eyes in a sexy, outlandish way as he moved, making Jo's breath catch in her throat. She knew that there wasn't a girl in the entire school who had not, at one time or another, gone after Robbie and now she knew why.

Jo waited with butterflies in her stomach for the slow dances, and each time they danced, he held her a little closer. By the end of the evening their bodies had merged into one rhythm, and Jo was in heaven.

She had never met anyone like Robbie before; he made her laugh, and he made her feel beautiful.

The evening was over in a flash, and when it came time to say goodbye, Jo felt desperate, believing with all her heart that she would never see him again.

They moved to the doorway together, saying little. Robbie turned to Jo and reached for her hand.

"I had a great time, thanks. I'll see ya, kid," he said whimsically as he walked away.

* * *

Jo tossed and turned all night, pretending that she was still in his arms. She wanted him to touch her, to kiss her, to love her, and in her dreams, he did.

As the sun peeked over the horizon, she got out of bed and stood in front of her bedroom mirror talking to herself.

"You're just a dumb country bumpkin who doesn't know the first thing about how to act with a boy in order to get him to like you, especially someone as sophisticated as Robbie," she said sullenly to her reflection.

Her friends had told her about his family in Boston and about how he spent his summers at the Kennedy Compound in Hyannis Port.

Why would he even bother with someone like me? He won his stupid five dollars! That's all he wanted, Jo thought as a tear slipped down her cheek. Angrily she wiped it away.

Jo didn't take a shower before class that morning so that his smell would linger on her skin. And for the first time in her entire life she didn't pay attention in class. When her teacher asked her a question, she actually said, "I'm sorry. I don't know the answer." Everyone in the room was shocked, but no one was more shocked then Jo.

* * *

She was lying on her bed that night when the hall monitor came and knocked on her door, "Jo, you have a phone call."

Damn, I don't want to talk to father right now. I'm really not in the mood to hear about how important my education is, and how important it is that I be accepted to Smith.'

Padding into the hall in her bare feet she picked up the dangling phone. "Hello, Father, how are you?"

"Hello beautiful. This isn't your father. This is an admirer who'll drop dead if he doesn't see those fabulous eyes of yours before the sun sets on another day."

Jo laughed, gloriously happy to hear Robbie's voice.

"You're outrageous, do you know that?" she asked breathlessly.

"I may be outrageous, but I'm also serious," Robbie replied gravely. "I'm going crazy, Jo. I've got to see you. We have to talk."

"That's impossible, I'm not allowed off campus."

He hesitated. "Sure you are. Just ask one of your friends how they manage it. I'll meet you at the soda fountain on Main Street at ten thirty. Please be there, Jo, please," he said, hanging up the phone.

Jo had always enjoyed listening to her schoolmates describing their ingenious plans of escape from campus after lights out, but she had never joined them simply because it had never occurred to her to partake in such folly; until now.

* * *

Jo had fallen in love, and she met Robbie that night and every night thereafter for the remaining two months of school.

They spent their evenings talking about everything: their pasts, their futures, their likes and dislikes, no matter how insignificant. Occasionally Robbie would manage to borrow a friend's car, and then they would spend hours necking in the back seat, steaming up the windows and their libidos.

"God, Jo, I want you. Please don't stop me," he begged, sliding his hand between her legs.

"Stop!" Jo insisted, pushing away his hand.

"I can't stand this, Jo. You have no idea how much pain I'm in when I leave you?"

"Oh Robbie, I understand. I'm in pain when we're not together also. I miss you so much."

"That's not what I'm talking about, Jo. It's not my heart that hurts it's…" Robbie stopped, not wanting to offend her.

Jo was aghast as it finally dawned on her what he was talking about.

"Listen, I'm sorry. I didn't mean to embarrass you. Men are just not the same as women, and when we get aroused and don't get relief, we hurt."

Jo was even more confused now. "Does that mean I'm suppose to lose my virginity so you won't have pain?"

"No," Robbie said angrily. "It means I love you, and I want you. Believe me, if it was only relief that I wanted, I'd have plenty of takers!"

Jo felt hurt. She'd never argued with him before.

"I love you, Robbie, but I'm saving myself for my wedding night."

"Why the hell did I have to fall in love with such a prude?" he said, tickling her playfully.

* * *

Robbie grew up in a privileged and happy home as the only child of an oil baron millionaire father, who dreamed of his son becoming President of the United States, and a socially prominent mother who could trace her genealogy back to the Mayflower.

As a young boy Robbie had been pressured to excel by his mother, who was intent on making sure that her husband's dreams became reality. Robbie found his mother's straight-laced behavior and stodgy attitudes tiresome, but as he matured he came to realize that it would be her connections, not his fathers that would open the doors to power–doors that would have otherwise remained closed.

Robbie's father had been born and raised in Texas, the son of poor dirt farmers. His deep accent led people to believe that he was a simple country boy, but Anderson Taxton was assuredly not that, having attended Yale, where he graduated first in his class.

The people who knew Anderson Taxton feared and revered him, as did his son.

"If my past was a little cleaner," Anderson loved to say to Robbie, "I might have been President of these United States; but hell, I had just too good a time growing up, and your mama was mortified at the thought of the papers revealing all of that. And damn, I just couldn't hurt your mama. But you, Son, well; you're a different matter. You'll go to the best schools, and you'll keep your nose clean, and then when the time is right, you'll enter politics. You got your mama's blood, and it runs blue, my boy. Blue enough for you to be President one day."

* * *

Robbie was going to Yale in the fall, and he was pushing hard for Jo to change her school from Smith to Wesleyan University in Middletown, Connecticut so that they could be together.

"It isn't that easy. My father's had his heart set on me going to Smith since I was a little girl, and you have no idea how stubborn he can be."

"Jo, I'm talking about our life together. You're going to have to stand up to your father, and make him understand!"

She had promised Robbie that she would talk to her father, and that had seemed so plausible when she was with Robbie, but now as she floated on her raft, it seemed an impossibility.

Jo faltered as she thought, *Father will be really angry. But, if I don't tell him today that I'm going to Wesleyan, I'll never have the nerve to tell him.*

* * *

Hans and Otto were sitting by the pool, deep in discussion when Jo sauntered over to them. She was covered in sand from the beach, and her hair was snarled and hanging in her face. She bent over and kissed her father and then her uncle.

"Uncle Otto, how's that gorgeous new wife of yours?"

"Elaine's fine. She went to Miami shopping with your mother. I'm afraid I'll be a poor man by the time they've returned."

Jo pinched his cheek, "Marriage agrees with you, uncle. You've never looked better."

Otto blushed, smiling. Hans had introduced Otto to Elaine, a small time actress, with a desire to marry well and settle down. At Hans's urging, Otto had married her.

The first time Otto had sex with Elaine, he had hypnotized her, insisting that she perform all sorts of perverted acts with him, but Otto found that unexciting because she was much too willing a victim. After that, he took her by force, sodomizing her as she begged for mercy. Threatening to kill her if she ever tried to leave him, Elaine remained, terrified for her life. As a reward for her silence and obedience, Otto spoiled her with expensive jewelry and a magnificent home. All in all, Otto was quite happy with the arrangement.

Jo remained the only person Hans and Otto really loved, and their manipulation of her was their only reason for living.

"Uncle Otto, I hope you don't mind, but I need to speak with Father alone," Jo said gently.

"I have a phone call to make anyway," Otto said, hiding his hurt feelings for Jo's sake.

As soon as they were alone, Jo began without preamble.

"Father, we've got to talk. I've met a wonderful young man, and I've made some decisions I want to discuss with you," Jo said, shaking visibly. To keep from striking her, Hans had to keep reminding himself that this was his child speaking to him in such a manner because he never allowed anyone to tell him what they were going to do. People in his life asked his permission and did what he said! Biting his tongue hard to keep from interrupting, Hans waited for her to continue.

"His name's Robbie Taxton. I met him at school. Father, I know you'll like him. He comes from a wonderful family and he's even going to Yale in the fall." Jo took a deep breath. "I want to go to Wesleyan University in Connecticut so that we can continue to see each other." *There, I said it*, Jo thought as she waited for her father's response.

Hans looked directly into Jo's eyes.

"So, my daughter is in love. It's quite obvious that you're happy, so…if this is what you want, this is what you'll have."

Jo jumped from the chair and threw her arms around Hans. "Oh, Father, I love you so much. Thank you, thank you, thank you!"

"Go get dressed, young lady, before you get sick. We'll finish our conversation over lunch and you can tell me all about this young man of yours."

Jo ran up to her rooms and grabbed the phone. The moment Robbie came on the line she yelled, "I did it! I really did, and he gave us his blessings. You're stuck with me now!"

Robbie laughed a deep, masculine, confident laugh. "I miss you so much. I want to hold you in my arms and smother you with kisses."

"So why don't you? "

"Angel, are you serious?"

"Are you coming or not?"

"Damn right, I'm coming. See ya soon, kid." Robbie said as he hung up the phone.

Jo knew him well enough now to know that he would be on the next plane to Florida, and she couldn't wait.

Lunch was an event for Jo as she chattered nonstop about Robbie. Hans and Otto looked knowingly at each other. They were aware of Jo's relationship with Robbie; she was followed everywhere, and had been from the moment she first left home.

"Liebling, we couldn't be happier. You have chosen well and we certainly are pleased. We look forward to meeting the young man," Hans said, grinning wildly. Jo had found the perfect man all by herself: ambitious, connected and destined for politics.

* * *

The Taxton ranch sat on 2,500 acres of prime Texas real estate. It had a shooting range, bowling alley, private movie theater, tennis courts, 3 swimming pools and a private airstrip.

Robbie's quarters were in the east wing, a 10,000 square foot section of the mansion complete with it's own kitchen and gymnasium. His room was filled with football memorabilia, and books. He pressed the intercom on his desk, his father answered immediately.

"Have you a moment to see me, father?"

"I always have time for you, son. You just hightail it right over here and we'll have ourselves some nice sweet tea," Anderson said, his voice booming with enthusiasm.

* * *

Robbie knocked on the door to his father's study.

"Come on in, my boy. It's so good to have you home." Anderson hugged his son and kissed him lovingly on the cheek, always greeting him as if they hadn't seen each other in days instead of hours. "The place isn't the same when you're gone. Now, what can I do for you?"

Anderson moved back to his desk. Robbie sat in the chair across from him.

"I need to borrow some money, dad."

"You do? You in some kinda trouble, boy? You go and knock up some pretty young thing?"

"No. It's nothing like that. I've met a girl; her name's Jotto Wells. I love her. Now, just hear me out. I don't plan on getting married until I graduate from college but I want to get engaged now."

"Well I'll be God damned! My boy in love," he said slowly, his southern drawl intensifying with every word. "Won't your mama be happy? You tell me all about this young lady of yours," he said, his sarcasm a mean and ugly thing.

"Jo's brilliant and beautiful," Robbie said stubbornly, disregarding his father's unexpected attitude. "She's strong-willed, which should fit right in with this family; she loves sports and wants a big family," Robbie said, feeling unexplainably threatened.

"And her family?" Anderson asked, his eyes angry and challenging. "Just what do you know about her family?"

"She's from a small town in Florida. Her father's a psychiatrist and she's an only child. What's going on?" Robbie could see the darkness in his father's eyes and he felt cold.

"Do you know what makes a great first lady?" Do you know what it means to come from a good family? I love you son, but you're a God damned fool sometimes!" his father shouted, exasperated.

"What are you talking about?" Robbie yelled back. "You don't even know her!"

"I know what I need to know. I've spent 18 years of my life making it my business to know what my boy does. And you can't marry this girl, no matter what your dick says."

"I can't believe you!" he stood up, intending to leave.

"You listen. Your young lady may be a very sweet young thing. I hear she's pretty as a picture and I've no doubt she's smart as a whip. But her father's a kraut! Got that, son? He's a German." Robbie sat, his knees suddenly weak. "We need the Jews if you're gonna get elected to anything in this country. And there's no way you'd get elected dogcatcher with a Nazi father-in-law. "

"He's a doctor, not a Nazi!" Robbie insisted.

"He's a Kraut. Forget about it. Fuck her if you want but you can't marry her. Not if you're serious about becoming President one day. You think about it, son. There's plenty of other woman. You're a good looking fellow and you'll fall in love a hundred times before the right one comes along. Think about it. It's your decision."

* * *

Twenty-four hours later Robbie Taxton picked up the phone on the desk in his room; it was after drinking a half a bottle of Scotch. He had spent the day in turmoil, speaking again with his father and then with his ever elegant, always in control mother.

"I know you're hurting and that breaks my heart," his mother had said, her jewel like eyes brimming with tears. "And I know that you think you'll never be happy again. But In this life we have to be willing to make compromises if we aspire to greatness, my son. You're handsome, brilliant and moneyed. You'll fall in love again. Just tell the young lady it's over. Believe me, that's the most humane way to do it. Just call and end it."

He dialed Jo's number. While waiting for her to come to the phone he rehearsed his lines, hoping that the numbness would remain and his brain would not defer to his heart.

"Robbie, where are you? When are you coming?" Jo asked, breathless and excited.

"I"…he faltered, the sound of her voice creating the vision of her. "I don't know how to tell you this. I've given our relationship a lot of thought and I'm convinced that we've rushed into this too quickly. We're too young, Jo. We haven't had enough life experiences. And I'd never forgive myself if you changed schools because of me." He heard her stifle a cry and felt wounded. But Robbie knew that the final words must be said. "We both need to see other people."

"I don't understand," Jo said, her voice a whisper. "I thought you loved me."

"I'm sorry, Jo. I'm really so very sorry. It's just not going to work. Take care of yourself."

"You too."

Jo hung up. Her hands were trembling, and her eyes burned from the tears that threatened to fall. She willed them away. *He doesn't want me. Well, the hell with him. I don't need him. I don't need anyone.* And then the tears came; her safety net evaporated and the loneliness and rejection set in–her world and dreams crumbled.

Chapter 37

───────── ★ ─────────

Smith College, founded in 1871 as a liberal arts college for women, was the largest college of its kind in the United States. Located in the picturesque city of Northampton, Massachusetts, on the Connecticut River, it offered Jo a place for solitude and contemplation; and it's tradition of high academic excellence both stimulated and challenged Jo's intellectual curiosity.

No longer the rebellious teenager, she worked hard and played little, graduating magna cum laude. Pleased with her compliant behavior and excellent academic achievements, Hans encouraged Jo to attend the school of her choice—New York University Law School.

New York City was a dream come true for Jo. She became instantly smitten with the exotic flavors of its diverse population and cosmopolitan trappings. And just like the mother she never knew, Jo was enchanted by and drawn to the theater.

On the few free evenings afforded her by her demanding law school schedule, she headed for Broadway to watch the performers weave their magical webs.

One such performer, for whom Jo quickly developed an addictive fascination, was the famous French Broadway actor Robert Osborne. She never missed an opportunity to see him perform, often standing in line for hours to buy tickets for his shows. Her law school friends teased her about her infatuation, but Jo remained undaunted and unaccount-ably attracted to the aging actor.

* * *

As a gift for Jo's twenty-fourth birthday, her best friend Merrill's father, a Broadway producer, arranged backstage passes for the girls to meet Robert.

As she sat in the darkened theater, only five rows from the stage, Jo's stomach churned while she worried endlessly what clever thing she might say to Robert to make him notice and remember her.

When the performance ended, Jo joined the audience in a standing ovation, ecstatic that she was about to have her greatest fantasy fulfilled.

Robert bowed, delighting in the applause. His stage presence had not diminished over the years, and at fifty-five he still retained his lean, hard body and the enchanting smile that radiated a sexiness and danger women of all ages found irresistible. The curtain fell and was then raised again. As he accepted the accolades graciously, his mind turned to Morgan. Although almost thirty years had passed since he had last seen her, he never took a bow without thinking of her.

He left the stage finally and hurried to his dressing room, where William, still his constant companion, was waiting for him.

"Great performance."

"Thanks."

"You've got a crowd waiting to meet you."

As Robert changed into a pair of navy slacks and an alpaca sweater, he replied, "Then let's get it over with."

* * *

In the reception area of the theater, Robert was lifting a glass of wine to his lips when he saw her. His hands began to tremble and the glass slipped through his fingers, crashing to the floor. An excruciating pain shot through his left arm and chest, squeezing off his breath and causing him to stagger. "Good God, man, what is it? Are you all right? Call an ambulance!" William yelled, his own heart pounding as he helped Robert to a nearby chair.

"Look at her. My God, look at her!" Robert said in a strangled whisper.

William scanned the room, and when he saw Jo he gasped.

"Do you see her?" Robert asked.

"There must be a logical explanation, a remarkable coincidence or something," William said.

The security people had begun to move the visitors out of the area. Robert reached for William's arm.

"Stop her! You've got to stop her," Robert said, momentarily oblivious to the pain gorging in his chest.

"OK. But please, you must calm yourself," William said as he rushed into the hallway.

* * *

Jo was moving towards the door when she felt someone touch her arm.

"Excuse me, Mademoiselle. Before you leave, Mr. Osborne would like a word with you," William said, trying to appear calm.

"He wants to see me? Are you sure?" she asked.

The cadence of Jo's voice caused William to flinch. This young woman not only looked like Morgan but sounded like her as well.

"I'm quite sure. Please..." he said, taking her arm.

The sight of Jo approaching thrust Robert backward in time.

"What's your name?" he asked weakly.

"Jotto Wells, but my friends call me Jo."

The sound of her voice shocked Robert as much as it had William.

"Take it easy, an ambulance is on the way," William said, noticing his friend's face turn a steely gray.

Terrified, Jo backed away. "I hope you feel better," was all she could say.

"Your number…give William your number. I must see you again, Jo Wells," Robert said as his vision blurred and his breathing became more labored.

"Let us through, out of the way!" the paramedics ordered, rolling in the stretcher.

William took Jo's arm.

"Is he going to be all right?"

William looked at her, but didn't answer. "Do you have transportation home?"

"Yes, thank you. My friend is waiting for me."

"Are you listed in the phone book?"

"No, I'm not. Do you think he's really going to call me?" Jo asked.

"As soon as he's feeling better, you can count on it."

Jo took a scrap of paper from her purse and jotted down her phone number.

* * *

Robert remained in the hospital for two weeks, having suffered a minor heart attack that had caused no permanent damage. But his recovery had not gone well. His constant worry and agitation over the encounter with Jo Wells continued to take its toll.

Vowing to stay away from her until he knew more, Robert hired a team of private investigators. Seven weeks after his meeting with Jo he was handed a fifty-page dossier on Dr. Hans Wells and his wife Ilya Milch Wells.

Clyde Turner, the head investigator, summarized for Robert: "As far as we could ascertain, Dr. Wells was with the resistance forces during the war. And if the Wells' did have a child born during that time, we couldn't locate the birth certificate. But I must tell you that doesn't prove anything, since the German government denied us access everywhere we turned. I had the definite impression that Dr. Wells must have had some very strong political connections. What we do know is that Jotto Wells has a Florida birth certificate that states she was born at Lee Memorial Hospital in Ft. Myers, Florida. Unfortunately, the obstetrician who delivered her has died. You'll see in my report that the girl was raised in Naples, Florida. Her father, the good doctor, has a penchant for beautiful women and is in the habit of seducing his patients. We also know that the wife, Ilya, has battled a drug and alcohol problem for years.

"We thought our most promising lead was Ilya's twin brother Otto. According to our connections in Bolivia, Otto Milch was supposedly involved with the SS during the war; but again, it was only hearsay. We could find no concrete evidence.

What we do know for certain is that both men worked with the United States government after the war. Many of my CIA friends swear that the United States helped relocate hundreds of Nazis in return for information about the Russians. But proving that would be next to impossible. I'm sorry I don't have better news, sir."

* * *

"She has to be Morgan's child. And if she is, Morgan didn't die when the Nazi bastards said she did. William, she might even still be alive," Robert said, once they were alone.

"If she were still alive, my friend, don't you think you would have heard from her?"

"I don't know, damn it! All I know is that Jo has to be Morgan's child," he repeated. "They must have bribed some official to get their hands on a forged birth certificate. But who could the father have been? How? Tell me, William, how could she have been with someone else?"

"Terrible things went on during the war, Robert," William offered. "After she was captured, anything could have happened."

"My God, that's what I can't bare to think about," Robert said, his voice breaking.

"Robert, you must get a hold of yourself before you get sick again. And you must begin to accept that there is nothing you can do to change anything."

Robert looked at him incredulously. "What do you mean, there's nothing I can do?"

"I mean just that. Do you plan on telling Jo that her parents aren't her parents and that her father is a Nazi? Do you plan on ruining her life? What will that accomplish? These people obviously don't want her to know about her past, and it's not up to you to tell her," William said.

"I have to tell her. Can't you see that?"

William put his arm gently around Robert. "No, my friend, I can't. Just be her friend, Robert. That's really all you can do."

* * *

The phone rang in Jo's apartment while she was studying for final exams.

"Hello," she answered distractedly.

"Jo, this is Robert Osborne."

Jo gasped, unable to find her voice.

"Are you there?" he asked, thinking the connection had been broken.

"I'm sorry. Of course I'm here…I was studying."

"Do you want me to call back later?"

"No. I mean, it's fine…I can talk. How are you feeling?"

"Back to normal." Robert was trembling, and he was glad she couldn't see him. "I was wondering if you'd have dinner with me tomorrow night?"

Why now? Why in the middle of exams? "I wish I could, but I have finals all week," she said, holding her breath.

"How about next week?"

"Next week would be great."

Robert felt relief wash over him. His greatest fear was that she might refuse him.

"How about a week from Sunday, around eight?"

"Perfect," Jo said, giving him her address.

They spoke for a few more minutes, and when Jo hung up she immediately phoned Merrill.

"I can't believe it!" Jo screamed. "He called, he really called. I'm having dinner with Robert Osborne."

* * *

The week dragged for Robert, and by the appointed night he was irritable and nervous. He was putting on his coat when William came into the room.

"I want to talk to you before you go," William said, motioning Robert to sit beside him on the couch. "We've been friends for over thirty years and I'm worried about you."

Robert began to speak but William held up his hand. "Hear me out first. Since the heart attack, you've not even had the strength or desire to go back to work; and now, by seeing this girl, you're placing yourself under the very strain that brought about the heart attack in the first place."

"Bull shit," Robert said. "You heard the doctors. I was a time bomb. It was going to happen no matter what. Sure the shock might have brought it about a little sooner, but that wasn't what caused it."

"Why not humor me a little and let me tag along?"

Robert shook his head. "I've never had a chaperone, and I sure as hell don't need one tonight. Thanks anyway. Besides, if I remember correctly, you weren't much help that night. You almost had a heart attack yourself."

"Yeah, right," William said as he walked with Robert to the door. "Don't scare her, Robert. Don't say too much."

"Jesus, you really have so little faith in me. I told you I wouldn't tell her, and I won't."

* * *

Conversation flowed easily as they rode to Robert's favorite French restaurant, L'Ami Louis, on the upper west side of the city. The bistro was quietly elegant; and the patrons, used to being around celebrities, barely glanced up from their dinners as Robert and Jo passed by.

Robert ordered champagne and then they discussed the menu. He was impressed by her easy command of French, as she ordered her dinner. A bottle of Dom Perignon was uncorked, and Robert sipped and nodded his approval to the waiting bar steward.

"To new friendships."

They touched glasses. Jo drank quickly, hoping to quiet her nerves. The conversation turned to the theater and Jo's finals.

"May I ask you something?" Jo said.

Robert nodded. *How much like her mother she is—curious and forthright.*

"I'm really flattered, but why are you so interested in me?"

He looked at Jo for what seemed an eternity before answering. "You remind me of someone, someone I loved very much."

"What happened to her?"

"She was killed during the war."

"I'm so sorry," Jo said.

"She was an incredible woman," Robert said, wishing he could tell Jo he was speaking about her mother.

"War ruins peoples lives," Jo said.

"Yes, my dear, it does. But you see, it's men that cause those wars. You would think we would learn our lesson, so many needless deaths. But enough about all of that, I want to hear about you," Robert said, determined to lighten the mood.

Jo chatted easily, painting the picture of an idyllic life. At times she seemed to be reciting her words by rote. Robert felt uneasy.

"And what will you do once you graduate from law school?" Robert asked.

"Enter politics," she said.

"That's certainly an unusual career for a woman," Robert said, feeling an unexpected chill as he thought about what Dr. Hans Wells might be planning for her future.

"I guess it is, but not for me. I was spoon fed that notion from the time I was a small child. My father had this idea that a woman could be anything she wanted to be. When most children were being read bedtime stories, I was being read the world news."

"And that didn't bother you?"

Jo seemed confused. "It's just the way it was in my house. There wasn't much time for childlike behavior. I was always being given deadlines for projects my father created. He couldn't stand mediocrity and I guess I just accepted that," she replied, a sadness slipping across her face.

"And what will you be, Jo Wells—Senator…President?"

Jo's face burned red. "Are you making fun of me?"

"Making fun? Absolutely not, my dear. It's important for this country that idealistic, bright young people go into government. I'd very much like to help you when you're ready."

"That's very kind of you, but why would you do that for me?"

"Maybe it's ego. I love being seen with a pretty woman."

Their laughter came easily.

"We're going to be great friends, Jo," he said.

* * *

From that night on Jo saw Robert almost every day. And for a very long time, despite herself and their age difference, she had romantic inclinations towards him. But because Robert never allowed her romantic illusions to take wing, she gradually accepted that they were to be nothing more than close friends.

Chapter 38

———— ✱ ————

Jo's years at New York University law school were a test of her endurance and determination. By her final year she had memorized so many case studies that she felt her brain had reached some kind of critical mass. To make matters worse, many of the men in her classes felt threatened by Jo's intelligence, and their chauvinistic attitudes made Jo's life miserable. But she persevered, becoming stronger with each passing year.

Drawn to criminal law, Jo had hoped to apply to the Public Defenders office after graduation. Committed to helping the less fortunate, she spent her few free hours doing grunt-work research for the Legal Aid Society.

Three months before graduation Jo finally mustered the courage to tell her father she wanted to practice criminal law. He reacted as she anticipated—he was infuriated. Jo argued that criminal law was an excellent stepping-stone into politics, but Hans refused to consider her assertions, and in the end she acquiesced.

* * *

Two days after graduating in the top five percent of her class, the prestigious New York firm of Stubengoord, Wurth and Brandt interviewed Jo. The interview was strictly a formality; enormous funds had been spent over the years to insure Jo's future. Not only had her employment been assured, but also a five-year plan was in effect to make Jo the firm's youngest and first female partner.

* * *

Jo was twenty-six when she joined Stubengoord, Wurth and Brandt in 1967. The United States was in the quagmire of the Vietnam War. The U.S. troop deployment neared 500,000 and the body count continued to escalate. In response, the frustrated took to the streets in antiwar demonstrations. In New York City 300,000 people marched from Central Park to the United Nations headquarters. Robert was among them. Jo had wanted desperately to join him, but her firm and her father forbade her to participate in the demonstrations.

In 1969 Richard Nixon became President of the United States. The end of the Vietnam War was in sight, and the mood in the country began to change.

* * *

Jo was her firm's political liaison, and for the next two years she attended every important fundraiser in the city, making contacts and positioning herself firmly within the highly cliquish Democratic Party. Enormously popular, she began being mentioned as a possible political contender for the State House of Representatives.

In 1970 Hans and his comrades decided that the time was ripe. Cajoling and maneuvering behind the scenes, the Nazis called in their favors. Jo's nomination was secured.

* * *

Jo avoided telling her father about her complicated relationship with Robert, because she knew he would never approve. She also knew she could no longer hide the truth.

Sitting in the Park Avenue apartment Hans had given her as a graduation present, she told Hans about Robert. Of coarse Hans all ready knew–he knew everything Jo did.

"Robert Osborne's endorsement will be a wonderful asset to your campaign," Hans said, outwardly calm, inwardly frantic. Over the years Jo had grown to look more and more like Morgan; and while Otto and Ilya never mentioned the resemblance, Hans lived in constant fear. Now that fear intensified ten fold.

* * *

Hans did not know that the twins had known the truth for years. They had discovered it the year Jo turned fourteen and came home for the summer. She had grown and changed greatly over that school year, and as Otto and Ilya sat by the pool watching her take long fluid strokes through the water, the truth became evident.

"She's absolutely magnificent," Otto said.

"You really love her?" Ilya asked, more out of curiosity than jealousy.

"Yes, I really love her. I guess I'll always be partial to women who look like Morgan."

The twins looked at each other and gasped.

"My God, that's it! She looks just like Morgan," Otto said, bounding out of the chair. "I'll kill that lying, no good son of a bitch!"

Ilya grabbed Otto's arm. "No you won't. Sit down this minute," she ordered. "We have to talk."

It didn't take them long to figure out what had really happened in the camp fourteen years earlier.

"It's our turn now," Ilya said. "It's our turn to use him." Her eyes glistened with hate and anger. "Hans isn't dispensable yet, but one day he will be. You have your work cut out for you, Otto. You must ingratiate yourself with his friends so that they begin to think of you and Hans as one. That way, when the time comes for me to eliminate him, you can simply take his place. It may take twenty years, but one day..."

Otto looked intently at his sister, sensing her power for the first time. "It will be me who watches the life leave that bastard's eyes. It will be me who kills him—me and me alone. I want your word that you won't interfere," Ilya said.

Otto nodded, understanding finally that her soul was indeed as black as his.

* * *

Jo was thirty years old when she ran for the New York State House of Representatives. Once that nomination had been secured, Hans went immediately back to Naples, insisting that he had to return home in order to care for his patients. In fact he feared his German accent might hinder Jo's election in a predominantly Jewish district. He was also intent on trying to postpone his inevitable encounter with Robert Osborne.

Robert immersed himself in Jo's campaign, taking great pride in introducing her as the first woman to ever run for the House of Representatives in the State of New York. Jo's oratory style was exceptional. Her self-assured presence and her outspoken honesty captivated the press and electorate. She won the election in a landslide and went off to Albany in a flurry of accolades and excitement.

Then Hans reappeared, deciding it was now time for him to take a more active roll in Jo's life, regardless of Robert Osborne's presence. But once the two men met and Hans saw the absolute hate in Osborne's eyes, he returned to Naples.

Meeting Hans and intuitively believing that he was Jo's father devastated Robert. For years he had held tightly to Morgan's memory. Now the memories were being obliterated by the hate he felt for Hans Wells.

* * *

Jo missed the City and Robert, but she adored her new life in Albany regardless of the long hours and low pay. While she sat in her office on a beautiful fall day, lost in paper work, her secretary Maggie buzzed the intercom.

"Mr. Blumenthal is here, Representative Wells."

Jo straightened her skirt and came from around the desk, waiting for Maggie to show him in.

Aaron Blumenthal was a very important man in the Democratic Party, representing that all-important Jewish vote in the State of New York.

"Aaron, how wonderful to see you again," Jo said, extending her hand.

Aaron hesitated, having never quite gotten use to shaking a woman's hand. Fighting his natural urge to resist, he shook it.

"It's so good to see you again, Jo. I always forget how magnificent you are. In fact, you're the most beautiful woman I know," Aaron said, his eyes sparkling.

"Will you stop," Jo said, blushing brightly.

"I can't help myself. You always have this effect on me. Maybe it's because you also happen to be the smartest woman, maybe even the smartest person I know, and that still bothers the hell out of me."

Jo grinned. "Aaron, you're absolutely hopeless. You know, being a male chauvinist in 1971 is not exactly in vogue. In fact, your limited flexibility towards women underscores why change is so desperately needed and so hard to come by."

Aaron feigned a hurt expression. "See, all you women are the same. You throw the insults around and then men of good breeding, like myself, have to smile and continue to act like gentlemen."

They both laughed.

Aaron Blumenthal filled the room with his presence. At 6'4" he was broad-shouldered and solidly built. His hair was black with streaks of premature silver and his eyes were dark and mischievous. He had a cleft in his chin and his nose was a bit too sharp, but it all went together strikingly, giving him an air of easy sexuality and confidence. And when he smiled, which he did often, his face looked almost cherubic. Jo thought he was one of the most appealing men she had ever known.

He took a seat in the chair opposite Jo's desk.

"Would you like a cup of coffee?" Jo asked, reaching to buzz her secretary.

"No, thanks. I have to go back to the City as soon as we're finished, so I'll save my coffee till later."

Jo tried to mask her disappointment. She had been nurturing a secret infatuation for Aaron and had been looking forward to spending the evening with him.

Aaron felt pensive and nervous, emotions that were foreign to him. "One of these days we'll have to find time for a quiet dinner together." He smiled. "Now, if you'll excuse me for being somewhat abrupt, today I'm here to do some recruiting on behalf of the United Jewish Appeal."

Jo threw her hands up in the air, doing her best imitation of Humphrey Bogart. "OK, OK, you can have my money. You can have as much as you need, sweetheart."

"Funny, very funny. Maybe you should give up politics and go on the stage."

Jo gave him a sheepish grin. "I'm sorry, I just couldn't resist. Go on, please. I'll behave."

"I've come here to extend an invitation for you to join me and a group of business people and your fellow legislators as our guest in Israel." Jo caught her breath as Aaron continued. "We want you to go to Israel so that you can learn about the country firsthand, forming your own ideas and reaching your own conclusions. The truth is, Jo, we need friends, and I believe your friendship will be invaluable to us in the years ahead."

Jo barely heard Aaron. Her mind had been flying over her life. She remembered well the first book she had ever read about the Holocaust and Israel, Leon Uris's *Exodus*. All during high school, despite her subtle anti-Semitic upbringing, Jo had been obsessed with what had happened to the Jewish people. She had grown to believe that if one single act in history had meaning to her, it was that time when all reason and all humanity seemed to have died. In her dreams Jo would hear the children calling to her from their graves, begging her to help them. She kept this obsession to herself, never understanding why she felt so compelled when it came to the Jews.

Aaron watched Jo closely, refusing to admit to himself how badly he wanted her to be with him on the trip.

"I'm honored you've asked me, and I would very much like to go. When are you leaving?" Jo asked, openly excited.

"The nineteenth of April. Israel is its most beautiful then, and it's also our holiday season."

"I'll have Maggie block the time off. I'll take it as a vacation."

Aaron smiled. "Thank you, Jo."

"Thank you for asking me."

Aaron rose.

"Do you really have to leave so soon," Jo asked, as she accompanied him to the door.

"I'm afraid so." Impulsively, Aaron brushed his lips across Jo's cheek. "Next time, try kissing me hello. You just might learn to like it.

Hand shakes are a man's business," he said, winking at her before leaving the office.

∗ ∗ ∗

Aaron's driver was waiting by the curb. The weather had turned chilly, but Aaron didn't feel it. He wasn't sure what he was more excited about, the fact that Israel would have a new friend or the thought of being with Jo Wells for ten days.

"The airport, please," he said, moving easily into the car.

Leaning his head against the smooth leather on the back of the seat, Aaron closed his eyes…remembering.

He had been a small child on that cold November night in 1939 when his mother held his trembling hand while walking through the town of Tourmai, Belgium. Aaron had been so confused, trying to understand why his parents were crying. Arriving at a tiny cottage on the outskirts of town, Aaron was introduced to the Grunwalds. He could still remember the tension that had filled the Grunwald's home that night. He was haunted by the look on his parents' faces as they smothered him with kisses, making him promise that he would always be a good boy. He had been too young and too distraught to realize what was happening to him that night, but he had never been able to forgive himself for not telling his parents how much he loved them.

The Blumenthal's had sacrificed their only child; and in return, all they had asked was that Aaron be given the Grunwalds' Christian name so that he would be protected from Hitler's grasp.

The childless Grunwalds were good people who loved Aaron unconditionally, never allowing him to forget who he was and where he had come from. He returned their kindness by never giving them any trouble and always being respectful. But Aaron felt destiny call, and when the war was finally over and he was old enough to leave, he did.

He traveled to America with money in his pockets, given to him by his adoptive parents. Passing through customs on Ellis Island, Aaron had given his name as Blumenthal, thereby resurrecting the memory of his family. And upon arriving in New York City, he had gone directly to a synagogue. He had picked up a prayer book and said a prayer for his dead parents, reading aloud and stumbling over the transliteration of the Hebrew words. Out loud he had prayed, carrying out the long overdue duty he had felt towards his dead parents. But to himself and to the God he had grown to hate he said, my people lived on the brink of hell, begging for your mercy, but you didn't help them. You've destroyed everything I ever loved, but you haven't destroyed me. If this was some sort of competition, you lose.

He had stood up then with tears running down his cheeks, crying for the past, for his dead mother and father and for the millions who had no one left to cry for them. Aaron had left the synagogue that afternoon determined to succeed.

He studied English at night and drove a cab during the day, and when he had perfected the language, he applied to City College and was accepted.

The next four years flew by. He commanded attention wherever he went, as people were immediately drawn by his charm, mannerisms, and good looks. At graduation Aaron Blumenthal stood at the podium as President of his Senior Class.

Finance degree in hand, he fielded dozens of offers, finally accepting a position with The Chase Manhattan Bank.

Aaron had used his first paycheck as a down payment on a Brooks Brothers suit, at the time a symbol of success. He fully intended, even though he lived in a fifth-floor walkup with no hot water, to portray himself as a successful businessman.

Before long Aaron had established a network of wealthy friends who looked to him for financial advice. He began by advising them on minor investments, but soon they were turning to him for major capital investments. Aaron was extremely insightful and his friends had made enormous amounts of money.

Now, fifteen years later, as he sat in the back of a Cadillac limousine headed for the Albany airport, Aaron Blumenthal had gotten his reward. He was president of one of the most prestigious banks in the country, Overland Mutual.

An idealist, he was a dedicated Zionist who loved both Israel and his adopted country, America. Infused with a passion for politics, Aaron had cultivated many important friends, giving generously to the campaigns of like-spirited candidates.

Arriving at the airport, Aaron was suddenly hit with an idea. *I should ask Jo to invite Robert Osborne to join us? If he agrees…talk about publicity!*

Aaron stopped at the first pay phone he could find and dialed Jo's number.

"Listen, I just had a great idea. Why don't you invite Robert Osborne to join us?"

Jo could almost see the Cheshire smile on Aaron's face. "What a brilliant idea. They always said you were a genius, Aaron."

"OK, so I'm transparent. What can I say? I just thought that…"

"It's all right, Aaron, I'll ask him. I'll even beg him if you'd like."

"Beg, Jo. Israel needs some good press."

Jo hung up the phone, feeling a sudden chill in the room, as if she weren't alone. *I wonder if I can convince Robert to go with me. It's time he began to face his past.*

For years Robert had shared the letters he received from Claire and Saul with her, delighting in the fact that they had named their first child after Robert's dead wife Morgan.

Wouldn't it be wonderful if I could get him to visit them? Maybe it would help him to finally close the wounds. He might refuse me, but

I won't let him refuse easily, she promised herself, rising to greet her next appointment.

* * *

Two weeks later, Jo arranged to spend the weekend in New York at the Park Avenue apartment. She instructed the housekeeper to put fresh flowers in every room and then told her to remain out of sight as much as possible during the evening.

Jo eagerly met Robert at the door.

"You look ravishing," he said.

"It's so good to see you," Jo said, throwing her arms around him. "Are you hungry?"

"I'm always hungry."

"Then let's go right into dinner," Jo said, reaching for Robert's hand and leading him into the dinning room.

The Herend china and Grande Baroque sterling silver set an elegant table. Drinking wine from Baccarat crystal glasses, they chatted easily as they hungrily demolished their lobster bisque soup and roasted hen with truffles.

An hour and a half later, sitting on the sofa, Jo snuggled against Robert. She began talking to him in a lazy, little-girl voice that made his ears perk up. He instantly knew she was up to something.

"You know, I had the nicest invitation extended to me a few weeks ago. I was invited to Israel," she said.

Jo saw a black shadow pass across Robert's face. Frightened, she was about to ask him if he was all right when his face suddenly relaxed.

"Sorry, I was just a little surprised, but now that I think about it…I'm happy for you. As a matter of fact, I think it would be good for you to go."

She gave him her brightest smile. "You've been invited to go along."

"Oh, and who extended this invitation?"

Jo smiled proudly. "The United Jewish Appeal."

Robert looked at Jo and laughed. "Your friend Aaron Blumenthal wouldn't be behind this, would he?"

"He's looking for media attention, and you can help get him that attention."

Robert looked troubled. "Jo, our taking a trip together would put our faces on every gossip tabloid in the country. Is that what you really want? It might not be good for your career."

Jo shrugged. "Like they haven't been speculating for years. Have you read the latest story in the *Mirror*? They say we're secretly married, and that I'm going to have a baby. But let's stay with the issues. You've always told me how you would love to see your godchild and your friends. Why not go?"

Robert wondered how he could articulate what he had trouble even thinking about. "What's all this really about, Jo?"

She hesitated, not wanting to hurt him. "I want you to face your past and let go. It's wrong to only love one woman your whole life. I can't believe that Morgan would have wanted that. Maybe if you go to see Saul and Claire, you'll be able to get some type of closure."

Robert got up and began to pace. Jo's words had catapulted him into the past and he could see Claire standing on the train platform so very long ago, with tears streaming down her face as they hugged good-bye. He could almost feel the warmth of her cheek against his face.

He thought about how much courage it took for his friends to remain in Israel. It had been a difficult life. Claire had suffered and survived malaria, their kibbutz had been attacked numerous times by the Arabs, and worst of all, their second child had died. Robert should have gone to see them years ago, and he realized he had run out of excuses.

He sat down next to Jo and took her hand in his. "I'll go with you," he said quietly. "And I'll try to find the soul I guess I lost somewhere along the way." "That's all I ask, Robert. Just try."

They sat quietly for a few minutes and then Jo began to giggle.

"What's so funny?"

"I forgot to tell you a story I heard about Saul." She hesitated, allowing Robert's curiosity to build. "A senator friend of mine, who will remain anonymous, went to Israel on a Finance and Funding Mission for the President. Saul was the head negotiator representing Israel. Anyway, as my friend tells it, they walked into this sterile hotel room, and when Saul shook hands with the senator, he said, 'I have a friend in your America—a big star. His name is Robert Osborne.' Well, guess what happens next? The moment he says your name, he gets all emotional and excuses himself from the room. My friend figures he has easy sailing ahead, and that your friend is going to be a pushover.

"As it turns out, he was in for a big surprise. Now, don't get angry, but my friend said Saul was the most pigheaded, unreasonable man he'd ever met. Protocol meant absolutely nothing to him. He told them point blank, 'We're Jews. We've learned the hard way that we have to take care of ourselves because no one else gives a damn. History has proved that to us time and time again. Your government wants to "loan" us money because they need to have our friendship in the Middle East. They loan us money for their own interests. We all know that; so don't try to dictate policy to us. Just give us the money and go away.'"

Robert laughed. "I guess he hasn't changed much over the years."

Jo looked deeply into Robert's eyes. "He sounds terrific to me. I'll bet you fifty dollars we become best of friends."

"No bet. I have no doubt you will."

"It's so strange–like I'm a part of them already." Her vacant expression changed to a smile. "I spook myself sometimes. How about taking me dancing? I need the exercise."

* * *

Later that night Robert lay in his bed visualizing Morgan, speaking softly to her, as was his nightly custom. "She sure is your daughter. I said I'd go, but I don't know why. Why is everyone trying to take you away from me? Why can't they just leave it as it is?" He sobbed into his pillow. "If only I could touch you. If only I could hold you just one more time, to smell your fragrance, to touch your hair."

He fell into a deep dreamless sleep that night, his first sleep not maddened with nightmares in over twenty-five years.

Chapter 39

——————— ★ ———————

A deeply troubled five year old who suffered from nightmares and bed-wetting was Claire's last patient of the day. After putting her final comments on the child's chart, Claire searched through a pile of papers until she found Robert's latest letter. She reread it, still finding it difficult to believe that he was actually coming to Israel after so many years.

Claire looked around her office, realizing that Robert would see it as a total mess. But it wasn't a mess to her; it was the product of years of begging, hoarding, and bargaining—what it took to obtain possessions on a kibbutz.

In the far corner was a child-size table and chairs where Claire's patients sat to draw pictures that gave her insights into the workings of their young minds. A dollhouse large enough for the children to crawl into faced the courtyard window, and dolls of every description lined an entire wall. Stacks of coloring books were haphazardly piled on a rickety old table. Overflowing file cabinets occupied every available nook and cranny, and on the floor next to her desk sat years of reference books and medical journals.

* * *

Claire closed her eyes, blocking out everything. She took a deep breath in order to relax as the vision of Morgan appeared in her mind's eye. She too had never forgotten the light and joy of Morgan's spirit, and just like Robert she had never gotten over the loss. What Claire never admitted to anyone was that she believed Morgan was still alive, stranded inside some Communist country, unable to escape.

Claire patted at her hair absentmindedly, tucking in stray hairs that had come loose from the braid she wore twisted into a bun at the base of her neck. Her strawberry blond hair had faded with time, but it was still thick and lustrous. Tiny lines crinkled around her bright green eyes when she smiled, and her deeply tanned, freckled face was still inviting and vibrant. At fifty-six, Claire was a stunning woman.

* * *

Shortly after her arrival in Palestine, Claire had taken a Hebrew name, as was the custom of the newly arriving Jewish immigrants. She chose Rebecca, the name given to her by the old rabbi who had married her and Saul. And then, despite Saul's objections that it wasn't necessary, Rebecca had gone through a full-fledged Orthodox Jewish conversion. Becoming a Jew hadn't been all that difficult for her, but understanding what it meant to be one of "the chosen people" had been.

As a Jew living in the State of Israel, Rebecca had become strong and tough, but she had never lost her keen sense of humor or her ability to laugh at herself. She soon learned that as a Jew, if one didn't laugh, one couldn't survive.

Her children, all eight of them, had also been raised within the yoke of Judaism. And just as she had promised, her first-born daughter had been named Morgan, despite pressure that such a name was not in any sense of the word a Hebrew name. When her other daughters had been born, Rebecca followed the tradition of her newly adopted religion by naming them after the Prophetesses: Devora, Rifka, and Esther. And her four boys she had named after great men in Jewish biblical history:

Yaakov, Abraham, Moshe, and Hillel. Ranging in age from eighteen to twenty-eight, her children were her glory. They were all Sabras, born into and unto the State of Israel. Indeed, Saul had done to her just what she had sworn he would not do—he had kept her pregnant for almost nine years.

Rebecca's head began to pound, and her hands began to shake as she remembered Miriam. *Yes, my little one, my sweetest, I'm not leaving you out of the count, nor do I ever forget you.* Their second child had been a daughter—so sweet, so happy, and so very sick. They had watched her die, moment by agonizing moment, from leukemia.

Rebecca didn't know how they had survived that ordeal. The children continued to be born and the world had gone on, but something in Saul and Rebecca had died when their child died. Rebecca had fought the demons that had threatened to destroy her life, and she had eventually won, but the scars had remained.

She went on to raise strong, independent, and totally self-sufficient kibbutzniks who had now begun their own lives. Rebecca fiercely loved her family and she had given them deep roots, love, and then wings to send them on their way. They had their lives to live, and she and Saul had theirs.

Rebecca's professional accomplishments had been hard won, and a source of great pride. Rebecca Lipinsky was a nationally recognized, many times published psychologist whose specialty had always been small children. But in the past few years Holocaust survivors began to seek her out. The survivors of the Holocaust were tortured people, and for some reason as they aged the memories and nightmares had returned and become unbearable. Rebecca couldn't refuse to see them.

Rebecca was often absent from the kibbutz, traveling to Europe and Scandinavia, speaking about the psychological effects the Holocaust had on the survivors, especially those who had been in the camps as children.

Rebecca had recently concluded an extended stay in Jerusalem, after completing a workshop for survivors. And Saul, who constantly worried that she was pushing herself too hard, had insisted on picking her up at the King David Hotel. After kissing her on the cheek, he had loaded her papers and luggage into the trunk of their five-year-old Mercedes, surprising Rebecca with a well-deserved vacation in the seaside city of Eilat on the southernmost tip of Israel.

The road to Eilat cut through the Negev Desert, a barren landscape of valleys and mountains. It was during a particularly tedious stretch of road that Saul decided to vent all his pent up concerns and frustrations.

"Rebecca, you can't take on the entire Holocaust problem by yourself. Have you looked in the mirror lately? Do you see how tired you look? Am I supposed to sit by and watch you work yourself to death?" As Saul spoke he grew angrier, and by the time he had finished his monologue he was shaking so badly he had to pull his car to the side of the road.

"I brought you here. I feel responsible for what you're doing to yourself. And it's not just me, Rebecca; the children are just as worried. Every time you give one of these workshops, you seem to age five years. I'm asking you to please slow down. Please learn to say no once in a while."

Rebecca had been wounded by Saul's words. As a doctor who studied human behavior, she understood what he was and was not saying. *Had she neglected him? Was she being a bad wife?*

"I can't stop, Saul, and you know that. If I drop dead from exhaustion, so be it. Know that if that happens, I died a contented woman. I'll face our God and I'll tell Him I tried to right the wrongs. I tried to lift the veil of pain that covers so many of the innocents."

She had taken Saul's hand in hers. "I love you. For every moment of pain I've suffered, I'd do it all again just to be near you, to share my life with you."

She began to cry then, softly at first and then with total abandon. "I'm so tired. Sometimes I think I would welcome death. I would smile at her and say, take me. I want to talk with God. I have so many questions I want answered. Damn it, Saul, when I leave these seminars, I feel like I've viewed hell. No matter how many times I hear the stories, I just can't desensitize myself."

"Talk to me about it. Can't you tell me anything? I feel so left out and so inadequate. You used to share your pain with me. Now you simply tuck it away. Why?" Saul had asked.

Rebecca thought for a moment before answering.

"I don't want to drag you into this hell with me. I want you to stay focused on the work you're doing. It's too important. You live for today and work for tomorrow. I live in the past, reaching out my hand to people who are trying to keep from falling into the abyss."

Saul had listened patiently, saying nothing. Rebecca didn't know if he understood or if he ever could, but it didn't matter, she knew she could never stop.

* * *

The intercom on her desk buzzed, bringing Rebecca rudely back to the present.

"Father John is here," her secretary Kaveva said, announcing her next appointment.

For years Rebecca had met with priests and ministers when they came to Israel. Because of her knowledge of Christianity, she had become a sort of ambassador to the religious gentile community, establishing a rapport that helped bridge the gap between Jew and gentile.

Rebecca was amazed by how little the Christian ministry really knew about the Holocaust. But when she finished with them, they knew a lot—sometimes more than they could handle. And when that happened, she availed herself to them as a friend and a doctor. She was sure that was why the American priest, Father John, had made an appointment to see her today.

"Father, it's so nice to see you again. I hope I didn't keep you waiting long," Rebecca said, extending her hand to the cleric. "You were vague with my secretary as to why you wished to see me. How can I help you?"

Rebecca was never sure how to begin these sessions. They always left her exhausted and frustrated, and as she looked at Father John, the old feelings of anger and frustration began to emerge. She had never been able to understand the role played by the Catholic Church during the war years, and she had never been able to reconcile herself as to why the Pope hadn't spoken out against Hitler or tried to stop the slaughter. Jesus had been born a Jew and raised to be a rabbi, and she had always felt that that alone should have been enough reason for the Church to speak out. But the priests were coming to Israel now, and Rebecca had taken it upon herself to educate them by repeating stories told to her by the survivors.

"Doctor, I know you're busy and I really appreciate your seeing me on such short notice," the priest said. "As I'm sure you know, I came to Israel on a pilgrimage, and I've become enamored with this land and its people. But I've become deeply troubled. You see, I've always believed that I was a good example for my parishioners. As a matter of fact, my parish in the United States has grown to over a thousand families." The priest hesitated, the pain clearly visible on his face.

"I thought I understood about the Holocaust, but I didn't." His face paled and he seemed to be unable to go on.

"Would you like a shot of whiskey, Father? It sometimes helps to take the edge off."

Rebecca poured him a drink from the bottle she kept stashed away in a file cabinet drawer. On more than one occasion, she had reason to pour herself a drink as well.

Father John drank down the whiskey in one swallow and after a few moments he continued. "Eight hundred thousand innocent children were slaughtered. I still can't believe it. I didn't know."

Rebecca understood. She didn't have to encourage him to continue; she knew he would.

"Over the years, I've officiated at many marriages between Catholics and Jews, and I've seen the pain on the faces of the Jewish parents. I had always discounted those feelings because it was my contention that with Jesus their children would be saved and that they should thank me for giving their offspring a chance at redemption. I know now that I was wrong.

"Please don't misunderstand what I'm telling you. I believe the Lord Jesus is the Savior, and I believe the acceptance of him is absolute and necessary. But my religion also teaches us that we must be compassionate. In this area I know that I've sinned.

"I should have understood. I should have been gentler with the parents. Millions of their people died for the right to be Jews, and I plucked more away without a second thought. I shouldn't have acted so callously. How do I make amends to the families? How do I live with myself?" "Father, I can't absolve you of your pain," Rebecca said. "That's between you and God. You did what you felt was right at the time, and who's to say that you were wrong? Yes, maybe you could have been more understanding towards the parents, but I don't think it would have eased the pain. What I can tell you from my own experience is that once someone's a Jew they're always a Jew. Oh, they may not practice their religion, and they may even take the vows of another, but in reality being a Jew isn't something you can ever walk away from. You're here in Israel at this time for a reason. Go back to your parish and try to help people understand what really happened. If you want to help the Jewish people, try to remember just one thing: when someone tells you that they're tired of hearing about the Holocaust, you make them understand. Remind them that we must never forget. Only in the forgetting can it ever happen again. One more thing, Father, when two people are in love, religion is only a minor obstacle. They won't listen;

they never have. If we have one hope, it's that one day religion will serve to unite the peoples of the Earth instead of driving them apart."

The Father rose to his feet, taking Rebecca's hand in his.

"Thank you for your help."

"Thank you, Father."

Rebecca sat pondering their conversation after he left, wondering why God had put him in her path. And then upon opening her journal to begin the outline for her next symposium in England, the answer came to her. She would organize a panel of priests and rabbis to begin a long overdue interchange of thoughts on Catholicism and the Holocaust, and she would invite Father John to sit on that panel.

She glanced down at her watch and jumped up from her chair. *I've been sitting here for an entire hour, and now I'm going to be late for dinner. I must really be getting old. Young people don't sit and meander through time when they're supposed to be eating. Maybe I should straighten all of this up before Robert comes?* Then she said aloud, "Ack! I'm a mess. My office is a mess. Who cares?"

"Who cares indeed?" Saul said as he entered the room.

"You scared me to death. I thought I was alone."

"Darling, if you're going to talk to yourself, you really should say kinder things. And you're not a mess. As a matter of fact, I think you're the most beautiful woman in all of Israel," Saul said, taking Rebecca into his arms and kissing her.

"And you, sir, are as blind as a bat, but I thank you for the compliment. Now, what are you doing here? Why aren't you at dinner?"

Saul looked at her with concern. "I was at dinner, but when you didn't show up, I became concerned. So here I am. Now tell me, what happened? It's not like you to miss a meal."

Rebecca handed Saul Robert's letter.

He read it once, and then reread it. "I'll be damned!" he said. "Finally he comes. I'm glad, really glad. And you, my dear, are you OK with his coming?"

Rebecca bowed her head, concealing her tears.

Saul gently lifted her face and kissed them away.

"It's time to bury Morgan. Perhaps together we'll all be able to do that."

His words hurt Rebecca. She had buried her child and grieved, but Morgan had never been buried, and Rebecca had never been willing to let her go. But the truth remained—she would never see her friend again and it was time to face her grief once and for all.

Three weeks before Robert was due to arrive in Israel, Saul was hand-delivered a letter through diplomatic pouch. It read as follows:

* * *

Dear Saul,

I look forward with great anticipation to our meeting. I can't explain and I don't expect that you will understand, but I must insist that you do not meet me at the airport in Tel Aviv. Arrangements are now being made for us to have a private reunion. You will be notified in advance of my arrival as to when and where.

Until then,
Robert

Chapter 40

————————— ★ —————————

By pulling up their collars and turning their heads, Robert and Jo managed to slip by the first group of reporters and photographers at Kennedy International Airport, but as they neared the El Al counter, they were spotted.

"Mr. Osborne, are you and Miss Wells secretly married?" a reporter shouted.

"I'm old enough to be her father," Robert said. "We're simply good friends."

"Then why are you going on this trip, Mr. Osborne?"

Aaron felt a slight pang of guilt when he saw the look of displeasure cross Robert's face.

"Do I have to answer these questions?" Robert asked, looking forlornly at Aaron.

"Just answer the ones you want to answer," Aaron said.

Jo prodded Robert playfully. "Don't be such a grump. It'll only be for a few minutes."

Robert spent five minutes more with the reporters.

"You've missed your calling, Aaron. I haven't been this exploited since my dalliance with Elizabeth," he said as they moved away.

Aaron looked sheepishly at Robert. "Sorry."

"No you're not," Robert said, laughing as they entered the lounge area designated for El Al passengers. The businessmen, politicians, and their aides, having already passed through the throng of reporters, were milling around, waiting to board.

Robert's presence caused a stir, and Jo could see how much that pleased Aaron. Excusing herself, she walked to a seating area far away from the excitement. Between her father and preparing to leave her office for two weeks, Jo had been under tremendous pressure; she was exhausted and glad to have a few moments alone.

* * *

Her father had read about the trip to Israel in the papers before Jo had a chance to tell him that she was going and that Robert would be going as well.

"How dare you make those kinds of plans without consulting me first? You have no business going there," he had said.

"I want to go," Jo responded. "Besides, I believe it's an excellent decision politically. Are you forgetting that a very large portion of my electorate is Jewish?"

"Forgetting?" Hans screamed, his voice quaking.

Jo had to bite her tongue to keep from shouting back. She knew she had stepped over the line, and the terror she felt towards her father returned.

"If I upset you, Father, I'm sorry. I just wanted to take a vacation."

"We'll talk about it later," Hans said, hanging up the phone.

* * *

Twenty-four hours later Hans appeared unannounced at Jo's Albany apartment. He had spent hours in discussion with his comrades, eventually deciding that it would be auspicious for Jo to be seen in Israel, although, to their great dismay, it put Robert Osborne's ultimate demise on hold yet again.

Still, Hans was furious with his daughter's insolent and disobedient behavior and he had lectured her for hours, while Jo sat docilely, agreeing and apologizing as necessary. But Hans remained angry.

"Father, I made a mistake. It won't happen again," she said finally.

"See that it doesn't."

Jo had grown accustomed to her independence and she resented her father's overbearing behavior. Yet, instinctively Jo knew that she had to indulge him.

* * *

A hostess offered Jo a glass of wine, which she accepted and drank too quickly; it made her dizzy.

"Hello, Jo."

"Robbie?" Jo went cold, her body reacting to his voice as she stared into the eyes of the man she'd almost married.

"It's been a long time. May I sit down?"

Jo nodded.

His nearness was disconcerting; it brought back the rejection and pain—the years of never understanding why.

And even though she never spoke of Robbie, she had continued to follow his career, privately pining for her lost dreams. When he was elected as the youngest member of the United States Senate, Jo felt proud that he had accomplished his goal and sad that she wasn't by his side. And despite her resolve that she was over him, Jo had been devastated when his picture appeared in the *Washington Post* with his new wife, the socialite, Ashley Merriweather, with a caption that read: "Will Camelot Reappear?"

Jo felt as certain then, as she did now, looking into his doe-like eyes, that Reginald Taxton would sit behind the desk in the Oval Office one day.

Robbie, who thought he was prepared for this encounter, watched Jo intently, his heart burdened with regret. Over the years he too had nurtured the fantasy of what might have been: sneaking into crowded rallies to hear her speak, watching silently, unable to stay away.

"You must be very proud of yourself. My spies tell me you've been slated to run for the Senate. Perhaps we'll be colleagues," he said. "As a woman, you're blazing new roads, but then again I always knew that you would. "

"Senator, I do believe we've both achieved a modicum of success. You have a fabulous looking wife and a career that's skyrocketing. I guess we both accomplished what we set out to do," Jo said, giving him her most beguiling smile.

Robbie felt the sarcasm and visibly flinched, suddenly fearful that his going was a huge mistake.

"I guess we have to be careful what we wish for," Jo continued. "I have everything I ever dreamed of, and yet I often feel like I'm running on empty. Does that surprise you, Senator Taxton?"

Robbie held his breath, wanting to hear more but afraid of what she might say. *If only I could be as honest as she's being. If only I could tell her how I never stopped loving her.*

Jo hesitated, knowing that she had already said too much; but she couldn't stop herself. "I've been in love exactly once in my entire life." Her voice choked with emotion; her eyes brimmed with tears. "After that, I never even got close. There were men in my life, but something in me was dead. I guess I kept looking for someone who could make me feel the way you had made me feel, but it never happened."

"Listen, I know I hurt you but I never stopped…"

"Please," Jo said, standing abruptly. "It's a lifetime too late."

"I just want to be your friend, Jo."

"I'm not sure that's going to be possible, Senator," Jo replied, moving away.

Robert was deeply engrossed in conversation when Jo joined him, slipping her arm through his for support. He could feel her trembling. He had been watching her out of the corner of his eye, and he had never seen her look at anyone the way she had been looking at Senator Taxton. *Was there something between them?* Robert put his arm around Jo.

"Are you all right?" he whispered.

"Yes, I'm fine."

Aaron was also watching the exchange. He glared at Robbie. He knew of his reputation as a womanizer and he was worried that he might be making a move on Jo.

* * *

Robbie sat on the couch watching Jo; sadly comprehending the damage his rejection had caused the only woman he had ever loved.

His wife flashed in his mind, and Robbie felt the pathos of indescribable regret. Ashley had wanted to be First Lady, and Robbie had needed a wife who would help get him to the White House. Ashley was beautiful, talented, bright, and her family was the *right* family. He had not married out of love, but Robbie admired Ashley and their relationship actually worked out for a while. But when they settled into the routines of daily living, their personalities clashed; Robbie was miserable and in need of some true passion in his life. He hoped to find it with Jotto Wells.

Jo knew that Robbie was watching her. She also knew that a fire was rekindling, making her alive with desire, and that desire made her feel sick inside. Jo lived by a strict set of principles, and at the top of that list was her rule that she never dated a married man.

* * *

In the first class section of the El Al jet, Jo cuddled up next to Robert, sleeping fitfully. Her dreams were filled with haunted visions of Robbie touching and kissing her and then in an instant he was kicking and punching her. Grotesque images of her father haunted the dream. His lips were moving but his words were unclear. Uncle Otto was in the dream as well, sneering and holding the silver cigarette case, its haunting music screaming in her ears. He kept telling her that she was to listen, listen, listen. Jo began to moan.

Robert shook her awake. "What is it? What's wrong?"

"Nothing, just a bad dream. Sorry if I disturbed you."

Robert took Jo's hand. "Go to sleep, child. Think about pleasant things. I'm here with you, and you're safe."

* * *

The plane touched down in Tel Aviv at 7:30 P.M. but the group didn't arrive at the King David Hotel in Jerusalem until well after eleven. Reporters and dignitaries greeted them at the hotel, and by the time Jo finally got to her hotel room she was exhausted. Yet sleep eluded her. The eight-hour time difference had been debilitating. She decided to call Robert's room. But he didn't answer the phone, which didn't really surprise Jo; from the moment they had arrived in Israel, Robert had seemed to collapse into himself. When she had asked him when they were going to see Rebecca and Saul, he had told her it wouldn't be for a few days. That had seemed strange to Jo, but she said nothing. He must be in the bar drinking, she now thought sadly.

Jo lay in bed tossing and turning, frustrated with her inability to sleep when the phone rang. She reached for it, happy to know that someone somewhere was also not sleeping.

"Hi, beautiful. Did I wake you?"

"Aaron? Thank God you called. I wish I'd been sleeping. I'm going crazy!"

"That's what I figured was happening. How would you like to throw on a pair of jeans, a heavy sweater, and meet me in the lobby?"

"I'll be there in ten minutes."

She washed her face and dressed. And when the elevator opened into the lobby, Jo was greeted with her first lesson in Israeli behavior—Israelis don't sleep. It was three o'clock in the morning: glasses clinked, cigarette smoke billowed, and conversations were loud and animated. Aaron was leaning against the wall waiting for her.

"I'm so glad you called," Jo said, kissing him on the cheek.

"So, finally I get kisses," he said. "I'm most definitely coming up in the world."

Aaron was thirty-seven, yet tonight, dressed in a bulky woolen sweater and jeans, his hair messy, his eyes sparkling mischievously, he looked years younger.

"Where are we going?"

"I'm taking you to one of the most unique places on earth," Aaron said, leading Jo out into the chill Jerusalem night.

"And where exactly is that?" Jo asked.

"We're going to the Wailing Wall."

"Don't you mean the Kotel?"

"You've got to be kidding? How did you…?"

"As I recall, it's the western wall that surrounded the ancient Temple." Jo smiled, child-like in her ardor. "It's all that remains of Jewry's holiest shrine. Your people have been praying there for thousands of years." She smirked, taking Aaron's hand. They walked slowly through the winding streets of the Old City, eerily quiet, surrounded in a golden darkness.

"This is a magical, God-like place. I can almost feel a presence," Jo said dreamily.

"Some people say that."

They were nearing the holy sight, and as the courtyard opened in front of them, Jo caught her first sight of the golden dome that sat atop the ground that was once the holiest Jewish Temple.

"Tell me about the Mosque," she said, thrilled by the vision.

"I thought perhaps you'd tell me."

"I don't know much about it. It's not my area of expertise." Her smile was playful; she punched his arm. "Come on, tell me."

"It's called the El Aksa Mosque. The Moslems believe that the Prophet Mohammed ascended to heaven on a white stallion from that very spot."

They looked at each other and smiled.

"I'm overjoyed by your knowledge. You must have really hit the books before the trip," Jo said.

"Actually, I didn't. Jewish history's been a hobby of mine for years. Come on. Let's go."

They descended the long, uneven stone stairway that led to the massive courtyard. Dozens of people, mostly men in uniform, milled around, some praying in front of the wall, others talking in hushed tones.

"Ah, the notorious fence." Jo said, her tone edged with disapproval.

"One side's for the men, and the other for women. It's just how it is," Aaron said as if that explained everything.

She watched as a young, machine-gun-toting Israeli soldier covered his head with a prayer shawl and moved towards the Wall. The soldier began to sway back and forth in a mystical rhythm that seemed so strangely familiar and comforting to Jo. An old man was also praying, and rocking back and forth in the same eerie fashion.

The incongruity of it all sent chills down Jo's spine as she looked around at the obviously tense soldiers guarding the perimeter of the area.

"This is always the first place I visit when I come back to Israel. It reminds me of who I am and just how blessed I am to be able to come here," Aaron said, interrupting Jo's thoughts.

"Tell me, Aaron, do you have to be a Jew before you can approach the Wall?"

"No, as long as you follow protocol, which is really no big deal. You have to cover your head and be dressed modestly...which you are. Would you like to walk down?"

"I think I would."

"We Jews, who I must admit are somewhat superstitious, consider it good luck to write a wish down on a piece of paper and then place it in a crack in the wall. Would you like to do that? It couldn't hurt," he said, looking at her sheepishly

Jo found a scrap of paper in her purse and quickly jotted down her wish, asking God to help her remain true to herself.

Aaron took a skullcap out of his pocket and placed it on his head. "I didn't have a Bar Mitzvah as a kid but I did have one as an adult. This is the yarmulke I wore when I officially became a man, and I wear it whenever I come to Israel."

He took out his piece of paper and walked away from Jo. As he neared the Wall, an old rabbi handed him a prayer shawl. She watched with admiration and respect as Aaron began his ritual of prayer.

Jo walked through the opening in the fence on the women's side. An old lady sitting in a makeshift little booth smiled and handed her a scarf. Jo took it, nodding her thanks as she put the scarf over her head before walking cautiously towards the Wall.

The women's side was almost empty, and as Jo neared, she noticed an entrance into a stone building off to her right. A young woman was sitting in the corner near its doorway on a chair that faced the Wall. In her trembling hands she held a tattered prayer book, and she was crying uncontrollably. Jo sensed that the young woman was in mourning.

Tentatively Jo touched the wall. Standing there for a moment holding the paper in her hand, she felt the cold stone beneath her fingers. As she searched for a crevice to put her paper in, a sensation of sheer joy enveloped her.

Jo stood for a very long time at the Wall, eventually touching the stone to her lips and then to her cheek. The stone felt like the kiss from a warm summer sun, and Jo lost all sense of time. She was being awakened…called…invited.

Chapter 41

───────── ✶ ─────────

Jo backed away from the wall. Her emotions were playing havoc with her intellect and she was desperate to resolve the conflict. Spotting Aaron sitting on the steps at the back of the square, she rushed to his side. Aaron took the pale and obviously frightened Jo into his arms, holding her tightly.

"Are you OK?"

"I don't understand what's happened to me," she said. "First I was cold, then I was hot, and then all these voices started talking to me. It's like I went away or something. I feel like I'm losing my mind."

Aaron gently touched Jo's cheek with his open palm. "You're exhausted, and when people are exhausted, their imaginations and their emotions can get the best of them. I shouldn't have brought you here at this hour."

Jo looked curiously at Aaron, trying valiantly to clear her head. "Look, I realize all this sounds totally outrageous, but I could hear them," Jo said. "You've got to believe me!"

"I do believe you. Sit here with me for a moment and try to calm down," Aaron said, pulling Jo down beside him on the steps.

As they sat side by side, Jo slipped her arm through Aaron's, wondering if she dare confide in him.

"Aaron," she said finally, deciding to trust her instincts, "something else really strange happened to me, and I know if I don't talk about it right this moment, I'll convince myself that I made it all up," she said. "When I put my cheek against the wall and closed my eyes, I saw a woman. She looked exactly like me—the same eyes, the same features, only her hair was different. It was like looking at myself…only it wasn't me. She just stared at me. And when she smiled, I thought my heart would explode from the love I felt.

"She kissed me on the cheek," Jo said, reaching up and placing her trembling hand on the spot where she'd been kissed. "Right here. I've never felt such love. And when she spoke to me, her voice was so soothing and kind. I wish you could have heard her. She kept saying that she and I were one and that she prayed for my life and my happiness every day.

"Right before she disappeared she said, 'We will meet again.'" Jo watched Aaron's expression carefully. Sensing no scorn, she continued. "Logically, I want to say it was my alter-ego trying to tell me something, but I know it wasn't. Aaron, what does it all mean? It felt so real; I'm so confused."

"Perhaps if I tell you what happened to me the first time I came here, you won't be so frightened," Aaron offered, deciding to share with Jo an experience that had been the turning point of his adult life.

"I came here when I was a very angry man. I remember approaching the Wall in 1968 as if it were the enemy, thinking to myself what a joke it was that people came here to pray. Because of the Holocaust, I believed that God was deaf to a Jew's prayers. I hated him for giving us the Commandments. I had come to the Wall to tell him that. I didn't write a prayer. I didn't cover my head.

"As I was approaching the Wall, an old man walked over to me and put his hand on my arm; I pulled away. He stared at me and then he removed his prayer shawl. Kissing the words written on the edge, he placed it over my head and shoulders; I was furious. I had no intention of giving in to the ways of the Orthodox Jews.

"'Your heart is cold as ice, my son,' he had said. I was mortified by the truth of his words; I didn't move. 'Is your life so tragic that you believe you have a right to close out the Almighty?' I remember the unexpected tears as I listened to his next words. 'Is this what your parents would have wanted? Will you give the Nazis the ultimate victory—your soul?

"'Recite the Kaddish with me, Aaron, so that the God of Abraham, Isaac, and Jacob will know that you've learned to forgive.' When he said my name, I was sure I was going crazy. And then the old man whispered in my ear, 'Remember the words of Isaiah. "When the soul is sick, we begin to believe that evil is good and good is evil, that darkness is light and light is darkness. We take bitter for sweet and sweet for bitter." You must not live your life like this, my son. Come now. Come and pray the words of our ancestors.'

"And I did, Jo. I walked to that Wall, and just like you, I got lost there as the generations reached out and touched my heart. I had no book, but I had the vision of my father and mother, and they helped me to remember the words."

Aaron was unable to continue. He turned his face away from Jo so that she wouldn't see his tears, and they sat that way for a long time.

"Walk with me, Jo," Aaron said finally, putting his arm around her.

Day was breaking, the sky turning a resplendent pink and gold. The sounds of people beginning to stir throughout the Old City served as a wondrous background; Aaron continued. "The old man gave me back my faith, and from that day on, everything became clearer to me. I began to understand why I was here.

"I believe you were given a message tonight as well. You may not understand what that message means right now, but someday you will."

Aaron stopped and turned toward Jo. His ruggedly handsome face was tense and drawn as he bent down, kissing her gently, lingering, lost in the sweetness of her.

"You're my adorable little shiksa, and if things were different, I would throw my hat in the ring," Aaron said.

"It wouldn't be much of a fight, Aaron Blumenthal…not much of a fight at all," Jo said tenderly.

They walked on in silence, each lost in their own thoughts. At the door of her hotel room Aaron took Jo into his arms, kissing her hungrily, longing for intimacy.

Then the voices began to scream in Aaron's head. Tidal waves of guilt washed over him. He willed the sounds and feelings away, but to no avail. Using every ounce of his willpower, he pulled away from her.

"It's late. I'd better go."

Alone in the hallway, Aaron leaned heavily against the wall. Jo was a shiksa, a gentile, and he knew he could never have her.

Jo was distraught, confused by Aaron's abrupt departure. She collapsed on the bed, sobbing. She had been so sure he had also experienced how right they were together. Hurt by Aaron's seemingly flippant remark about her being a shiksa; she tried to rationalize her feelings for him. Perhaps it was seeing Robbie again: maybe she just wanted to be wanted. Her mind was swimming in confusion from a day too wrought with emotion; she drifted off into an exhausted sleep.

* * *

The Mosad agent was waiting for Robert when he entered his hotel room.

"Shalom, Mr. Osborne. My name's Dov. When you're ready, I'll drive you to the American Embassy," he said in the telling Israeli accent of a Sabra.

"Thank you. I'd appreciate the opportunity to change my clothes and take a quick shower first. It's been a long trip, and I feel like shit."

"I'll be waiting," the agent said, his expression unreadable.

A half-hour later Robert was sitting in the back seat of a black Mercedes, speeding through the hilly countryside on his way to Tel Aviv.

* * *

It was midnight, April 16, 1971. Rebecca and Saul sat in the living room of the United States Embassy. Their nerves were raw as they waited.

"May I bring you something to drink?" the Embassy aide asked solicitously.

"I'd love some coffee," Rebecca answered.

"Nothing for me, thanks," Saul said, his gentle, sun-creased face darkened in worry. "Rebecca, are you all right?"

"I'm really nervous, but I'm determined not to fall apart when I see him."

Saul smiled knowingly.

"You'll fall apart, Rebecca. Accept it."

"Thanks for the encouragement," she said, moving to the window.

Saul watched her as he lit his fourth cigarette in less than half an hour. He couldn't wait to see Robert: to finally show him what they had created with their vision and determination—a land where their children could be proud to be Jewish, a country that by its very existence could have served as a safe haven for Morgan, saving her and the millions of Jews who had perished in the Holocaust.

The door opened, startling Saul out of his musing.

"If you're not a sight for sore eyes!" Rebecca said, jumping up and running to Robert. She threw herself into his arms, kissing and hugging him tightly. "Let me look at you," she said, holding him back, examining, her eyes flooded with tears. "My God, my dear God, how I've dreamt of this day."

Saul approached his friend. They shook hands: tentative, shy, and then they hugged, boyish, child-like, loving.

"Look at us! Finally together again after so many years," Rebecca said, hugging them both. "Now come and sit down, you must be exhausted."

Robert smiled at her.

"The years have been good to you, Claire. He stammered self-consciously. "Sorry, I meant to say Rebecca. It takes some getting use to. Anyway, you're even more beautiful than I remember. My God,"

Robert said, "I still can't believe I'm really here. Your children, tell me about the children?"

Rebecca smiled. "They're Sabras, Robert—Israelis. What more can I say? They were born in the State of Israel and raised as soldiers. They're tough, courageous, and consumed with Nationalism that boarders on fanaticism. You'll understand better when you meet them."

"Your parents must be so thrilled…eight wonderful grandchildren."

"I don't get to see them very often," Rebecca said sadly. "When the children were small I used to go back to Paris at least once a year, but as the children grew they began showing less and less interest in going. It hurt me but I understood why. I'm afraid my mother and father never managed to establish much of a rapport with their grandchildren. I don't think they liked that their grandchildren—or their daughter for that matter—were such zealots. For years I tried to get them to visit, thinking that was the only way they'd ever really understand any of us. But they were too afraid. I've learned to live with their decision," Rebecca said. "But at least we have Saul's parents," she added brightly.

"I know, and I think that's terrific," Robert said, remembering Rebecca's letters about Saul's family.

"It really is," Saul said, recalling the events that had led up to his parents' coming.

Before the Nazi storm the Lipinsky's liquidated their ample resources, tucking the money safely into a numbered account in Switzerland. They then fled France, moving to the United States where they purchased an enormous estate in the wealthy suburbs of Long Island. They soon settled into the same insulated and assimilated life they had known in Europe.

But when the truth about the war began to emerge, Saul's father had become racked with guilt. He began going to the synagogue daily and took to writing ten-to fifteen-page letters to his estranged son. Eventually father and son managed to establish a loving and trusting relationship through their correspondence.

"They came for a short visit and never left," Saul said. "I brought them to our home in the mountains of Israel, where I gave them my most precious possessions—my children, their grandchildren."

Robert said, "I'm happy it turned out like that, Saul."

"Thanks. So am I."

"I don't think either of you will ever know how much I worried for your safety. I never understood why you stayed," Robert said.

"All we ever wanted was a homeland for our people. When Israel became a state in 1948 and the Arabs attacked, we had no choice but to fight."

"We had to grow up fast," Rebecca said. "We had two small children hidden away in the Children's House when they attacked our kibbutz. We were forced to take up guns in order to protect our families and ourselves. And I admit that I considered leaving Israel and Saul after that first Arab attack. We had spent years turning the flooded malaria-filled swamps into lush farmland, and the Arabs came and needlessly set our crops on fire. But my fellow kibbutzniks took that act of terrorism in stride, pointing out to me that the fields could be replanted." Rebecca sighed. She touched Saul's arm, and he took over.

"It was in the burying of our dead that we cried and felt the true agony of war. Dozens of our settlers, who had managed to cheat death in the concentration camps, were killed; the pain of those losses was excruciating. The entire population of our kibbutz tore their clothing and mourned. It was—"

"It wasn't all bad, Robert," Rebecca interrupted. "We had our glorious moments as well: harvesting our first crops, sitting on the sweet-smelling grass at sunset while our fellow kibbutzniks preformed a concert musicale. We even got to see Arturo Toscanini conduct the Israeli Philharmonic Orchestra. I guess you could say that those were the moments that made our lives worth living."

"Unfortunately," Saul said, "peace never seems to last long, and I'm worried about my country's complacency. I think the Arabs are up to something."

"Maybe you're being overly pessimistic?" Robert said, easy in the conversation, as if a lifetime hadn't passed.

"Not if you look at the history of this country. In 1956 we had the Sinai Action; and in 1967 we had the Six-Day war. We quadrupled the size of our territory, and the world took note that Jews could be fierce warriors when need be.

"The problem today is that too many Israelis believe we've fought our last Arab war, but I don't think the Arabs are through with us."

"Maybe they're not," Rebecca said, "but they'll never drive us out."

Robert had always been impressed by their accomplishments, but being here and feeling the energy of their commitment kindled a fire in his own soul.

Rebecca took Saul's hand. "I'm sorry if we sound so maudlin. The truth is, we've had a good life together, Saul and I. I've never been sorry that I came here with him."

"She was nuts to come with me, and she's still nuts," Saul said. "It hasn't been easy for her; I've been away from the kibbutz more often than I've been here."

"And I hear you're very good at what you do. I hear you're one of the toughest negotiators the Americans have ever had to deal with," Robert said proudly.

"Ah," Saul said, waving his hand. "I speak for my people. I'm not great. I'm just me. I came here filled with idealism and dreams that could have easily died the very first winter we spent in the Golan. But people like David Ben Gurion and Golda Meir and love for the State of Israel kept me going when I faltered."

"I'm so proud of you both. I'm only sorry that Morgan's not here with us," Robert said, needing to mention her name, needing to acknowledge his love.

"I owe her so much," Rebecca said. "Every time I wanted to give up and every time I felt lost, I saw Morgan's face and remembered how brave and determined she'd been. That always reminded me that I could do it too."

Saul stood up and began to pace. "I spent hundreds of nights wading into the Red Sea to help new immigrants to shore. Every time I reached for a hand, I imagined I was reaching out for Morgan. More than anything, I wanted her to be among those who had survived."

"Thank you for that," Robert said. "She's as alive for me today as she was on the night I first saw her perform thirty-eight years ago."

"I've never stopped missing her," Rebecca said, swallowing hard to push away the tears.

"You were the sister she never had, and she loved you very much. That night we left you at the train station, she cried for hours."

After a brief silence, Robert continued.

"I asked to meet you here tonight instead of at the airport because I have some incredible news to share with you both," Robert said, struggling to find a gentle way to break the news. "Perhaps you had better sit down, Saul. Robert took a deep breath. *God, give me the strength.* "Morgan had a child; I've brought her here with me."

"Oh my God!" Rebecca cried. "I don't understand."

It took Robert almost an hour to tell them his entire story, including everything he suspected.

"I need your help," he said in conclusion.

Stunned, Rebecca and Saul sat silently.

"Whatever happened," Rebecca said finally, trying to regain a composure that was rapidly disintegrating, "I know that Morgan never stopped loving you. And I know she'd have never willingly let another man touch her," her accusatory tone not lost on either man.

Saul reached for Rebecca, enfolding her in his arms. "Calm down, darling; I know this is difficult for you." Looking at Robert, Saul continued, "If this man who's posing as Jo's father is in fact the father, what then? Will you kill him? How will you live with the knowledge that might be uncovered?"

Robert felt himself grow tense. "Honestly, I don't know. But I can't continue on like this. I need answers."

"I don't know about you," Rebecca said, "but I need a drink." She went to the side table and poured herself vodka neat.

The two men followed her. "I need to get drunk," Saul said, "and I would if I didn't have so much to do today."

Robert reached for a glass. "I'm on vacation, so start pouring." He took a deep swallow before continuing. "I hired the best private detectives money could buy but I'm getting nowhere. They tell me that so far the Israeli investigator that they hired has hit a stone wall and hasn't been able to find out anything about Morgan."

"Impossible! What kind of a schmuck is this?"

"Saul," Rebecca interrupted.

"I know for a fact that she...,"

"Saul!" Sara shouted.

"What's going on?" Robert asked, his voice terse, his eyes blazing.

"The German's kept impeccable records and Morgan's name was never listed with the deceased. I know because I've been searching for years," Saul said with stubborn determination.

"Why didn't you tell me?" Robert asked, hurt prevailing, his voice edged.

"I didn't tell you because if we couldn't find her than I knew you couldn't find her. Why give you false hope. But what I don't understand is why your Israeli investigative source didn't tell you."

"I don't even know who the Israeli source is. I get my reports from the American team."

Saul began to pace, his body tensing. "I don't like it. I want the name of the Israeli." They returned to the couch; Saul continued, "The Simon Weisenthal Foundation has the most extensive files on earth regarding the Nazis. I have a friend who works with Weisenthal. If inquiries have been made, he'll know. I'll set up an appointment for you to meet with him."

"I'd appreciate that," Robert said, his voice passive, deflated, sad. "For years I simply denied the possibility that she may have survived. I was terrified that she might be starving and hungry in some God-awful place, so I buried her. God forgive me, I needed to believe that she was dead; I needed to believe it so that I wouldn't go crazy. But then when I saw Jo," he said, his color rising, his breathing labored.

"No more for now," Saul said, putting his arm around Robert. "We don't want you getting sick again. I'll help you, my friend. You're not alone in this anymore."

"Thank you," Robert replied, his pounding heart beginning to regulate, the pain easing in his chest.

"When do we get to meet her?" Rebecca asked, kneading her hands, pulling on her skirt, her face pale, and her eyes wild.

"Soon," Robert said, touching Rebecca's face with trembling fingers. "Very, very soon."

Chapter 42

───────── ★ ─────────

The cheap motel room on the Tamiami Trail about 5 miles outside of Miami smelled of stale cigar smoke and disinfectant. A single lamp cast an eerie light over the group: Werner Brest, the ex-S.S. officer, Viktor Docheff, Hans and Otto. Huddled around a chipped wooden table, sipping vodka from paper cups, Brest, his beady black eyes twitching expectantly, scratched his nose and cleared his throat before taking control of the meeting.

"It's the chance we've been waiting for and all we have to do is play God," Brest laughed, his jowl face shaking with the movement. "We get rid of the wife, and in good time, Taxton marries Jo." He sat.

"And how can you be so sure that Taxton wants to marry Jo? He's walked away from her once already, remember?" Otto said sarcastically. Hans nodded his head in agreement.

"Because we have Anderson Taxton in our pockets and soon we'll have his son as well," Docheff said, smoothing the lapel of his thousand-dollar suit.

"You've gotten to Anderson Taxton? How?" Hans asked, his palms sweating, his lip beginning to quiver in anticipation.

"It was easy. Anderson Taxton has some very incriminating skeletons that he wants kept tightly locked in the closet." Docheff smiled, showing teeth with pointed, dog-like incisors. "Our oil baron was a close business associate with Henry Ford during the War. They shared similar beliefs–they both hated Jews and worshiped money.

And as you may or may not know, Ford and the Fuhrer were very good friends. The Fuhrer regarded Henry Ford as an inspiration and kept a life-size portrait of the man next to his desk. As a matter of information, it was Ford's plant in Berlin that produced our "Blitz" truck.

"That would be of little consequence had Ford not openly bragged of his relationship with Taxton in letters to the Furher. And we just happen to have copies of those letters."

He took a moment to gaze at the men before continuing. "Ford helped our War effort as much as any industrialist did and so did Anderson Taxton. He invested hundreds of thousands of dollars into Ford's coffers." He rubbed his hands together, his eyes dancing.

"He belongs to us. And, as it happens, he just can't imagine anything sweeter than his son marrying the only woman he ever truly loved." He snickered. "The son would sell his soul to be president; and we're doing the buying."

The men all began to talk at once. Hans jumped from his chair, knocking it over.

"The implications are staggering," he shouted. "But how can we be sure that the younger Taxton will fall in line."

"We have no fear of that," Werner Brest interjected. "The boy does his father's bidding. And, according to the father, the boy hates the Jews. He blames their political influence on his having to give up Jo in the first place. The point is, all we have to do now is get rid of Taxton's wife."

Otto stood, his blue eyes glistening, his once muscular body tensed. "I'll take care of her. Don't concern yourselves."

"Excellent!" Brest exclaimed.

"We still have another problem," Hans said, wiping the perspiration from his face with a linen handkerchief. "Robert Osborne has too much influence over Jo. It's a problem. And his being in Israel is dangerous to our entire project," Hans said tightly. "If he goes to the Israeli's for help we could be exposed. We've waited long enough. It's time to get rid of the son-of-a bitch."

Docheff studied his fingernails as he spoke. "We've all been in agreement that eventually Osborne would have to be disposed of; and I agree that perhaps he has outlived his usefulness. Consider him as good as dead." He laughed. "But I'll be the one to handle it. You're too emotionally involved and your judgment is clouded."

Hans tightened his fists, working to control his rage at the implication that he was not competent. "I've given this a lot of thought and I..."

"I said I'll take care of it and I will," Viktor Docheff said, staring at Hans, the promise of violence flushing his face.

* * *

The Jerusalem sky was glistening hues of white and blue. A breeze whispered, cascading through the window of Jo's suite like the caress of a lover. She stirred, kicking off the covers before slipping back to sleep.

The phone rang; she reached for it, her eyes unfocused, her mind unfamiliar with its surroundings. She mumbled unintelligently into the receiver.

"Jo, did I wake you?"

"Robbie?" she sat up, his voice jarring her awake. "What time is it?"

Robbie laughed. "It's noon. The bus pulls out in an hour. I was expecting to see your beautiful face at breakfast, and when you didn't show I was worried."

Jo was flattered by his easy familiarity, and immensely uncomfortable as well.

"I guess I was really tired. Thanks for calling. I'll be down in a little while," she said, trying to sound more distant than she felt.

As she showered and dressed, Jo's thoughts returned to the previous night. *It was all a big mistake. We're destined to be nothing more than friends. That's what Aaron wants, and I must respect him for his decision.*

She wanted to believe that she could avoid the pitfalls of a wounded ego and stay away from both Aaron and Robbie, but in her heart she wasn't sure what she would do.

* * *

She arrived downstairs in less then half an hour and was the first person on the bus. Robbie entered a few moments later and slid in beside her. "Good morning, beautiful." he said, studying her unabashedly.

"Good morning," Jo replied a bit too abruptly.

Their jet-lagged traveling companions began to straggle into seats in front and behind them. Jo saw Robert coming down the aisle. She smiled, but he frowned in response.

"Excuse me, Senator Taxton, but I believe you're in the wrong seat," Robert said, sounding more like a jealous suitor than a friend. Jo cringed.

Robbie stood, obviously embarrassed. "Sorry, Mr. Osborne. If you'll excuse me," he said, moving into the aisle.

"Robert Osborne, that was so rude. What's gotten into you?" Jo said as soon as Robbie was out of earshot.

"Look, I'm sorry. It's just that you seemed so upset by him yesterday. Besides, a married man shouldn't look at a woman the way he looks at you," he said, intent on protecting her.

"I'm a grown woman, and if I wanted or needed a chaperone, I would have brought my father," Jo snapped.

"I guess I deserved that," Robert said, frowning.

"I'm sorry. I sound like a shrew," Jo said, pecking him on the cheek. "I'm just tired. Let's just forget it. Did you speak to Saul and Rebecca?"

"Yes."

"When are we going to see them?"

"They both were unavoidably detained. We'll see them at the kibbutz. Rebecca wanted me to—"

"Good afternoon," Aaron said enthusiastically from a microphone at the front of the bus. "Welcome to Israel, the land of milk and honey."

The sound of Aaron's voice startled Jo. She craned her neck to see him and then fell back into the seat, thankful he hadn't noticed her. Her heart pounded, warmth filled her. It was both disconcerting and exciting. She closed her eyes and listened, pretending he was speaking only to her.

"Over the next several days we're going to do our best to introduce you to this country and her people so that when you return to the United States you'll have a fuller understanding of exactly who and what Israel stands for. Many of you will be meeting with officials of the Israeli government and we hope that you will have open and honest discourse. It's not our intention to bombard you with political propaganda. We're simply going to show you the country: her heart and her soul. And then we'll allow you to draw your own conclusions. Of course, in the end we hope you'll have fallen in love with her."

Polite laughter followed and Aaron's demeanor grew more serious. "A hundred million Arabs surround this land, and they've vowed not to rest until every Jew has been pushed into the sea. Those threats have turned the Israeli soldier into the fiercest fighter on earth.

"This country is small, no larger then Rhode Island, and Israel's soldiers, her sons, know how vulnerable their families are. The Israelis know that if their front lines are ever breached; the Arabs would be at their mothers' doorsteps within hours. So they fight, not to conquer but to survive.

"Today,' he continued, "we'll be traveling into the Judean Desert on our way to the ancient city of Beer Sheva. In Beer Sheva we'll be hosted by representatives from Ben Gurion University.

"From there we'll check into the world famous health resort, Ein Bokek, and go for a swim in the Dead Sea, the lowest spot on earth at approximately 1,300 feet below sea level. People come from all over the world to swim in its healing waters. The extremely high gravity of the Dead Sea waters makes it possible for you to float freely on its surface, and I think you'll find that to be quite an experience. After your late afternoon swim, we'll return to the spa, where you'll be pampered for the remainder of the evening."

As the bus pulled away from the curb, Aaron began walking up and down the aisles, shaking hands and making small talk. When he came to Jo and Robert, he nodded politely.

"Did you have a good night's sleep, Jo?"

"Very good, thank you."

"And you, Robert? Did you sleep well?"

Robert nodded and Aaron moved away, his eyes having spoken an unwitting love song to Jo.

Eventually Aaron moved back to the front of the bus.

"You'll all be happy to know that I'm not your guide," he said, laughing easily into the microphone.

"We'll pass out the rest of our itinerary now. We intend to expose you to the sights, sounds, and flavors of this country as best we can. You'll be meeting with dignitaries and with the people on the streets. We're proud of what we've accomplished here, and we're going to attempt to share those accomplishments with you.

"It's now my distinct honor to introduce you to Major General Jacob Perlman. He'll act as our guide, companion, and expert on both the Jewish and the Christian sides of Israel. Jacob, if you please?" Aaron said, thankful to turn over the responsibilities.

* * *

Robbie spent the day trying to decide what he would do about Jo. He did not intend to tell her that his marriage was in a shambles for fear that she might think he had an ulterior motive. But he remained determined to somehow reestablish a relationship with her.

"How about climbing Masada with me in the morning?" Robbie asked Jo after dinner that evening.

"Are you serious? I planned on taking the cable car. Aaron says it's really a very difficult climb."

"Go with me, Jo. It'll be fun," Robbie urged, his eyes flashing mischievously.

"Oh, why not. I'll go. But you have to promise me that if I hate it, you'll take me back down."

"You have my word. I'll wait for you in the lobby. Now how about a nightcap before bed?" he asked.

Jo hesitated. Because Aaron had scarcely spoken to her all day, she was feeling insecure—an emotion foreign and uncomfortable to her.

"I'd like that," she said finally, taking his arm and disregarding instincts that were screaming at her to refuse his offer.

Watching Robbie's maneuvers from afar, Robert could see that Jo was getting caught up in a game that could only have a dreadful conclusion. He was surprised and concerned that she was so foolishly falling victim to Robbie Taxton's charm. But he remained silent, respecting her request that he not interfere.

* * *

On day-three the group arrived in the mountains of northern Israel. Robert, missing Jo's presence, became nervous and irritable as they neared Saul and Rebecca's kibbutz. He was contemplating their arrival when Jo slid into the seat beside him.

"I can't wait to meet them. I'm so excited," Jo said.

Robert smiled but said nothing.

"You're mad at me. I haven't been spending enough time with you," Jo chided, feeling sad, selfish and guilty.

"Don't be silly," Robert replied, feigning annoyance. "Why would I be angry with you? I'm just concerned that you've been spending so much time with Senator Taxton. I just don't think it's appropriate for you. . ."

"We're just friends," she said cutting him off. "You don't have to give it another thought. I would never let myself get involved with a married man."

"I know that, Jo." Robert said, taking her hand. "I guess I'm overly protective. Now put that smile back on your beautiful face, and let's forget all this senseless chatter."

The bus pulled up in front of the administration building, where it was met by a group of casually dressed kibbutzniks. Rebecca and Saul had concealed themselves in the back of the group, wanting a chance to deal with the shock of seeing Jo before they were actually introduced. Saul was holding tightly to Rebecca.

"There she is. Oh my God, Saul, she looks exactly like Morgan."

Rebecca began to tremble.

"We've got to get a hold of ourselves. The girl will think we're crazy if we don't. Here they come. Smile, my darling. Smile and be brave," Saul said softly.

Robert hugged his friends, instantly concerned at how pale they both were. As he hugged Rebecca, he whispered, "Unbelievable, isn't it?"

Rebecca flashed her eyes at him and whispered back, "I still can't believe it."

Jo smiled warmly and hugged each of them. "I can't believe I'm finally meeting you."

"We're going to be the best of friends, and that's all there is to it. Now come with me and I'll introduce you to our family," Rebecca said, putting her arm around Jo. "Oh, you can come along too," she said, reaching for Robert's hand. "They haven't stopped talking about finally getting to meet the famous Robert Osborne in person."

Jo loved Rebecca on sight. And as they walked along the paths of the kibbutz, chatting easily, Jo felt strangely at home and at peace.

* * *

They spent the rest of the evening in a flurry of noisy conversation. Robert immersed himself in easy repartee with each of the Lipinsky children; he couldn't help but think about the children he and Morgan might have had if she'd lived. Exhausted from the onslaught of too many emotions, melancholy seeped in like a rising tide. Desperate to be alone, Robert excused himself, making his way into the garden.

As the evening grew to a close, the family began to disperse.

"Come sit next to me," Rebecca said gently to Jo, once they were finally alone. "I want you to tell me about yourself. What do you like to do in your spare time? What kind of clothes do you like? What's your favorite movie? What types of books do you read?"

Jo laughed. "Why do you want to know about me? I'm nothing special. Tell me all about you. You're the one who's remarkable."

Rebecca pointed her finger playfully at Jo. "Listen to me, young lady. I decide who's remarkable and who isn't. You're special—very, very special. It doesn't matter why I think so. It only matters that I do. Now tell me about your life."

* * *

Robert sat inconspicuously on a bench watching the Lipinsky children leave. His heart ached for Morgan.

"This is your family, my dear one."

Robert looked around, trying to locate who was speaking to him. He soon realized that no one was there. Morgan's words continued to drift into his consciousness. His head throbbed and he buried his head in his hands. Saul quietly approached.

"Are you all right?" he asked.

"I'm fine."

"Then let's go. He's here."

Chapter 43

———————— ★ ————————

In the cool Israeli night, Robert and Saul crossed over bridges and walked down long winding paths until they reached Rebecca's office.

"You'll have to forgive me for not having a more appropriate place for us to have this meeting," Saul said, "but kibbutz living doesn't have many amenities. When I want to pretend that I'm an important person, I have to go to Jerusalem or Tel Aviv, because here I'm just another kibbutznik."

Strain was on both their faces as they walked into Rebecca's domain. Saul flipped on the light and said to Robert, "I'm afraid you could never accuse my wife of orderliness, but rest assured if we moved even one thing, she'd know, and have a fit. Now sit down and relax for a moment while I go and bring Natan here."

Robert was anxious to speak with the Nazi hunter. He paced. He sat. He stood. Ten minutes later Saul returned with Natan.

Robert was disappointed by Natan's appearance, expecting him to look more menacing. Instead, he found a slightly built, scholarly looking man in his mid-forties who looked more like a literature professor than a Nazi hunter.

"I've read the dossier," Natan began without preamble. "First of all, I've located the investigator that's been working for you in Israel; his name is Jacob Aronowitz. He's made great progress and found out some very interesting things…things I might add that are quite obviously omitted from the reports you've been receiving from the American investigative team."

"I don't understand," Robert said, his head pounding, a headache looming.

"You don't understand? It's really quite simple. Someone doesn't want you to have the information. My bet is that it's the Nazis," Natan said softly. "They want you fed misinformation and that's exactly what you've been getting. Your investigation is compromised."

"Jesus Christ!" Robert's pulse quickened. "Did he find out anything about Morgan?"

"Does the name Jacob Gold ring a bell?"

Robert gasped. "My God! I stayed at his home in Vilnius when I first met Morgan. He went on to become a doctor. But what does he have to do with this?"

"He was a prisoner at the death camp where we now believe Morgan was held. Survivors were found that remember him. They said he hid a very sick young woman, with the help of the other prisoners. From the descriptions, it was Morgan."

Robert began to tremble. "What was wrong with her?" he asked, his heart threatening to break.

"Robert, perhaps it's enough for one night," Saul interjected.

"What was wrong with her?" Robert repeated, ignoring Saul.

"She suffered dire physical problems from childbirth and I'm sorry to say this, but from the eyewitness reports…she was mentally ill as well."

"I'm sure most of the survivors were mentally ill." Robert said, anger causing his head to pound. "You didn't know Morgan. She was strong, resilient." He took a deep breath, and began to pace. "You think she's alive! That's what your telling me, isn't it?"

"Yes. I think she may be. Gold disappeared after the liberation. No records have been found on either one of them; and that could mean that they're both still alive."

"Oh my God." Robert closed his eyes. *Is this really happening?* He envisioned Morgan as she once was: vital, spirited, his lover and companion. "If she were still alive they would have contacted me!" Robert said, his practical, pragmatic self taking hold.

"That might depend on where they're living, if in fact they're able to get a communication out. It also depends on whether they want to."

"What are you talking about?" Robert snarled, stepping angrily towards Natan.

"You don't shoot the messenger," Natan said softly. "She was damaged, and perhaps she wanted to spare you the agony of that."

"I want her found! I don't care what it costs or what you have to do. I want you to find her!"

"Mr. Osborne, I would like nothing better than to locate your wife for you. And if she's still alive, I will. But you must also be practical. If they've decided not to be found, then our task is going to be even more daunting. You're going to have to be infinitely patient." Natan looked at Saul. "There's more. Mr. Osborne could be in real danger. The Nazis don't want Mrs. Osborne found, and if they feel threatened they could certainly decide to eliminate him."

"Then we'll just have to protect him," Saul said softly. "I'll arrange for a body guard."

"What are you talking about?" Robert asked, incredulously. "Do you think for a moment that I'm afraid of those bastards?"

"If you're not then you're a fool," Natan snapped. "Let's understand something; if you want my help then you're going to have to do as I say. One has to think like an animal in order to corner one. To be a hunter, one must understand his prey. I understand how they think. I should. I've been living and breathing their foul smell for years."

Natan stared at Robert. "I watched the Nazis tear my infant brother from my mother's arms and smash him against a brick wall. When my mother tried to save her baby, they shot her in the back. The only reason I'm alive today is because a Christian neighbor took me in and hid me. I vowed that I'd avenge my mother and brother's death, and I've done that. But I've done it my way, by tracking the Nazi bastards down and bringing them to trial." Beads of perspiration dripped from Natan's brow.

He had told his story hundreds of times over the years, but it never got any easier. "Now, can we get down to business?" Natan asked, determination flaming in his voice. "I have a lot of questions that need to be answered."

He was an expert interrogator, and Robert found himself responding with dispassionate preciseness until Natan asked, "Have you considered the possibility that she may have willingly become another man's mistress?"

Robert jumped to his feet.

"How dare you?" he screamed.

Natan also stood up, leering at Robert.

"You wouldn't believe what people are capable of doing in order to survive. So don't judge what you can't possibly understand. If you're really interested in finding out the truth, then I suggest you begin to accept the fact that the woman you loved was not the same woman who had this child. If you can't accept that, then I'll leave. It's your choice."

Robert felt the blood drain from his face. It took all of his will power, but he managed to apologize.

Natan's face softened.

"You must rise above your own emotions if we're to be successful."

Robert answered Natan's questions for another hour, and when they were finished, he was numb and exhausted.

"We'll do this slowly and methodically. You just go about your life and forget about everything for a while. My contact will be Saul. He'll keep you informed," Natan said, gathering his papers.

"I'm sorry, but that's not acceptable to me," Robert said. "This is my problem and my wife we're talking about. I want you to contact me."

Natan shook his head. "That's impossible."

Before Robert could say anything in rebuttal, Saul intervened.

"Natan is used to doing things his own way, Robert. I'm sure you can understand why he doesn't trust many people," Saul said, walking over to Robert and putting his arm around him. "You have my word that I'll keep you informed every step of the way."

*   *   *

The night sky glimmered with stars, and the full moon lit his way as Robert moved along the well-traveled walkway. Seeking solitude under the giant arms of an olive tree, he sat on the damp ground and cried.

After the hours of interrogation and introspection, Robert realized that it was time to let someone else take over. *I'm so tired. I want to love again and be loved. I want the pain to go away. And...if you're alive, my darling, then I just want to know that you're okay.*

*   *   *

At 4:00 AM, a persistent knocking at his door awakened Aaron.

"I'm coming, I'm coming," he said, pulling on his robe.

"Mr. Blumenthal, there's an urgent call for you from the United States, and they said we were to awaken you," the messenger said.

Pulling his bathrobe tightly around him to stave of the damp night air, Aaron followed the young kibbutznik. By the time he reached the telephone in the kibbutz office, Aaron was deeply agitated.

"Aaron, is that you?" the voice on the other end asked.

"Who in the hell do you think it is? Do you know what time it is here? Let me tell you something, Steve, this better be important, because I've just aged five years."

"I'm afraid it is. You're going to have to be the bearer of some really bad news," Steve said. "Senator Taxton's wife was killed in an automobile accident about three hours ago." Steve had been Aaron's administrative assistant for several years, and he knew that his boss would take this news badly.

"Tell me what happened," Aaron said so softly Steve could barely hear him.

"All I know, sir, is that she was returning home from a dinner party at her parents' estate when she apparently lost control of her car. It went off the side of a mountain and exploded on impact."

"Dear God! That's horrible," Aaron said as he pictured himself telling Robbie.

Steve continued, "I don't know if you're aware of this, sir, but the President is very close friends with Senator Taxton's in-laws. He's become personally involved with the situation. There's an Air Force jet on its way from England as we speak. I've been told it'll arrive in Israel in about three hours. The Senator will then be taken directly to New York, where a helicopter will be waiting.

"Thanks, Steve. I know you must have had a hell of an evening. I'll call you later."

Aaron went back to his room and dressed, wondering how one prepares to tell a man that his wife is dead.

* * *

Robbie awakened with a start. Realizing that someone was knocking on his door, he stumbled out of bed.

"Who is it?" He asked.

"It's Aaron Blumenthal, Senator. I'm sorry to disturb you, but..."

Robbie opened the door. "Please come in. What's wrong?"

As the two men stood facing each other, all Aaron could think about was that what he was about to say to this young man was going to ruin his life.

Robbie braced himself, realizing that something terrible had happened. *Is it father? Is it mother? Dear God, please no, not yet, they're too young.*

"There's been a terrible accident. Your wife…I'm sorry, Robbie…she was killed."

Robbie shook his head. "Ashley's dead? There must be some mistake."

Robbie allowed himself to be led to the chair as Aaron's words began to sink in. Ashley had been a part of his life for years. She was a kind, good woman. He had never wished her any harm.

"Tell me what happened? What kind of an accident?" Robbie asked, his voice breaking.

"After leaving her parents home she apparently lost control of the car. It went over the side of a mountain."

"Dear God, my in-laws. This is going to kill them. You don't know how close…she was their only child. I must go to them immediately."

"It's all taken care of, Senator. An Air Force jet is on its way here to take you back to the States. I'll leave you now so that you can dress. If you'd like, I could have someone come in later to pack for you."

"No, thanks. I'll take care of it myself."

As Aaron turned to leave, Robbie stopped him.

"Thank you, Aaron, for being the one to tell me."

* * *

Robbie watched as his things were loaded into the car. Nodding to the driver that he was ready to leave, he reached for Aaron's hand, smiling sadly.

"Please don't let this ruin the mission for everyone," Robbie said. "Some of these men are good friends of mine. I want you to tell them that I don't want them coming back to the States for the funeral. And please tell Jo that I'll be in touch with her very soon. Thanks for everything, Aaron."

* * *

Three hours later Robbie sat alone in the dimly lit airplane. He was deeply shaken, and feeling deplorably guilty. *Maybe I never really loved her, but she didn't deserve to die, not now, not like that.*

* * *

Aaron knocked on Jo's door after deciding she would want him to awaken her.

"What are you doing here at this hour? Don't tell me," she said, pulling her bathrobe closed. "You've decided you can't live without me."

If she only knew how true that was, he thought.

Jo was about to continue her teasing, hopeful that he had in fact come to be with her, when she noted the strain on his face.

"I'm afraid I have some bad news. Robbie's on his way back to the States. His wife was killed in an automobile accident last night."

"Oh my God, that's horrible!"

"I came here to ask if you'd like to go have a cup of coffee with me. I don't feel much like being alone right now. It's been a horrendous night."

"Of course I'll go with you. Just give me two minutes to throw something on."

* * *

Three days later Aaron stood by Jo's side in the Knesset, the legislative body of Israel.

"I'm so nervous," Jo said.

"You'll do just fine. Just relax and be yourself."

I still don't know why they selected me.

She walked to the platform, swallowed hard, and placed her prepared statement on the lectern.

"To the State of Israel, to her people and her government, we salute you. Arriving here we thought that we were well educated and sophisticated, and that we understood the concerns and dynamics of your country. How foolish we were. How little we knew.

"We visited your universities and research centers, marveling at the advances you're making in the fields of medicine and agriculture. We traveled to the Negev Desert, where we tasted wonderfully delicious tomatoes grown miraculously from the once barren desert soil. We walked the ancient streets of Jerusalem, watching in awe as you lovingly excavated beneath her streets, reaching back into the mysteries of the past.

"From the ashes of Triblinka, Majdanek, and Auschwitz, a great nation emerged. And although it's time for us to leave you now, I can assure you that we're going back to the United States enriched and inspired by what we saw here.

"We will never forget you, our Israeli friends. We came here strangers, we're going home feeling like family."

The applause was thunderous as 120 members of the Knesset rose to their feet.

Aaron moved to Jo's side. "Thank you, thank you from the bottom of my heart," he said.

"No, Aaron, thank you. You've opened a whole new world to me."

Saul sat with Robert in the back of the Knesset.

"She's incredible. It's too bad that she'll never know she's one of us," Saul said.

"What do you mean?" Robert asked.

"By Jewish law," Saul said, "when a child is born to a Jewish mother, the child is a Jew. It's divine providence that has brought her here to us."

Robert nodded.

"Natan called today," Saul said matter-of-factly. "Weisenthal is interested in Jo's case and willing to get involved."

"That's fantastic," Robert said.

"Natan thinks so." Looking very serious, Saul continued, "You must never forget how dangerous these Nazis can be. Having a body guard is some protection, but you're going to have to be very careful who you trust."

Robert smiled at his friend. "I will. Don't worry." As they rose to leave, Robert touched Saul's arm. "Just knowing that I'm not alone in all of this has meant more to me than I can ever tell you."

"It's time for you to go home now and begin your life anew. The mystery surrounding Morgan will eventually be unraveled, and when it is, we'll be there to help you. One day with God's help perhaps we'll be able to tell Jo who she really is. Until then, just be with her and protect her as best you can."

The two men hugged, and then they stood staring into each other's eyes.

Saul spoke first. "May God protect you, my brother."

Robert fought back his tears. He whispered, "You too, my friend. Until we meet again."

Chapter 44

———————— ★ ————————

Vladimir was sitting at the desk in his study contemplating the events of the past few days when he absentmindedly picked up one of his wrestling medals. Polishing it on the felt writing pad, he allowed himself a moment of reflection.

It had been twenty-five years since the war's end, and he had managed to replace David, the valiant survivor, with Vladimir: an accomplished athlete, a brilliant scholar.

Feeling restless, Vladimir opened the desk drawer and removed the key he kept hidden inside. He stood and walked to the glass display case nestled between shelves laden with papers and books. Unlocking the cabinet, he reached inside, removing the Olympic gold medal that he had won for Russia in London, England in the Games of 1948. He held it, marveling at how many doors that little piece of gold had opened for him.

Because of the gold, Vladimir had been allowed to select his course studies at Moscow State University. His first five and a half years he majored in chemistry and computational mathematics. During the following three years he expanded those studies to include physics. He was awarded the *kandidat nauk* degree as a doctor of science after successfully completing his thesis. The University had then offered him a job, and Vladimir went on to become a full professor and department head.

Now, as he stood holding the medal, his eyes wondered around the room. Framed newspaper articles and photographs of himself with famous politicians and athletes stared out at him from the walls. He had kept this shrine-like room not for his ego, but as a reminder that he had managed to survive his masquerade and had become a success along the way.

Placing the medal over his head, Vladimir turned his thoughts to Anna. He envisioned her soft brown eyes and lovely face. Her mouth was heart-like and she had high cheekbones that gave her a doll-like appearance. Her hair was a lustrous chocolate brown and she wore it in a braid down the center of her slender back. She had been one of his students, and even though she was twelve years younger then he, Vladimir had become smitten by her fiery disposition and brilliant mind.

But Anna was Jewish, and that had caused many difficulties from the onset. The KGB watched Vladimir closely. He was considered to be one of the leading experts in the world on nuclear fission. And because Russia was an openly anti-Semitic society, Vladimir had avoided making Jewish friends, fearful always of exposing his true identity.

But after meeting Anna he threw caution to the wind. He wanted her and he made the decision to disengage himself from the web of lies and risk everything by pursuing her.

During the more than three years Anna worked side by side with Vladimir, he did his best to win her over. But Anna had remained standoffish, denying even to herself that she had fallen in love with her roguishly handsome professor.

Then one day Vladimir was notified that he was being sent to a nuclear research facility at the foothills of the Ural Mountains in Western Siberia. He was ecstatic for the opportunity to monitor the Soviet project, hoping to help avoid the possibility of a nuclear calamity. But he was desperately unhappy about leaving Anna. Fearful that she would find someone and fall in love, he used all his influence to have her assigned as his assistant.

* * *

Only days after their arrival at the top-secret facility, the weather turned nightmarishly frigid, and Anna, hating the cold, became equally frigid toward Vladimir. Realizing that the possibility of establishing a relationship with her had become as remote as the hellhole they were living in, Vladimir had become despondent.

When he was sitting alone one evening in his laboratory, bundled up against the freezing Arctic temperatures, Anna had wandered in.

"Vladimir Vloriscoff, you might just as well know that I'm never going to forgive you for bringing me to this horrible place," Anna had said without hesitation or embarrassment. "I have no intention of having a relationship with you, and I'm tired of your advances and innuendoes. I'm a Jew. I only go out with Jewish men," she had said. "And besides, you have a terrible reputation as a womanizer, and I wouldn't be caught dead with someone like you."

Vladimir stood, knocking over the chair he was sitting on. He grabbed Anna roughly by the shoulders, his face only inches from hers. Darkness filled his eyes and Anna's pulse quickened.

"What do you know about my reputation? Is it such a crime that I like women? Have you ever asked yourself why I never married?" he asked angrily, his fingers biting into her shoulders.

Anna stifled a cry, inexplicably excited by his roughness and the danger she saw in his eyes.

"You don't know me because you've never bothered trying to get to know me."

"I'm no fool," Anna insisted, her resolve beginning to crumble. "I may be a woman but I'm every bit as smart as any man you'll ever meet. And I won't be taken in by your charms. You can't make me love you."

"Make you love me? If only I could," Vladimir said. "Do you know about love, Anna? Do you know about desire? Do you know what it's like to want something so badly that the wanting of it only brings you pain?"

Anna's eyes filled with tears. "I know, Vladimir," she said, her voice barely audible. "And I wish to God that things were different. It can't work between us. You must try to understand."

"You're wrong. It can work," he insisted.

"I have to go, Vladimir."

"No," he said, tightening his grip on her shoulders.

Anna cried out in pain.

"My God, I've hurt you! I'm sorry, Anna. I would never intentionally hurt you." Mortified by what he had done, Vladimir took her trembling body into his arms. "Forgive me, Anna...please forgive me," he said. Taking out his handkerchief, he tenderly wiped away her tears. *I must tell her. It's the only way.*

"Come and sit for a moment," he said, seating her in a chair directly facing him. "I have a story to tell you. I'm not...I'm not a Russian," he said. "I'm Viennese."

"I don't understand," she said.

"My family lived in Vienna. My father was a respected doctor, a brilliant man, a kind and caring man. When Hitler invaded Austria, I was studying at the University. I had hoped to follow in my father's footsteps. I was so innocent and filled with dreams then.

"They came for my father. When my mother tried to stop the Nazis from taking him, they killed her. But not before raping her in front of my father, little sister, and me." Turning his face from her, he fought to hide the hate.

"I was so filled with rage. It was an anger that devoured me. I only wanted revenge. But my father's brother refused to let me destroy myself. He insisted that I be sent away. I protested. But I was young and had very little choice.

"I was smuggled onto a boat with hundreds of Jews fleeing to Palestine. But when the boat arrived, the English wouldn't allow us entry. We were sent back to Germany. I escaped, thanks to the kindness of the ship's captain. But I'm sure the rest of my fellow passengers perished in the camps.

"I spoke fluent Russian," Vladimir said, needing to purge himself of the nightmare. "I disguised myself as a Soviet soldier and eventually made my way to Russia. I've chosen to hide my identity all these years in order to survive. They wanted me to survive, and that's exactly what I've done," he said. "So you see, my darling Anna, I too am a Jew—a damaged, angry, disenchanted Jew, but a Jew all the same."

"My poor, sweet Vladimir. How much you've been forced to endure. If only I'd known," Anna said, caressing his face with her eyes.

She moved into his arms. He breathed in her sweetness.

"I love you, Vladimir. I've loved you from the very first moment I saw you," Anna said. Then she kissed him deeply, surrendering her resolve.

* * *

Anna walked into the study, pulling Vladimir back from his wondering memories.

"What are you doing sitting here in the dark?" she asked, walking over and kissing him gently on the lips. "Is something wrong?"

"No, my love, nothing's wrong. I was just thinking."

"About what?" Anna asked, fully expecting him to tell her about the project he was working on.

"I was thinking about us, Anna. I was thinking that it's time for us to go."

"Not that again," Anna said. "Come on, Vladimir, I'm tired of this foolishness already. How many years have you been saying this? Won't you ever stop?"

Vladimir crossed his arms over his massive chest.

"Sit down, Anna. I want to tell you about my day," he said, a dark look crossing his face. "We had an accident at the plant, and one of my colleagues was mortally burned."

"What happened?"

"I was alone with him while the doctors were being summoned. Anna, he was dying, and with his last breath he said, 'Don't waste your life; you must get out before you become the Angel of Death.' I begged him to tell me what he was talking about but he died before he could answer. Don't you see, Anna? We've got to get out. Something's going to happen. I feel it in my bones."

"Vladimir, you're too sensitive. The man was dying. I'm sure he was delirious and didn't know what he was saying. Anyway, this doesn't change anything. We have no way out of here, and it's time you faced that reality."

"I received this today," he said, handing her a letter.

"An invitation to Sweden. How nice," Anna said after reading it. "And of course you're going to accept. But I don't see how this changes anything."

"It changes everything," Vladimir said. "Finally, after all these years, I've convinced them to allow you to travel with me. When we get to Sweden we're going to ask for political asylum. And then I'm going to make you my wife," he said.

Anna shook her head.

"They won't let us leave," she said. "Can't you get that through your head? If we try to leave, they'll kill us both. We know too much. Why can't you see that? The KGB will track us down no matter where we go. I don't want to die. I'm happy this way. It's all I need. Do I ever ask for more? Do I seem unhappy? For God's sake, Vladimir, I'm almost forty years old. It's too late to have children, so what difference does it make if we marry or not? At least the KGB has turned a blind eye on our relationship, allowing you to keep a Jew as your mistress. It's that stupid promise you made to the man on the ship that's driving you so crazy, isn't it? Do you think he remembers you? Do you think he ever expects to see you again?"

Vladimir looked at her with tears in his eyes. "Anna, I want to go to Israel. I have to go."

"Look, we can't always have what we want," she said gently.

"We can, Anna. Just trust me."

"You know it has nothing to do with trust," she said. "I've trusted you with my life, for God's sake." Seeing his crestfallen look, Anna decided to relent. "OK, let's pretend for just one moment that it's possible. Tell me your plan."

Vladimir stood and began to pace.

"In Stockholm we always stay in a large hotel in the center of the city. There is a myriad of exits. I'm sure we'll be able to find a way to slip out one of the doors and go to the American Embassy. When the Americans find out who we are, they'll protect us. I'll tell them everything I know, and then I'll insist they send us to Israel."

"My poor, sweet, naive Vladimir. If it were that easy everyone would do it."

Vladimir persisted. "Anna, I must try. I won't leave you behind, so you must try with me."

"Fine!" she said. "And what about Boris Blanchack and Sadie? Will you just leave them? Is that how you'll thank them?"

"That's exactly how I'll repay them for all the years of love they've given to me," he said. "We'll live the dream they had for themselves by fulfilling that dream. With you as my wife, living freely in the land of our people, what greater gift could I ever give to them? God knows I'll miss them. But we must do this, and we must do it now," he said, striking his fist on the desk.

"I've hurt you, and I'm sorry," Anna said. "Please try to understand. I don't have your courage. I'm simply a scientist, nothing more. But I can't live without you so if you insist on going, I'll go with you."

Vladimir took Anna in his arms and held her tightly. "One day you'll thank me, Anna. I promise you that."

* * *

Unavoidably late and knowing that Anna had come early to help Sadie with the Sabbath meal, Vladimir walked rapidly up the three flights of stairs to the Blanchack's apartment. Climbing laboriously, he thought tenderly about the people who had become as dear to him as parents.

Over the years the once vivacious Sadie had grown frail and forgetful. Vladimir knew that her oncoming senility would protect her from the pain of Anna and his leaving. But Boris was another story. And as Vladimir neared the top of the landing, he became terrified at the thought of telling him. Boris's mind was still keen even though his body was now ravaged with arthritis. The thought of causing Boris any more pain overwhelmed Vladimir.

An all too familiar tightness closed around Vladimir's chest, and he sat down hard on the stairs. "Angina," the doctors had said. "Nothing to worry about as long as you don't get too upset over things."

* * *

Ten minutes later Vladimir sat watching as Sadie and Anna said the blessings over the candles. As was the tradition, they covered their eyes, singing out in loud, clear voices. Then Boris said the blessing over the wine, and after welcoming in the Sabbath, they all began to eat.

Vladimir tried to make light conversation over dinner, but he had difficulty remaining focused. Thankful when the dinner was finally finished, he helped Anna and Sadie clear the table. Then, rather than face Boris alone, he leaned against the wall in the kitchen, listening to the two woman gossip.

"OK, Vloriscoff, if you want to hang out in the kitchen with us girls, you help," Anna said, throwing the dishtowel at him.

"Spit it out," Boris said the moment the three of them walked out of the kitchen. "You think I don't know you? You think I trained you for the Olympics, taught you how to pray again, taught you how to study for exams, and now I don't know you? What's going on?"

"Leave them alone. It's not our business," Sadie said fearfully.

My God, they know, Anna thought, looking helplessly at Vladimir. Seeing his obvious distress, she reached for his hand and squeezed it.

"The opportunity to escape Russia has finally presented itself," he said stoically. "I've been invited to Stockholm, and Anna's going with me. We're going to seek political asylum."

No one spoke. The silence was long and painful. Finally Boris reacted.

"Israel. It's no good unless you go to Israel."

"Yes," Vladimir said, "we're going to Israel."

"We'll miss you," Boris said.

Sadie looked at Anna in bewilderment.

"Does this mean you won't be here for Shabbat dinners? What will I do?"

Anna seemed to understand the way Sadie's mind worked these days, and she responded gaily, "You'll invite Mr. and Mrs. Rosenstein from downstairs. They're a lovely couple. She has told me many times how she wished she had a family to be with on Friday nights."

"What a good idea!" Sadie said with glee.

Boris looked at his wife and smiled. "Don't worry, Sadie. You'll have a house full on Friday nights, just like always."

Boris moved his chair closer to Vladimir's.

"In some ways, she's lucky," he whispered. "Nothing much bothers her these days. But you do understand that she loves you?" he asked.

"Of course I do. And I love her," Vladimir said, taking Boris's shaking hands in his own.

Promise me just one thing," Boris asked quietly so that Sadie couldn't hear.

"I'll promise anything you ask of me," Vladimir said.

"Promise me that when I die, you'll say Kaddish for me."

He embraced Boris, his eyes blinded with tears.

"I love you, Boris. You have my word."

Chapter 45

The plane touched down in Stockholm on December 5, 1971. Vladimir's delegation of six scientists and four assistants were escorted through the airport by a group of KGB agents. Whisked through customs, they were ushered into Mercedes limousines and taken directly to the Russian Embassy. Debriefed and warned about unnecessary contact with capitalist opportunists, the exhausted group was taken to their hotel, the Gamla Stan, a ten-minute ride from the Embassy. The KGB agent assigned to Vladimir and Anna watched closely as the hotel valet carried their luggage into the room.

"You have enough clothes to stay gone a year," he said.

Anna cringed, convinced that he was suspicious of them.

"Have a good sleep, comrades. I'll be right outside your door if you should need anything."

They entered the room and Anna watched Vladimir throw himself down on the bed.

"Damn it!" he said, slamming his fist into the mattress.

Seeing the desperation in Vladimir's eyes, Anna rushed over to him and put her hand across his mouth.

"You must say nothing," she whispered. "They may be listening."

Vladimir slapped his forehead angrily. Grabbing Anna's hand, he pulled her into the bathroom and turned on the water in the tub to block the sound of his voice. "I should have known it wouldn't be easy," he whispered. "I kidded myself into believing I'd find a way to get us out."

"You'll find a way."

"I need time to think."

"I will leave you."

* * *

Vladimir knew he had to calm himself. His whole life had been one of survival and competition and he knew that with proper planning he would find a solution.

I have to use the resources at hand. Sitting on the edge of the tub, surrounded by the stark white of the bathroom, a plan began to slowly germinate in his mind. He painstakingly played out several scenarios, disregarding some and mentally pursuing others as he measured the unavoidable risks.

Two hours later, convinced he had a plausible plan, he brought Anna back into the bathroom.

"It just may work," Anna said cautiously after hearing his explanation. But there is still a very big problem."

"What?"

"I'm terrified! You're depending so much on me, and I don't know if I can do it."

"I'm scared too. But even if we fail, at least we'll know we tried," he said.

"If we're caught, will they kill us?"

"No. We're too valuable to them."

With Vladimir's arms around her, Anna began to feel a strength she had doubted she possessed.

"All right, my darling. But now you need your sleep. Tomorrow will be a big day."

* * *

Sometime in the middle of the night, Anna reached out for Vladimir. Sensuously kneading his muscular back, she felt him stir. Stroking his hardening penis, she coaxed the sleep from him. Normally reticent, Anna became the aggressor. She teased him with her mouth, kissing and gliding her tongue over his body. Vladimir exploded in ecstasy. Riding the wave, they clung to each other, lost in their passion. The physical contact served to strengthen them. Drifting back to sleep, they were ready to accept their fate.

* * *

The Swedish government sponsored the Conference of International Physics. One thousand of the world's most acclaimed scientists had gathered to confer on the latest theories and hypothesis.

Arriving at 10:00 AM, Vladimir and Anna were seated in the front of the auditorium. The first speaker of the morning was to be the 1970 Nobel laureate in physics, Alfven Hannes of Sweden. Following Hannes, Neel Louis Eugene of France would give his presentation. Also a Nobel laureate, Neel was a man Vladimir had spent his entire career emulating.

Vladimir was slated to be the third speaker. Following such esteemed colleagues, he was understandably nervous. Holding tightly to Anna's hand, he tried to remain focused. If his speech was not flawless, he would become immediately suspect.

At 12:30, his body damp with sweat, Vladimir took the podium. At first his words were stilted and he faltered momentarily. But his vision of the future and his abounding knowledge of nuclear fission soon dispelled his case of nerves. He spoke articulately, holding his audience spellbound.

After a standing ovation he returned to Anna's side. Looking forward to mingling with his fellow scientists, Vladimir began to make his way into the crowd at the close of the morning session.

"Where are you going, comrade?" the KGB agent asked, firmly grasping his shoulder.

"I intend to visit with my colleagues," he said.

"Follow me and do not make a scene," the agent said.

Herded like prisoners, Vladimir and his Russian delegation were spirited into the waiting limousines.

"You were wonderful, darling," Anna said.

"Professionally, it was the greatest day of my life."

With sirens screaming from their police escort, the Russian delegation was taken to Operakallaren. With its turn of the century interior and its magnificent view of the Royal Palace and surrounding water, it was considered to be one of the world's most beautiful restaurants. The delegation was taken to an elegant private dining room on the west side of the building.

Once seated, Vladimir's comrades began discussing his paper. Anna pretended to listen, but she was much too nervous to follow their comments. She forced herself to eat so that she wouldn't draw any unwanted attention from the KGB. As coffee was being served, Anna excused herself and went into the restroom. A KGB agent followed, waiting by the pay phone at the entrance to the restaurant.

Moments after Anna entered the bathroom, the agent heard a loud disturbance coming from the private dining area. Panicked, he left his post by the front door. Vladimir, having knocked over the table in his fall, was lying on the floor clutching his chest.

Anna peered out the bathroom door. Seeing that she was alone, she moved quickly to the pay phone. With trembling hands she deposited coins and dialed the number of the American Embassy, a number she had memorized from the telephone book in her room earlier that day.

"You've reached the American Embassy. May I help you?" the operator asked.

"My name is Dr. Anna Stein, and I'm here in Stockholm with Dr. Vladimir Vloriscoff. We're coming to your Embassy tonight in order to defect from the Soviet Union," Anna said in rapid Russian before hanging up the phone.

It had taken less then twenty seconds, and Anna doubted that the operator had any idea what had just transpired. But Vladimir had assured Anna that all incoming calls would be monitored and recorded and that the proper people would be notified of their impending arrival.

Entering the dining room, she rushed to Vladimir's side.

"Get out of my way. He needs his medicine!" Anna ordered, realizing instantly that Vladimir wasn't acting. His face was a pasty white and he was shaking uncontrollably. Anna slipped the nitroglycerin tablet under his tongue as she held him tightly in her arms. Within moments he stopped clutching his chest and the color returned to his face.

"I'm OK now, there's nothing to worry about," Vladimir said to his concerned colleagues as he moved to stand. "It was just an angina attack."

"Call a doctor," the head agent commanded.

"No, that's not necessary," Vladimir assured the agent. "This happens quite often, and now that I've taken my medicine I feel much better. Can we please get back to lunch?" he asked, rising unsteadily to his feet.

* * *

Later that evening, as the rest of the delegation was retiring for the night, Anna locked herself in the bathroom. For over an hour she worked. She applied eye shadow, liner, and cherry red lipstick with a heavy hand, making her look garish and cheap. Undoing her braid, she allowed her lustrous hair to fall wildly around her face. Taking up scissors and needle, she cut six inches off the hem of her skirt before turning the fabric and stitching it in place. Having shaved her legs for the first time in her life, she slipped into the now skimpy skirt. She then unfastened the first three buttons of her blouse, exposing the tops of her breasts. When she finally emerged from the bathroom, she was barely recognizable.

Vladimir feigned a whistle, smiling his approval. He had slicked his hair back, removed his necktie, and opened the color of his shirt.

"Are you ready?"

"As ready as I'll ever be."

Moving to the door, Anna held up both hands with her fingers crossed before opening it and moving into the hallway.

"Comrade, come! You must hurry. Dr. Vloriscoff's ill again," she said, pulling the agent into the room.

The moment the agent had both feet inside the door, Vladimir struck him at the base of his skull with the bedside lamp. Unconscious, he fell to the floor.

"My God, we've killed him!" Anna whispered, her body tense, shocked.

Vladimir felt for the fallen KGB agent's pulse. Standing up, he grasped the shaking Anna by the shoulders.

"Anna, listen to me…he's going to be fine. We've got to hurry."

"You're right of course. We've got to hurry," she said, grasping for Vladimir's arm as they quietly opened the door.

The night manager looked up from his desk as the lift opened, watching as the man, apparently one of his guests, kissed a woman passionately, rubbing her slightly exposed breasts. Realizing he hadn't seen this hooker before, he memorized every curve in her body.

The KGB man sitting in the chair reading his newspaper also glanced up as the couple passed. The magnificent legs of the hooker immediately aroused him. He watched lasciviously as she moved through the lobby and out the doorway, never lifting his eyes above her swaying hips.

A taxi with its driver dozing at the wheel was parked in front of the hotel. Vladimir and Anna got into the car and instructed the driver to take them to the American Embassy.

The Embassy was on full alert, having been told by Washington that they were about to take part in one of the most important defections in years. As the taxi came into view, the Embassy gates were thrown open. The exterior spotlights were switched on, and soldiers with drawn pistols directed the taxi into the secured area of the compound. One of the soldiers assisted Anna and Vladimir out of the car.

"Hurry! We must get you inside," the American said in Russian. "You're not safe out here in the open."

They moved into the main building, where the American ambassador was waiting for them.

"Welcome," he said, extending his hand first to Vladimir and then to Anna. "My name is Wesley Bass. It's my duty to formally ascertain exactly what your intentions are."

The American soldier interpreted, adding, "Sir, you must state your intentions decisively and clearly for the record."

"We are requesting political asylum," Vladimir said.

Ambassador Bass was given the interpretation.

"Welcome to the Embassy of the United States of America," he said, smiling broadly. "I'm afraid you won't be safe here for very long. We'd like to move you out tonight if you feel up to it."

"We go now!" Vladimir said, understanding the Ambassador's words.

"You speak English. That's good. Yes, you'll go now," the Ambassador said.

"You'll be taken to a private landing strip about three hours drive from here. A United States transport plane will be sitting on the runway waiting for you. It's in transit as we speak," the interpreter said.

"That is good," Vladimir said, taking Anna's hand and kissing it, sending a signal to the Ambassador that was instantly understood.

I must call the States and forewarn them that they're much more than just colleagues, the Ambassador thought as he led them out to the waiting transport.

* * *

Nine hours later in a secured building in London, Vladimir and Anna found themselves being interrogated by what were obviously high-level American agents and government officials. They kept refusing to answer their queries, insisting that the Israelis be present at the debriefing. One American, dressed in the uniform of a full general, grew angry.

"You came to us for help, and now you insist that you won't talk unless the Israelis are present. It doesn't make any sense; and it doesn't work that way. You answer my questions, and then we'll arrange a meeting."

"I'll tell you only one more time," Vladimir said. "I have information invaluable to your government, and I'll give you that information in joint participation with the Israeli government. You go to your people and tell them what I said. This is not open for discussion."

The men moved out into the hallway.

"Son of a bitch! What do we do now?" Andrew Madison, a CIA deep cover agent with over twelve years experience, asked General Buford. "I've dealt with the fucking Israelis before, and I'm telling you, General, it's a mistake to bring them in. You just give me a few hours alone with these Russians and I'll have them singing like canaries."

"You'll do no such thing," General Buford said. "I want them taken to the safe house, where they can get some rest. I'll contact you as soon as I've heard from Washington."

* * *

The call came into Golda Meir's office at three o'clock that same afternoon.

"I understand, Mr. President. I appreciate your call, and we'll be more than happy to assist. Please allow us twenty-four hours to make arrangements and to deliver our people," Golda said, hanging up the phone and smiling. She rang the buzzer on her desk, instructing her assistant to arrange a meeting with the head of the Mosad.

A few hours later, files were being analyzed and a group was being assembled. In attendance would be Israel's top nuclear scientists as well as a select group of trusted non-government officials. The President of the United States had been insistent that no one directly representing the Israeli government could be in attendance at the debriefing. The search was on to find highly placed civilians with security clearance and fluency in Russian.

* * *

Saul's phone rang. He listened without speaking, finally saying, "I'll be ready to leave in fifteen minutes."

He went in search of Rebecca.

"You'll never believe this, but Golda just called. I've been selected to go to England to debrief some Russian scientists that have defected to the Americans. The interesting thing is that the Russians are refusing to cooperate unless representatives from Israel are present."

"Maybe they're Jews," Rebecca speculated. "Wouldn't that be something?"

Saul laughed, "You know, I bet that possibility never even dawned on the Americans."

* * *

Twenty-four hours later, the Israeli team arrived in London. The group was taken directly into the debriefing.

Saul's group entered the room and was shown to their chairs. The General, standing at the head of the huge oval table, welcomed them and conducted the formal introductions. Eventually Vladimir and Anna were brought into the room.

"I have a statement to make," Vladimir said in Russian without waiting for the General to even sit down. "We'll tell you everything we know, but in return we want to be guaranteed safe passage to Israel, where we can be with..." he took a deep breath, "with our people."

Saul's eyes clouded over. Could this be possible? he wondered, feeling as if he'd been transported back in time to the hellish bowel of the ship that had brought him to Palestine so many years earlier.

Riveting his eyes on Vladimir, Saul stood, causing his chair to overturn. He walked quickly to Vladimir and put his hand on the Russian's shoulder. The two men looked deeply into each other's eyes.

"My God, it's really you," Saul said, recognition and shock setting in simultaneously.

"Is it possible? Oh, my God, you're the man from the ship." Vladimir lifted Saul, hugging him as tears unashamedly slid down his face.

"Yes, from the ship. It's really me, David. You're safe now; I'm going to take you home," Saul whispered, kissing him tenderly on the cheek.

Chapter 46

──────── ★ ────────

Jo dropped her bags by the front door of her Albany apartment and immediately went around opening windows, allowing the cool April air to circulate through the stale-smelling rooms.

In the bedroom, she stripped off her clothes and collapsed on the bed, having traveled for almost twenty-four hours. But before giving in to sleep, she dialed Robbie's home.

"Hello."

"Robbie, it's Jo."

"When did you get back?"

"I've only been home a few minutes. I'm so sorry about your wife. I tried to reach you from Israel several times. Did you get my messages?"

"Yes, I did, and thanks. It meant a lot. It's been a nightmare. Can I ask you something, Jo?"

"Of course."

"I know I don't have the right to ask you this, but would you consider coming to Washington? I could really use a friend right about now."

"I could probably work it out, " Jo said, exhausted and wishing she felt more enthusiastic than she did.

"Listen, I don't want to impose, if it's even slightly inconvenient we could do it another time."

"No, no. It's okay. You just took me by surprise. I'll come for the weekend."

"Thanks. I can't tell you how much it means to me. It's been hell."

"Do you want to talk about it?"

"To tell you the truth, I'm not sure I can. I'm so closed off I feel as if I'm going to explode. Sometimes I think I'm fine and then I just…well, I lose it. Death is so final, so damn final and she was a good woman. She didn't deserve this," he said, his voice heavy and sad. "But anyway, it's happened and I'm trying to learn to live with it. Listen to me, I'm being selfish as hell; you must be exhausted. We'll talk when we see each other. And Jo," he continued cautiously, "I'm afraid I'll have to send my driver to pick you up when you arrive. I'd come myself, but the reporters follow me everywhere. They're having a field day playing up this tragedy—Camelot destroyed and all that. I think it would be best if I didn't have to explain our friendship just yet. I hope you don't mind?"

"Don't be silly. Of course I don't mind," Jo said, her hands trembling in anticipation.

Returning to her office the next day, Jo found that her staff had done an excellent job of keeping everything under control. On Wednesday she called Robbie.

"I'm all caught up. So, if you'd still like me to come, I'm available for Friday."

"That's wonderful news, " he said, taking down her flight information. They spoke for a few more minutes before hanging up.

* * *

Jo barely slept Thursday night, haunted by memories from their past relationship. He was no longer married, and that meant that everything would be different. The question that she kept asking herself, was did she want it to be different?

* * *

Arriving in Washington, Jo felt horribly insecure and her stomach kept knotting in cramps as she made her way through the crowds.

At the end of the concourse, a well mannered, impeccably dressed elderly gentleman waited, holding a card with her name on it.

"I'm Bennett, Miss Wells, Mr. Osborne's driver. I hope you had a pleasant flight." He was solicitous and fatherly, and Jo liked him instantly.

"It was fine, thanks for asking."

* * *

The Mercedes limousine was parked at curbside, the government plates assuring that the tow truck would pass by.

"You just sit back and relax, Miss Wells. We'll be there in no time," Bennett said, his thick Texas accent drawing out every word as he slid into the front drivers seat.

Jo loved Washington. She knew it well and felt exhilarated as they drove north from Washington National Airport. Crossing the Potomac River, they headed east past the Washington Monument and the Mall, finally arriving at the Senate offices.

"We're here, Miss Wells. Safe and sound," Bennett said, opening the door. "You just go on in and tell the man at reception that you're looking for Senator Taxton's office. He'll give you directions. I'll see you later."

* * *

Jo found Robbie's office easily.

"Representative Wells, I'm so very glad to meet you," Robbie's secretary, a silver haired woman with piercing green eyes and a lovely smile said after Jo introduced herself. "The Senator is expecting you."

Jo had tried to envision what Robbie's office would look like. It was a game she often played with herself. She was usually quite good at guessing, but not this time. She expected it to be ultramodern. Instead, Robbie had chosen the sleek lines of contemporary American furniture. Floor to ceiling cherry wood bookcases filled with leather-bound books and spectacular period pieces covered one wall—all obviously selected by someone with exceptional taste.

Hanging on the wall behind Robbie's enormous Georgian antique desk was a photograph of President Kennedy with Jacqueline, Robbie and Ashley. Photos of the Senator's family and other famous friends surrounded that photo.

Jo studied Robbie as he approached her. When she looked into his doe-like eyes, she saw the sadness. It was so intense that she actually flinched.

"It's good to see you, Jo," he said, kissing her tenderly on the cheek. "Would you like some coffee or perhaps something a little stronger?" he asked, leading her to a sofa facing widows that overlooked the magnificent Washington skyline.

"Coffee would be fine."

Robbie buzzed his secretary. By the time the coffee arrived, they were so deep in conversation, they hadn't noticed that time had passed.

Robbie shared the details of the funeral with Jo.

"I guess it's been hardest on my in-laws. Ashley was their only child," he said, biting back tears.

He stood up abruptly, turning his back on Jo.

"I hate this! I hate being so damn vulnerable. It's as if I've been caught in some horrendous downward spiral I can't get out of."

Turning to face her, his eyes burning with anger, he continued, "I'm so pissed off. Why do these things happen? She never did anything to hurt anyone in her entire life."

Jo instinctively reached for his hand. The contact seemed to frighten Robbie, and he pulled his hand away.

"My parents," he stammered, "keep a year-round suite at the Parker Hotel. I've made arrangements for you to stay there if you'd like."

"Thanks, but Aaron has been kind enough to invite me to stay with him. I think I'd be more comfortable there," Jo said, noticing the skepticism in Robbie's eyes. "Aaron and I are just good friends, Robbie," Jo said, immediately growing angry with herself for finding it necessary to explain her motivations.

A dark look crossed Robbie's face.

"It's very kind of Aaron to offer his home. I hope you know that I'd like nothing better than to have you stay at my home, but I'm afraid it's out of the question. The press would misconstrue our relationship, and that wouldn't be good for either one of our careers."

Jo was taken aback. *Nothing's going on between us. What's his problem?* She thought moodily, smiling through gritted teeth.

"There's a great little Italian restaurant in Bethesda. We could have dinner there tonight if you'd like?"

"That would be lovely," she replied stiffly.

Robbie removed a piece of paper from his breast pocket with the name of the restaurant and its location written on it.

"Would you mind meeting me there? I'm afraid I'm going to be tied up in a meeting until very late."

Before Jo could respond his secretary entered.

"Sir, your appointment has arrived."

"I'm so sorry, Jo. Believe me, I'd have gotten out of this if I could have. Bennett will be at your disposal for the rest of the day," he said, rising.

How magnanimous of you, Jo thought, furious, having expected him to clear his calendar as she had cleared hers.

"Give me five minutes," he instructed his secretary, "and then show the Congressman in. I promise I'll make this up to you. I've had this appointment scheduled for weeks. He's a very important contact for me. I couldn't chance alienating him. You do understand?"

"Don't give it another thought, " Jo said, moving toward the door.

"Wait!" Robbie said. "Use the side door. The elevator is just down the hall on your right and Bennett is out front waiting for you."

As Jo waited for the elevator, she rationalized his paranoid behavior as a reaction to everything that he'd gone through, berating herself for being so self-centered.

Once in the limousine, Jo gave Aaron's address to Bennett. He had recently moved from New York to Silver Springs, Maryland, and she had yet to visit his new home.

* * *

Turning into Aaron's driveway, the limousine was stopped from entering by a gate. Pressing an intercom, the driver announced his passenger, and the gate slid open.

Jo looked out the window in wonder. The sprawling mansion was complete with antebellum verandas, stained-glass windows, Japanese cherry trees, and crawling ivy vines. *It's perfect,* Jo thought as she spotted Aaron standing in the driveway.

"Hi beautiful, I've missed you," Aaron said, helping her out of the car. He kissed her gently on the cheek. "Well, what do you think of my humble abode?" he asked. "Not bad for a once penniless immigrant, is it?"

"Aaron, what can I say? It's absolutely fabulous."

"You don't think it's too ostentatious; you know, noveaux riche and all that?"

"Absolutely not," she answered, dazzled by the beauty of the surroundings.

Taking her by the hand, Aaron led Jo up the steps.

"My butler will see to your luggage," he said, squeezing Jo's hand. "

Jo was awestruck as she wandered around the mansion with Aaron. He had turned his home into a museum filled with priceless objects. And yet, in all its opulence, there was warmth that permeated every room, making Jo feel as if she never wanted to leave.

The walls were covered with Judaic art and very old photographs, not of famous people, but of people just doing what people do. And through those photographs Aaron managed to tell the story of the survival of the Jewish people. Every room seemed magical to Jo, revealing another side to Aaron's personality.

"Where in the world did you find all of this?" Jo asked, holding what was obviously a very old silver candlestick.

"From collectors, from my travels, from friends who heard what I was trying to do here. What do you think?" he asked.

"What do I think? I think I've never seen anything as perfect," Jo said "And I also think that I'm honored to be your friend."

Aaron laughed self-consciously as they moved out to the veranda that overlooked the back gardens of the mansion.

Sitting comfortably in an old-fashioned rocker, Jo began to giggle. "I love this. I may never leave."

Aaron laughed. "Just wait until you see what happens next."

With that, the butler appeared, carrying a silver tray of pink lemonade and home-baked cookies.

"Aaron, this is right out of *Gone with the Wind.*"

"I know. It's intentional. But enough already. Tell me, how was your first week back at work?"

"My staff did a great job without me. I guess I'd kind of hoped that they'd have missed me more," Jo said. "How about you?"

"About the same. I think we make ourselves more important than we really are," Aaron said, seeing a troubled look cross Jo's face. "What's the matter? You look like you lost your last friend."

"I don't know. I guess I'm just being silly, but I don't like the way Robbie treated me. I know I should give him the benefit of the doubt, but he was terribly rude. I almost felt dirty. It was as if I were doing something wrong by being his friend," Jo said, as she proceeded to tell Aaron every detail of her encounter with Robbie.

Aaron had always known that Robbie was a notorious skirt chaser, and since his wife's death, rumors had begun circulating that there had been no love lost between them.

"You know people do change, and you really don't know him anymore. So why don't you give yourself some time to see if you like the person he's become."

"You're right, of course. After all, we were only kids when I knew him."

"Go with your instincts," Aaron said, glancing at his watch. "I can't believe it's almost six. You better get moving, or you'll be late."

He kissed Jo on the cheek; then he watched as she moved inside, thinking all the while how beautiful she was. Just as he was about to sit down, Jo came back outside and ran to Aaron, hugging him tightly. Then, without saying a word, she was gone again.

* * *

Entering the guest room that Aaron had specified as hers earlier in the day, Jo was delighted to find that all of her belongings had been meticulously unpacked.

The huge room, obviously decorated with a woman in mind, had a four-poster bed adorned with a rose-patterned down comforter and matching pillow shams. Freestanding wardrobe closets stood open, and alongside her own clothing she found an exquisitely hand-embroidered silk bathrobe. Putting it on after showering, she applied some fresh make-up and dressed in her favorite Yves Saint-Laurant evening suit. Feeling pampered and relaxed, she went to find Aaron.

"You look lovely, Jo," he said, leading her out to the driveway. His chauffeur was waiting. "I must be crazy sending you off into another man's arms," he teased, wishing he had the courage to ask her to stay. "Have a good time. I'll see you tomorrow."

Aaron stood in the shadowed light of the driveway for a very long time after Jo left, trying to understand the turmoil he was feeling. He hadn't wanted Jo to leave, but he couldn't tell her that. Theirs was a relationship that could never be; he was a Jew, and he had a responsibility to the memory of his dead parents, and to the six million of his people who had been lead to their slaughter because of their beliefs. Jo wasn't one of his people, and he couldn't break with the covenant. But still he didn't want Jo to have a relationship with Taxton, of that he was certain.

Returning to the house, Aaron admitted to himself that what he was feeling was pure, unadulterated jealousy. Lonely and depressed, he poured himself a stiff drink.

* * *

As the limousine moved rapidly through the light Maryland traffic, Jo was filled with self-doubt. For years Robbie had been the object of her every fantasy, remaining her one true love. But now that he was here and available to her, Jo couldn't understand why she felt so reticent.

* * *

"Welcome, Representative Wells," the maitre d' said, greeting Jo warmly as she entered the restaurant. "Please follow me. The Senator is waiting."

Jo was surprised to be called by name, especially after all the fuss Robbie had made earlier in the day about their friendship remaining secret.

The maitre d' led her to a secluded table in the back of the restaurant. Seeing her approach, Robbie stood, looking relaxed and very handsome.

"You're magnificent, absolutely magnificent," he said, holding the chair for her. "I've been sitting here like a nervous school boy, trying to make sense of everything that's happened. I hope you're not angry with me for the way I acted today."

"Don't be silly. Why would I be angry?" Jo asked, her voice cold.

"Look, I can explain."

"That's not necessary, Robbie," Jo retorted.

"You are angry."

"You were rude and you made me feel cheap." Jo's eyes blazed; she hadn't intended to be so bold.

"My God, I never meant for you to feel cheap. I guess I'm acting irrationally and I really am sorry."

Jo stared at him, her eyes squinting, her mouth tight. *He's being sincere. I'm just being an overly sensitive ass.*

"Do I remember that look?" Robbie said playfully. "I can even remember when you used to use it."

"So do I," Jo replied, laughing despite herself, remembering all the times he had tried to seduce her and all the times she had given him the *look* .

Her anger dissipated; they discussed what food to order and what type of wines they liked. Robbie talked about the funeral but he did so begrudgingly.

"You know, I've talked and thought about nothing else for days. Please, don't think me uncaring, but I'd like to talk about something else–anything else."

"Well, let's see, religion and politics are off bounds according to proper etiquette," Jo chided sarcastically.

"The hell with that! We'd have nothing to talk about." He smiled. "Tell me Miss Wells, what are your views on the Watergate scandal?"

"I'm angry and disappointed," Jo said.

"I think Nixon is guilty as hell," Robbie said. "The only good thing is that the son of a bitch has made it almost impossible for a Republican president to be elected for years to come."

"Why not cut the man some slack?" Jo responded. "Whatever happened to due process or innocent until proven guilty? And if he is found to be guilty, don't you think there are issues here far more important then the future of the Republican Party? My God, think of the repercussions. I still can't even begin to comprehend that the President of the United States could be involved with such abuse of power. On the other hand," she said, vacillating slightly, "I think it's important that we remember some of the fantastic accomplishments the man has had, not the least of which is how he negotiated a peace agreement in Vietnam."

The first revelations of just how serious Watergate was had occurred while they had been in Israel. President Nixon had announced the resignations of his Chief of Staff H. R. Haldeman and his Domestic Policy Assistant John Ehrlichman. Shortly thereafter FBI Director Patrick Grey had resigned when it was revealed that he had destroyed Watergate records given to him by White House Counsel John Dean.

Then Jo and Robbie allowed themselves to become enmeshed in a discourse on Vietnam. But their ideologies were diametrically opposed, and it didn't take long before Jo's liberalism and Robbie's hawkish views clashed.

Robbie made some disparaging remarks about peace protesters and how they had torn at the fabric of everything America stood for, and Jo retorted with some livid remarks of her own. Realizing how badly their evening was deteriorating, Robbie tried unsuccessfully to change the subject, but Jo refused to be distracted, stubbornly continuing her rebuttal.

"You know, we don't have to agree on everything in order to be friends," Robbie said finally, interrupting her tirade.

Embarrassed and realizing that he was right, Jo apologized. Finally finding a subject of mutual interest, they turned their discussion to a book that they had both recently read and enjoyed.

"Well, what do you know? We're having a conversation that's mutually satisfactory," Robbie said. His mood changed quickly and his eyes took on an intensity that frightened Jo. "I want us to find a lot more things we can agree on. I want us to be much more than friends." Jo squirmed in her seat as he continued.

"We have to start with a clean slate, so you might as well hear this from me instead of from someone else. My wife and I were not exactly a match made in heaven. I'm ashamed to admit this to you, but it was a marriage of convenience; I needed a wife, and she wanted a husband who was going places. It was really that simple."

"Simple? I don't understand. Are you telling me that you married a woman you didn't love?" She asked, finding his motives reprehensible.

"We were good together. We had a lot in common—we enjoyed the same people, we traveled in the same circles, and our families were thrilled. At the time it seemed like the right thing to do for both of us. I admit I took the easy way out, but now that you've come back into my life, everything's different."

"It's getting late, Robbie, and I really think I should go," Jo said, doing little to hide her displeasure.

"Listen, I don't expect you to understand. I've given up a lot to get where I am today. And looking back, perhaps I shouldn't have. But fate has given me another chance and I want to try and do it better this time," Robbie said, reaching for Jo's hand. "Just give me a chance, please."

Despite herself, Jo smiled.

"So, how about a picnic at the zoo tomorrow?" he asked while waiting to pay the check.

"Look, Robbie, this is all happening too quickly. I need time."

"I'll back off. I promise. I just want to spend time with you, Jo."

The longing she saw in his eyes disarmed Jo, and she found herself agreeing to see him again.

When they reached her waiting car, he reached down to kiss her, but she turned away, offering him her hand instead.

"I'm sure this is much more appropriate," Jo said softly. "Thank you for a lovely evening."

"I'll call you tomorrow," Robbie said, furious with himself for how the evening had turned out.

* * *

Jo spent the next day and evening with Robbie. And she actually found herself enjoying his company. They spent hours talking about their lives. He intended to run for the presidency, and Jo was convinced that he had a very good chance of winning.

Returning to Aaron's late Saturday night, Robbie took Jo into his arms. He kissed her deeply and she responded hungrily.

"I've dreamed of this moment for so long, Jo. I've never stopped loving you."

"Please, Robbie. You promised," Jo said, pulling away.

"You're right. I promised," Robbie said, cautious now, intent on winning her affections. "Thank you for a terrific weekend. I'm going to miss you."

* * *

Once Robbie's car had pulled out of sight, Jo went to the front door. Aaron opened it before she could knock.

"Hi, beautiful. How was your date?" Aaron asked, sipping a drink, his speech slightly slurred.

"Aaron Blumenthal, are you inebriated?" Jo teased.

"That's entirely possible."

"Have you been waiting up for me?"

"Guilty as charged. Did you have a good time?"

"It was OK."

"Only OK? What happened?"

Jo wasn't sure. Her mind kept flashing back to the way it used to be between Robbie and her. She found the memory of that love titillating. There was no question in her mind that she was attracted to Robbie, but she didn't know why. And she couldn't help but question whether she really liked him. Jo was glad to be going home.

"I'm just not sure how I feel about him. Things are moving too quickly. I need some time to think."

"That's probably a good idea," he said, relieved that she would be out of Robbie's grasp.

"I'll miss you, Aaron," Jo said.

Aaron smiled.

I'll miss you more than you'll ever know, he thought, touching her face tenderly.

Chapter 47

──────────── ✦ ────────────

Hans and Otto sat on the sofa in Jo's Albany apartment awaiting her return. They had decided to take no chances; they would intervene and assist in Jo's relationship with Senator Robbie Taxton.

"We need to talk," Otto said, turning his attention away from the television show they were watching. " I've been thinking a lot about Robert Osborne, and the best way to eliminate him. I'm not particularly worried about the body guard, that can be handled," Otto sneezed; he delicately removed the monogrammed handkerchief from his pocket and wiped his nose.

"I've been thinking about it as well," Hans interjected. "And I've some grave concerns. Putting aside my own personal wishes, and looking at this strictly from the viewpoint of a psychiatrist, I'm convinced that at the very least Jo would go into a sustained mourning period if something happened to Robert Osborne. And God only knows how long that mourning would last if Osborne met a violent death. If the goal here is to have her marry Taxton, and to have that happen within the year, then I think we have to reconsider our original plans. I think we have to wait."

"But the danger to us and the others…"

"I know it's a calculated risk, but we're too close to reaching our goals to let the fucking Israeli's scare us into making a mistake. We can't risk it. I'll call the others. All I'm asking for is a little time, just until they're married."

* * *

On the plane ride home Jo found herself thinking more about Aaron than Robbie and that confused her. By the time she arrived at her apartment, she had given herself the beginnings of a migraine.

"Welcome back, Miss Wells," Andrew, the doorman, said, taking Jo's luggage from the trunk of the taxi. "Did you have a nice trip?"

"Yes. Thank you."

They entered the elevator. "By the way, your father and uncle are here. They arrived yesterday."

Damn it! That's the last thing I need right now.

Standing outside the door of her apartment, Jo handed Andrew a five-dollar bill.

"I can take it from here," she said, slipping the key into the lock. Jo pushed open the door. Her father and uncle were watching television.

"This is a surprise," Jo said, doing little to mask her annoyance as she brought her luggage inside.

Disregarding Jo's obvious displeasure, her father approached. He kissed her cheek.

Otto watched, saying nothing.

"Where have you been?" Hans asked, even though he knew.

"I went to Washington to see friends," Jo said.

"We've had this discussion before, Jotto. I want to be kept informed where you are at all times," her father said, anger causing his face to redden.

"Must we begin with such unpleasantness?" Otto said.

Hans shot him a murderous look, but Otto disregarded his brother-in-law.

"Come and sit next to your uncle. I've missed you," Otto patted the seat beside him. "We've a lot to talk about. We want to hear all about your trip to Israel."

Jo cringed. The cadence in his voice frightened her and she pressed herself against the wall.

"Come, my child," he said, opening the silver cigarette case. The music tugged at Jo's mind.

She moved trance-like to the couch.

"Close your eyes...relax..."

Damn it. I'm too tired. But I won't give in. I won't listen!

* * *

Jo awoke the next morning with a memory lapse and an all too familiar ache in the pit of her stomach. While standing in the shower the tears suddenly came, her chest heaved; she was furious.

Why? Why couldn't I resist? What did they do to screw up my head?

Dressing quietly, she slipped from the apartment.

Determined to throw herself into the work at hand, and to put aside all thoughts of her family and Robbie, she began reading a new bill that would be coming up in the House. But she was unable to concentrate. Instead Jo had a manic compulsion to hear Robbie's voice. Driven mad by her compulsion, Jo dialed his private number.

"Hello, Robbie."

"Jo?" he asked. "I tried all last night to reach you but the phone was continually busy."

"My father and uncle paid me an unexpected visit. I guess the phone must have inadvertently been left off the hook. "

"Listen, I feel like I owe you an apology for the other night. I know I'm moving too quickly and the last thing I want to do is to scare you off. It's just that you drive me crazy; I feel like a love-sick school boy all over again."

"I didn't especially like the way that particular romance turned out," Jo chided. "You broke my heart, remember?"

"Someday soon I'll explain it all to you. I swear it. But for now, just take my word that I never stopped loving you."

"I don't think I ever stopped loving you either," Jo said, drawing out each word, unexplainably emboldened.

"God, how long I've dreamed of hearing you say that? When can I see you again?" Robbie asked, his voice husky, gentle.

"Soon. Very soon," Jo said, knowing that nothing would be able to keep her from his side.

* * *

Jo began commuting to Washington on the weekends and to Robbie's family estate for holidays. Robbie's mother was joyous that her son seemed himself again. Due to her husband's change of heart toward the relationship, she was now convinced that Jo would be an excellent partner and First Lady.

Robbie, overjoyed by the relationship, showered Jo with extravagant gifts: a diamond and emerald ring, each square-cut stone 2 karats, an ermine full-length coat, dozens of Hermes scarves. At first she was reluctant to accept the gifts, but she eventually acquiesced.

Reveling in the addictive emotions of being so loved, Jo was intent on sharing that happiness with the two other men in her life whom she adored: Robert and Aaron.

Robert would take the shuttle from New York to Washington a couple of times a month. And then Aaron, Robert, Jo and Robbie would go out, attending the theater, opera and ballet.

But Jo knew down deep, that neither Robert nor Aaron particularly liked Robbie. And she understood why. After all, Robbie and Aaron could find little to agree upon, having diametrically opposed beliefs on just about everything.

As for Robert, Jo felt that he was simply being over-protective and perhaps a little jealous. He had always been the one to give her lavish gifts, and he had been the object of her affection, platonic as it was, for years.

Jo was also very concerned about the turn of events in Robert's life. He had come back from Israel with a bodyguard in tow, Manny, a 6'4", 250 pound gorilla who never smiled or spoke. Robert explained that he had been pestered by fans lately and felt that his lifestyle and safety were being encumbered. Jo understood his concern but the bullet-proof limousine and the bullet-proof glass on all the exterior windows of the townhouse, the movement sensors and alarm systems, seemed a bit neurotic; more the behavior of a wealthy eccentric then the Robert Osborne she thought she knew so well. But despite everything, Jo was determined to keep her little family together.

* * *

Aaron and Robert's friendship grew. The two men met whenever Robert came to Washington or Aaron went to New York.

"I'm telling you, she's infatuated. She doesn't love him; she couldn't. They have absolutely nothing in common," Aaron said as they sat on his veranda, drinks in hand, months into Jo's courtship with Robbie.

"I'll be damned if I can figure it out," Robert said, frustrated. "I suppose he's a nice enough young man, but he's not right for Jo. I just can't believe she doesn't see that." Robert shaded his eyes with his hand as he spoke, the setting sun causing a glare.

"Maybe she's been taken in by the thought of becoming the First Lady," Aaron offered as he moved the umbrella to get the sun out of Robert's eyes.

"I refuse to believe that. There's something else going on here. Perhaps it's family pressure."

"That's a possibility," Aaron said. "Jo's father and uncle have been invited a number of times to the Taxton mansion."

Robert paled. "How do you know that?" His voice was terse. His hands trembled.

"Jo told me."

Robert's heart pounded, he clenched his fist. "I wonder why she never told me?"

"She probably thought she did."

Robert's head swam. *The Nazis are grabbing for power and Jo's the unwitting pawn. I'll call Saul. He'll tell me what to do.*

"Are you okay?" Aaron asked, seeing the terror in his friend's eyes.

Robert nodded, looking at his watch. "We'd better go; I don't want to keep William waiting. The agent in him has never done well with anyone keeping him waiting," Robert said, rising on unsteady legs.

* * *

William was sitting on the barstool at the Vandam restaurant when they entered. He often accompanied Robert on his weekends. Smiling, he stood, waving enthusiastically. Pushing his horn-rimmed glasses securely back over his prominent nose, he moved gingerly toward them despite his broad girth.

Robert and Aaron waved. Manny followed, never more than a foot from Robert's side. And as they approached, a hush fell over the noisy bar. People turned to stare at Robert.

At sixty-five Robert Osborne was still magnificent. His dark hair was dashed with silver streaks, his cobalt eyes remained intense, and his body was lean and hard. He walked past with panther-like grace, an air of danger and sexiness radiating from his every move.

Nodding now and again to acquaintances, the group made their way to an isolated table in the far corner of the restaurant. After they placed their drink order, a lovely young girl boldly approached them.

Manny moved to block her but Robert waved him aside.

"Mr. Osborne, may I have your autograph?" she asked, handing him a slip of paper.

Robert asked her name and then jotted her a note, signing it in big scrawling letters.

"Call me sometime and I'll make you dinner," she said, handing him her business card.

"I don't get it," Aaron teased, after the young woman had moved away. "You're not bad looking; I'll give you that. But you're old enough to be her father."

"Maybe she likes her men older," Robert parried, his eyes filled with mirth. "You know in my day, I was quite the lover. But now they're just old stories…just like me. Ten minutes with that beauty and they'd have to bury me."

"Who are you kidding?" William interjected. "You'd find a way."

"You're right, you old dog," Robert said. "I'd damn sure find a way."

* * *

Alone in his office, the phones turned off, Robbie sat eating his lunch while reading the newspaper and contemplating the events of the last few weeks. A public that was enchanted with the image Robbie had so carefully created met the announcement that he, considered one of the country's most eligible bachelors, was to marry New York State

Representative Jotto Wells, with insatiable curiosity. He was poised and waiting to announce his Presidential candidacy, and in the mean time he was doing his best to capitalize on all the media attention, parading the magnificent Jo around like a prized possession.

"Sorry to disturb you, Senator, " his secretary said, interrupting his musings.

"I'm having my lunch," Robbie snapped, angered by the interruption.

"It's Miss Wells' father and uncle, sir."

"Oh, Jesus," Robbie said, quickly throwing his food into the garbage. "Show them in, and bring coffee."

Hans entered first, and Robbie was again struck by his future father-in-law's exceedingly handsome good looks. His neatly trimmed beard and hair were pure white, perfectly accentuating his dark-green eyes, that radiated an intensity Robbie found frightening. He wore a white shirt, Hermes tie, and black wool suit, exceptionally expensive and beautifully tailored.

Otto followed. In contrast, he was dressed more flamboyantly: gray suit, black silk shirt left casually open at the collar, and black Ferragamo loafers. His high cheekbones and meticulously cut silver hair made Robbie think that Otto was perhaps prettier than he was handsome.

"What a nice surprise," Robbie said, shaking their hands.

"We were in the area and decided to come by and personally welcome you into our family," Hans said. "I hope we're not interrupting anything too important, Senator."

"No, not at all. It's always a pleasure to see you both. Please, make yourselves comfortable," Robbie said, moving back behind his desk.

"We thought the time was right for you to get to know us a little better," Otto said, as he and his brother-in-law sat.

Robbie watched as Hans and Otto unhurriedly prepared cigars, first snipping off the tips and then wetting them with saliva, obviously enjoying their ritual.

"We understand," Hans said finally, lighting his panatela, "that before her death your late wife's family had been using their enormous political influence in Washington to help insure your future. It's most unfortunate for you that you've lost their backing now that you've decided to marry my daughter," Hans said, watching for Robbie's reaction.

Robbie had known that his decision to marry Jo would alienate his in-laws and financially impact his candidacy. But his father had assured him that it would be a very small bump in a very long road and that other arrangements had already been made."

"I love your daughter, sir. We all make choices in this life, and I've made mine."

Hans and Otto were pleased at Taxton's devotion to Jo, delighting in how much easier that would make their job.

"How far would you be willing to go to become President of the United States?" Hans asked, his narrow lips taking on a sinister smirk.

"I don't understand what you mean, sir." Robbie frowned.

"I think I'm making myself extremely clear. How far would you be willing to go?"

"I guess I'd do just about anything this side of the law," Robbie said, not the least cowered by Hans' tone.

"That's good. That's what I wanted to hear. You see, Senator, my brother-in-law and I happen to be in the position to hand you the presidency."

"And how are you going to do that?" Robbie asked, enthralled.

"The same way it's always done. We're going to buy it for you. You see we have some very powerful friends who'll do just about anything we ask of them. And we also happen to have more money at our disposal, Senator, than we know what to do with."

"And in return, gentleman?" Robbie asked, fascinated.

"Just a little cooperation on your part."

Robbie grew cold. "I really appreciate your offer, gentleman, but I don't care to be put in a compromising position. I believe I'll secure the nomination of my party on my own merits. Now perhaps we could discuss something—"

Hans brushed a piece of thread from his jacket before looking up. His eyes burned brightly. "You have little choice. You'll do as we say or you'll not only loose the nomination of your party but you and your family will be ruined."

"Are you threatening me, sir?"

"Pick up the phone and call your father."

"I don't know what this is all about but I take great exception to…"

"Call him," Otto growled, the nerves jumping in his left eye.

Robbie dialed his father's private number. Anderson answered on the first ring.

"Father, Jo's father and uncle are here. They're making threats about ruining me, and I'm about ready to call…"

"Do you want to be president, son?" Anderson asked.

"Yes, sir," Robbie replied.

"You just listen to them, boy. And you do whatever they say. You're going to be President of the United States, and that's all that matters. It's what you've worked towards your entire life. Call me after they've gone and we'll talk."

"Yes, sir." Robbie hung up the phone. His throat was dry. He trusted his father's political savvy, and he knew that if his astutely ambitious father trusted these men, he must trust them as well. Buzzing his secretary, he instructed her to cancel all appointments for the rest of the day.

"Why don't we sit over here," Hans said after Robbie turned off the intercom, moving toward the leather sectional sofa, "so we can talk."

Robbie moved to the couch, watching curiously as Otto pulled a chair from across the room. He placed it directly in front of Robbie.

"Turn the radio on," Han's ordered.

"Robbie reached over and tuned into a classical station.

"We can never be too careful. Now tell me, how do you feel about the Jews running the country?" Otto's voice was conciliatory, testing, cold.

"Excuse me?" Robbie asked, incredulous at the audacity of the question.

"We think it's time to stop them. All I want to know is if you agree."

Robbie looked from one to the other. He took a deep breath. "I think they're shit under my feet. They have their filthy little hands in every newspaper, bank and business in the country. Their liberal views are ruining this country and I'd do anything to stop them. Is that what you were hoping to hear?" Robbie said, taunting them.

"That's exactly what we wanted to hear," Otto said, smugly. "Now, why don't you just sit back and relax. Look at me, Robbie…look into my eyes and just relax."

Robbie smiled self-consciously, feeling silly. That was the last thing he remembered before being drawn into the overpowering depths of Otto's gaze.

* * *

The wedding was scheduled for July 4, 1973, and it was to be held in the private gardens of Robbie's close friend and associate, Peter Newel.

Ilya took an intense interest in her daughter's wedding, interviewing florists, caterers, and musicians. And Jo was thrilled by her mother's involvement, noting joyfully that her mother had even stopped drinking.

Ilya derived incredible satisfaction from the joyous look on Hans' face whenever she discussed Jo's impending nuptials with him. And she remained euphoric, knowing that all she had to do now was wait until the wedding took place, and then she would finally get to exact her revenge upon the unsuspecting Hans. The thought of killing him at the happiest moment in his life kept Ilya sober.

* * *

The inevitable announcement of Jo's wedding had devastated Aaron
and Robert; they got wildly drunk together. And when they parted the
next day, hung over and heartsick, they vowed that the friendship they
had forged would endure despite Jo's decision.

It was because of that friendship that Robert was now faced with a
dilemma. Saul had sent a telegram on June 1, 1973 that read:

"Urgent! Information available. Must see you at once.

Meet at Aaron Blumenthal's 6-4-73."

Robert was shocked and confused by Saul's decision to expose their
friend Aaron to a potentially dangerous situation. *Saul's always so
cautious. What's changed? What's happened?*

Chapter 48

─────── ★ ───────

Standing in front of the credenza in the foyer, Robert picked up the script delivered to him earlier in the day. Chastising himself for not reading it sooner, he took the lift to his bedroom on the third floor of his brownstone. After arranging the pillows so that he could sit comfortably on the bed, he put on his glasses and began perusing the manuscript. For a short time he managed to comprehend what he was reading, but eventually the words began to swim in front of his eyes and he found his mind wondering.

Why did I ever tell Aaron about Jo? Throwing the manuscript aside, he thought back to the circumstances surrounding his decision to confide in Aaron.

* * *

Only weeks before Jo's engagement, Aaron had come to New York on business. He had called Robert and invited him for dinner at the Plaza Hotel, where he was staying.

Both men had been understandably upset by the inevitability of Jo's impending engagement. And as they sat in the bar drinking more than either was accustomed to, Robert had told Aaron everything.

"Wait a minute!" Aaron said. "Are you telling me that Jo's the child of a Jewish mother?"

"Yes. That's exactly what I'm telling you. My wife was Jo's mother, and I convinced her father is Dr. Hans Wells."

"And you think Hans Wells is a Nazi?" Aaron asked.

"You're damn right I do! But we haven't been able to prove that...yet."

"And if you do?" Aaron asked. "What then? My God, Robert, the implications are devastating."

Robert hadn't answered Aaron. He just sat there staring into space.

Respecting Robert's silence, Aaron ordered another drink.

"To Jo," he said, slurring his words.

"Are you all right?" Robert asked, hearing his own thickened words.

"The night we arrived in Israel I took Jo to the Wall," Aaron said, his face pale and drawn. "She stood in front of the Wall for over an hour, Robert, and when she finally returned to where I was sitting, she was distraught. Jo had said that she'd had a vision of a woman who looked exactly like her. She said the woman talked with her..."

"Morgan came to Jo! I knew she would one day," Robert.

"My God, Robert, do you think...?"

"Do I think it's possible? Yes I do, Aaron...I do."

* * *

Robert got out of bed, deciding that it was futile to try to read the manuscript. He knew that it was right for Aaron to be present at his meeting with Saul and Natan, but he was angry that contact had been made behind his back and he was even angrier with himself for telling Saul that Aaron knew about Jo.

Cursing Natan, certain that the underhandedness of it all had been his doing, Robert called Aaron.

"I've received a telegram from Saul this afternoon. Tell me what's going on, Aaron? Why has he been in contact with you instead of me?" he asked.

"He called because he knows we're friends, that's why," Aaron said. "And you must have been the one to tell him that I know everything, because I haven't seen or spoken with him since Israel. He asked if he could use my home to meet with you. He said it would be too dangerous to meet anywhere else. What did you want me to say, Robert? Should I have said no? They've obviously found what they've been looking for, and you should be happy. As a matter of fact, you should be jumping for joy. What's wrong with you?" Aaron asked.

"I guess I'm afraid," Robert said. "I've created my own scenario over the years, but what if I'm wrong? What if Morgan willingly went—"

"You've got to stop thinking like that, Robert," Aaron said, continuing to talk soothingly to his friend. "You're not alone in this. I'm going to be with you no matter what happens."

* * *

After arranging to meet, Aaron fixed himself a drink and took it out to the veranda. As he stood gazing at the stars, his mind whirled with thoughts of Jo.

He wanted desperately to go to her, to protect her and make everything right, but he knew that Jo was with Robbie. And even though Aaron tried to deny his feelings, every time he thought about Taxton touching Jo, it made him crazy with jealousy.

He realized that his emotions were futile, but he couldn't control them. Ever since he had found out that Jo was born of a Jewish mother, thereby making her a Jew, he had been unable to keep himself from fantasizing about a life with her.

Maybe it's time for me to find a wife.

* * *

On June 4, 1973, Saul and Natan boarded El Al's flight 1624. The jumbo jet touched down in London to refuel before heading for New York City.

Having been warned by Israeli intelligence that his inquiries into the pasts of Dr. Hans Wells and Otto and Ilya Milch had caused alarm in certain German circles, Natan watched intently the boarding London passengers.

A man, his hair cut unfashionably short, wearing dark aviator glasses, his hands empty, moved down the isle. Natan's ulcerous stomach began to burn.

* * *

Making their way from customs through the busy La Guardia Airport, Natan turned to Saul.

"We're being followed," he said casually.

"He got on in London, right?"

"You knew?"

"I could smell the fucker," Saul said.

"We'll proceed as planned," Natan said, casually stopping to purchase a newspaper before boarding their plane to Washington.

Saul had been hoping he wouldn't have to expose Robert and Aaron to the danger that he and Natan were used to. They lived in an area of the world where violence and treachery were a way of life, but Robert had grown vulnerable, and Aaron, for all his experiences, was still naive as a child.

"Do we have any alternatives?" Saul asked as they moved down the concourse.

"I'm afraid not. Osborne's already in the house. We won't get another chance like this. As it is now, they'll never tie you in with Osborne. And that's the only hope we have of bringing them out into the open. Now act a little more natural and smile at me when you talk."

* * *

Upon their arrival in Washington, the two men secured a cab. Giving the driver Aaron's Silver Springs address, Natan looked sternly at Saul.

"You're sure you followed my instructions to the letter? You told Aaron to keep Osborne away from the windows and doors, and that he's not to come out to meet us."

"You know," Saul said, "I'm not a dolt."

"One can never be too careful," Natan said, nonplused by Saul's reproach. "I expect you to do as I say without hesitation, because as you said so succinctly to your friend Robert not very long ago, I don't trust people, not even you, Saul. It will be best for both of us if you remember that."

It was nearing midnight when the taxi passed through the security gate at the Blumenthal mansion. Aaron and his butler were waiting in the driveway as the cab approached.

"How was your flight?" he inquired, shaking hands, as the luggage was unloaded into the butler's capable hands.

"Uneventful," Saul said.

"Shall we go in?"

The three men entered the house.

"Is Osborne here?" Natan inquired.

"Yes. I'll take you to him now," Aaron said, leading the men through the cavernous rooms of the mansion.

"Any problems?" Aaron asked.

Saul nodded. "We were followed from London." Turning toward Aaron, Saul put his hand on his friend's shoulder. "I want you to reconsider your involvement in all of this, Aaron, before it's too late."

Aaron smiled. "We've talked about all of this on the phone, Saul. I'm here because I also care very deeply about Jo. There isn't anything I wouldn't do to help her. So why don't we cut the bullshit and get down to business," he said, moving to the study door.

Saul patted Aaron on the back.

"You're a good friend, Aaron. I only hope you won't regret your decision one day."

When the three men entered the study, they found Robert pacing the room, his face pale and his eyes blazing. Shaken, he embraced Saul. "God, it's good to see you, my friend."

"Are you OK?" Saul asked, watching as Robert shook Natan's hand.

"I'm nervous as hell. That's all. Did you have a good flight?"

"Nothing out of the ordinary," Natan answered.

"How are Rebecca and the family?" Robert asked, fighting to calm his frayed nerves.

"As I wrote to you, she has David and his wife to take care of now, and that's keeping her very busy. And of coarse, she's expecting to be here in less than a month for Jo's wedding. Don't ask how excited she is about that."

"It'll be good to see her. You must both be exhausted," Robert offered, noting the dark circles under Saul's eyes and the drawn look on his face.

"Would you like some coffee?" Aaron asked.

"I think we should begin," Natan said, taking out a note pad filled with pages of information written in Hebrew.

Robert, having forgotten how much he disliked Natan's imperious attitude, had to literally bite his tongue to keep from speaking out.

"Before I begin," Natan said, glancing one last time at his notes, "it's imperative that all of you understand that the information I'm about to reveal could put your lives in danger. I have to be sure that each of you understands and accepts that responsibility?"

"This is crazy," Robert said. "You have no business being here, Aaron. I want you to leave."

Aaron crossed his arms over his chest, glaring at Robert. "You're forgetting something, Robert. I'm a Jew and that makes it my business."

"Are you two quite through?" Natan asked. "If that's settled, I'd like to continue.

"As you know, my goal was to substantiate both the Wells' and Otto Milch's Nazi past. I worked with three of my colleagues from the Weisenthal Center in Vienna. Pouring through hundreds of files, we took a two-pronged approach. First we searched through testimonies given by survivors after the war. And then we went to Washington, where we got permission to research transcripts of interrogations that the Allies had held on displaced persons after the liberation, focusing primarily on those misplaced persons who had been given refuge in the United States.

"We decided to begin with Dr. Wells. It took weeks, but eventually we located the dossier on him. He was interrogated along with tens of thousands of others. He produced identity papers that listed him as a prisoner of war, part of the Free Polish Forces. The U.S. government processed him, along with his wife, Ilya Milch Wells, and their infant daughter. They were released.

"At the back of his file, inside of an envelope marked 'CONFIDEN-TIAL,' we found a picture of Wells as he had looked when the Allies interrogated him. That in itself seemed highly unusual. And as we continued to study his file, we found several entries that made no sense at all. There were other interviews, coded entries, and dates—all very mysterious. And then we found documents showing that three months after his release, Hans had been given a prestigious position within the United Nations Relief and Rehabilitation Agency in France. Confused, we went back to Israel. We began showing his picture to a cadre of survivors. Within a month we had ten positive identifications."

Natan hesitated, enjoying with anticipation the impact of his next words. "Hans Wells was a doctor at the Dachau concentration camp during the war."

Aaron and Robert gasped.

"Then how in the hell did he get into the United States?" Robert said. "The Americans must have known that."

Natan held up his hand to silence him.

"Let me try to explain. You see, after the war the government of the United States became convinced that they had a new enemy, the Soviet Union. American intelligence networks established proof that the Soviets were developing an atomic bomb. The Americans were terrified. They let it be known through the underground that they were looking for cooperative Nazis who could supply information.

"The United States government established a Nazi spy network within France. Nazi collaborators came out of the woodwork. Obviously, Hans Wells and Otto Milch were among the collaborators willing to help.

"We know now, of course, that the Nazis deceived the Americans. They forged intelligence reports in order to convince the United States that they had a wealth of information on the Soviet Union, when in fact they had very little. Unfortunately the Allies not only believed the information, but as a reward they even allowed a very elite group of Nazis to immigrate to America. Allowing this immigration was a direct violation of laws passed by the Congress of the United States. So, many collaborators, denied entrance to America, relocated in South America. We believe that's why Otto Milch wound up in Bolivia.

"According to Israeli intelligence, the Nazis had hidden, in secret vaults throughout Europe, priceless paintings stolen during the war— Greco, Cezanne, Monet, and others.

Collectors were willing to pay millions to own one of these great paintings. For that right, they signed agreements requiring them to keep their acquisitions out of sight for at least twenty years.

"We know for a fact that the Nazis have hundreds of millions of dollars deposited in numbered accounts in Switzerland," Natan said.

"This is absolutely unbelievable," Aaron said.

"Perhaps, but it's true," Natan said.

"It's just so hard for me to believe that the Americans would work knowingly with the Nazis."

Natan stared at Aaron, envious of his naiveté.

"I digressed so that you would be able to understand the rest of my report. I'd like to continue now, if you don't mind.

"One of the survivors, a Jewish doctor who worked for a time in the hospital, told us that while most of Dr. Hans Wells' work was done under a great cloak of secrecy, it was common knowledge that he was working on something to do with mind control. We understand that he often attempted surgery using hypnosis instead of anesthesia; only it didn't work very well. I'll spare you the details," Natan said.

Glancing at Robert, whose face looked gray and drawn, Natan began to fidget with his papers, hesitant to continue.

"We began asking questions about Morgan, hoping that someone would remember her. As luck would have it, it was our same Jewish doctor who filled in the missing pieces for us."

Robert held his breath, terrified to hear Natan's next words.

"Our informant said that Morgan was brought into the hospital after an apparent suicide attempt, and that Doctor Wells cared for Morgan himself. Eventually he even allowed her to wander among the hospital staff unsupervised."

Robert gasped and put his hands over his ears to block out the sound of Natan's voice.

"For God's sake, Natan, you've just told the man that his wife tried to kill herself. Show a little compassion," Aaron said.

Natan looked from Aaron to Robert.

"It was his wife. For me it was my mother, father, and baby brother. And for you, Aaron, your entire family. I'm sorry if this hurts, but I don't have the time, heart, or desire to soften my words. We're involved in a situation that stinks. If you can't take it, feel free to leave."

Robert wiped at his eyes with the back of his hand.

"Go on," Robert ordered, his voice tired and angry.

Natan began again, staring into space as he spoke, fighting to sound devoid of emotion, because even he feared what his next words were going to do to Robert Osborne.

"Dr. Hans Wells fell hopelessly in love with Morgan. Hospital gossip had it that he couldn't keep his hands off of her. She became pregnant and carried full term. No one seemed to know what happened to Morgan after the delivery."

Robert felt strangely disoriented. His vision blurred.

"As far as our informant knew, the baby was destroyed. All Jewish babies were. And if I hadn't seen the photos of Morgan and Jo for myself, I would have changed directions at that point. But I knew Morgan's child was still alive. What I didn't understand was why Wells would have taken the child as his own.

"The gossip mongers around the hospital—and there were plenty of them—told another informant of ours that an SS man named Otto Milch had sent Morgan to the camp to be protected and cared for by his twin sister, Ilya Milch, and her then fiancé, Dr. Hans Wells. It became very apparent to us at that point that Otto had been in love with Morgan as well."

Robert's protective cloak of denial shattered. His weakened heart began to palpitate irregularly and the roaring in his head became deafening. The room grew dark, and gasping for breath, Robert clawed blindly for something to hold onto as he tried to stand. Saul reached for Robert just as he collapsed.

Kneeling beside him, holding his hand and crying, Saul begged Robert to hold on. But it was too late. He was gone.

Chapter 49

———————— ★ ————————

The alarm clock buzzed annoyingly. Jo reached across Robbie to turn it off as he mumbled something about how ridiculous it was for her to go home so early. Quickly slipping out of bed, she padded barefooted into the kitchen.

She put two pieces of rye bread into the toaster, and while waiting for the coffee to finish percolating, she called the airport to be sure her flight back to Albany was on schedule. Then she turned on the television and changed stations until she found the morning news. She buttered her toast and poured her coffee, barely listening to the drone of the newscaster's voice in the background.

Carrying her breakfast to the table, she stopped dead in her tracks.

"At 3:00 A.M. today Robert Osborne was pronounced dead on arrival at Bethesda General Hospital," the newscaster said.

Jo dropped everything she was holding. The coffee splashed up and burned her legs.

"No! My God, please make it a nightmare," she screamed.

Robbie rushed into the room, pulling on his bathrobe.

"Jesus Christ! What's going on? Are you all right? Did you burn yourself?"

"It's Robert…he's dead," she mumbled almost incoherently.

"Oh no. My poor darling, I'm so sorry," Robbie said, moving toward Jo.

"I've got to talk to Aaron, he'll know what happened," she said pushing past Robbie and reaching for the phone, her hands trembling so badly she could hardly dial.

"Hello, Blumenthal's residence."

"Haddie, this is Jo Wells," Jo said, recognizing the maid's voice. "Is Mr. Blumenthal there?"

"No ma'am, he's out making arrangements to fly Mr. Osborne's body back to New York."

"But I don't understand. Why didn't he call me?"

"He tried to reach you at Senator Taxton's last night. I was right here making coffee when he called," Haddie said.

"That's impossible," Jo snapped, feeling a black fury beginning to build in her gut. "I was here all evening."

"All I know is that he talked with the Senator, ma'am."

Jo hung up the phone without saying goodbye.

"Last night, it was Aaron who called, wasn't it?" she said, remembering that when the phone had rung, awakening them both, Robbie had told her it was nothing.

"Now, darling, it was the middle of the night, and I simply suggested that whatever he wanted could surely wait until morning. How was I to know that it was something so serious? There's really no reason for you to be angry. After all, what could you have done last night? As it is, you've had a good night's sleep, and you'll be able to handle all of this so much better."

Jo slapped Robbie's face hard enough to leave her palm print on his cheek.

"How dare you? You insensitive bastard!" she yelled, pushing Robbie away, her mind numb, her heart exploding. "I've got to get out of here. I'm calling a cab, and don't try to stop me!" Jo sobbed between words.

While she quickly dressed, Robbie tried to reason with her. "I was wrong and I'm sorry. Just sit down a minute and let me talk to you."

"I have nothing to say to you."

"Come on, darling, you're just upset. You don't mean that."

"Please, just leave me alone," she begged.

"If that's what you want, then fine. Just remember I love you and I'm here to help you."

* * *

Jo stumbled from the cab, her eyes burning and blurred from crying. Aaron ran down the steps to greet her, taking her gently into his arms.

"Why, Aaron? Why did this have to happen?" she cried.

"I don't know, Jo. But it was over quickly and he didn't suffer," Aaron said, leading Jo into the living room. She spotted Saul and gasped, her confusion and shock so encompassing that she was too distraught to even ask him what he was doing in the States.

William was sitting on a sofa by the fireplace, looking off into space. He stood, his eyes bloodshot and somehow empty. Jo went to him, and he held her in his arms. Saul came to her eventually and when he embraced her she felt as if her heart had shattered.

"He loved you like a daughter," Saul said finally.

"I'm going to miss him so much. How am I going to live without him?"

"He had a good life," Saul said, looking deeply into Jo's brimming eyes. "He only wanted you to be happy, Jo. That's all he ever wanted."

William stood, putting his arm around Jo protectively.

"I'll be fine, William. I really will," she said, breathing deeply. "The funeral…when is it? Where?"

"The day after tomorrow at Saint Patrick's Cathedral," Aaron said softly.

"That's good. Robert would have liked that. Will Rebecca be here in time?" Jo asked, looking at Saul.

"She's on her way."

"Listen, I hope you'll understand this. I'm going away until the funeral. I need some time alone."

"What's going on, Jo?" Saul asked.

"I'm all confused. I don't think I want to marry Robbie, and I'm frightened."

"Of what, Jo? Did he threaten you? If he did, I'll kill the son of a—"

"It's not like that, Aaron," she said. "It's just that I…I feel like…damn it, Aaron, sometimes I do things I really don't want to do and I don't understand why. But I want it to stop." Tears streaming down her face, she turned and walked toward the doorway.

"Jo," Aaron said, blocking her path to the door, "please let me help you. I swear I'll protect you. Just don't go running away like this. I'll get you to New York. And I promise, no one will find you. You've got to trust me," Aaron said, fearing that if she walked out the door, he might lose her forever.

"If you really want to help me, then get me out of this city now, before they come for me," she cried, her instincts screaming that she was in danger.

"Who, Jo? Who are you afraid of?"

Jo looked at Aaron blankly. "I need some time alone to think," she said, not answering his question as her mind swirled in confusion.

"It's going to be all right. Sit here," Aaron said, leading Jo to the sofa. "William and Saul will stay with you while I make some phone calls."

He returned half an hour later, after making arrangements to have Jo flown to New York on his friend Michael Rosenthal's Lear jet.

"You'll land on a private runway near Bridgeport, Connecticut. A driver will be waiting there to take you to the Seville Hotel. It's not exactly the Plaza, but it's clean and no one will think to look for you there," Aaron said. "I also talked with Father Donovan at Saint Patrick's. He's agreed to let you have a private viewing."

"Thank you," Jo said, her eyes again filling with tears.

* * *

Agonizing over her loss and fearful of being spotted, Jo remained isolated in her hotel room. At noon Aaron called from the Waldorf.

"Arrangements have been made for one of Father Donovan's priests to let you into the church at midnight. I don't expect you'll have any problems at that late hour. But just in case, I'll have someone there watching the church."

"Thank you, Aaron."

"Are you sure you don't want me to go with you?" he offered.

"I have to do this alone."

* * *

It was midnight. Standing alone at the side door of Saint Patrick's Cathedral, Jo gathered her courage and knocked. A young priest opened the door only wide enough for Jo to enter.

Leading her into the eerie stillness of the main sanctuary, the priest touched her shoulder.

"There," he said, pointing to the altar.

In the dimly lit church she could discern the silhouette of the open coffin. Standing at the first row of pews, she could clearly see Robert's profile protruding from the coffin like a waxen caricature. The room began to spin and she grew light-headed.

You can do this. You have to do this! Her breathing labored, she walked to the coffin and gazed at Robert's waxen face. His mouth was frozen, ageless in its expression. Bile rose in her throat. *Why?* Tears clouded her vision.

She placed her hand against Robert's face. *My God, you're so cold!* Standing there in the ghostly silence of the enormous cathedral, touching the only person who had ever allowed her to be exactly who she wanted to be, Jo was overcome with grief.

Jo placed her hand over Robert's unyielding hand. *I'll miss you, Robert. I'll miss you so much. You were my best friend.*

The room began spinning in a surreal kaleidoscope of color. Jo held onto the side of the coffin.

"Damn you, damn you, Robert Osborne! Why did you leave me? How could you do this?" she screamed in rage at his lifeless body. She knelt on the floor, and buried her head in her hands.

The priest walked silently toward the front of the church. "It's time to go now," he said.

Jo looked at him with vacant eyes.

"Come."

Leaning into the coffin, Jo pressed her lips against Robert's forehead. "Be with the angels, Robert. I will always love you."

A gentle breath of warm air caressed Jo's face. She lifted her eyes heavenward. *Is that you, Robert?* Stronger this time, the heat surrounded her entire body. *It is you.* She allowed the priest to lead her from the sanctuary.

* * *

Hans and Otto were frantic when they heard that Robert Osborne had died and that Jo had disappeared.

"Can't you control her? You should never have let her out of your sight. Find her and find her now!" Hans ordered Robbie before he slammed the receiver down.

"The man's an incompetent fool. We'll have to move to Washington so we can keep tighter controls on their lives," Hans told Otto. "Still, what luck!" he said, smiling broadly as he slapped his brother-in-law on the back. "Robert Osborne's dead. The last obstacle is out of our way."

* * *

Heydrich Rict glared at his comrades, his face contorted with anger. He had called a meeting after being notified of Robert Osborne's death.

"This is all very unfortunate, and I'm deeply disturbed to be put in this position," he said. "The Israelis were seen entering Aaron Blumenthal's house, and a short time later Robert Osborne was taken out by ambulance, dead from a heart attack. The Jews must have found something, and we can't take any more chances, especially since we now know that Robert Osborne was involved.

"We've been very lucky up till now, gentleman. We have our good friend, Kurt Waldheim securely installed as the United Nations Secretary General and we are about to have control of the White House.

"And as of this moment, besides Robbie, Anderson Taxton and Jotto Wells, Hans Wells is the only person that we still need. Hans has always been smart, never needlessly exposing himself, covering his tracks meticulously; I'm sure of his loyalty. But Otto's another story. He walks around Miami—where hundreds of survivors live—as if he has nothing to fear. We can't risk exposure. The publicity would destroy the girl. We must eliminate Otto!" Rict said, pounding his fist on the table.

The men all knew what was at stake. They had spent their lives building political connections and setting the stage for their rise to political and financial domination. Now it seemed to be hanging precariously.

"We never should have let him leave Bolivia," Rict said. "I tried to tell Hans it was a mistake, but he insisted that he couldn't continue without Otto. But now he'll have to. We have no other choice. Rict snubbed out his cigar. "Nothing will change. We have everything in place and we have nothing to worry about. Taxton is with us, and the girl is a pawn in her father's hands. Hans will be able to handle the situation. I want Otto eliminated as soon as possible."

* * *

On the day of the funeral the weather had turned angry. Rain pelted the streets and thunder reverberated from the skies. The CBS evening news had done a biography of Robert's life the night before, and thousands of his fans lined the avenue outside the cathedral. Sheltering themselves under umbrellas, they stood silently watching, as dignitaries and friends from around the world gathered to pay their last respects.

Aaron, William, Saul, Rebecca, and Jo sat in the front row. Beyond sorrow, their eyes drained of tears; they listened in dazed silence as the priest eulogized Robert.

"And now," the priest said, "Miss Wells, a young woman Mr. Osborne considered his surrogate daughter, would like to say a few words."

Rebecca squeezed Jo's hand. "Are you sure you want to do this?"

"I'm sure."

Pale and trembling, Jo stood. Aaron rose with her, taking her arm and walking with her up the stairs to the podium. Moving off to the side, Aaron remained close by.

"I hope you'll bear with me," Jo said, squaring her shoulders. "We've all come here today to bid farewell to our beloved friend, Robert Osborne." Jo looked over at the coffin. "This is so hard, Robert," she said. "Most people knew you as a great actor. But Rebecca and Saul, who knew you for almost forty years, knew you differently, as did William, your agent and best friend. They knew you as a devoted friend, as a loving and gentle man. They shared the agony of the war with you, and they shared your heartbreak when you lost your beloved wife, Morgan.

"I came into your life long after that. I was an infatuated fan, madly in love with you, the actor. You became my friend and let me get to know you, the man. That was the most cherished gift in my life." The pain in Jo's heart threatened to choke off her words. "Robert, I know God is with you and I know you're here with us now. Look into the hearts of your friends. We love you."

Her resolve crumbling, Jo turned toward Aaron. She said nothing, but Aaron knew she was in trouble. He strode to her, placed his arm around her shoulder, and all but carried her to her seat.

The priest's closing benediction ended the service, and the five moved to the waiting limousines that would take them to the cemetery.

Robbie approached as Jo was leaving the church.

"My darling, I've been so worried about you," Robbie said. *How in the hell could she allow herself to appear in public looking like that? She has so much to learn; I have so much to teach her.* "I'm here for you now," he said, reaching for Jo's arm.

"Here for me? No, Robbie, you're not here for me," she said, pulling her arm from his grasp. "It's all about image. It was when we were kids and it still is."

"Now, now darling, you're just upset. You don't mean that," he whispered, glancing around to make sure no reporters overheard. Realizing how damaging a public outburst could be to his career, Robbie backed away. "I'll see you later, darling," he said in a loud clear voice, walking rapidly away.

Aaron took Jo's ice-cold hand in his.

"Hold on, Jo. It'll be over soon," he murmured.

The friends sat in the car on the way to the cemetery in silence, then they watched, stunned, as the pallbearers lifted the coffin from the hearse. None of them would be able to recall the exact sequence of events that followed. Time became as distorted as Dali's watches, as each second of heartache seemed an eternity.

* * *

Hundreds of people came to Robert's townhouse after the funeral. They ate, drank heavily, talked loudly, and laughed a lot, creating a carnival-like atmosphere.

Jo spent the afternoon clinging to Aaron, speaking rarely. As evening began to fall, she searched for Rebecca. She found her sitting alone on the leather sofa in Robert's study.

"He loved this room. He used to study his lines with me in here sometimes," Jo said. She sat down next to Rebecca on the sofa. It was warn from years of use and it felt cool and soft against Jo's legs. Kicking off her shoes, she tucked her feet under her.

"When Robert was young," Rebecca said, "he was so handsome. And when he and Morgan were together...you should have seen them...they were so in love."

"Tell me about them," Jo asked.

"He never told you?"

"He did, but I want to hear it from you."

Rebecca smiled, remembering the story as if she had been there through it all.

"He was a famous actor, stopping in Vilnius on his way to Warsaw, because he had friends there– the Gold's.

"Jacob, the son, convinced Robert to go to watch Morgan perform in a local theater production.

"She was a great actress even then. And they fell madly in love. Morgan was only seventeen when Robert took her to Paris with him.

"She gave up everything—her family, her religion, her home—to follow her dream. They were such a charismatic team on stage that soon they became the toast of Paris. And off the stage they were inseparable." Rebecca paused. "I loved them both so much, and now I've lost them."

Jo put her arms around Rebecca and together they cried.

"Do you really think we've lost them, Rebecca?" Jo asked.

Pensive, trying to capture the essence of her faith, Rebecca hesitated before answering.

"No, Jo. We haven't really lost them. I believe with all my heart that they are watching over us. They're going to be our guardian angels. I never lost Morgan and I won't lose Robert. Neither will you."

"I know," Jo said. "I know."

"Do you want to talk about Robbie?" Rebecca asked.

"There's nothing to talk about. I'm not going to marry him. It was a mistake from the beginning."

Saul had told Rebecca everything, and she was relieved that the marriage would not take place.

"You've been through so much. You must be exhausted, sweetheart. You need a rest."

"I need a rest and a change. I've been giving this a lot of thought, and if you wouldn't mind, I'd like to go back to Israel with you for a little while."

"You're always welcome in our home," Rebecca said. "But you know running away is not the answer. Eventually you're going to have to face Robbie and put closure on the relationship."

"I know. I'm just not capable of facing that right now. And I need just one more favor, Rebecca. Please don't tell anyone I'm going to Israel."

"What are you so afraid of, Jo?"

"I'm afraid they'll try to stop me."

"Who are they?"

"My father and my uncle Otto," Jo said, vocalizing her fear for the first time.

Chapter 50

─────────── ★ ───────────

At 10 o'clock that evening Aaron took Jo back to her hotel, turning down side streets and alleyways to evade anyone who might be following.

"Would you like some company?" he asked in front of the hotel.

"Not tonight. I'm so tired, I can barely keep my eyes open." She leaned over and kissed him on the cheek. "Thanks for being my friend. I don't know how I would have made it without you."

* * *

Driving back to Robert's townhouse, Aaron allowed his thoughts to meander. He vowed to himself that no matter what he would tell Jo exactly how he felt. That thought led to others and he was soon contemplating the implications of the information Natan had given to them.

Do I have a chance in hell with her? How do I keep her away from Taxton and her family? he shuddered.

Parking his rental car in a garage a block from Robert's townhouse, Aaron began walking, reliving the events of the past few days. He thought about Natan and wondered if the man felt any sense of guilt.

Saul, William, Rebecca, and Natan were deep in conversation when Aaron entered the townhouse. Natan was just finishing a recap for Rebecca, having decided that as a psychologist, her expertise would be invaluable to the group.

"How's Jo?" Saul asked.

"She's Okay." Aaron said.

"I want you to know how sorry I am about Robert's death," Natan said, the pain clearly evident on his usually impassive face. "And I'm sorry I couldn't be at the funeral."

Aaron poured himself a scotch, a response obviously not forthcoming.

"I think we should get to the business at hand," Natan said. "As I explained to you the other evening, we clearly established that Hans Wells was a doctor at the Dachau Concentration Camp. We also established that some type of weird emotional connection existed between Morgan, Otto, and Hans.

"Witnesses affirmed that a child was born to Morgan. And we know that weeks earlier, Ilya Wells, Hans's wife, also gave birth. Now it is obvious that Morgan's child was not murdered, as were other Jewish babies born in the camps."

Natan took a deep breath, remembering his own baby brother's death. He turned away; they waited.

"Jo's father, Hans Wells, with the help of the United States government, covered his tracks well. I don't think we can touch him. But Otto Milch, he's another story entirely.

"One of my assistants kept insisting he had heard the name Otto Milch before, but he couldn't remember where. We decided to play along with his hunch, and as impossible as it seems, we found the file my assistant had actually read years earlier.

"Some Nazis escaped by masquerading as survivors of the camps, but one of these 'pass off's' got caught by the Americans during routine questioning when a survivor recognized him as an SS Black Shirt.

"During interrogation the Nazi, Schmidt told the Americans that he had worked under a man named Otto Milch. He said that Milch used hypnosis in ways never before thought possible. According to Schmidt, family and friends were hypnotized and actually turned on each other.

"The American's brought in a psychiatrist to interview Schmidt. Afterward the psychiatrist submitted a report stating unequivocally that it was impossible to make a person under hypnosis do anything to harm oneself or someone they love. And so, the information on Otto Milch was disregarded and the file was closed."

Aaron began to ask a question but Natan stopped him.

"When I'm finished, you may ask questions," he said, glancing back at his notes before continuing. "We went to the prison and interviewed Schmidt. He couldn't wait to cooperate with us," Natan said, pausing– his mind reeled with the images of the stories the Nazi had told them about Otto.

"Otto Milch is a monster who'd do anything to get what he wants. And although we have no proof, you'll have to take my word–Doctor Hans Wells is just as evil. They must be stopped!"

"You don't think they'd hurt Jo?" Aaron asked.

"No, they obviously need her. What I do think is that she's somehow involved in all of this although she's probably not even aware of her involvement. Think about it. Jo was slated to marry a man being groomed as President of the United States. The implications are terrifying."

"But what could she possibly have done as the First Lady?" Aaron asked skeptically.

"Not much." Natan said. "It's her family's involvement. It would have given the Nazis front door access to the White House."

* * *

A black sedan was sitting in front of Otto Milch's favorite Miami restaurant. When Otto emerged from the restaurant with his wife Elaine, the sedan's darkened windows slid open and two shots rang out. The sedan screeched away, leaving burned rubber on the pavement.

Both shots found their mark. He was hit once in the chest and once in the head. Death came instantly.

Elaine, splattered with Otto's blood and brains, vomited on the sidewalk next to her slain husband. She screamed hysterically until the police and the ambulance arrived. A paramedic injected her with a sedative, taking her to Jackson Memorial Hospital.

She awoke from the heavy sedation early the next morning, slowly comprehending that it was all finally over. She'd been forced to live under Otto's control for years, and the only regret she now had was that she hadn't been the one to pull the trigger. Finding her wrinkled and bloodstained clothes, Elaine dressed and snuck from the hospital.

After buying a new wardrobe at a small Coral Gables boutique, she went directly to the airport. Elaine Milch was never seen or heard from again.

* * *

The phone call came just as Ilya was getting ready for bed. She picked up the receiver and heard Hans speaking with the officer. The officer's words made her fragile mind snap. She screamed, dropped the phone, and ran for the bathroom. Reaching for a loose razor blade, she slashed at her wrists.

Hans might have let her die if he hadn't been so worried about the effect her suicide would have on Robbie and Jo's careers. Desperate to maintain some appearance of normalcy, he stitched up Ilya's bleeding wrists himself and gave her a shot of morphine.

* * *

Hans sat in his darkened study for hours trying to calculate his next moves. He was infuriated by Jo's refusal to see him, even though she did call periodically to tell him she was all right. But now, with Otto gone, Jo would be coming home for the funeral. And when she did, he would bring her back into the fold.

Feeling confident about Jo for the first time in weeks, Hans turned his thoughts to his dead brother-in-law. Hans had warned Otto dozens of times to stay away from Miami. There were too many Jews living there who might recognize him. But Otto had refused to take those warnings seriously. *You should have listened to me. If you had you might still be alive.*

He picked up the phone and dialed the Osborne home, having learned that Aaron, as executor of the estate, had temporarily moved into Robert's townhouse.

"Hello," Aaron said, the sound of his voice sickening Hans–this Jew who could contact his daughter when he could not.

"This is Dr. Hans Wells," he said tersely. "I know you're in touch with my daughter. I need to contact her immediately."

"I'm sorry, sir, but I can't give you her number. I'll forward any message you wish for me to forward, but I'm afraid that's all I can do," Aaron said emphatically.

"Fine." Fury enveloped him. "You tell my daughter that her Uncle Otto has been murdered, and that her family needs her," Hans said, breaking out in sweat as he slammed down the receiver and smashed his fist against the desk. "Who does that fucking Jew think he is?" he screamed. *By tomorrow she'll be home. I'll fix everything then.*

Hans reached deep inside to gain control. He called his pilot, arranging an immediate flight to Washington. He then called Robbie and told him everything, instructing him to leave for the airport as soon as he was packed.

"My jet will be waiting for you. I want you here when she arrives. This fucking wedding is going to happen no matter what it takes."

* * *

Aaron held the dead receiver in his hands, hardly believing what he had just heard. Going immediately to Saul's door, he knocked loudly.

"Come in."

"Hans Wells just called. Otto Milch was murdered tonight."

"Bullshit!" Saul said, throwing off his covers. "It's just a ploy to get to Jo. Let's go talk with Natan."

After waking Natan with the news, they all moved into the study.

"It will take exactly one phone call to find out if this is true," Natan said, dialing a Miami number.

"It's true," Natan said after hanging up minutes later. "He was gunned down outside a Miami restaurant. It must have been his own people, because it wasn't ours." He wiped the perspiration from his forehead with the back of his hand. "Aaron, I think you should go to Jo and bring her back here. In the meantime Saul and I will try to figure out what to do."

Aaron dressed quickly and walked to the corner, where he hailed a passing cab. At Jo's hotel, he knocked on her door.

"Who is it?" Jo asked.

"It's Aaron."

She opened the door. "Oh, my God! Not again," she said, recognizing the darkness of Aaron's eyes. "Don't say anything. I don't want to know. I can't take any more...I can't!"

Aaron took Jo into his arms.

"Jo, I'm so sorry...it's your Uncle Otto. He's dead."

Jo pulled away, pale, uncomprehending.

"Uncle Otto, dead? How? What happened?"

"Your father called and said he was...murdered."

She began to pace. "I have to go home. I have to go to Naples," she mumbled, her voice brittle, fearful, laden with sadness. "I have to go back there!" she began to sob.

"It's going to be all right. I'll take care of you."

She grasped his wrist. "Just promise me that no matter what happens, you won't let them make me stay in Naples. Promise me!"

"I swear to you." He took her gently by the shoulders. "Listen to me, Jo. I need you to get dressed now. You're coming back to the townhouse with me. You'll be safer there."

* * *

Saul, Aaron, Rebecca, and Natan were sitting in Robert's library. Rebecca had given Jo a sedative and she had drifted off to sleep on the guestroom bed.

The four were arguing.

"Are you fucking crazy? You can't let her go there," Saul said. "This isn't a game. They murdered Otto to protect Jo. Once they get their hands on her they'll never let her leave. We can't take the chance."

"Keep your voices down," Rebecca said. "You'll wake her."

"What do you want her to do? For God's sake, he was her uncle. She believes it's her duty to go home," Aaron said, throwing up his hands in disgust.

"Maybe it's time to tell her everything," Saul said.

"What will you tell her, that her father's a Nazi and that she's been used her entire life? It will kill her," Aaron said.

"There may be another way," Natan offered. "Hans is going to try to keep Jo in Naples. Have no doubt that he will try to use hypnosis to gain control of her mind." He scowled. "Tell me, Aaron, have you ever given an injection?"

"No." Aaron's face paled.

"Then you'll have to learn. I'm going to give you a syringe filled with Valium. When it's time to leave Naples, if she tries to stay, you'll inject her."

"This is beginning to sound ridiculous. It's going to look like I'm trying to kidnap her," Aaron said.

"Not if we plan this correctly."

"I believe," Rebecca interjected, "that Jo is beginning to break free from her father's influence. But time is critical. In Jo's weakened emotional state, she'll be much more susceptible to Hans' hypnotic suggestions."

"If we lose Jo now, we'll lose her forever," Natan offered, staring at Aaron.

"I won't let them take her away from me again," Aaron said, squaring his shoulders. "I'll do whatever it takes."

Chapter 51

─────────── ★ ───────────

Aaron's head ached as he sat in Robert's study trying to focus on everything he had to do before accompanying Jo to her uncle's funeral.

The first item on his agenda was the reading of Robert's will. He asked Saul to have Rebecca and William in the study by seven that evening, regretting having to expose Jo to even more emotional strain. But Saul and Rebecca were about to return to Israel, and he had no other choice.

Fighting a headache, Aaron pushed away from his desk. *I've got to take a shower and take some Aspirin.*

* * *

Aaron opened a bottle of champagne, carefully filling five crystal Baccarat glasses, explaining to Saul, Rebecca, William, and Jo how Robert had insisted that the reading of his will be accompanied by Dom Perignon.

After handing each of them a glass, Aaron lifted his.

"To our friend Robert Osborne, may he rest in peace."

They all drank, silently making their own toasts. Aaron noted a disturbing dullness in Jo's eyes. Moving to her side, he placed his arm around her.

"Are you sure you're up to this, Jo? I can always go over it with you another time."

"I'm fine, Aaron. I just want to get it over with."

As Aaron sat down behind Robert's desk he nostalgically thought back to the moment when Robert had asked him to be the executor of his estate. He had felt honored at the time, never imagining how soon he'd be serving in that capacity.

Coming back to the present, Aaron took another sip of champagne before picking up his notes.

"A will is a legal document written to dispose of a person's property after their death," Aaron said, wanting to be sure that everyone understood the proceedings that were about to transpire. "In most instances the executor reads the will in its entirety, but Robert had an enormously diverse and complicated will. So I've taken the liberty of condensing it, and at a later date when we're all less stressed, I'll go into the finer details."

"'To my lifelong friends, Rebecca and Saul,'" Aaron quoted directly from the document, "'I leave the enormous responsibility of overseeing the establishment, in the State of Israel, of an acting school—The Morgan and Robert Osborne Theatrical Institute—and a theatre—The Morgan Rabinowiszch Theatre of The Performing Arts.'

"Robert wanted to resurrect Morgan's familial name, Rabinowiszch, a name he said he'd tricked her into dropping when she came to Paris." Aaron noted the quiet look of satisfaction on William's face. "But more than anything else," he continued, "Robert envisioned the building of this project as his way of bringing Morgan back home to her people," Aaron said.

Hearing Aaron's comments, William was momentarily transported back to the hotel bar where he and Robert had discussed how they could protect Morgan from the possibilities of a German invasion. He remembered well what it had taken to expunge all traces of Morgan's heritage. *Thank God she never found out.*

"Robert bequeathed fifteen million dollars to this endeavor," Aaron said. "He also stipulated that if either one of you were unable to oversee the project for any reason, your eldest son and daughter were to be designated. Of course, there are boards to be appointed and a foundation to be established as well, but we'll discuss all of that at another time."

Looking intently at William, Aaron smiled.

"'To William, the brother who stood by me through thick and thin, I leave you the sum of one million dollars. Enjoy! We had great times. You kept me sane and I loved you.'"

Aaron paused as he watched the tears fill William's eyes. William stood, walking quickly to the door. "If you'll excuse me, please?" he said, leaving the room.

Rebecca and Saul were holding hands, whispering, and Jo was watching them, her face completely devoid of expression.

"Go on, Aaron," Saul urged.

"'To my Jo,'" Aaron said, swallowing hard, "'to the daughter I never had. I leave you my home in New York and all its possessions, along with all the other assets of my estate.' Robert left a considerable amount of money to his favorite charities, Jo, but all in all he left you an estate worth well over six million dollars."

Jo's eyes glazed over. "What am I going to do with all of that money?" she asked, incredulous, bewildered.

Rebecca reached for Jo's hand.

"It will allow you to be who you really are, who you really want to be," Rebecca said.

Jo was confused by Rebecca's comments, having always believed that she had choreographed her own life. But she was too distraught to think about any of that now. Jo turned her attention back to Aaron.

"I think that about wraps it up," Aaron said, as William walked back into the room.

"You know," William said, "Robert would have hated all this maudlin crap. I say we all have another drink."

"I'm with you," Saul said, reaching for the champagne. To our beloved friend, Robert Osborne."

They raised their glasses and drank.

Aaron put his arm around Jo and eased her away from everyone.

"I've been thinking, Aaron. Maybe I overreacted. Sure my father's controlling, but he loves me, and I don't think he'd really try and stop me from leaving Naples."

"You may be right," Aaron said, trying to think of a way to convince Jo that she had to remain committed to her initial instincts. "And if you are, no one will ever know. But if you're wrong, Jo, we need to protect you. Just trust me on this. There won't be any cloak and dagger drama unless we have to."

"Okay, I suppose it can't hurt to take precautions," she said, noting the deep look of concern in Aaron's eyes. "Now, I hope you won't think I'm rude, but I'm really tired. I'd like to lie down for a while."

"You go and rest," Aaron said, hugging her. "I'll wake you when it's time to go.

* * *

Jo climbed the stairs–Robert's stairs–her stairs now. Feeling a thousand years old, she went into Robert's empty bedroom. Moving to the king-sized bed, she carefully removed the coverlet he had purchased at an antique auction in London. She was about to lie down when she remembered the room adjacent to his bedroom. She had asked him about it once and he had replied, "It's where I do my best thinking. It's off limits to everyone."

It would be OK for me to go in there now, Jo thought, realizing it now belonged to her.

She tried the door, found it locked, and then remembered that he kept the key in his desk. Retrieving it, she unlocked the door and felt around for the light switch. The room filled with the glare of iridescent lights.

A poster caught her eye, announcing the opening of Romeo and Juliet. A photo of Robert, young and virile stared back. Her eyes left his face–drawn to the image of a woman. It was Morgan's face–Jo's face. *Oh my God. This is crazy. I'm loosing my mind* She moved into the room, studying the walls. They were covered with posters, pictures, and newspaper articles about Morgan. Jo was disoriented.

Stunned, Jo slipped to the floor. She cowered in the corner, hugging her knees, afraid to move. After a long time she stood, perusing each photograph, trying to comprehend.

Aloud she read, "October 27, 1939. Vilna-Poland. It is with great sorrow that the Government of Poland announces the death of one of its most famous citizens..." *Who is she? And why do I look so much like her?* Ripping a picture of Morgan off the wall, Jo stumbled from the room.

* * *

Aaron saw Jo standing in the doorway glaring at them, holding a picture of Morgan against her heaving chest. He rushed to her and put his arms around her; she pushed him away.

It took only seconds for the psychiatrist in Rebecca to realize what had happened. She went to Jo. "Look at me, Jo," she said.

Jo shook her head like a petulant child. Rebecca repeated her words again, seeing how quickly Jo seemed to be emotionally retreating. "Jo, look at me now!"

Her perceptibility blurred, Jo reached out for Rebecca.

"Help me, Rebecca, help me please," she cried.

"I will, my darling. We all will."

Jo allowed herself to be led to the sofa, but just as she was about to sit, she pulled away.

"Who is this woman to me?" Jo asked.

"She's your mother," Rebecca said, knowing how critical absolute honesty was at this moment.

"My mother? I don't understand. I don't understand any of this. You all knew?" Jo said. "You lied to me—every one of you. Isn't there anyone I can trust?" She backed away.

Rebecca grasped Jo's arm and held it tightly.

"We didn't tell you because we wanted to protect you. Maybe we were wrong, but we did it out of love for you, Jo."

"Tell me. I want to know," Jo said, understanding finally why she had felt so unloved by Ilya, the woman she had thought was her mother.

"When Germany attacked Poland," Rebecca said, "your mother, Morgan was alone at a villa on the French Riviera. Robert and William were in England, making arrangements for a command performance in front of the King. Your mother became frantic because her parents, your grandparents, were still living in Poland.

"She left Paris by train, returning to Poland in the hopes of getting her family out. We're reasonably certain that because she was so famous, she was recognized and detained."

Rebecca stood up and walked to the desk. She fingered one of Robert's pens for a moment. "Saul, please, tell her the rest."

"It appears that Otto Milch was one of the first Germans to interrogate Morgan. He became obsessed with her. We know this because when Morgan was sent to the Dachau Concentration Camp Ilya Milch became her protector.

"Now, we don't know what precipitated it, but your mother attempted suicide before arriving at the camp." Saul closed his eyes, forcing aside the images. "Your father met Morgan at Dachau." He stopped.

Jo didn't move. *This can't be happening. It's a dream–an ugly, horrible, impossible nightmare. But it's not. They're all watching me, waiting. But I'll show them. I'll make the bastards pay!*

"Please, Saul, go on."

"Your father married Ilya, although from what has been reported to us from survivors, he was infatuated with Morgan. Ilya and your mother were pregnant at the same time. We don't know exactly how Hans managed to do it, but after you were born he passed you off to Ilya as her child."

"But as I grew, Ilya must have seen the resemblance to my mother," Jo said.

Aaron spoke for the first time. "She must have. And yet Ilya continues to play along with the charade. She wouldn't do that unless she had a very good reason. There must be something in it for her."

"What are you talking about?" Jo asked.

"Your father and uncle were involved in mind control during the war. They developed techniques with hypnosis that allowed them incredible control over their subjects. We still have no idea what they're up to but we do know they are up to something."

"Mind control?" Jo sighed, anguished, picturing her father sitting beside her bed night after night speaking softly to her while she drifted off to sleep. "I tried so hard not to listen. I knew. I always knew and I never said a word."

"Jo, I want you to listen to me carefully," Rebecca said, authoritative yet gentle. "You are an intelligent young woman so I know you'll understand what I'm about to say to you. This is very much like being a battered or abused child. You were deceived by those you loved most and you simply retreated into denial. It's how our psyche deals with some things; it's how we learn to survive."

"But you don't understand, Rebecca. Uncle Otto and my father were waiting for me at my apartment when I returned from seeing Robbie in

Washington right after my trip to Israel. They hypnotized me that night even though I tried so hard to resist.

"After that night, I found myself becoming more and more involved with Robbie. Somewhere down deep I knew he was wrong for me, but I couldn't stay away. Is that it? Are they trying to get themselves into power by using me? My father and uncle are Nazis. My God, I'm a part of all of this, aren't I?" she said, wanting to flee, feeling as if her body and soul were filth.

"There was nothing you could do to stop it, Jo. You were a pawn," Saul said, his voice rising in fear. "You're Morgan's daughter: her flesh and blood. You have to remember that!"

"We don't know what they've buried in my brain. We don't even know what I'm capable of? I could be some horrid creature that's been—"

"Stop it, Jo," Rebecca snapped. "Why do you think they brought Robbie into the picture? It's because they've never been able to take total control of your mind. If they had, do you think you'd be standing here talking to us now?"

"But how can we stop them? And who killed my uncle?"

"We're still working on that," Aaron said. "Robert hired a man named Natan to make inquiries into your father and uncle's pasts. Perhaps some of their fascist comrades got nervous about those inquiries and decided to eliminate your uncle. He was the weakest link. But now that Otto's dead, we're worried about Ilya and what she might do."

"How she must have hated me and my father." Jo closed her eyes. "If we can get to Mother…I mean Ilya," she said as if speaking to herself, "I know she'll tell us everything. We'll get them and then we'll get Robbie!"

Aaron sat down next to Jo. "If you expose them, you'll be signing a death warrant on your political career. We can't let you do that."

Jo's face turned crimson. "Do you think I care about that? Do you think I would trust myself? I'm going to get as far away from politics and America as I can. They'll never touch me again."

"There may be another way, Jo," Saul said. "I think we can come up with a way to isolate them without making headline news out of it. We just need some time to think."

William was sitting off by himself in the corner, his face solemn, frozen in pain. "Are you OK?" Aaron asked, going to him.

"If only we hadn't gone to England. If only we'd stayed in France. I was his agent, and I should have known better."

Jo walked over to William and began to straighten his tie.

"If only the world hadn't gone insane. You and I have to find strength. It's not the past that we have to fight anymore, William. It's the present. I need you to fight it with me," Jo said, kissing him softly on the cheek.

"We'll get those bastards."

"You're damn right we will," Jo said.

Natan knocked and without waiting for a reply, he entered the room. Jo looked curiously at him.

"This is the man we told you about," Saul said, introducing Natan to Jo.

Jo nodded. "I suppose I should thank you. Ugly work you do," she said.

"Not when we win," Natan said.

His strange accent, a mixture of Hebrew and German, caught Jo by surprise. But his determination and obvious desire for revenge ignited her.

"It's the desire for justice that drives me," he said. "Nothing more, nothing less. I don't get personally involved in vendettas. I simply do what needs to be done."

"We all have to have our motivations," she said, having found a renewed strength and purpose. "And I can assure you that mine is purely revenge. But I guess our motivations aren't what matters here. All that really matters is that we accomplish what needs accomplishing."

"Now that that's settled, " Saul said, smiling at the tempestuous exchange, "Will everyone please sit down. I think we have a plan that just might work."

✷ ✷ ✷

Saul and Rebecca reached the hotel well after three in the morning. Lying in bed, they snuggled, and Rebecca whispered, "Aaron's in love with Jo, isn't he?"

"I think he's been for years. And now that he knows she's Jewish, maybe he'll tell her." Saul shook his head. "I think we have to be realistic. She was born to a Jewish mother, so by law she's Jewish. On the other hand, her father's a Nazi, and that may be too big an obstacle even for someone like Aaron to ever overcome."

Rebecca sat up and switched on the light. "You're forgetting, my darling. Think back. You and I would have died for the right to be together. I wasn't a Jew. Would that have stopped us? And Morgan and Robert, could anything have ever stopped them?"

Saul held Rebecca in his arms, and as he felt the warmth of her body next to his, he was reminded that above all things in life, he loved this woman.

Chapter 52

————————— ★ —————————

As Jo, Aaron, and Natan walked through the mobbed Miami airport terminal, they were being bumped constantly.

"Stay close to me, Jo," Natan ordered, his eyes darting nervously.

When they arrived at the baggage claim area, Natan immediately spotted his contact, whom he introduced simply as Udi. "Take them to the car and I'll see to the luggage," Natan ordered.

Udi led them to the waiting limo just as a policeman was placing a ticket on the windshield.

"Oh shit," Udi said, taking the ticket and throwing it through the open window. Reaching inside the car he retrieved a chauffeur's cap, which he placed on his head.

Aaron and Jo settled uneasily into the back seat. A short time later Natan appeared with a porter in tow. After loading the trunk with luggage, he slid into the front seat beside Udi. He closed the partition between the front and back seats as they pulled into the noon traffic on the 836 Expressway.

Jo and Aaron looked at each other knowingly.

"You know damn well that man's not a chauffeur," Jo said. "So why the charade?"

"I don't know. I'm a nice Jewish banker from Washington, so I don't get too carried away with all this intrigue," Aaron said, immediately ashamed of his offhanded comment. "God, Jo, I'm sorry. I sound like an insensitive baboon. I know this is far from intrigue for you. Please don't misunderstand what I said."

"It's OK, Aaron. I know what you meant."

Jo turned and stared out the window, taking comfort in the familiarity of the passing vistas. They sped along the Palmetto Expressway until they reached the Tamiami Trail, where they exited, heading west on U.S. 41.

Jo had traveled this route hundreds of times in her life. As a child her father arranged marvelous shopping excursions to Miami, taking her to Renee's, an exclusive children's store on the Miracle Mile in Coral Gables. And when her Uncle Otto moved to the states, he joined them on their outings.

Otto had always taken an enormous interest in Jo's emerging and unique sense of style. And as she matured, he had encouraged her to select where they should shop. Jo delighted in that freedom, soon discovering the 5,7,9 Shop and Burdines.

But for Jo nothing compared to Teresa, the Cuban dressmaker whom Uncle Otto had introduced Jo to on her fourteenth birthday. Jo would bring Teresa pictures of the latest styles from *Seventeen* magazine, and weeks later when they returned, Teresa would have miraculously reproduced exact replicas of those designs.

As the limousine fought its way through traffic, Jo recalled with fondness the evenings she had spent with her father and uncle Otto at El Centro Vasco, their favorite place for the exotic flavors of Cuban cuisine. She remembered her father and Uncle Otto smoking contraband Cuban cigars, drinking fruit-laden sangria, and joining in with the boisterous Latinos as they tried, without much success, to teach Otto the merengue.

How could they have done this to me? Why would they pretend to love me only to use me?

Since finding out about Morgan, Jo had focused all her attention on the divisiveness of her upbringing, and that had made her more miserable than she had ever believed possible. But now as she thought back on those enchanting times from her childhood, she realized how important those memories were if she intended to survive the impending ordeal.

Heading west toward Naples, they moved through the heavy traffic for another ten minutes. Then the road ahead cleared, offering them ninety miles of flat, straight highway that cut through the profusion of wildlife and flora known as the Everglades.

"A penny for your thoughts," Aaron said.

"I was just thinking about Uncle Otto. I was so sure that he loved me; he was always so kind and gentle. I can intellectualize what I've been told, but in my heart it's so damn hard for me to accept that he was such an evil man."

Aaron took Jo's hand but remained silent.

"When I was a young girl, he was my champion. He made me believe I could do anything, be anything. But he was weak, my father's pawn, and I always knew that. That's why I can't hate him.

"But my father…how could my own father use me? How could he willingly sacrifice his own daughter? Do you have any idea how I feel knowing my father's a murdering Nazi? I hate him so much! I hate him for making me feel so black and dirty inside," she said, her pain-stricken face a refection of the agony. "All this…and Robert gone too. God, I just don't know how I'm going to ever feel whole again."

"If I could take the pain away I would," Aaron said, putting his arm around Jo. She snuggled against his shoulder. They remained silent for a long time. He thought she had fallen asleep, so he was surprised when she began to speak again.

"I love it out here. It's so peaceful, this river of grass," she said dreamily.

He looked around, seeing a flat expanse of monotonous wilderness that he didn't find particularly enthralling.

"It's lovely," he said with gentle sarcasm.

"No, I'm serious. Appreciating the Everglades takes some effort because the animals camouflage themselves among the mangroves. But they're here...hiding...waiting to be discovered. Look at the anhinga over there," she said, pointing to a large bird that stood majestically drying its wings in the Florida sun. "Look! Alligators. In the water." Jo craned her neck for a better look at the canal running beside the road.

Jo continued to identify the various species of flora, birds, and other animals, and soon Aaron was making his own discoveries: eagles nesting atop telephone poles, and giant turtles, oblivious to danger, crossing the road. Passing Seminole Indian villages and airboat ride tours, they became lost in the vast expanse.

Overwhelmed by the closeness of Jo, Aaron leaned over and kissed her softly on the cheek. She smiled. Their eyes held. They moved together, the kiss passionate, hungry.

"Can we do this, Aaron? Can we make it together?" she asked, her breathing short, her longing unbearable.

"I can't make it unless we're together. I know that now. I always knew. But I was too stupid and too afraid of the ghosts from my past to tell you. I'll do whatever it takes to be with you, if you'll have me. I came so close to losing you and I'm never going to let that happen again."

Jo lowered her eyes, too wounded to think about her future. Aaron, on the other hand, was too in love with her to think about anything else.

An hour and fifteen minutes into their crossing they passed a sign alerting them that they were entering Collier County. Jo's mood radically changed.

"Why did everything have to go so wrong?" she asked, twisting and pulling at the hem of her dress.

"I don't know, Jo, but it'll be over soon."

"Over? How can it ever be over?" she said, her voice agitated, her face ashen.

Naples was a tourist Mecca with a population that swelled by tens of thousands during the winter season. In the summertime its pristine streets were normally deserted except for the diehard locals who endured the ninety-plus temperatures. Going up Fifth Avenue and then turning south on third, Jo was aghast to see cars lining both sides of the street.

"It looks as if the entire city has turned out. My uncle was a loner so you can be sure they're not here because of him," she said bitterly.

As they neared her beachfront home, the traffic became so dense they were forced to take a detour.

Natan slid the partition open.

"This is exactly what I thought would happen. They've turned the funeral into a circus. Jo, when you get out of the car, I want you to stay close to Aaron and me."

The car eventually made its way through the traffic and pulled into a neighbor's driveway.

"Are you ready?" Natan asked.

"I think so," she said, her stomach knotting spasmodically.

"I think so is not good enough. You have to be stronger than that if you intend to succeed," Natan said.

Aaron's first instincts were to protect Jo from Natan's bullying, but he knew that Natan was right; he kept quiet.

Jo drew on all the resolve she possessed. Taking out her mirror, she applied fresh lipstick, then brushed her hair and snapped closed her purse.

"I'm ready. Let's go." Squaring her shoulders, she stepped from the car.

The three of them cut across the neighbor's lawn, maneuvering their way through a hedge opening that Jo had used since childhood. Once through the hedge, they walked headlong into the throng of waiting reporters.

Immediately recognizing Jo, the press closed in, pushing and shouting questions at her.

Natan and Aaron cleared the way for Jo to the front porch. From that vantage point Jo looked out at the journalists, some of the best and brightest from the *New York Times, Washington Post,* and the *Miami Herald.* She steeled herself, knowing full well that the only reason they were here was because they thought she might one day be the First

Lady. And now that her family was involved in a murder, the possibilities were just too titillating to pass up.

Jo held up her hand to quiet them.

"The murder of my uncle has been a terrible tragedy for my family," she said, sounding strong and determined, yet looking vulnerable. "But the police have assured us that they'll find the people responsible for this hideous crime."

"Now, before I go inside to be with my family, I have a short statement to make," Jo said. "Due to irreconcilable differences, Senator Taxton and I have broken off our engagement."

"Has this got anything to do with the death of Robert Osborne and the murder of your uncle?" the *Herald* reporter shouted.

"Absolutely not," Jo said, shocked by the audacity of the question. "I've lost two people that I loved in a very short time but I can assure you that this decision is not a result of those tragedies. Now, if you'll please excuse me," she said coldly, turning to enter the house.

Robbie was standing inside the foyer when Jo opened the door. His face was crimson.

"What was all that about? Are you trying to ruin us both?" he hissed. "And what in the hell are you doing here?" he said, turning his attention to Aaron. "Is he the reason? Are you in love with this Jew?"

The words slipped out before Robbie could stop himself, and the moment he uttered them, he knew that he'd made a huge mistake. He looked around nervously to see if anyone that mattered might have heard, but there was only the butler. Figuring no harm had been done; he reached for Jo's arm.

"Come with me. We need to talk in private."

Jo pulled her arm away.

"I'll be happy to talk with you, Robbie, but don't touch me. Don't you ever touch me again."

She turned and walked into the sitting room off the main hallway. Robbie followed, slamming the door behind him.

At that moment, Aaron, the gentle, kindly man who had never lifted his hand against another human being in his life, wanted desperately to kill Robbie Taxton.

That son of a bitch! His eyes raged with hate.

Natan put his hand on Aaron's shoulder. "Stay focused. Now's not the time to let your emotions get the best of you. If you hear anything out of the ordinary, go in. I'm going to find Ilya."

"Good luck," Aaron said, feeling a kinship toward Natan that he hadn't felt before.

Natan looked at Aaron and gave him a rare smile.

Once the door was closed, Robbie turned on Jo.

"You stupid bitch! How dare you humiliate me like that?" he said.

"I have a few things to tell you, Robbie. I think you'd better sit down and listen," she said, her voice cold steal.

Her composure frightened him. He sat.

"When you were young, Robbie, you had such high ideals, such dreams. And I really believed that you were going to make a difference. But you became greedy and power-hungry. And then you made the ultimate mistake—you allowed yourself to be taken in by my family. You're not stupid, so let's not pretend that you didn't know they were Nazis."

Robbie tried to formulate a rebuttal that Jo might accept, but he couldn't find the words to justify the decisions he had made over the past year.

Soon after Hans and Otto's Washington visit, Robbie had gone home to see his father, the consummate strategist. Anderson Taxton had told his son everything; his relationship with Henry Ford, the money that he'd given, knowing it was to be filtered into Hitler's numbered accounts in Switzerland, and the roles Hans and Otto had played in the Third Reich. Robbie had listened to his father that day and made a decision–a pact with Satan–and even now he had no remorse.

"It's really so very sad and such a waste," Jo said, interrupting Robbie's reverie. "You were never right for me, but you actually might have made a decent president. But now that's never going to happen."

Robbie bounded from the couch and grabbed Jo by the shoulders.

"Take your filthy hands off me," she ordered.

Robbie dropped his hands as if he'd been burned, the depth of her hate shocking him.

"You can't stop me, you silly bitch. No one can!"

"I can stop you. And I will if it becomes necessary," she said. "I've indisputable proof of your involvement with my family. They're Nazis, Robbie, and you knew that. I've documented it all and put it in a safe place. You'll never be President. You're finished. It's over."

"Really? And what about your career? Do you think you can destroy me without destroying yourself?" he said.

"My career is over. It was over the moment I learned the truth about my family. Believe me, I would never seek political office again. I don't deserve it and neither do you. Think about what I've said, Robbie."

For a split second Robbie believed she had in fact managed to destroy him. But then he smiled, realizing that she didn't have the capacity to completely neutralize him.

"You fool! You can't stop destiny. If it's not me, it'll be someone else. There are others like me. And you can rest assured that some day one of them will be in the White House," he said, his words echoing, the room darkening.

Jo turned and walked into the hallway, praying that his ominous predictions were nothing more than bravado. The encounter left her trembling and numb, her eyes vacant.

"My God, are you all right?" Aaron asked, fumbling in his pocket for the syringe Natan had given him.

Looking askance at the needle, Jo pulled away. "Get that thing away from me!"

"Thank God," he said smiling. He placed the syringe back into his pocket. "Let's go find your father. We don't have much time."

Chapter 53

─────────── ★ ───────────

In the upstairs master bedroom, Ilya was dressing for the funeral under the close observation of a male aide when they heard a faint knock on the door.

"Who is it?" the aide called.

"A friend of the family. I've come to see Ilya."

Not expecting company, he opened the door only a crack. Natan leaned his shoulder against the door, pushing his way in before the aide could react.

Natan took in the surroundings in seconds. The room was sparsely furnished with a hospital bed in the corner, a single chair, and a dressing table. The smell of disinfectant permeated the air. Ilya was busy buttoning the sleeve on her dress, and in her drugged stupor she didn't even bother looking up when Natan entered.

"No one's allowed in here," the aide said.

"I was a very close friend of Otto. I'd like to talk with his sister for a moment. Would you deny me that?" Natan asked, smiling.

"You have exactly two minutes."

Natan approached Ilya and leaned close to her ear. "We must talk. I can help you," He said in German to Ilya.

The sound of her mother tongue brought her momentarily back to the present.

The aide, who understood Natan's words, moved quickly. Bounding across the room, he put a strangle hold on Natan, applying deep pressure to his windpipe.

"You have made a very grave mistake. I thought I recognized you, you stupid Jew. Did you really think you could get to her that easily?" the aide growled, tightening his hold.

Natan turned to his right and struck the man in the stomach with his elbow. The Nazi gasped for air, momentarily loosening his hold. Natan dropped to his knees, dislocating the Nazi's shoulder as he flipped him to the ground.

Screaming in pain, he struggled for the gun in his shoulder holster. Natan put his knee on the Nazi's chest, and the fallen man cried out in agony.

"Keep quiet you piece of shit or I'll kill you!" Natan hissed, squatting down and applying pressure to the artery in the Nazi's neck, cutting off the blood supply to his brain. When the stunned aide lost consciousness, Natan released his grip. Satisfied that his advisory was neutralized, Natan turned his attention toward Ilya.

She began to laugh, making great booming sounds. Walking unsteadily to the dressing table, Ilya picked up a brush and began to tear fitfully at her tangled hair.

"I used to be so beautiful, everyone said so," she whined, her words a drugged slur.

"You're still lovely, Ilya," Natan offered gently.

"Who are you?" she asked, looking at his reflection in the mirror.

"I'm here to help you, but first you must help me."

"Why?" She asked dully.

"Because I know who killed your brother; and I know that Hans is keeping you here against your will."

"My brother is dead, and now Hans must die," she sneered.

"Yes, Ilya. They've killed your brother, and you're going to be next unless you tell me what they're planning. Tell me, Ilya, and I'll protect you."

For a moment Ilya's eyes seemed to clear, but then they glazed over. She hummed a tuneless verse. Then, just as quickly as she had lost her concentration she became coherent.

"Are you a Jew?" she asked.

"Yes."

"Hah!" she said. "That's perfect. It should be a Jew who stops him: the ultimate insult, the ultimate shame." She continued brushing her fading blond curls. "There're going to infiltrate the government from within—the best families…a 1,000 year Reich…one Germany…power reborn. That's what they're doing," she said, her eyes that of a madwoman.

"Who, Ilya? Who's planning this?"

"Hans, the bastard, can tell you who; only he won't," she said.

Natan took the brush from Ilya's hand and looked into her eyes. "What about political power? Where?"

Ilya began to laugh again. "Everywhere, you fool. They're working to destabilize governments. And you can't stop them."

"How are they going to do it?"

"With money. Tons and tons of money!" she said, sweeping her hand across the makeup table, sending her perfume bottles crashing to the floor.

"What did you mean when you said 'one Germany'?"

"They're planning to reestablish the Mother Country. No East and West Germany—one country. You Jews, you'll see and you'll cry again; of that you can be certain."

For a moment she was contemplative. "I want that bastard dead!" she bellowed, pulling the gold band off her left hand and throwing it across the room. "He's a fucking liar! He stole my baby and made me raise that Jew whore as my own. He must die. You have to kill him. You have to help me!"

"No, the funny thing is I don't have to help you."

"But you promised. You can't leave me here!" She screamed. "Take me with you. If you don't they'll kill me."

"I'm a Jew, remember? I don't owe you anything," he said, his voice ice. Natan turned and walked out the door, closing it softly behind him.

* * *

Once alone, Ilya continued to sit at her dressing table. Her drugged mind clear; she began to cry. Remembering how her brother had always protected her, first from her father and then from Hans. Anticipating a future that held only loneliness, she dropped to her knees, cutting them badly on remnants from the smashed perfume bottles. But she was barely aware of the pain that tore at her body as she picked up a jagged chunk of crystal.

She studied the multicolored glass curiously for a moment, lost in the swirling colors, relishing the thought of putting an end to the agony. Then she remembered Hans.

Not before I see him in hell. Crunching the broken glass under her feet, she went back to her dressing table to wait.

* * *

Natan headed down the long hallway toward Udi, who was standing guard at the stairway.

"Any unusual activity?" Natan asked.

"I'm afraid so. We've got to get the hell out of here now," Udi said decisively.

"Where are Jo and Aaron?"

"With her father by the pool."

"Let's go."

* * *

Jo found her father in the living room, surrounded by his friends. When he spotted Jo, he rushed to her side.

"My poor child," he said, hugging her. Jo did not return the embrace; her aloofness staggered Hans.

"We have to talk, Father," Jo said.

"Of course we do, and we will, right after the service."

"No, Father, we must talk now."

Jo's disrespectful behavior infuriated Hans, but his fear that she might cause a scene kept him under control.

"We'll go out by the pool, where you might be able to explain why you seem so incapable of acting properly," Hans said, turning to his guests, who were pretending they had not overheard the bitter exchange. "Excuse us, please."

He took Jo's arm and led her out toward the pool. Jo wanted to pull away, but was too cowed by his touch. Aaron came to Jo's side.

Hans waited until they were well away from his guests before he turned on Aaron. "Perhaps you don't understand. My daughter and I want to be alone."

"I want him here," Jo said.

"Since when do you dictate to me? We'll talk alone!" Hans ordered.

"No we won't," Jo snapped.

Fearful that Aaron might cause the scene he was so determined to avoid, Hans glared but said nothing. Forty feet outside the back door, surrounded by lush hedges of hibiscus and bougainvillea, Hans lead them up three steps to an enormous thatch-roofed platform that the Wells' used for parties. Interspersed among the brightly painted picnic tables on the platform were potted palm trees and bamboo cages inhabited by parrots that squawked loudly when the threesome approached. Wicker chairs and sofas overlooked the pool and the aqua waters of the Gulf of Mexico.

Hans sat in one of the canvas-covered sofas and he motioned for Jo to join him.

Aaron took a seat a short some distance away from them.

"It's good to have you home. I've missed you," Hans said. "I'm sorry it's under such miserable circumstances, but we'll overcome this crisis," he said, reaching for Jo's hand.

"Damn it, Father, drop the pretense. It's too late…I know everything."

Hans looked from Jo to Aaron and then back to Jo.

"I don't know what you're talking about," he said.

"Yes you do. What would you have done once Robbie got to the White House? Are you stupid enough to believe you could destroy democracy? This is America, for Christ's sake, not Nazi Germany. Did you really think for even one moment that you could resurrect your fascist hyperbole? Would you have tried to reestablish the Third Reich? Would you have begun the slaughter again? How many more children would you have murdered? And why? My God, why would you even want to try?"

Hans shook his head. You've no idea what you're talking about. You must understand it's our destiny. Reaching for his cigarette case, he opened it. The music invaded Jo's thoughts. "Just listen to me, my darling child," he beckoned.

"I won't listen. Damn you to hell, I won't listen!" Jo screamed, the veins on her neck protruding, her face scarlet.

"Leave her alone, you bastard!" Aaron said, grabbing Hans by the arm and jerking him from the sofa.

Jo stood, her face only inches from her father's. "I'll never forgive you for what you've done. I'm leaving, father. I'm leaving and I never want to see you again."

"Don't be a fool. I can give you everything." Suddenly Hans seemed to shrink, the color drained from his face.

"Looks like you need some help here," Natan said, approaching slowly. He pointed a gun at Hans' heart.

"My God, is that necessary?" Jo cried.

Natan lowered his gun, aiming it at Hans' crotch, his mind blocking out everyone and everything but his target.

"Nothing would give me greater pleasure than to blow your balls to hell."

"There's no need to act foolishly," Hans sputtered.

"Act foolishly? No. You're right. I'm not going to stoop to your level." He lowered the gun with trembling hands. "Walk away, you son of a bitch, before I change my mind," Natan ordered, his voice menacing.

Hans riveted his attention on Jo. He desperately wanted to tell her that he would always love her, but he refused to give the Jews the satisfaction of seeing him squirm. Instead he lifted his head high, squared his shoulders and walked away.

Hans Wells, his movements regal, entered the crowded room. He took a seat in the front row, and signaled the minister to begin the service.

You mother fucking scum. You can't take my daughter from me. We'll kill you all. You can't stop us. We're the true reflection of humanity. It's only a matter of time.

* * *

"Let's get out of here," Udi said, leading them from the platform. "I've moved the car, so no one will see us leave."

Lost in their own thoughts, they didn't speak again until they were well on their way to Miami. Natan broke the silence, turning from the front seat.

"Ilya made some remarkable accusations: infiltrating governments...a 1,000 year Reich...a reunited Germany. If what she says is true, we're in big trouble."

"I have friends on the President's staff. I'll call and make an appointment. I think they'll help us."

"Help us? No, Aaron, you're kidding yourself. What they'll do is laugh in our faces," Natan said. "Do you really expect them to believe a story like this?"

"We have to do something," Aaron said harshly.

"We will," Natan said, turning around, dismissing him.

Jo said nothing, her eyes vacant, her breathing shallow.

* * *

It was hours before Hans realized that Ilya had not been at the memorial service. He went to her room, a knot of apprehension tugging at his gut.

"Why wasn't my wife at the service?" Hans asked the aide, seeing Ilya sitting at the dressing table, unmoving, staring.

"You dare question me, old man? If you'd kept better control over your family, success would be in our grasp." The Nazi had already contacted his superiors about the fiasco at the mansion, and the decision had been made to eliminate Hans.

"How dare you speak to me in such a tone." Hans leaped at the man, shoving him against the wall. The aid's dislocated shoulder sent spasms of pain throughout his entire body.

"You're finished, old man," he howled, reaching for the gun inside his shirt, its silencer in place.

Hans reacted instantly, throwing his full weight into his injured adversary. The gun flew from the Nazi's hand. He fell, smashing his head on the steel corner of the hospital bed. He slumped to the floor, unconscious.

Ilya turned from the mirror, her eyes wild with hate. Seeing the gun only inches away, she picked it up swiftly.

"Good girl, Ilya. That son of a bitch was going to kill us. Now give it to me," Hans said, approaching her.

"No! Don't come near me," she cried.

"Don't be a fool. Give me the gun."

"I'm going to kill you, Hans. Just like you killed my brother."

"Ilya, listen to me," he pleaded. "I didn't kill Otto. I swear to God I didn't have anything to do with it. You have to believe me."

"Believe you? Next you'll be telling me that Jotto's my child. You're nothing but a fucking liar."

Hans' eyes bulged.

"Are you afraid, Hans? I see your fear. I smell your fear," Ilya snarled, delighting in the control. "I'm going to do the world a favor by killing you."

"Ilya, I didn't kill Otto. For God's sake, I loved him like a brother."

"Liar…fucking liar!" she said, shooting blindly, her rage preventing her from holding steady.

Hans lunged; she fired again, hitting him point blank in the chest. He crashed to the floor.

"Help me! Help me, please," Hans gasped, pathetically trying to stem the flow of blood from the gaping hole in his chest.

Ilya watched in fascination as Hans wheezed and gasped for breath.

The Nazi, his head pounding, came to. He watched, not daring to even blink for fear that Ilya would turn the gun on him.

"Die, you bastard," Ilya said, smiling as the blood spurted through Hans's fingers. She aimed the gun at his genitals. "This one's just for me."

The Nazi aide closed his eyes and shuddered.

Ilya fired two shots into Hans's groin. Laughing wildly, splattered with blood, she placed the gun barrel into her mouth. *I'm coming, Otto.* Shards of skin, bone, and brains rained down. It was over.

* * *

Once back in New York, a lethargic Jo was given over to Rebecca's care. Natan, Saul, and Aaron, frightened and confused cloistered themselves in Robert's home, spending hours in heated contemplation.

"How in hell could Germany ever be reunited?" Saul asked for the hundredth time.

"Just look at what they've accomplished since the war; they're the wealthiest economy in Europe, and if you talk to the young people, you'll see a familiar nationalism emerging. Have they learned? Have they changed? Only God knows," Natan said, exhausted.

"We've looked at this from every angle. I've had enough. We need help. We'll go to the Israeli government, Aaron," Saul said, his own exhaustion hanging heavy.

* * *

The day before they were to leave, Rebecca made an appointment to see Aaron at his office.

"It's so good to see you again, Rebecca. Please, make yourself comfortable."

"I've been so worried," Aaron said, crossing and uncrossing his legs. "I want to help and I just don't understand why she refuses to see."

"She's refusing to see anyone," Rebecca said, readjusting her skirt as she sat. "She's met with only one person—William—since the events in Naples. She's asked him to move into Robert's home. You have to try and understand. Jo's living a moment at a time, her world one of terror and distrust."

"But she can be helped?"

"Yes. But it's going to take time. She sent a letter of resignation to Albany. Aaron, she needs to feel safe. I'm taking her back to Israel with me."

Aaron felt as if he were breaking apart. "Rebecca, I can't let you take her. I can't lose her again."

"You won't lose her. She'll get well, Aaron. I promise you that."

Chapter 54

————————— ★ —————————

Thickly foliated trees turned Ayelet Haba-ah a lush green, and vibrant orange, red, and yellow wild flowers filled the cool mountain air with fragrant sweetness. When Jo arrived at Rebecca and Saul's kibbutz on June 26, 1973, she barely noticed the resplendent countryside.

Jo settled into her new lodgings: a tiny room furnished with a single bed, nightstand, and a three-drawer dresser. The undersized bathroom had a stall shower, sink, and toilet.

* * *

Trying to remain alone, Jo resisted participating in the daily routine of the kibbutz, but the nature and ideology of communal living made total isolation impossible. If she wanted to eat, she had little choice but to join Saul, Rebecca, David, and Anna for meals in the huge communal dining room.

David and Anna, now very much a part of Rebecca and Saul's family, opened their hearts to Jo. But Jo was unyielding, remaining sullen and unapproachable, refusing their friendship and the opportunity to participate in the rich family life of the commune.

* * *

The kibbutzniks created a park—a kind of animal sanctuary—where they would go when needing solitude. It was here that Jo took refuge and spent hours each day. The deer and rabbits peeked out at her from behind the dense brush. The squirrels, brave and curious, would scurry past her feet looking for handouts, as families of birds sang out melodiously.

Late one afternoon, sitting on the sweet-smelling grass, leaning against a fallen log, Jo was startled by a noise.

"Who's there?" she asked in English.

A male voice answered her in Hebrew. Even though Jo couldn't understand the words, displeasure was evident in the tone of the voice.

She rose to her feet and stood toe to toe with David.

"What are you doing in this place? This happens to be my private log, and I'm not willing to share it with you," he said in German, their only common language.

Jo was taken aback by David's attitude.

"I wasn't aware that private property was a viable concept on a kibbutz," she said, confused by David's aggressive behavior.

"That only applies when you're a member of our collective, and from what I've seen, you're not a member of anything."

"And what makes you such an authority on my life?" Jo asked.

David laughed. "Saul's my best friend. I know everything about you," he said. "Do you think you're the only one who's ever experienced pain and disappointment in your life? This entire country is filled with people who have survived much worse than you. Do they sit around feeling sorry for themselves? No. There's just too damn much to do."

Jo felt her lethargy evaporate. She grew angry. "What could you possibly know about my pain? You have a common bond with these people. I have nothing."

"If you want common bonds, then become a part of us."

Jo's eyes filled with tears, and David softened. "Sit on my log and we'll talk," he said.

His stubborn claim on the log was not lost on Jo, and she found herself smiling as she joined him on the fallen tree trunk.

"You know, in a way you and I are comrades," he said. "I've also known great desperation and hopelessness. There was even a time when the sight of a dying man meant nothing to me. It was an ugly time in my life, but that's all behind me now." His doe-like eyes glistened. "Love, Jo. It's all about love. I found it a long time ago while hiding inside a log a lot like this one." David caressed the fallen tree trunk with his calloused hands. "I was a young man running from the Nazis, when a little Gypsy girl found me, injured and delirious. She healed my body with a cure concocted from some of God's crawling creatures taken from the very log I was living in." He smiled, remembering the spider the Gypsy had added to his poultice. "But more than my body, my mind and heart needed healing. She gave me her love, Jo, and through it I rediscovered my humanity."

Looking skyward, he continued, "I made so many mistakes. While living in Russia, I wouldn't even admit to being a Jew. I live with the shame of that denial every day of my life, but I survived. Now I'm here with my wife, Anna. We have chosen to live, and so must you. If you allow the light back into your life and let the people around you love you, then you too will heal."

"How do I live with myself when I don't even know who or what I am? I've been programmed with some sort of diabolical evil that can be triggered with a sound. I'm like a hand grenade with its firing pin about to be pulled. What can I do? How can I ever trust myself? My God, David, I have the blood of a Nazi running through my veins."

David shook his head. "Is that who you are? Are you really evil?"

Before she could reply, David continued, "You're not, and you know you're not. Life isn't easy, but sometimes we get lucky enough to make choices. You have that opportunity right now if you'll just open your eyes and see. The answers are in the smile of a child, in the fragrance of a flower, in a touch." David took Jo's trembling hand in his. "It's time to begin again. Give yourself a chance. Life is filled with the possibilities of miracles. Each day, we are blessed with those possibilities. Learn to see with your heart, to hear with your eyes, and to love with your soul. I'll help you."

The facade Jo had built over the past month had no room for tears, but when David took her in his arms, rocking her gently, she sobbed.

They continued talking quietly as the sun set on the Golan Heights. A friendship formed.

* * *

In October 1973 catastrophe struck. Egypt and Syria, intent on recovering land taken by the Israelis during the Six-Day War of 1967, launched an attack against Israel on her most holy day, Yom Kippur.

Fierce and determined, it took only three weeks for the Israeli army to repel the Arabs. During that time, Jo lived in a bomb shelter while rockets reined down from the mountains. When it was over, many had died. The country mourned, and she mourned with them.

* * *

In December, sitting across from Saul at a table in the busy coffee shop at the King David Hotel in Jerusalem, Natan thumbed through his papers. Knowing that Jo's safety depended on their protecting her from her father and realizing they had to know how their confrontation had impacted Hans, Natan had gone back to Naples. Now he was ready to give his report.

"When I arrived in Naples, I went directly to the house—or what remained of it. An unfortunate accident had all but burned it to the ground." His sarcasm was evident as he continued.

"The fire chief said that the blaze had begun in the kitchen. I asked why the damage had been so extensive. He said that gale-force winds had buffeted the city that night. That was a little too coincidental for me. So the next day, posing as a journalist, I questioned some of the neighbors.

"A cook at the neighboring house, who had gone to help out for the funeral, told me that the entire staff had been fired the night of Otto's funeral by someone claiming to be Hans's brother. She also said that she had seen a lot of unusual activity at the house after the firings—suitcases loaded into cars, lights on in the house at all hours, and then no activity at all. She never actually saw the Wells' leave, but she was sure they had, because she hadn't seen Hans out for his daily walk since the funeral."

"Where the hell are they?" Saul asked.

"I was told this morning by my contacts at the Israeli Embassy in Miami that Hans and Ilya apparently left the United States for Bolivia just days after Otto's funeral."

"Shit!" Saul said.

"I'm going to find them, Saul," Natan said. "I'll go to South America. If they're there, I'll find them."

"You're not going to Bolivia by yourself?" Saul said.

"No. The Israeli government is interested in pursuing war-crime charges against Hans. Apprehending him in Bolivia and bringing him back to Israel will be much easier than going through extradition hearings in the States."

"I hope the bastard's dead," Saul said, worried about what the ordeal of a trial might do to Jo's precarious recovery.

* * *

The Israeli team, consisting of Natan and two Mosad operatives, traveled to La Paz, Ilya and Hans's reported city of entry. For weeks they searched for the Wells' with the help of a sophisticated network of agents who had infiltrated every facet of the Bolivian government.

* * *

With Rebecca at Jo's side and Saul nervously pacing Rebecca's office, dodging dolls, toys, and medical magazines, Natan read through the daily log he had kept while in Bolivia.

"We couldn't find them," he said. "We showed their picture to hundreds of people, and I'm now convinced that they're dead—eliminated by a hierarchy that considered them both expendable."

"I don't understand," Jo said. "You said they went to Bolivia."

"I think the Nazis had your father and Ilya's passports doctored, and then they sent two imposters into Bolivia. I'm certain Hans and Ilya never left Naples. But it's far from over."

He's dead. What do I feel? Do I care? He was my father–I loved him.

* * *

Jo wandered around the kibbutz for hours before heading up to the Children's House just as they were preparing for bed. She changed diapers, dusting round little bottoms with powder. She helped toddlers to the bathroom, undoing their pajamas and helping them wipe clean.

As she was fastening a toddler's pajama bottoms, she spotted a young girl standing in a corner all alone and obviously frightened. Jo approached her, realizing immediately that the child was one of the new "Olim" freshly arrived from Russia.

Jo took the child's hand. "Come with me. It's time to brush your teeth," she said softly, although the bewildered child couldn't understand a word she was saying.

Jo's eyes were warm and caring. The child felt safe. She allowed Jo to lead her to the sink. While brushing her teeth, she never took her eyes off of Jo.

She allowed Jo to tuck her into bed. Leaning down, Jo kissed her on the cheek, intending to leave but the little girl reached out, pulling Jo into her arms.

"It's all right. I'll stay here with you," Jo said, holding the little girl to her breast. Eventually the child's breathing steadied and she fell asleep. Holding the sleeping little girl in her arms, Jo began to understand how badly she was needed and how much she had to offer.

"I'll be back, little one...I promise," Jo said, gently placing the slumbering child's head on the pillow.

* * *

On a frigid winter morning, as rain pelted the rooftops of the kibbutz, David's forty-two-year-old wife Anna gave birth to a seven-pound, six-ounce baby boy. David, feeling decades younger than his fifty-four years, sat with Jo after seeing his wife and child. He cried unashamedly.

"When I took the name of Vladimir and denied my religion, I was so sure God would punish me. But instead, he has forgiven and blessed me. With the birth of this child, my father's name will be carried on. He represents the future and the hope of our people. And I'll teach him to remember. I'll tell him all about my parents, my grandparents, and the old rabbi whose clothing Saul buried on the grounds of Hebrew University. There's always hope. Life can always be more than we expect it to be. You must never give up."

Jo began to understand.

* * *

Jo spent two years on the kibbutz, rotating jobs with her fellow kibbutzniks. She learned Hebrew and studied Judaism. On her thirty-second birthday she declared herself a Jew, taking her mother's religion as her own.

In the quiet times, when the work was finished and the babies had gone to sleep for the night, Jo wrote to Aaron. The letters were long and often disquieting, but she wrote because she loved him. Aaron's letters to Jo were filled with promise and hope. However, after being betrayed by her uncle, her father, and the only mother she ever knew, Jo had difficulty trusting anyone.

Rebecca kept reassuring Aaron that Jo was making progress, but two years was a long time to wait, and Aaron was discouraged by Jo's refusal to see him. His life in Washington kept him busy, and he dated occasionally to keep his sanity, but he was miserable. Still, he waited–reliving the desperation and loneliness from his own childhood.

* * *

Sitting in the garden behind Rebecca's cottage, Jo pulled off her sandals, wiggled her toes in the newly mown grass, and watched as the dew-covered blades lodged between her toes. She smiled at Rebecca, who poured lemonade from a thermos and handed it to her.

"It's going to be hot today," Rebecca said, noting how quickly the rising sun was drying the dew-laden grass.

Jo watched dreamily as a robin busily built its nest in the olive tree that shaded Rebecca's yard.

"I've been thinking," she said, "that God must have spent extra time creating this place."

"I've thought the same thing myself many times," Rebecca said.

"I checked some books out of the library the other day," Jo said.

Rebecca nodded, opening her notebook. After working two years with Jo, Rebecca had come to know her ways. That kind of an opening, "I've checked some books out of the library," could only mean that Jo had something really important to say.

"They're books about Vilna—Vilnius, since it's part of Lithuania now. It's taken months and I had to pull a dozen strings but I finally received a visa," she said, waiting for Rebecca's reaction. When Rebecca didn't respond, Jo continued. "I've learned all I can about my mother from you. Now I need to touch something she's touched—a doorknob, a sidewalk. I want to look at the things she looked at, to walk where she walked."

Rebecca put her notebook aside.

"It's time for me to leave Israel, Rebecca."

"Yes, Jo, it's time, I'll miss you very much. You're a remarkable young woman. I love you as I loved your mother. She taught me to have the courage of my conviction. If not for her valor, I might never have come to Israel with Saul. And you…you helped me make peace with her death, something I had always been afraid to do.

"When I said good-bye to Morgan at that train station in France so many years ago, I had a premonition that I would never see her again. But I know that you and I will be together again," Rebecca said, turning her face away from Jo.

"Are you all right?"

"Yes, I'm fine. Just a few too many memories have come flooding back. She would be very proud of you, Jo."

Rebecca saw a look cross Jo's eyes that she had never seen before.

"There's something you're not telling, isn't there?"

"I'm going to call Aaron," Jo answered, her eyes sparkling, "to ask him if he'll join me in Vilnius."

Rebecca hugged Jo tightly. "He's waited so long and he loves you so much."

"How can I ever thank you, Rebecca? When I have children, I want you to stand in for my mother and be their grandmother. Would you do that for me?"

"I wouldn't have it any other way."

At that moment, a desultory wind blew the pages of Rebecca's journal and raised goose bumps on both women's arms.

Rebecca perceived Robert's presence.

Thank you for helping, the breeze seemed to whisper.

"You're welcome," Rebecca said aloud.

Jo looked at Rebecca knowingly, as if she too had heard Robert's words.

* * *

Rebecca accompanied Jo to the pay phone in the lobby of the kibbutz guesthouse, where Jo placed her call to Aaron. When the connection was finally completed and Jo closed the door to the booth, Rebecca moved away.

The sound of Aaron's voice paralyzed Jo.

"Hello, Hello! Is someone there?" he asked, his voice heavy with sleep.

Frightened that he might hang up, Jo finally spoke.

"It's me, Aaron. It's Jo."

The words he had so often-fantasized hearing resounded in Aaron's head. He turned on the bedside light to reassure himself that he wasn't dreaming.

"Talk to me, Jo. Just let me hear the sound of your voice. I've been drowning without you. I love you so much."

"I know. I've always known," Jo said. "Do you remember what you promised me that night at the Wall?" she asked.

"I remember every moment I ever spent with you."

"You told me that if I ever needed you, you would be there for me. Well, I need you. I need you desperately."

"I'm here. My God, I'm here and I always will be," Aaron said.

"I'm leaving Israel to go to Lithuania, to Vilnius, where my mother was born. I have so many things to find out about my past, and I want you with me when I do. Will you meet me in Vilnius?" She asked.

"Of course I'll come. I'll help you find whatever it is you're looking for, and then we'll go home, Jo."

Home. The word filled Jo's mind with glorious possibilities.

"I'm leaving a week from Thursday. You're going to need a visa, which will mean asking for some very serious favors. It took me months to get mine but it should be a lot easier doing it from Washington."

"A lot of people owe me favors."

"Do you have a pencil?"

"Go."

"I'll be staying at the Lietuvana Hotel. Just leave a message with the desk telling them when you'll be arriving. And don't worry about me, I'll be fine."

"I love you, Jo."

"And I love you."

"Shalom, my beloved."

Barefooted and dressed only in his underwear, Aaron got out of bed and went into his library. He switched on the light and picked up the daily prayer book that was sitting on the side table next to the sofa. Turning to a passage he had always refused to read, Aaron solemnly repeated aloud the words of his forefathers: "'I love that the Lord should hear my voice and my supplications. For thou hast delivered my soul from death, mine eyes from tears, and my feet from stumbling. I shall walk before the Lord in the land of the living.'"

Aaron looked upward, thankful that his personal war with God had finally ended.

Chapter 55

————————— ★ —————————

The noon sun was unmerciful and Saul was sweating a river. He reached for a thermos of cold water, splashed his face, and wiped off the excess with the back of his hand. The construction site on the grounds of the Hebrew University campus, where Morgan and Robert's theater and school were being built, was alive with activity. Saul put his hard hat back on and snaked through the girders in search of the project foreman.

Twenty minutes later, sitting on a huge boulder, eating yogurt and a hard-boiled egg, Saul smiled as Jo approached him.

"What a nice surprise," Saul said, kissing Jo on the cheek. "I suppose you just happened to be in the neighborhood?"

"It's been a while since I've seen the site, so here I am," she said. "It's pretty incredible, isn't it?"

"Robert would be pleased."

Saul stuffed the remainder of his lunch back into his briefcase.

"You've done a remarkable job, Saul."

"Thanks. I've grown to love this place," he said, pride and satisfaction clearly showing on his face. "There's something so honorable and noble about a building. It will outlive us all, and God willing, hundreds of thousands of people will discover pleasure and knowledge inside its walls. It's a bit like writing; the author dies but his words don't. I believe Robert knew that."

Jo touched Saul's face. "You're a very special man, Saul."

"Thank you. And you–you've come such a long way and we're all so very proud of you."

William, spotting Jo from across the field, rushed to her side.

"What a wonderful surprise," he said, gathering her into his arms. "What do you think, Jo? Isn't it fabulous?" he asked.

"It's overwhelming."

Jo delighted in William's robust and youthful appearance, remembering how differently he had looked when he had arrived in Israel six months earlier.

* * *

Saul had returned from New York, after getting Aaron and William's approval on the architectural plans, gravely concerned about William's mental and physical condition.

"He's become an old man since Robert's death. Looking after the house is simply not enough of a challenge for him, Jo," Saul said.

"Is he well enough to travel?"

"I'm sure with the right motivation he could. Why?"

"I think it would be good if we brought him here and got him involved in the project."

William had been a part of the life that Jo had shared with Robert, and she really missed him.

"That's a wonderful idea," Saul had said. "I'm sorry I didn't think of it. But I know he feels obligated to care for the house. You'd be the only one who could talk him into leaving it."

Jo had no contact with anyone other than Aaron in the States since leaving, and the thought of reestablishing those ties terrified her. It took her days to gather the courage to make her call. When William heard her voice, he broke down crying.

"We need you here in Israel," Jo had said. "No one here knows the first thing about theater. This project just won't work without you. I know it isn't fair for me to ask you to disrupt your life, but I have no one else to turn to. Will you come?" she had asked, realizing how true her words really were.

"But the house?"

"The housekeeping staff can take care of it. Will you come?"

"I'll be there," he said finally, delighted at having a reason to get up in the mornings.

* * *

That had been months earlier, and now as William held Jo in his arms, his renewed vitality and strength was evident.

Taking William and Saul's hands, Jo led them to a grassy area not yet trampled by the construction workers. She sat, pulling them down beside her.

"We're having a picnic without a blanket or food…or ants. This isn't any fun," William teased.

"You expect her to bring sandwiches? She hates the kitchen," Saul said.

"I'm so glad you're both having such a good time at my expense?" Jo said, smiling broadly. "I don't hate the kitchen. I just hate the kitchen on the kibbutz. I intend to become a very good cook one day. But you can take bets that I'll never peel another potato in my entire life," she said recalling the thousands of potatoes she had peeled on kitchen detail over the past two years.

"Some Jewish wife you'll be! No potato latkes, no Kugels, no knishes…"

"Stop! You're making me hungry," Jo said.

"No brisket with browned potatoes simmering in broth…" Saul continued.

"Enough!" Jo said, punching him playfully.

"OK, I'll stop if you tell us just what brings you here at high noon in the middle of summer. I know you too well. This isn't a social call."

"I'm leaving Israel. I'm going to Vilnius to see where my mother was born. Aaron is joining me there. And then…we're going home."

William laughed. "Today I feel young again. God has smiled on us all. This is wonderful!"

"Your mother would have approved of Aaron. He's a fine young man," Saul said. "I wish you nothing less than the kind of love I've known with Rebecca.

"I love you both so much and I'm going to miss you."

* * *

Jo slept little that night. She tried to quiet her roving mind, but she kept wondering what her life was going to be like with Aaron, what she would find in Vilnius, and how she would ever bring herself to tell David. When the sun finally rose, Jo was exhausted but happy to be getting out of bed.

Directly after breakfast she went to David and Anna's apartment. David answered the door.

"Come in, Jo. It's so good to see you. Anna is always complaining that you don't visit us often enough."

Jo kissed David on the cheek. He put his arm around her and led her into his home. Its once antiseptic sparseness was now filled with the smell and necessities of a newly arrived infant.

Anna was sitting on the couch, pillows stuffed behind her, as she fed Moshe. She patted the seat, and Jo joined her.

"Mazel tov," Anna said with a laugh when Moshe burped.

"May I hold him?" Jo asked.

"Of course you can," Anna said, handing Moshe to Jo.

Jo held the baby, delighting in his contented gurgles and sweet smile. Wanting to hold the memory of him in her mind's eye forever, she mentally recorded how his fingers, his nose, his eyes looked. "I'm leaving," she said.

"As I knew you would," David said.

Anna understood the melancholy look on David's face. She went to her husband and put her arm around him.

"We've been through this before, Jo…Anna and me. When we left Russia to begin our lives here, we left behind everyone we loved. It was painful then, and it's painful now. You've become a part of us, and we'll never be the same once you've gone. But we understand that it's time for you to get on with your life."

Anna took the baby from Jo and placed him into the bassinet under the window. "You're going back to be with Aaron, I hope?"

"Yes, but first I'm going to Lithuania. Aaron's going to meet me there," Jo said.

"And then you'll go back to Maryland and marry Aaron and have a pleasant and peaceful life, right?" David asked, his eyes narrowing as he watched Jo.

"You know what I'm going to do," she said, her face reddening. "It's taken me two long years to reach this decision. But now that I've decided, nothing's going to stop me. I'm going to expose those Nazi bastards if it's the last thing I do."

"For God's sake, why?" David asked. "We've talked about this before, and I thought that—"

"You know I'd like nothing better than to go back to the States, have children, and be a good wife, but I can't do that."

"It's because of that article in the paper, isn't it?" David said.

"Yes, damn it!" she said, looking to Anna for support. "There are professors in America, Anna, teaching their students that the Holocaust never happened, that it's a Zionist ploy to gain world sympathy. What's going to happen when there are no more survivors left? Will people begin to believe it never happened? I have to be a witness. I'm not going to rest until I've exposed my father and uncle's unconscionable duplicity to the world. People must be told what the Nazis are up to.

"Once I began to think about the people who were involved with my campaign, I realized just how deeply my father's connections reached into our government—senators, congressmen, judges. Some journalists were literally in his pocket. I know of one who was promised my father's help in getting his own syndicated television talk show if he wrote favorable commentaries and gave me enough coverage in the newspaper.

"I hated everything that journalist stood for, and when I confronted my father about having someone like him involved with my campaign, he said, 'We need him. Don't worry about it.'

"At the time I shrugged it off. But now I realize just how dangerous that journalist and his friends might be one day. It won't be tomorrow–maybe not even ten years from now–but I'm convinced that one day they'll be chewing at the very fabric of democracy and decency.

"I'm going public with the names of every person who ever made the fatal mistake of aligning with my father and uncle."

"They'll kill you," David said.

"They won't kill me," she said.

"But why must you do this to yourself?"

"Don't think for a moment that I relish living my life like that. I would much rather be like everyone else. I didn't ask for any of this, but it was given to me, and now it's my responsibility. There are people still out there working to see that Hitler's ideology is perpetuated. If that ideology is allowed to spread again, it'll surely destroy us all. It's way beyond my choice now; it's my destiny."

"Fight them, Jo, if you must," Anna said. "Fight for Moshe and all the children of the world, but don't let hate be the emotion that drives you. If it is, in the end it will be you who's destroyed. You must fight with love as your companion. Promise me you'll try to do that."

Anna's words touched Jo deeply. "I'll fight with a love for justice, not revenge," Jo vowed.

* * *

Going back to the garden, Jo sat in a patch of golden field poppies. She had come to Israel a shell of a woman, lonely and full of despair; but that was all behind her now.

She smiled, as a rabbit she had seen many times before came close enough for her to touch. She reached out to pet it, and for the first time he allowed her to stroke his fur. The world was just as David had said—filled with the possibility of miracles.

Chapter 56

———— ★ ————

Darkness obscured the kibbutz as the old Mercedes bumped along the dusty rode. It was stifling and Jo breathed a sigh of relief when David finally reached the open highway and opened the windows. Jittery, she rambled on about nothing in particular. Not wanting to interrupt her obvious ploy at keeping them both distracted, David nodded at the appropriate moments, smiled intermittently, and interjected a word occasionally.

Despite lapses into melancholia that unwittingly caused David to drive more slowly, they still managed to arrive at the airport in Tel Aviv two hours before Jo's scheduled departure. While waiting in the security line for the luggage to be searched, Jo said, "How can I ever thank you, David?"

He swallowed, biting back tears. "Just be happy," he said, embracing her.

* * *

The trip was tedious. She had to change planes in London, and foggy weather delayed her plane for three hours. When she finally touched down in Vilnius, her nerves were frayed and she was exhausted. Gathering her camera, tape recorder, and briefcase, she disembarked.

The antiquated air terminal was disorganized, noisy, smoke-filled, and crowded. Jo was forced to stand in a customs line for over an hour, dragging her luggage along as the line inched forward.

Jo took in her surroundings, a hunter, searching for the illusive thread that would tie her to Morgan.

After getting through passport control, Jo found a porter to take her luggage outside. She watched her fellow travelers being greeted with back slaps, warm handshakes, kisses, and tears, all the time hoping to see the light of recognition on one of the unfamiliar faces. She smiled in relief when a young man pushed through the throng of people, calling out her name.

"Sorry. The crowds are impossible," he said, reaching out to shake Jo's hand.

He was dressed in a white T-shirt, khaki pants, and sandals. His hair needed cutting, which only served to accentuate his wholesome good looks.

"My name's Paul," he said, hoisting her luggage, arms bulging from the weight of them.

"I can't tell you how much I appreciate your help."

"Think nothing of it. Heard you had some difficulties with the weather, Miss Wells?" he said in heavily accented English.

"Call me Jo, and yes we did, but it wasn't that bad."

"Let's get out of here. My car is parked just a few minutes away."

The car was a dilapidated wreck. Jo slid in carefully, mindful of the seats that had been taped to prevent the springs and stuffing from falling out. The window on her side was missing, but Paul said nothing in way of an apology as he loaded her belongings into the trunk. Tying a cord around the latch on the trunk, he attached it to the bumper.

"Welcome to Vilnius, hell hole of the earth, " he said, getting into the car. He pulled into the intermittent traffic, popping the clutch too quickly and sending the car into jerking spasms. "They didn't tell me you were so beautiful," Paul said, unabashedly studying Jo.

Jo's hair, bleached to white gold by the Israeli sun, was gathered at her neck. She wore a turquoise sleeveless blouse and an eggshell linen skirt that highlighted her long elegant legs, tanned and muscular from her years of working out of doors.

"I take it you're not too fond of Vilnius," Jo said.

"What's to like? The city is filled with communists and collaborators."

"Then why do you stay?"

"I have my work," he said curtly, dismissing further conversation on the subject.

Jo looked out the open window at a city steeped in neglect. Three- and four-story apartment buildings lined both sides of the street. They were old and badly in need of painting. Women were hanging laundry out to dry, taking advantage of the warm afternoon breezes. And smells from simmering food drifted out to the open streets. The unseasonably warm summer wind loosened her hair from the chignon, causing blond wisps to fall into her eyes.

"I can't remember the last time the weather was this perfect. You couldn't have picked a better time to come. We'll be at your hotel in a few minutes."

"If it wouldn't be too much of an imposition, I would really like to take a walk before going to the hotel."

"It's certainly no imposition. There's a nice park not very far from here on Gora Zomkova."

Five minutes later Paul pulled onto the shoulder of the road and opened the door for Jo. "Welcome to Bernadner Gargin. Take your time. I'll wait here for you."

Jo walked slowly through the billowing grass, relishing the sensation of the tall blades tickling her bare legs. Children were at play all around her: jumping rope, playing tag, sitting on swings, watched by attentive mothers.

Not far from the swings, the smaller children were playing in a sandbox. Jo kicked off her shoes, stepped into the sandbox and sat down in the sand. The mothers, sitting on benches, stared on in disbelief, too repressed to ever consider doing such a thing.

A little boy no older then two toddled over to Jo. His bucket was filled with sand. Deliberately, he dumped it into her lap, grinning mischievously. Jo laughed as she brushed herself off. The mortified mother rushed over and scolded the little boy. Jo tried to tell the woman that she was not upset, but verbal communication was impossible. So Jo patted the sand, inviting the child to sit. She refilled the bucket, allowing him to spill it in her lap at will. The mother went back to her bench to watch.

"You're so adorable and this place looks so lovely," she said. The child looked at her in delighted confusion. "How could a place so lovely have harbored such horror? Tell me, little boy; was your grandfather a collaborator? Did Jews live next door? Did he help round them up?" Her words were met by the gentle, trusting eyes of innocence. It's all so very sad, she thought, trying to imagine the madness that must have overtaken the city.

The child lost interest in Jo and moved away. She dusted off her feet and put her shoes back on, then decided to sit for a moment under a giant birch.

Mother, did you play here when you were a child? Did you ever sit in the sand box or play on the swings? Jo drifted into a half-sleep.

✳ ✳ ✳

The woman watched from afar. In her youth, her hair had been a lustrous blue-black. Now it was streaked with white. Her porcelain complexion was deeply etched with the fine lines of her years. Thin and fragile looking, she was a woman defeated by the burdens of time, but her eyes were still bright, revealing the essence of her once-great beauty.

She watched in fascination as the stranger played with the child in the sandbox. Smiling, she thought that in her youth she might have done the same. Her eyes strained to see the stranger more clearly as Jo moved to sit under the tree. Deciding that she wanted to meet the lovely stranger, she walked slowly from the nearby bench.

When she got close enough to make out Jo's features, the woman's heart began to race. Turning away, she staggered to a nearby tree and slipped to the ground. *I'm dying. God is allowing me to see myself as I once was, and now I'm going to die.* Closing her eyes, she waited for the angel of death to appear. Instead, the palpitations diminished and she opened her eyes. She glanced in Jo's direction. *I'm here and she's still there. Dear God, dare I hope? Is it possible?*

When Jo made her way back to the car, Morgan followed.

I know that young man, Morgan thought. *I can call him. All it will take is a phone call. A thousand nights I've prayed for this moment.* Her body trembled with the greatest feeling of joy she had ever known. Morgan began to cry the first tears she had shed in twenty years.

* * *

The Hotel Lietuvana was located fifteen minutes from the park on Mickiewitz Street.

"Welcome to the best Vilna has to offer," Paul said sarcastically as they pulled into the driveway.

Jo detested the place on sight.

When Paul untied the trunk, a surly porter, his uniform stained and faded, took the luggage and grunted as he took it inside.

"Arrogant fool," Paul whispered as he retied the trunk. "Try and get a good nights sleep. I'll pick you up at ten tomorrow morning."

Jo watched Paul drive away. She entered the hotel, heading directly to the registration desk in the far corner of the lobby. Everything about the place reeked of neglect, from the threadbare carpet to the worn wood of the reception desk.

After filling out the registration, Jo followed the unfriendly bellhop to her room. Exhausted, she sat on the bed. The mattress springs angrily dug into her buttocks, and sick to her stomach from the smell of stale cigarettes, Jo opened the doors to the balcony. Venturing out, she was greeted by rusting furniture covered in pigeon droppings. Stepping back inside, she undressed, leaving her clothing piled on the chair. Too tired to shower, she placed an overseas call to Aaron.

Forty minutes later, her eyes heavy with sleep, the phone rang.

"We have your party on the line," the operator said.

"Aaron?"

"Jo, darling, is that you? Are you OK? Was your flight on time? Did you eat? I've been so worried. Was there someone their to meet you?"

"Aaron Blumenthal, just listen to you go on. I'm fine. I'm just tired and confused."

"Confused? I don't understand. What's the matter?"

"I'm surrounded by murderers, Aaron. These are the same people who led the Jews to their slaughter. I expected the people to be hateful and ugly. That's what I wanted. God help me–that's really what I wanted. But they're not monsters. They're just people. And I don't understand how that's possible. I don't know what to do?"

"There's nothing for you to do. You went to Vilnius to connect with the spirit of your mother. You need to focus on that and try to block out the rest. I don't think it's possible for us to understand why a child grows up to become evil or why mankind is so willing to follow the path of evil. Perhaps it's not for us to understand."

"It's so damn hard to accept that."

"You know, I have this mantra I say whenever I'm loosing sight of things. Maybe it could help you as well. Today I pray for the wisdom to build a better tomorrow on the mistakes and experiences of yesterday."

"Build a better tomorrow–that's what I'm trying to do."

"And you will, my darling. You will. Now, I have some good news. "My visa is being processed as we speak. I should be on an airplane tomorrow night, or the next night at the latest."

"How in the world did you pull that off?"

"It wasn't easy, but when people have power and no money, then money has a way of getting to those powerful people. Now, you get a good night's sleep. You'll feel better in the morning."

"I'll feel better when you're here with me."

"I love you," Aaron said. And Jo,"

"What?"

"Nothing's ever going to hurt you again."

Chapter 57

──────────── ★ ────────────

Morgan sat on the balcony of the home she shared with Jacob Gold. Despite the heat, she was shivering. Jacob came with a sweater. He wrapped it around her shoulders. She looked at him, her lovely eyes saying everything Jacob needed to hear.

Morgan took his hand, touching it to her lips. *He gave up everything for me. I must take care; I must remember everything.*

* * *

Jacob saved Morgan after the birth of her child, risking his life daily: caring for her until she had been well enough to move from the concentration camp hospital, hiding her in the women's barracks under a false identity, feeding her with food from his own meager rations. And each time a "selection" took place in Morgan's barracks, Jacob would hide Morgan amongst the cadaverous patients being experimented on by the doctors of Dachau.

And then on a spring day in 1945 the 45th Infantry Division and the 42nd Rainbow Infantry Division entered Dachau and liberated 30,000 prisoners. It was finally over. Morgan was thirty years old at the time and weighed only eighty pounds. Dirty, starving, unwilling to speak and mentally confused, Jacob had stepped in, taking control, protecting her.

Their first stop had been the displaced persons camp, a no-mans land of confusion and despair. Jacob painstakingly nurtured Morgan, feeding her, dressing her, trying to reach into the enveloping darkness. Her physical strength began to return, but her mental state continued to deteriorate.

Finally making their way back to Paris, Jacob took Morgan from doctor to doctor, but the diagnosis was always the same; she needed long-term extensive therapy. His heart broken, Jacob committed Morgan to a psychiatric hospital, DeVille-Evrard, on the outskirts of Paris.

Jacob accepted a staff position at a local hospital only a few miles from Morgan. And everyday, morning and night for three years he visited. In time Morgan improved; she recognized Jacob, she began to speak, and the dragons that spewed fire into her brain began to disappear. Painfully shy and frightened, she spent another full year in the hospital before the doctors felt she was well enough to leave.

* * *

Accepting a position at a prestigious hospital in Paris, Jacob moved Morgan into a lovely villa he had purchased and renovated. She had a private bath and a bedroom of her own with a huge veranda that overlooked the Seine. She loved the house and seemed content, although she refused to meet any of Jacob's friends or enter Paris society. Instead, Morgan spent her time at inconspicuous coffee houses, listening and waiting. Then one day, Robert Osborne's name appeared in the newspaper, he was returning from America, he was coming to Paris.

"I knew it was mistake for us to come here," she said the moment Jacob entered the door, handing him the newspaper.

"You must see him," Jacob had said after scanning the article. "You owe it to yourself and you owe it to him."

"I can't," she cried.

"For God's sake, Morgan, he's your husband. We've had this discussion a thousand times. How can we ever hope to have a life, either one of us, if you refuse to put this behind you?"

"Look at me, Jacob. I was the whore of a Nazi. He thinks I'm dead and that's what I want him to think. If you won't come with me, then I'll go without you."

"What are you going to do, run away for the rest of your life?" he had asked, disappointed that after so many years of therapy she still thought of herself as a whore.

"I'm going back to Vilna."

"Why in the hell would you want to go back there? It's under Communist rule, for God's sake."

"It was my home once, and I want to go back there. I'll be safe. He won't ever find me."

Jacob tried to talk Morgan out of returning to Vilna, but in the end he had relented, and within a week the villa was closed and they were on their way to Lithuania.

* * *

Now, twenty-five years later, he saw the stunned and ashen look on Morgan's face. "What's the matter, darling?"

"That boy, Paul the one who came to your office to interview you—"

"What's he got to do with this? I told him to stay away from you."

"Shh. You must listen. I need you to call him for me."

"Why?"

"Ask him about the young woman who was with him today."

"And why would I do that?"

Morgan took a deep breath. "Sit down, Jacob."

"I don't want to sit. What's all this about?"

"I saw my daughter in the park today. And I saw her get into a car with that boy."

Jacob's hands began to shake. *Please, God,* he prayed, *not now. Don't take her mind away from me now.* He struggled for so many years to shield Morgan, guarding her fragile mind. He had won her heart; they lived as man and wife, he loved her.

"Jacob Gold! Get that look off your face. I'm not crazy. Just pick up the damn phone and find out who that young woman is."

Shaking his head, Jacob took out his wallet and shuffled through cards until he found Paul's telephone number. He dialed.

"Paul, this is Doctor Gold," Jacob said recognizing the man's voice.

"Yes, sir? What can I do for you?"

"You'll beg my pardon for this intrusion into your privacy, but my wife saw you with a young woman today. Can you tell me about her? Where's she from?"

"She's an American."

Jacob put his hand over the mouthpiece.

"She's an American," he whispered to Morgan.

"And?" Morgan said, exasperated by Jacob's timidity.

"Perhaps you would be kind enough to tell me why she's here?" Jacob asked.

"I'll do better than that. Why don't you meet us for lunch tomorrow, noon at the Lietuvana?"

"One moment, please." He looked hard at Morgan, deciding that she must face whatever it was she thought she saw. Again placing his hand over the phone, he said, "They want to meet us at the Lietuvana for lunch."

"Invite them to come here," Morgan said.

"Come here for lunch, Paul. Noon will be fine," he said before giving him the address.

* * *

Early the next morning, dressed in blue jeans and a T-shirt, Jo began exploring the city with Paul. They walked for miles, wondering up and down the narrow streets and alleyways of Vilnius.

On the Boulevard of Gora Zomkova a small dog, its tail wagging playfully, ran up to Jo. She reached down to pet it, and when she did, he barked.

"What is it, boy? Is something wrong?" she asked, playfully scratching the dog's neck. He continued barking, running in circles around her legs. Jo turned, intending to walk away from the dog, but he continued to bark, running back and forth trying to stop her.

"That's enough, boy. Get away," Paul said.

Jo studied her surroundings. Each house, totally unique in its design, was connected to the other by common walls. And on the other side of the Boulevard was the park she had visited the day before. Jo stared at the balconies that perched from the second story of every home, pulled by a feeling of familiarity.

"Get lost, you mutt," Paul said, kicking at the little dog.

"Stop that!" Jo ordered, scooping the animal into her arms and nuzzling it.

"Are you trying to tell me something, boy?" Then, putting the animal down, she said, "Be a good boy and go home."

The dog looked at her for a moment before running into the yard of a house down the street.

"Let's go," Paul said. "We'll be back here later. We've been invited to have lunch with Doctor Gold and his wife. They live in one of these houses. I thought you would enjoy meeting them."

* * *

Getting into the car, Paul continued, "I never met her, but he's a fascinating man. What I don't understand is why a doctor trained in the finest schools in France would want to come to a communist country. When I asked him about it, he was philosophical. Said they needed a good doctor. And then he said something about the affairs of ones heart, but I didn't understand what he was talking about. Anyway, you'll meet them soon enough."

They drove down Gora Zomkova.

"Right now I want you to see what was once the very center of Jewish mystical life in Europe–before the Germans came."

"What happened to the Jews of Vilnius? Were they sent to concentration camps?" Jo asked, again finding it so impossible to believe that Nazi murderers once occupied this pleasant little city.

"No, Jo," he answered, "They didn't have to send them anywhere. With the help of the villagers more than 100,000 Jews were slaughtered not more than 10 kilometers from where we're standing. There are massive death pits filled with the bones of the innocents.

"When the Russians finally pushed the Germans out of Vilnius, only 2,500 Jews had survived. Most of them survived by hiding in the forests, and a small number were concealed inside the city–a very small number. Some managed to escape to the Soviet Union. All four of my grandparents died here. And my parents would have died as well if their families hadn't pooled their money and paid a family to hide them."

"I'm so sorry. This must be a very difficult place for you to live."

"On the contrary," Ran said. "I'm a Jew. I'm alive. I have my own country now and someday I'll go there. They didn't win. Isn't that what matters? They didn't win."

"Is that what this is all about? Is it about winning?" Jo asked.

"God Damn right! We can't bring them back, but we can make sure it never happens again."

* * *

Morgan stayed awake most of the night. Terrified that what she had seen was an illusion, she spent the entire night speculating. At three in the morning she began cleaning: dusting, washing floors, and vacuuming. Jacob helped.

Jacob had acquired Morgan's childhood home for her by bribing Soviet officials. But it had cost him his entire savings, leaving nothing for home repairs or furnishings. But that didn't seem to bother Morgan. She saw her home as she had seen it as a child, and she was content.

At sunrise Morgan began preparing their noontime meal. And by early morning she was exhausted and euphoric.

"I'll wait in the kitchen. When they come in, you go and look. Then you come and tell me if she's my daughter."

"Darling, you're not thinking rationally. And you're setting yourself up for a terrible disappointment."

* * *

Gora Zomkova Street had changed little over the past half-century. The homes were still regal, regardless of the lack of fresh paint and repair. And on this day in the summer of 1975, the sun was shining brightly, and the air was sweet and cool.

"This is the house," Paul said, reading the number on the post. He pulled into the driveway.

"It must have really been lovely at one time," Jo said, getting out of the car.

"I'm sure that before the communists came, it was beautiful."

They approached the front door. A dog barked. Paul knocked.

"Welcome," Jacob said, recognition flashing through his head like cannon fire. He steadied himself against the doorframe. The little dog jumped on Jo, barking wildly. She picked him up, recognizing him as the same animal she had seen earlier in the day.

"Dr. Gold, are you OK?" Paul asked.

"Fine," he said, reaching out his hand to Jo. "I'm Jacob Gold."

"Jo Wells. It's a pleasure meeting you, sir."

The voice! My God, I delivered this woman. She's Morgan's child. "Please, come into the library. Make yourselves comfortable. I'll be right back."

He ran down the hallway, almost falling on a corner of an oriental rug. Bursting into the kitchen, he found Morgan cowering in the corner.

"It's her, isn't it?" she asked, her eyes brimming.

"It is," he said, putting his arms around Morgan, trying to stop her from shaking. "If I hadn't seen her with my own eyes, I would never have believed it."

"Take me to her, Jacob. Take me to my daughter."

Chapter 58

─────── ★ ───────

Jacob entered the library with Morgan clinging tightly to his arm. The sun bathed room reflected shards of white and gold, silhouetting Jo in billowy light. Morgan dropped Jacob's arm, her eyes riveted on the reflective angel-like image. The room was eerily silent as she moved trance-like toward her daughter.

Jo watched as the stranger approached, mesmerized, lost in Morgan's face. *Oh, my God. Those eyes, they're my eyes.* "Mother?" she asked softly.

"My child. My child," Morgan cried. Opening her arms; her eyes beseeching, begging the child she had lost to understand. Jo moved into her arms.

"Dear God, it's you, it's really you," Jo said, laughing, crying, kissing the salty sweetness as their tears mingled, their bodies trembling.

"I can't believe you're alive; my mother, my mother," Jo murmured, her words muffled against the warmth of Morgan's face. "I want to look at you," she said, wiping the tears from her eyes with the back of her hand. She took Morgan gently by the shoulders. "You're so beautiful."

"No, my child, not beautiful but finally whole."

They sat on the sofa facing each other, their knees touching, holding each other's hands.

"Come," Jacob said to Paul, "A little whiskey and lunch will do us both some good." He leaned down and kissed Morgan tenderly on the lips, "my angel," he whispered before moving from the room.

"I don't even know your name," Morgan said sadly.

"Jotto Wells but everyone calls me Jo."

"How did you come to be here? How did this miracle happen?" Morgan asked, her voice strained, her body rigid.

"I met Robert Osborne in New York while I was in law…"

Morgan's eyes filled with tears, the sorrow debilitating to see. "Robert knew," she sobbed, "he knew that I had another man's child."

Jo took Morgan in her arms. "Shh. Shh. It's all right," she cooed: rocking, patting, soothing. "He knew what happened in the camp. He knew; he understood; and he never stopped loving you."

Does Robert know you came here?" Her face radiated fear, but her eyes were suddenly child-like as she spoke of him.

Jo's mouth turned dry as sand. "He's…," she stammered, detesting the thought of inflicting more pain. "Robert passed away."

Morgan cried out, wounded. She put her hand to her mouth and seemed to pull inward, stifling her sobs. Disentangling herself from Jo's embrace, she buried her face in her hands. "I never stopped loving him but I couldn't go back to him," she said, her words muffled.

"I want you to understand why. You must understand why," she said softly. Morgan lifted her head, her resolve evident, her strength renewing. "My mind shut down for years; it was the only way I knew how to cope. Too many things happened. The murder of my parents, while I was off pretending to be some great actress." Morgan paused, tears streaming down her face. "I came back here after the Germans attacked, but I was too late to help my family. I was eventually captured and sent to Dachau where I became the whore of an SS doctor." Morgan's face went crimson. "Oh, my poor sweet child, I'm so sorry. I didn't mean to say that. "

"It's alright. I know what kind of an animal my father was. Please, just go on; I want to understand, I need to know."

"For years I blocked most of the memories from the Camp," Morgan said tentatively, the veins in her temple throbbing wildly. "When they took you away from me," Morgan continued, her mind wondering, the pain short-circuiting her thought processes, "I thought you were dead. If not for Jacob, I would have died too. He saved me, not only in the concentration camp but afterwards. I was sick and I spent a very long time in a psychiatric hospital. Jacob cared for me. He demanded nothing. You must try to understand. I thought you were lost to me forever and I knew I could never face Robert again, although Jacob begged me to either go to Robert or to finally put the relationship behind me. I was incapable of doing either.

"For years Jacob and I had a platonic relationship: sharing a home, being each others confidants. He loved me and I knew that but I had nothing to give to a relationship. But time dims memory and at some point, I don't even know when, I fell in love with Jacob. Perhaps not with the same passion I had for Robert, but it's the kind of love that endures. I hope you understand."

"How could I not understand?" Jo took Morgan's hand; never taking her eyes from her mother's face. "You're everything that everyone said you were: brave, caring, a good woman. I'm proud that you're my mother."

"Thank you, child. That's the kindest thing you could ever say to me. But now, it's your turn."

Jo sighed. After listening to Morgan, her own story seemed less tumultuous, less damning. She talked about her life: Ilya, her father, boarding school, Robbie, college, law school, her election to public office. "I've been living in Israel the past couple of years. Actually, I stayed with your friends Saul and Rebecca."

"Rebecca? I don't know a Rebecca."

"Wait. I'm sorry. Her name use to be Claire."

"Oh, my God. Claire. You know my Claire? You stayed with her? She's...tell me. Tell me all about her."

Jo rambled on, her sentences running together, wanting to fill the lost years for her mother. She talked until she was hoarse.

"And is there no young man in your life?"

"Yes, Mother. There is. Aaron is…

And so it went, hours on end.

* * *

As dusk fell, Jacob entered the room carrying a food-laden tray. The light was dim, the air damp and chilly. The two women glanced his way, his intrusion shocking them into the present.

"You should eat something," he said, wrapping a sweater around Morgan's shoulders. "Can I get you a wrap?" he asked Jo, moving to turn on the lamps.

"No thanks, I'm fine."

"Well, if you change your mind just let me know," Jacob said, leaving the room, closing the door quietly.

They picked at the food, neither one very interested in eating.

"Thank you for coming here, my child," Morgan said, her face pasty, her eyes shadowed and heavy with exhaustion. "This old body needs some fresh air?"

At the front door Morgan took a tattered sweater hanging from a hook on the wall. "Put this on. The nights get cool here."

Hand in hand they walked across the street into the park. The moon was full, and the sky was brilliant with stars. Birds sang their night call, trees rustled, and the darkness seemed bright. They didn't speak; they simply walked.

* * *

Later that evening, sitting side by side on the terrace, Morgan spoke of her earliest memories, painting a landscape so vivid that Jo felt as though she were there.

"How did your family act after you ran away with Robert?" Jo asked.

"What I did almost killed my father," Morgan said. "But I just couldn't allow them to marry me off to someone I didn't love. I wanted to be an actress." A searing pain tore through her chest. She tightened her grip on Jo's hand. "I was selfish, I broke with the tenets of my faith. And God punished me."

"No," Jo said. "You followed your destiny. You never meant to hurt anyone."

How nice. My child wants to protect me. The pain in her chest ebbed slightly.

"Before the war," Morgan continued, "before the German's and the communists, Vilna was a vibrant city. The streets were filled with people: yelling, bargaining, talking, and laughing. Everything was a celebration. When a baby was born, everyone was joyous, and when someone died, everyone mourned. The Jews of Vilna were a family. When the end came, they died together, a family united even in death. Then there was Dachau. You must understand what happened at the Camp."

For the next hour Jo listened. It was a detached commentary, an epic story told in third person. Jo asked no questions, debilitated by what she heard.

"Now, child," Morgan said finally, the catharsis complete, "it's very late and we're both exhausted." She rose, smiling, her eyes crinkling with joy. "Tonight you will sleep in your mother's home."

"Yes, mother. Tonight I'll sleep in your home. But I need some things from the hotel. And I need to see if there are any messages from Aaron."

"Oh, yes, the young man. Come on. Jacob will take us."

* * *

At the hotel a message was waiting; Aaron was arriving the following morning. Ecstatic, Jo reread the message, daydreaming the implications.

Morgan leaned heavily against Jacob. "Get me to a chair," she whispered, teetering, her legs threatening to fail. Jacob put his arm tightly around Morgan, supporting her weight.

"Relax, darling. Take deep breaths, you're going to be just fine." He led her to the nearest chair.

"What is it? What's the matter with her?" Jo cried when she finally looked up, watching as Jacob kneeled at her mother's feet.

"She just needs to rest for a moment. Your mother suffers from angina. She'll be fine in just a few minutes."

"I feel better already," Morgan said, the color returning to her face, the pain slipping away.

"Are you sure?" Jacob asked, his own breathing ragged.

"Enough, I'm fine." Morgan said, pushing the unwanted attention aside. "Now, let's get this hotel business behind us. You and Aaron should stay with us. We have plenty of room."

"Mother, I don't want to hurt your feelings but I haven't seen him in a very long time."

"How thoughtless of me. Of coarse you must have your privacy. But tonight you'll stay with us?"

"Yes, Mother. Tonight I'll stay with you."

* * *

Aaron's plane touched down in Vilnius at seven o'clock the following morning. Handing his passport to the customs inspector, Aaron nervously ran his fingers through his hair. Slipping the stamped document back into his briefcase, he straightened his tie before heading through the doorway.

At 6'4" he towered over the other arriving passengers, and Jo caught her breath as he approached.

"How I've missed you," Aaron whispered, taking her into his arms, kissing her deeply.

"Hold me. I need to feel your arms around me," Jo said, breathing in his strength.

Someone passed by, clucking disapproval. Then another disembarking traveler passed, snarling at their open show of affection.

"I think we'd better go get my luggage before we're lynched," Aaron said, laughing.

"First I have to tell you something," Jo said, pulling Aaron away from the disembarking passengers. Sleep-deprived and overwrought with emotion, Jo began to cry.

"What is it?" he asked.

"It's Morgan. I've found her, Aaron. She's alive. My mother's alive."

Chapter 59

———————— ★ ————————

Before Jo left for the airport that morning, mother and daughter had sat in the breakfast room, drinking a cup of coffee and talking. The simple ritual had been one of the most precious interludes in Morgan's life. Feeling exuberant and renewed, she had then gone upstairs to dress.

Jacob was putting on his tie when she entered. He turned, his eyes soft, his face at sixty-five still handsome. He smiled. *She's never been more beautiful.* Taking her in his arms, he kissed her.

"The time has come, my darling," he said.

"For what?" Morgan asked, drinking in the aroma of his aftershave and the feeling of his arms around her.

"I want you to marry me. Now, while your daughter's here with us."

Morgan pulled slowly away.

"Yes, darling. That's a wonderful idea. Robert was just a memory—a wonderful time of grace and happiness but no more than a memory. You are the one I've loved for the past thirty years, and I'd be honored to take your name."

* * *

Promising Morgan that she would, Jo took Aaron directly from the airport to the house. On the way, she talked nonstop; recounting everything her mother had said.

At the house, introductions were made. Jacob shook Aaron's hand, greeting him warmly.

"Mother, this is Aaron," Jo said proudly.

"You're so handsome," Morgan said, throwing her arms around Aaron, hugging him tightly.

"I feel as if I know and love you already," Aaron replied, taken instantly by Morgan's warmth.

* * *

Sitting in the living room, they talked about their lives, their dreams, and their disappointments. Morgan and Jo sat close together, touching every few minutes as if to assure themselves that they were not participating in an illusion.

Eventually the conversation turned to the possibility of Jacob and Morgan immigrating to the United States. None of them doubted that it would be a lengthy and difficult process. And they knew that more times than not the applications were denied, but Aaron felt certain he could help. Optimistically, they allowed themselves to speculate about what the future might hold for them all.

* * *

That evening, after a dinner of roast chicken, mashed potatoes and fresh chicken soup, Jacob cleared his throat, clinked his water glass with his fork and stood. "I have an announcement to make." Morgan blushed and giggled. Jo grinned at Aaron. "This," Jacob said proudly, "is the happiest day of my life. Would you like to know why it's the happiest day of my life?" he asked, teasing, thoroughly enjoying himself.

"Jacob Gold," Morgan scolded, "you're making such a fuss."

"Yes, I am, my beloved. I'm making a fuss. I'm entitled to make a fuss."
He pinched her cheek. "So, shh. Tomorrow, this woman, who I've loved
and adored for my entire life, has finally agreed to become me wife."

"Oh, that's so wonderful," Jo said, rushing to kiss her mother and Jacob.

"Mazel tov," Aaron said, raising his glass.

"A toast to my fiancée!" Jacob said boisterously.

This is how it should be. She belongs with this man. Jo pushed the
image of Robert firmly from her mind as she moved to embrace her
mother and Jacob.

* * *

Hours later, Aaron and Jo rose to leave. At the front door, Morgan
embraced her daughter.

"He's a good man," Morgan whispered while hugging her. "And he
loves you very much. Now, go. We've kept you long enough."

* * *

Jo felt embarrassed by the shabby hotel room. She stood in the
doorway scowling as the porter brought in Aaron's luggage and left.
Aaron laughed, pulling her into the room.

"I do believe you're a snob, Miss Wells," he said. "Think of tonight as
a communist version of the Plaza."

Aaron took Jo into his arms. Their emotions burning with hunger,
they came together. Touching, tasting, exploring one another, they
made love throughout the night. And then, as the sun peeked over the
horizon, spent and delirious, they drifted off to sleep.

* * *

Too soon, the alarm rang, awakening them rudely.

"Good morning, sleepy head," Aaron said, kissing Jo. She responded with a sigh, wrapping her arms around him.

"What time is it?" she asked.

"It's 8:30."

"I guess we'd better get up," Jo said, not moving.

"The sun is shining; it's going to be a beautiful day for a wedding."

"Yes, it is." Jo nuzzled his neck.

"I've been thinking. Since neither of us have any family, I thought it might be nice if we got married here, so you could be with your mother."

"Oh, my God!" she said. "Are you proposing?" She sat up, pulling the sheet over her naked body.

"I'm not only proposing, I'm suggesting we get married today."

"Today? But how?"

"We'll ask Jacob to do it; a symbolic wedding, with your mother giving you away. We'll make it legal when we get back to the States."

"What a marvelous idea. What a beautiful thought. What a thoughtful—"

"Is that a yes?" Aaron asked, laughing.

"That's a definite yes," she said, hugging him.

* * *

The civil ceremony between Morgan and Jacob took place in an office at City Hall. Morgan wore an aqua suit and carried a corsage of pink baby roses in her hands.

It made little difference that Aaron and Jo didn't understand a word of the proceedings, because Morgan and Jacob's eyes said everything either of them needed to hear.

* * *

Back at the house they ate a lunch of smoked fish and potatoes. The conversation was lively, the room spinning with happiness: the newlyweds touching, hugging, their faces shining with joy. And when they were finished eating the main coarse, they moved into the library for desert and coffee. Aaron reached for Jo's hand. He nodded to her, signaling that he felt the time was right.

"Mother...Jacob, Aaron and I have a favor to ask. Aaron has asked me to marry him. We would like to do it here, in your home, today."

"My kinder, my kinder," Morgan said, slipping into the Yiddish of her youth. "Now I will have a son and a daughter. Oh, Jacob, could we ever have a better day?" She slipped the diamond and emerald ring from her finger. Morgan had found the ring the day she and Jacob had moved into the house, under a floorboard in her parents' bedroom—one of Sara's favorite hiding places. It was the only possession of Sara's to survive the war.

"This belonged to my mother and to her mother before her." Morgan handed the ring to Aaron. "And now it will be passed to yet another generation. Now, Jacob, show the children how well you speak Hebrew. We'll make the blessings over the wine, we'll break the glass...we'll do it all. This is the happiest day of my life."

* * *

During the days that followed they became a family: sharing intimacies, idiosyncrasies and histories. Each moment became precious in days that slipped too quickly by. Before any of them were ready, it was over.

* * *

The noise from the airplane was deafening, and the flight attendant, anxious to have her passengers aboard, kept urging them to hurry. Jo began to walk up the stairs. She looked back at her mother.

Not yet. One more kiss. One more embrace. Did I tell her I love her? Did I tell her I'd be back? Did I tell her I'd get her out? She pulled her hand away from Aaron and fought her way back down the stairs. Crying, she ran into her mother's arms.

"It's going to be all right, my darling. I know what you're thinking. I know you love me and I know we'll be together one day," Morgan whispered, kissing the tears from Jo's cheek. "Go, child. Your husband's waiting for you."

Standing on the tarmac, watching as the plane pulled away, Morgan held tightly to Jacob's arm.

Chapter 60

─────────── ★ ───────────

August 6th, 1978. The sky danced white, the sun dazzled; it was a glorious day. Three chefs cooked and supervised the food preparations; while a dozen catering assistants set tables with the finest china and crystal on the lawn of the Blumenthal estate, under tents draped in white silk. Dozens of varieties of plants, trees and flowers, were flown in from around the world, creating an ambiance of fragrant beauty.

Two hundred guests looked on as Jo, dressed in a seed pearl satin and lace gown that swept off her shoulders became the wife of Aaron Blumenthal. It was a storybook wedding, replete with prince and princess.

Security was tight. Jo Wells was still news. A photographer and a reporter from the Washington Post, both friends of Aaron's were allowed a thirty-minute interview and photography session a week before the wedding, hoping that the public's curiosity would then peek and diminish. It was not to be the case.

* * *

Days after the wedding the supermarket tabloids and People Magazine wrote feature articles, showing a shunned Robbie Taxton resigning his Senate seat. Alongside that picture were photos of Jo and Aaron smiling and holding hands. Every talk show in America wanted Jo. Johnnie Carson called personally to ask her to appear.

Jo detested the attention. She needed solitude and refused every request, content to slip into the surrealistic cocoon of her new life. Passionately in love, she wove her life around Aaron: cooking, gardening, overseeing the household staff, and learning to integrate her life with his. To her friends she seemed well adjusted and content. Only Aaron knew of the greater turmoil that stirred within, coloring Jo's every waking moment.

* * *

In between letters and phone calls to her mother and Jacob in Lithuania, Jo bombarded the Department of Immigration and Naturalization with written requests. She met with members of the Soviet Union's embassy and spent hours with the USSR's United Nations delegation, begging them all for help. Simultaneously, she enlisted Saul in Israel, hoping that if all else failed, perhaps he could secure exit visas for her mother and Jacob.

But nothing was happening and Jo was rapidly becoming depressed and embittered by broken promises and hundreds of disappointments. Aaron tried to encourage Jo to give him and others a little time to see what they could do to help. But Jo refused to stop trying.

In desperation she turned to an old law school friend, Steven Stein, who had spent five years with the State Department before going into private practice. He was thrilled to hear from Jo and invited her to his McLean, Virginia, offices for lunch.

Jo took the train and then a taxi to Steven's prestigious Farm Credit Drive address. As they walked arm in arm into the executive dining room, Jo couldn't help but notice that prosperity and too many hours of work had taken its toll since last she'd seen him. His hair had grayed and his body carried an extra 25 pounds, adding years to his appearance. Still his eyes sparkled mischievously and his smile was warm.

Entering the dining room, all eyes turned toward Jo.

"You're quite the celebrity, Mrs. Blumenthal," Steven teased.

"And this is quite the room, Mr. Stein," Jo countered, noting the leather upholstered club chairs, heavy mahogany dining tables, and lavish brocade draperies. The smell of cigars permeated the air.

"This sure feels like a good-old-boys club to me."

"Now, now. Don't even think of going there with me. We have 10 female attorneys in our practice."

"I would expect nothing less from a friend of mine," Jo said as they made their way to Steven's table.

They ordered lunch and were soon lost in laughter as they reminisced. When lunch finally came it was served on hand-painted Limoges chinaware, and Chateaux Lafite Rothschild was poured into magnificent cut-crystal glasses.

"I can remember when Heinz vegetarian baked beans out of a can was the best meal of the day for you," Jo said, giggling.

"Yes, and I can remember when living like a pauper was a socioeconomic experiment for you," he responded slyly. "And you didn't think any of us knew. You reeked of class. You had what we wanted."

"You wouldn't want what I had," Jo said, her mind reeling–the small talk over. "Steven, I'm in trouble and I need your help."

"I'll do whatever I can to help you. Just tell me what it's all about."

"You may not be so anxious to say that after you hear my story."

"I'm not stupid, Jo. I knew something terrible must have happened. One minute I thought you would be the First Lady and the next I heard you were living in Israel. What's going on?"

Jo told Steven her story, naming names, sharing every detail, unburdening herself, watching his every reaction, wondering all the while if he comprehended the enormity of her dilemma.

"I was born in hell, Steven, on a day when the sky was filled with the ashes of human flesh. All I have left is my mother." Her eyes filled with tears, she wiped them away self-consciously.

"How can I help?" he asked, his voice tight, his eyes filled with furry. Steven was a Jew. The events of the Holocaust had shaped his life.

"I don't know yet. I only know two things: I want my mother out of Lithuania and I want to find out the truth. My father didn't get into the United States unaided. Who helped him and why?

"I've begun to accept the fact that I'll never be taken seriously. No one's going to believe that Nazis are infiltrating the government of the United States. They'll say I'm a lunatic."

He reached for a cigarette. "I'll do whatever I can to help you with your mother. I've still got some pull at the State Department. Also," he said, inhaling deeply, "There's someone I'd like you to meet. He's a lawyer with the Justice Department's Nazi-hunting unit. His wife and my wife were sorority sisters. He's been digging into declassified CIA and NATO files. He's not Jewish, but I still think he might be someone for you to talk to."

"Arrange it, please," Jo said without hesitation.

✳ ✳ ✳

John Lofts, an idealistic young attorney, met several times with Jo, finally agreeing to introduce her to some of his friends. One introduction led to another, and before long Jo was traveling thousands of miles, meeting with anyone who would talk with her, refusing to leave any stone unturned.

The duplicity reached even further than she had ever expected. Prestigious Western institutions, such as the French Curie Clinic, the Rockefeller Foundation, and the Carnegie Fund, and corporations like Dow Chemical, W.R. Grace, and Imperial Chemical all employed fugitive German scientists—the same scientists who had done advanced research into biological and chemical warfare during the war, the very same scientists who had used human beings for their experiments.

Important names like Count Folke Bernadotte, head of the International Red Cross, were given to her. Ex-CIA agents confided that the Count permitted the Red Cross to be used as a vehicle for Nazi intelligence during the war and that after the war he used the Red Cross to arrange passports for fugitive Nazis.

Having such volatile information and knowing that she could not go public with it, caused Jo untold agony. She and Aaron spent hours trying to find an outlet for the information Jo was compiling—information that, while coming from credible people, could not yet be verified.

* * *

Jo spent long days away from Aaron and her exhaustion and frustration were beginning to take its toll. Lying in bed together one winter night, the wind howling angrily, the rain stinging the windowpanes, Aaron turned to Jo.

"I've got an idea. It may not be the do all, end all, but it will be a way for you to divulge what you know."

"What are you talking about?" Jo asked, her voice high with excitement.

"A book. A fictional novel."

"Fiction, Aaron?" Are you crazy? You want me to trivialize what I know into fiction?"

"Think about it, Jo. Think of all the people you can reach. Someday all of this is going to come out. Until then you can tell your story. At least it would get people speculating."

Jo closed her eyes, trying to visualize turning all the horrific facts into fiction–trying to visualize herself as a writer. "I don't know."

"Yes, you do."

"But Aaron…"

"Jo, trust me on this. It's what you need to do. I'll take over the lobbying efforts on behalf of your mother and Jacob. I really believe it's only a matter of time now."

"I can't let you do that." Jo said.

"Why? Have I turned incompetent? What is it? Maybe you can't trust me with something this important."

Look what I've done now. He's hurt and I'm a stupid ass. "Of coarse I trust you. I love you."

"Then it's decided."

"That fast?" Jo asked, her head reeling.

"That fast."

"You're a real trip, Aaron Blumenthal."

"I know. That's why you love me."

* * *

Becoming a writer and establishing a writer's voice was a laborious process. Jo had to face a blank page every day and filling that page meant dredging up demons.

The storyline was simple; a young Jewish girl from Vilnius, Poland falls in love with a famous French actor. Claire, Saul, David, William, Otto, Ilya, Hans, Robbie, Natan and Aaron were all characters in her book–shrouded in other names.

Every evening after dinner Jo and Aaron poured over the day's writing. His reassurances became Jo's nourishment. He rarely criticized and when he did Jo brooded, learning how easily her ego bruised. It went smoothly until the day she had to write herself into the story.

Drinking hot chocolate, the fire crackling, Mozart in the background, Aaron read the day's work.

"I don't get it, Jo. There's no feeling."

"What are you talking about?" Her hands grew cold and her neck tensed.

"It's just words. You're not telling me how you feel."

Jo pulled the paper from Aaron's hand. "I'm doing the best I can."

"Listen to me, darling. This is about you. No speculation, no innuendo, just the truth."

Jo reread the pages, pulling at her hair and fidgeting the entire time. "This took me all day. I really thought it was good. But it's not. It sucks!" Her eyes filled with tears. "I don't want to talk about this any more tonight," she said. "I'm going to take a shower."

* * *

And so it went, 6 hours a day for almost a year. Her only diversions were the phone calls to her mother and the letters that she wrote. When the book was finally completed and edited, Steven found her an agent, who used Jo's fame to interest a publisher in New York.

At the Plaza on the day Jo signed with Loughton and Sweal Publishing, she awakened with a start, so sick that she thought she would die. Vomiting all morning, Jo was certain she had the flu. After meeting with the publisher and signing the contract, Jo took the first plane back to Washington. A week later the blood tests confirmed that she was going to have a baby.

* * *

A clock somewhere deep within the house chimed nine times.

"Damn!" Jo said, scolding herself for not realizing it was so late. She sat up, moving too quickly. Pain shot through her, cutting like a hot blade.

The caesarian section she had eight days earlier left the always energetic Jo weak and listless. She painstakingly made her way to the full-length mirror in the dressing room.

She studied her reflection before getting into the shower. *OK, so you're still fat, you need a haircut, and there are bags under your eyes. You look like shit. But when I'm finished with you, you'll look like a million bucks.*

The warm water soothed her aching body. Her mind wondered as she relived the telephone conversation she'd had with Rebecca upon returning to the United States from Vilnius.

"Did you find what you were looking for? Have you found some peace?" Rebecca had asked.

"Are you sitting down?"

"No," Rebecca replied.

"You better sit."

"What's this all about?"

"She's alive, Rebecca."

"What are you talking about? Who's alive?"

"My mother. My mother's alive."

Rebecca began to cry then, sobs mixed with laughter. And each time she tried to speak, she began to cry again.

"We'd have called you," Jo said, "but mother has a slight heart condition and Jacob felt it would be too much excitement for her after everything else."

"Jacob? Who the hell's Jacob?"

"Calm down and I'll tell you everything."

* * *

Smiling as she mentally reminisced, Jo turned off the water. Stepping gingerly out of the shower, she began brushing her hair, still lackluster from the anesthesia and childbirth.

Jo thought about Rebecca and William's arrival three weeks earlier. They were intent on sitting vigil, refusing to let Jo do anything that might tire her. They were a joyous threesome; spending most days: eating, drinking hot cocoa, daydreaming about the baby and talking about Morgan–letters had flown across continents and every letter was good for an hour's speculation.

Slipping into her dress, Jo smiled, allowing her mind to caress the most precious experience of her life—the birth of her daughter.

* * *

Aaron paced, dressed in scrub greens with a surgical mask hanging around his neck. Circumventing hospital rules, he had used his influence to be in the room when they brought the baby to Jo for the first time.

"You have a beautiful little girl," the nurse said, placing the baby into Jo's arms. "After you get acquainted, she needs to be fed." The nurse placed a bottle on the bed. She smiled at Jo and winked at Aaron. "I'll be back in twenty minutes. If you need me sooner, just press the buzzer."

"Hello, little one. Your daddy and I have been waiting for you," Jo said, holding the tiny bundle against her breast.

Aaron reached down and touched his daughter's hand. "She's so tiny."

"Take her. Hold your daughter," Jo said, handing the baby to Aaron.

"She's so perfect," he said, his eyes a blur of tears. "If only my mother and father could have lived to see this day."

"I wish I'd known them," Jo whispered. "And I wish my mother was here." She began to cry.

"Don't cry, darling. She'll come," Aaron said, placing the baby into Jo's arms. He kissed Jo's forehead, his lips warm and comforting. "Trust me."

*   *   *

That was exactly eight days ago, Jo thought as she began putting on her make-up. *And today I will take my daughter to the synagogue and give her the name of Aaron's mother. And her middle name will be for my grandmother. Today both Esther and Sara will be reborn.*

"I see my sleepyhead is finally awake," Aaron said, bounding into the bathroom. He kissed her cheek. "How do you feel?"

"Better."

"Really?"

"Really."

"Good. The caterer and florist have arrived and everything's under control. We won't be leaving for the synagogue until eleven. So just take your time and don't worry about a thing."

"I'm trying not to. What time did David and Saul arrive?"

"Around three this morning."

"Oh my God. They must be exhausted."

"I'm sure they will be. But right now all they want to do is get their hands on our daughter. David's never been a godfather before and he's so excited he hasn't stopped pacing."

"He'll do fine. Now get out of here. I've got to put myself together, and it's no easy feat."

"You're gorgeous just the way you are."

"Get out!"

"Pure perfection," Aaron said as he backed out of the bathroom.

Jo finished applying her make-up. Convinced that she was presentable, she headed to the nursery.

*   *   *

Furnished in white with accents of lilac and pink, the room was a gentle wonderland. Jo moved to the crib. She gently lifted her daughter as the nurse discretely left the room. Jo sat in the rocker, holding her tiny child in her arms.

"Today you'll enter into a covenant with your people," Jo said, rocking the baby gently. "Daddy and I will always love you and care for you, my precious. We're going to teach you to honor yourself and to honor others." She looked up to see Aaron standing in the doorway.

"She's a lucky little girl, our Esther," Aaron said softly.

* * *

William, David, Saul and Rebecca were standing in the hallway foyer when Jo entered.

"Motherhood agrees with you. You look wonderful!" David said, hugging her tenderly. His face flushed as he fought the tears burning behind his eyes. "I've missed you so much."

Saul stood off to the side, looking in wonder at the infant in Aaron's arms. "She's beautiful," he whispered, kissing Jo softly on the cheek.

David looked longingly at the child. He touched her hand, her face, tracing and memorizing every fold and curve. "My Jo a mother–a miracle," he said, winking at her.

"I think we'd better go," Aaron said. "They're going to do the naming after the Bar Mitzvah service and the Rabbi said that should be around noon."

"You go," Saul said. "Rebecca and I will follow. I have a couple of things to do."

* * *

During the limousine ride to the synagogue William, David and Aaron talked incessantly, their excitement disconcerting Jo.

"What's with you?" she quarried, her own nerves beginning to shatter. "I've never seen any of you like this. You're making so much noise it's amazing the baby hasn't awakened."

Their guilty looks and silence made Jo instantly sorry that she'd said anything. "Oh, never mind."

The prattle began again, as if she'd never spoken. Jo pulled inside herself, smiling despite the confusion.

* * *

The conservative synagogue, Temple Beth Shalom has a congregation of 1,000 families. The main sanctuary seats eleven hundred–expandable to twice that number for the High Holy Days. Cavernous, with high domed ceilings and stained glass windows rising in 12' sections, the main sanctuary still managed to maintain a feeling of warmth.

The Bar Mitzvah boy's friends and family filled the first rows of the sanctuary. As they entered the Rabbi was standing with the young man, complimenting him on the wonderful job he'd done reading his portion in the Torah.

Jo held Esther Sara in her arms, settling in a pew near the back in case the baby began to cry. Ten minutes later Rabbi Pomerantz motioned for the family partaking in the baby naming to come to the bimah.

As Jo rose to her feet Rebecca came up behind her. "Thank you for asking me to be the godmother. I'm so proud and I'm so proud of you," she whispered as the entourage–Aaron, Jo, Rebecca, David, Saul and William–made their way to the front of the synagogue where they climbed the three steps to the bimah.

"Such a beautiful baby," the Rabbi said, his voice rolling over the congregation. "Who are the godparents?"

Rebecca and David took a step forward.

"Would either of you care to say something before I begin?"

Rebecca nodded to David. "Go ahead. You talk."

David took a deep breath. Looking from Jo to Aaron, his eyes finally settled on his godchild.

"As a young man I wandered in the forests of Russia, lost, disheartened and embittered. And for many years I remained embittered. But then in the Judean hills of Israel I found my God, married my wife and was blessed with a healthy a son. For a man like me, this was enough. This was everything.

"And yet," he said, turning to Jo and Aaron, "I have been given another mitzvah–to become the godfather of your daughter. I don't have the words to tell you what this means to me. But I can tell you that I will love and protect your daughter all the days of my life. And if, God forbid, she ever comes to me in anguish, I will put aside my life to help her."

A silence fell over the room. Light filtered through the stain-glassed windows, filling the room in glorious streams of light. The sound of the rustling trees could be heard dancing against the glass.

Just then two people entered the isle leading toward the front of the synagogue. With quiet deliberateness they made their way forward.

Jo noticed how everyone seemed to be watching the isle instead of the Rabbi. She turned to see what was going on.

"Oh my God," Jo cried, her body trembling in disbelief. Aaron moved quickly to Jo, supporting her and the baby in his arms.

"I knew you needed me," Morgan whispered, as she moved to Jo's side, pressing herself tightly against her daughter's trembling body–encircling Aaron, Jo and the infant in her embrace. "It's all right. I'm here now," Morgan said, weeping despite her resolve not to. "Just look at her." She caressed her sleeping grandchild's face with her eyes.

"Take your granddaughter," Rebecca said softly. "She's been waiting for you."

Morgan took Esther Sara into her arms.

The Rabbi placed his hands in blessing over the infant's head.

"O my God, the soul which you gave us is pure. You created it. You fashioned it. You breathed life into it. Blessed shall you be in your coming.

"May the Lord bless you and protect you, Esther Sara Bat Yosefa V' Aharon. May the Lord cause His countenance to shine upon you and be gracious unto you. May the Lord bestow His favor upon you and grant you peace."

And so it was…A NEW BEGINNING.

THE END

Printed in the United States
54561LVS00006B/89